# The Dream Spinner

GAIL CREASE

JOVE BOOKS, NEW YORK

This is a work of fiction. Names, characters, places, and incidents are either the product of the author's imagination or are used fictitiously, and any resemblance to actual persons, living or dead, business establishments, events, or locales is entirely coincidental.

MAGICAL LOVE is a registered trademark of Penguin Putnam Inc.

THE DREAM SPINNER

A Jove Book / published by arrangement with
the author

PRINTING HISTORY
Jove edition / October 2000


For information address: The Berkley Publishing Group,
a division of Penguin Putnam Inc.,
375 Hudson Street, New York, New York 10014.

The Penguin Putnam Inc. World Wide Web site address is
http://www.penguinputnam.com

ISBN: 0-515-12929-1

A JOVE BOOK®
Jove Books are published by The Berkley Publishing Group,
a division of Penguin Putnam Inc.,
375 Hudson Street, New York, New York 10014.
JOVE and the "J" design
are trademarks belonging to Penguin Putnam Inc.

PRINTED IN THE UNITED STATES OF AMERICA

10 9 8 7 6 5 4 3 2 1

# Prologue

In a little-used corner of Wimpole-Barrett's Antique Shoppe in Springfield, Vermont, an old spinning wheel kept silent company with the spiders and dust motes that drifted down upon it.

The owner of the shop, Mrs. Wimpole-Barrett, had received the spinning wheel as part of a larger shipment of antiques from the estate of the dowager countess of Thelford in northern Yorkshire. This, along with an exquisite assortment of Sheraton and Chippendale tables, Hepplewhite chairs and settees, and an extensive collection of Sevres and Meissen porcelain, had been purchased as a bulk lot by her agent in London, England, and shipped to Mrs. Wimpole-Barrett sight unseen.

Thus, when the lady had unpacked the crate and found herself looking at an item that was for collecting purposes neither fish nor fowl, she had realized herself at something of a loss. As a reputable dealer of fine old English furnishings, Mrs. Wimpole-Barrett had never had any call for spinning wheels. People who wanted that type of thing invariably went to the farm auctions or local garage sales, which were held throughout the neighboring towns.

As a result, Mrs. Wimpole-Barrett had deliberated upon the addition of a spinning wheel to her prestigious collection of antiques with a good deal of ambivalence. How, for example, was she to display the unusual piece? She couldn't put it next to the delicately carved Chippendale chairs or the exquisite Sheraton secrétaire-bookcase. And it would not set off the polished silver candlesticks or Limoges plates to any advantage at all. In short, there was simply no way of displaying the spinning wheel without detracting from something else.

It was this ultimate decision which resulted in the relegation of the seemingly inconsequential piece to a dusty corner in the back room of the shop where, basking in the opalescent glow of light reflected down through the panes of a baronial stained-glass window, the Lockton spinning wheel sat in solitary splendor. Alone. Unseen. Unwanted.

Until the twenty-first day of June. The day upon which Mrs. Wimpole-Barrett inadvertently brushed against the antique, dislodging a small wooden dowel which held in place the large wheel, and caused it to turn one slow, complete revolution—thereby setting into motion a series of events which would ultimately affect the lives of all who came into contact with it.

"C'mon, Kate, haven't you seen enough of these darn things yet?" Matthew Pedigrew complained as he steered the truck down yet another winding country road. "I feel like some demented Prince Charming driving Sleeping Beauty around town until she finds just the right needle to prick her finger on!"

"Spindle."

"What?"

"Sleeping Beauty didn't prick her finger on a needle, Matt," Kate replied as she drew her attention away from the glorious autumn foliage all around them. "That was just part of the fairy tale. Old English spinning wheels didn't have needles. It was probably the spindle or something on the distaff."

"Oh yeah? And when did you become such an authority?"

"I've done a little reading, that's all." Kate slanted her older brother a good-natured grin. "Haven't you ever been interested in something for no good reason?"

"No, but then I don't believe in Santa Claus or the Easter Bunny either. Look, sis, you've already spent the best part of the summer digging through every dusty cellar and antique shop you can find, and here it is September and we're still trying to chase up spinning wheels. And all because of some stupid dream."

"It wasn't stupid," Kate replied defensively. "And it wasn't a dream. Exactly."

"Then what was it, exactly?"

"I don't know. I guess you could call it a feeling."

"A feeling that said go out and waste a perfectly good summer looking for a spinning wheel?" Matthew snorted disparagingly. "Come on, Kate, you're way too sensible for that kind of nonsense. Besides, you work with stained glass. What the heck do you need a spinning wheel for?"

It was a perfectly logical and intelligent question. And as a perfectly logical and intelligent woman, Kate knew she should have had an answer. But she didn't. In fact, she had absolutely no idea why the desire to own a spinning wheel had suddenly become such an all-consuming passion in her life.

Okay, so maybe Matt was right about her having had some kind of weird dream back in June, and yes it *had* involved a spinning wheel. But that didn't explain why this sudden and totally irrational desire to find one—and just the *right* one at that—had stubbornly lodged in her head. She'd dreamt about all kinds of things in her life but she'd never gone out *hunting* for any of them. So why was the spinning wheel different?

Kate rolled down the truck window and rested her elbow on the door. Maybe it was some long-repressed childhood fantasy coming back to haunt her, she mused. Sleeping Beauty meets Nineties Woman. What other explanation could there be for a dream in which she'd been standing in a medieval turret, looking down at a spinning wheel and fighting an almost overwhelming urge to touch it? What kind of dream would have her hanging out at antique stores and combing the back roads for weekend garage sales? If it had only been a dream, why was she so disappointed every time she went to check out a spinning wheel and found it wasn't what she was looking for? If it had only been a dream, why was she putting herself through this aggravation?

"Okay, so I don't *need* a spinning wheel," Kate conceded grudgingly. "That doesn't mean I don't want one. I think one would look great in that little nook beside the fireplace."

"You don't *have* a little nook beside the fireplace, sis," Matt drawled. "In fact, you don't have a little nook *anywhere.* You're jammed to the rafters as it is."

Unfortunately, that was also true. The beautifully restored stone church Kate called home was filled to overflowing with the antiques her mother had left her when she'd died, along with the other furnishings and craft supplies which were such a necessary part of her life. Kate really didn't have room for a spinning wheel. But nothing—not even a rare flash of insight on her brother's part—was going to stop her from having one.

"There'll be plenty of room once I've rearranged things," Kate assured him. "Now that the addition's finished, I'll be able to take my work out of the living room and move it into the studio. Then I'll have plenty of space for the—oh my gosh—Matt, there it is!"

"What?"

"Wimpole-Barrett's. The antique shop we've been looking for. Slow down, this is where we turn."

Matt frowned as he dropped the Chevy Blazer into second gear and pulled off the main road. "Wimpole Barrett. Isn't that the name of a writer or something?"

Kate grinned. "Way to go, Shakespeare. Barrett probably comes from Elizabeth Barrett Browning, and Wimpole refers to the street where they lived. The Barretts of Wimpole Street. Remember?"

"Oh yeah, right. Think these guys are any relation?"

"Not for a minute. The owners are probably just trying to invoke more of an English feel for their customers."

"Why? They're selling used furniture, not fish and chips."

Kate briefly debated the wisdom of explaining the value of a name like Wimpole-Barrett's to an antique store that sold fine English furnishings, and then decided against it. To Matt, antiques were right up there with New Age music and television evangelists. It would be a complete waste of time.

"Are you sure you want to go in?" Matt hooked his arms

over the steering wheel. "The place looks kind of expensive."

And it did. From the outside, Wimpole-Barrett's, with its white-washed walls and charming second-story gables, looked like most of the other antique stores that dotted the picturesque countryside around Springfield. But something about the neatly tended flower gardens now ablaze with a profusion of rust and gold marigolds, the charming hand-painted signs—and the gleaming black jaguar parked outside the front door—suggested to Kate that the contents of this store might just be a cut above what she had found elsewhere.

"Well, I guess there's only one way to find out," she breathed softly. "Are you coming?"

"Not me." Matt held up his hands as if to ward off evil spirits. "I've seen enough armoires and escritoires to last me a lifetime. But you go ahead. We didn't come all the way out here just to sit and wonder."

Kate slung her tan leather bag over her shoulder and leaned across to kiss her brother's smooth-shaven cheek. "You're too good to me, Matthew Pedigrew."

"Don't I know it. Have a ball."

And Kate did. Because Wimpole-Barrett's turned out to be a treasure trove of fine old English antiques and memorabilia. The interior was redolent with the scents of old wood and new wax, along with the slightly musty smell always associated with remnants from another time. The shop itself was divided down the center into two distinct halves. The area on the left contained the larger pieces of furniture which had likely come from old English mansions and stately homes, while the area on the right showcased the smaller pieces and accessory items. There were mahogany display cases filled with polished silverware and somewhat gaudy estate jewelry, along with delicate wing chairs, antique music stands and ornately carved cradles. There was even a harpsichord in perfect working order.

But not—Kate noted despondently—a single spinning wheel.

"Welcome to Wimpole-Barrett's, my dear. May I be of some assistance?"

The voice was quintessentially English and turning around, Kate found herself in the presence of a petite, elegantly dressed woman who would have looked more at home serving tea in an English drawing room than she did waiting on customers in an antique shop in rural Vermont. She had a round face and the warmest hazel eyes Kate had ever seen. Her gleaming silver hair was drawn back into an old-fashioned bun and fastened with a striking silver and jet clip. She looked like someone's much-loved grandmother.

"Mrs. Wimpole-Barrett?" Kate inquired.

"Mrs. Barrett will do, dear. I only use the hyphenated form for advertising now. Too much of a mouthful otherwise." The diminutive lady gave her a gracious smile. "Were you looking for anything in particular?"

"Well, yes I was, but I don't think you have one."

Mrs. Barrett's forehead puckered in a frown. "We carry one of the finest collections of English antiques in Vermont, my dear. I cannot imagine that we wouldn't have what you were looking for."

"Unfortunately, what I'm looking for *is* a little more on the rustic side."

"I see. And what precisely are you looking for?"

"A spinning wheel."

Mrs. Barrett didn't so much as bat an eyelash. "A spinning wheel. How interesting. We don't get much call for that sort of thing. As you say, it is somewhat more . . . provincial than the type of antiques I normally like to carry."

Kate sighed, disappointed but not surprised. "Yes, I was afraid that might be the case. Well, thanks for your—"

"I didn't say we didn't have one, dear," Mrs. Barrett said as Kate turned to leave. "I merely said we don't get a lot of call for them. As it happens, I do have a spinning wheel and a rather fine one at that."

Kate stopped dead. "You do?"

"Yes. It came in with a shipment of antiques from a large estate in the north of England. A titled family, you know, and as is so often the case, they had to sell everything to pay the death duties. Dreadful shame," Mrs. Barrett commented as she led the way towards the back of the store. "One can hardly afford to live in Britain these days, let alone die there. Especially if one has money."

Anxious to see what lay at the end of the hall, Kate paid little attention to what the woman was saying. Her search thus far had yielded up eleven spinning wheels, none of which had been to her liking. She had seen several large walking wheels, a Quebec upright dated somewhere around 1817, an early American Saxony, and even an East European Saxony. But most of them, like the more traditional spinning wheels she had seen, had been missing one or more key components, most often the distaff or the cross-arm.

"Is the wheel in good condition?" Kate asked now, thinking about some of those more dilapidated models.

"Well, I'm really not an expert on spinning wheels," Mrs. Barrett confessed, "but it seems to have everything it should. Do you spin?"

"No." Kate smiled. "I just happen to like them."

As they approached the back of the shop, Kate noticed that the light seemed to be growing warmer, and moments later, she understood why. High on the back wall of the building was a large stained-glass window. It looked to have come from an old church and it was a truly lovely piece of work. Perhaps not as detailed as some of the more elaborate church windows she had seen, Kate acknowledged, but it was certainly something the craftsman could have been proud of. And there on the floor below, captured in a beam of rose-colored light, stood the spinning wheel. A beautiful piece of workmanship, and complete to the last detail.

"Wow!"

Mrs. Barrett nodded proudly. "Yes, it is rather nice, isn't it."

"I'll say." Kate knew she shouldn't have sounded so impressed, but she couldn't help it. The spinning wheel, which stood about three and a half feet high, was exactly what she'd been looking for. And it didn't look to be missing a single part. The entire spinning assembly was there, along with the treadle and the long pole called the footman, which joined the treadle to the ten-spoked wheel. It even had its fragile pear-shaped distaff—the unit that held the flax fiber—still intact.

"Do you know anything about the spinning wheel, Mrs. Barrett? Where it came from, or how old it is?"

"Regrettably, no," the shopkeeper said, "though I have written to my agent in London requesting information. In most cases, a family's artifacts are documented, but this particular item was not."

Kate ran her hand lightly over the wheel part of the assembly, liking the feel of the wood beneath her fingers. It was incredible. After months of searching, she had finally found a spinning wheel that was perfect in every way—and one that was almost *identical* to the one she had seen in her dream.

"It's fortunate that you're not going to be doing any actual spinning," Mrs. Barrett said, "because I wouldn't be able to tell you the first thing about it. No doubt there are people in the area who can, however."

Kate nodded absently. It didn't seem important to tell the woman that she had absolutely no intention of learning how to spin. All she wanted to do was own a spinning wheel.

*This* spinning wheel.

"How much do you want for it, Mrs. Barrett?"

"Well, considering the value of the other items in the shipment, I would have to assume it to be of considerable age," Mrs. Barrett began in her best let-me-explain-why-it's-so-much-money-voice. "And it is, of course, the age of an item which goes a long way toward determining its value."

Kate's spirits took a nosedive. She knew what was coming. The owner was setting her up for a high price, and judging by the price tags she'd seen on the antiques in the outer room, she could only imagine what a splendid piece of workmanship like this was going to cost. Undoubtedly far more than her meager budget was going to allow.

Wistfully, she rested her hand on the top of the wheel. She hated the thought of losing it now after everything she'd gone through to find it, but there was no point in getting into debt over a piece of furniture. She could make a counteroffer, of course, but the woman already knew how badly she wanted it, and that definitely put her at a disadvantage.

Kate gave the wheel a gentle spin and watched it turn one slow, complete revolution.

A sudden breeze stirred the tendrils of hair at her temple. Mmm, that was nice. Autumn might be in the air, but that had definitely felt more like . . . a spring breeze. There was a freshness about it; a softness almost.

Kate closed her eyes and drew a deep breath of it down into her lungs. Funny how tired she felt all of a sudden, though. She'd probably been working too hard. Either that or she was coming down with something—

*. . . for you . . . the Chosen One . . .*

Kate slowly opened her eyes. "I'm sorry, Mrs. Barrett, what did you say?"

"Why . . . nothing, dear." The woman smiled at her in a polite, slightly vague fashion. "I was waiting for *you* to say something."

"But I thought I heard—" Kate didn't finish the rest of the sentence, because she wasn't sure what she'd heard. It had sounded like Mrs. Barrett's voice. But why would Mrs. Barrett say something, and then claim she hadn't?

"Sorry, Mrs. Barrett. I guess it must have been the radio." *Or else Matt was right and she really was starting to lose it.* "You were about to tell me how much you wanted for the spinning wheel."

"I was? Oh, yes, of course I was," Mrs. Barrett said with an embarrassed smile. "Well, as I was saying, one must consider the antiquity of the item, which alone would make it valuable. And given that the piece is in such perfect condition, I think—" She placed her hand lightly upon the still revolving wheel. "—one hundred dollars would suffice."

Kate stared at the woman in disbelief. "Did you say . . . one hundred dollars?"

"Yes, I did. Well as you can see, it really isn't in keeping with the type of thing I like to carry, and I could use the space—"

"Sold!" Kate pulled out her wallet before the woman had

a chance to change her mind. A *hundred dollars?* It was fantastic. It was . . . unbelievable.

It was fate.

"There you are, Mrs. Barrett," Kate said, handing over the money. "One hundred dollars cash."

"Thank you, dear. Do you live in the area?"

Kate put her wallet back in her shoulder bag. "Yes, about an hour from here. Why?"

"Because we deliver free anywhere within a hundred-mile radius of Springfield."

"Thanks for the offer, but I've got a truck outside," Kate assured her. Then, breathless with anticipation, she bent to pick up the spinning wheel.

"Oh, just a moment, I do believe something has dropped off." Mrs. Barrett stooped to pick up a small, narrow piece of wood that was lying on the floor beside the spinning wheel. "I wonder what this is."

Kate examined the intricately carved wooden dowel, and then glanced down at the wheel. "It looks like a restraining peg of some kind. You know, something to hold the wheel in place when it's being moved."

"Well, that would certainly make sense," Mrs. Barrett said, relieved that the wheel wasn't falling apart in front of her eyes. "Oh look, is that where it goes?"

Bending down, Kate fit the small piece of wood into the narrow slot between the wheel and the bench, and nodded in satisfaction. "You bet. The wheel won't budge an inch now."

"Well, I'm glad it was something so easy to fix," Mrs. Barrett said in relief. "I thought for a moment there I was going to have to give you your money back. Now, why don't you take it through the big door here and save lugging it all the way through the shop."

Grateful for the suggestion, Kate picked up the wheel. It was lighter than she'd expected, probably weighing no more than twenty pounds. "Thanks so much for your help, Mrs. Barrett."

"My pleasure, dear," the older woman said as she held the back door open for her. "Do come again."

Mrs. Barrett watched her customer walk toward a late-model truck, and smiled as a husky young man got out to help her. Good. She didn't like the idea of the young lady doing all of the lifting and carrying herself, no matter how thrilled she was with her new spinning wheel. The fact that she had been so concerned that it had all its working parts—when she didn't intend to use it—was a little strange, but then, there was no accounting for taste. And she *had* seemed a very nice young woman, even if her remarks about the voices on the radio had been somewhat curious.

Mrs. Barrett was so pleased to be finally getting rid of the spinning wheel that she hadn't even thought to tell her she didn't keep a radio in the shop!

Matt was about as enthusiastic as Kate had heard him be all summer. "Well, glory hallelujah! Does this mean we can finally go home?"

"We sure can. Open the back for me, will you, Matt?"

"You bet. So how much did that set you back?"

"One hundred dollars. Can you believe it? I thought I was going to faint."

"A hundred bucks! Jeez, Kate, I should think you would faint, blowing a hundred bucks on an old relic like that."

Kate rolled her eyes. "Do you have any idea how much spinning wheels like this are going for in New York?"

"How much?"

"Try eight hundred and up."

Matt whistled, and then stood back to survey the purchase again.

"So, what do you think now?"

"That they're crazier in New York than I thought. And that's saying something since we both used to live there."

Kate sighed as she climbed back into the truck. "You're such a philistine, Matt."

"Yeah well, I know what I like—and other people's cast-off furniture isn't it. Okay let's go. I promised Christian we'd watch the football game together."

"Matt, Christian's only five years old. Don't you think you're being a little . . . overzealous here?"

"What's that supposed to mean?"

"It means that just because *you* wanted to play professional football, doesn't mean your son will too."

Matt shrugged his big shoulders. "Who said anything about him playing the game? All I want him to do is watch it. I figure he's about the right age to start appreciating Doug Flutie's fancy footwork."

Kate shook her head as they pulled out of the parking lot. "And he says *I'm* the obsessive one!"

The church, as Kate liked to call her home, was situated on a scenic stretch of country road between Barre and Montpelier, and was bordered on two sides by stands of towering sugar maples. Though it was still possible to tell that the building had once been a place of worship, the additions and renovations Kate had carried out since buying it three years ago had turned it into a delightful and charming home. She'd replaced the long, narrow windows on either side of the front door with stained-glass panels of her own, and had done the same with the windows in the bathroom and den. Now, the quaint, Vermont–granite sided building was not only a home, but also a reflection of who Kate Pedigrew was.

"Okay, sis. One spinning wheel safely picked up and delivered," Matt said as he brought the truck to a stop in front of the arched entryway. "All at no charge to you."

"Thanks, big brother. I don't know what I would have done without you."

"All part of the friendly customer service." Matt grinned as he got out of the truck and headed round to the back. "Speaking of which, are you still coming over for dinner Sunday night?"

"You bet." Kate watched her brother easily lift the spinning wheel out of the truck and set it on the gravel driveway. "I wouldn't miss Meg's Sunday night pot roast for anything."

"Good, because we don't get to see nearly enough of you these days, Katie."

His words had Kate chewing on her bottom lip. "I know, and I'm really sorry about that, Matt. But between the business picking up, and then all the work on the addition—"

"Hey, it wasn't intended as a guilt trip," Matt assured her

quickly. "We miss you, that's all. Especially Christian. He keeps asking when his aunt Kate's going to take him to feed the ducks again."

Kate's eyes softened as she recalled the great time she and her nephew had had in the park back in July. Heavens, was it really that long since she'd been to her brother's for a meal?

"Tell you what. I'll come over early on Sunday and take him to feed the ducks before we eat. Deal?"

"Deal. Just make sure you give his mom and dad equal time." Matt gathered her close and gave her an affectionate squeeze. "See you Sunday, kiddo. And don't work too hard. You're starting to look as frazzled as me."

"Heaven forbid!" Kate punched him lightly on one beefy forearm and then waved as he got back into the Blazer and drove off.

In spite of what he'd said, Kate was delighted at how good her brother was looking these days. He might have been five years older than her but nobody would have guessed it by looking at them. They both had the same youthful features, the same engaging smiles, and even though his brawny six-foot-four, two-hundred-and-eighty-pound frame dwarfed her considerably more slender five-foot-five form, there was no mistaking the fact that they were brother and sister.

Matt had long since recovered from the physical injuries he'd sustained in the car accident that had ended his dreams of playing professional football, but more important, he'd recovered from the emotional pain as well. He could joke about football again, something he hadn't been able to do for a long time. At one time, even the *mention* of the game had been enough to send him into a deep depression, and Kate knew that the credit for pulling him out of it went to his lovely wife, Megan.

Yes, it was obvious that marriage and fatherhood suited him, Kate thought as she carried the spinning wheel into the living room and set it down next to the fireplace. Her brother might be a little tired from the long hours he was putting in at work, but he was happy—and that was all that mattered as far as she was concerned.

Kate put her shoulder bag on the couch and then turned to survey her purchase. She glanced at the fireplace, then at the wheel, and sighed. Okay, so Matt was right. It didn't exactly fit into the nook she'd boasted about having. That wasn't a problem. She'd find somewhere else to put it. All she cared about was that she had found it, and at Wimpole-Barrett's of all places. Who'd believe it? An old spinning wheel—at the most expensive antique shop in the area.

Kate ran her fingers lightly over the wheel and marveled at the skill and craftsmanship that had gone into the making of it. How amazing to think that hundreds of years ago, a young woman had sat at this very wheel, her foot pumping the board while her nimble fingers held the raw wool that would eventually be spun into yarn.

*Like straw into gold.*

The thought was so unexpected that Kate actually laughed. *Rumpelstiltskin?* Good grief, where in the world had *that* come from? She hadn't read that old fairy tale in a hundred years.

Eager to see the wheel in motion, Kate bent down and pulled out the dowel. She gave the wheel a gentle spin and watched it turn. It had an amazingly fluid motion. It didn't wobble or bounce, or pull to one side as so many of the other spinning wheels had. It just turned smoothly and effortlessly and in complete silence.

She watched it go round once, resting the tips of her fingers lightly against the rim. She spun it again and felt the whisper of a breeze against her face. It was soft and warm, reminding her again of a spring morning fragrance. Kate closed her eyes and inhaled a long, deep breath.

And then she fainted.

# Two

The ringing of the phone woke her from a deep slumber. Kate slowly opened her eyes and glanced around in confusion.

What was she doing on the floor? Her face was pressed up against the spinning wheel and her legs were doubled up under her. And she had absolutely no idea how she'd gotten there.

The phone jangled again.

"Okay, okay, I'm coming." Kate carefully got to her feet, wincing as she stretched out her cramped legs, and limped toward the kitchen. Had she fallen asleep? Impossible. She hadn't taken a nap in the middle of the day since she'd been five years old.

"Good afternoon . . . Pedigrew Stained Glass."

"Kate, honey, whatever's that matter? You sound like you're in pain."

The voice belonged to Madeleine Carstairs, a wealthy fifty-five-year-old widow. She was affectionately known around town as the Georgia Peach, but there was nothing soft or retiring about this Southern Belle. Madeleine was the driving force behind the local craft association. She had single-handedly gathered together an eclectic bunch of artists and crafters and formed them into a respected body of artisans. And Kate knew exactly what she was calling about.

"I'm . . . fine, Madeleine. Just a bad case of pins and needles in my legs. So, all set for the big party tomorrow night?"

"Lord, I hope so. Though I probably won't know for sure until everybody starts arriving. And by then it'll be too late to do anything if it isn't," Madeleine said in her soft southern drawl. "I just thought I'd call to see how things were going at your end. You are still coming, aren't you?"

"Would you forgive me if I didn't?" Kate teased.

"Not in this lifetime. I need someone with your style and sophistication to lend a little flair to the gathering. Have you decided which piece you're bringing?"

"Yes, and it's already wrapped and waiting in the front hall."

"Wonderful. I'll send someone around in the morning to pick it up. What about your speech?"

"Don't worry. It's written, rehearsed, and ready to go."

Kate could almost hear Madeleine's sigh of relief. "Honey, if they were all like you, my job would be so much easier. All right then, I'll see you tomorrow night. Eight o'clock or thereabouts. And wear something artsy, Kate. I've invited some very important people to this little get-together."

"You always do, Maddie. See you tomorrow."

Kate chuckled as she hung up the phone. Something *artsy*? Lord only knew what that meant. Depending on Madeleine's mood, it could be flowered skirts or Dior gowns. That's just the kind of person Maddie was.

Still smiling Kate walked back toward the living room—and then came to an abrupt stop.

Perfume. She could definitely smell perfume. But it wasn't any scent she owned. And the air was . . . different somehow. Cleaner. As though she'd been running the air purifier. But she hadn't turned it on once all day.

Kate gazed down at the spinning wheel and frowned. What a weird day she was having. First she'd thought she'd heard voices in the antique store, then she'd fallen asleep on the living room floor. And now, she couldn't even remember what she'd been doing just before she fell asleep.

Kate shook her head as she carried on into the living room.

At this rate, she was going to have to start taking gingko. She was way too young to be losing it this badly!

By seven forty-five Saturday night, Kate was in her car and headed for Montpelier. Even though Madeleine told her guests to arrive around eight o'clock, Kate knew she'd be expecting her earlier, and that was okay with her. She'd always been a stickler for punctuality. Besides, there was nothing she hated more than being the last one to walk into a room full of people. She turned onto Cherry Tree Close and parked her car as near to the house as she could get.

Madeleine Carstairs's home was the ultimate in gracious country living. The stately, two-story colonial mansion, which was situated in an exclusive residential area just outside Montpelier, had been featured in three home design magazines, and was probably worth in excess of a million dollars. It was certainly a far cry from the modest, three-bedroom bungalow Madeleine had grown up in in Atlanta, Georgia. Fortunately, Madeleine Templar, as she'd been then, had been one of the lucky ones. Her elevation to the ranks of the privileged had come about through a fortuitous marriage to the eldest son of an affluent New York lawyer.

A long-time devotee of the fine arts, Madeleine had met the charming and sophisticated Lawrence Carstairs III at a Broadway play, and had fallen in love with him on the spot. Fortunately, he'd felt the same way about her and the two were married within the year and spent twelve blissfully happy years enjoying everything life had to offer. But as quickly as it had come, fate had stripped Madeleine of her happiness. One cold December night, Lawrence had been struck down by a massive heart attack, something the doctors said had been brought on by the stress of his job and a lifestyle rich in overindulgences.

Naturally, Madeleine had been devastated. Her happy, orderly world had suddenly been turned upside-down by the loss of the only man she had ever truly loved. She had refused to go out, accepting visits from only her very closest friends, and she had shunned the New York social scene completely. So it had really come as no surprise to anyone when six months after her husband's death, Madeleine had sold their Manhattan apartment and packed her bags. She hadn't returned to her comfortable southern roots as everyone had expected, but had retired instead to the peace and tranquillity of Montpelier, Vermont, where she and Lawrence had spent so many happy summers together.

And there, Madeleine had begun to live again. She found a new focus for her life by involving herself in the local arts scene. She began cultivating sculptors and painters, and got to know the craftspeople who were such a big part of the area's tourist industry. She established special artistic events, and even donated her own money to causes she felt worthy of her support. And twice a year, Madeleine hosted elegant cocktail parties for her New York friends and business associates, with the express purpose being to introduce the craftspeople, who had become her personal *raison d'être*, to the executives and socially prominent people who could afford to buy their works.

Tonight was the second of her two annual events—her Fall Fling, as she liked to call it, and as always, it was well attended. Kate followed a stylishly dressed couple up the flagstone path to Madeleine's front door, and wrinkled her nose. The woman was wearing one of the new perfumes she'd been sprayed with the last time she'd been in a New York department store. She hadn't liked it then, and she didn't like it any better now. Nor did she care for the woman's sequined outfit, thinking it far too glitzy for one of Madeleine's elegantly understated receptions.

Kate glanced down at her own carefully chosen attire and knew that Madeleine would approve. While the black cocktail-length dress, with its long sleeves and low but not revealing neckline, wasn't exactly artsy *or* haute couture, it definitely suited her. As did the wide gold necklace inset with dramatic swirls of brass, copper and bronze she wore around her neck. The striking piece had been designed by one of the talented young goldsmiths in the area and it complimented the elegant simplicity of the dress to perfection. And if there was one thing Kate loved, it was simplicity.

She stepped into the marble-tiled foyer and was immediately enveloped in Madeleine's warm, Chanel-laced embrace.

"Kate, honey, I'm so glad you're here," Maddie greeted her. "Everything's going perfectly. For once, the caterers arrived on time and I actually have enough champagne on hand to—" She broke off in midstream and stared at Kate in confusion.

"What?" Kate asked, wondering whether she had lipstick on her nose. "Is something wrong?"

"Well, no, not exactly . . . wrong."

"Then what are you staring at?"

"Was I staring?"

"Yes," Kate replied, laughing. "Come on, Maddie, what's up? Did I forget one of my earrings?"

"*You* never forget anything, honey, but there's definitely something different about you tonight. I just can't put my finger on what it is. *Have* you done something different to yourself?"

"Well, I'm not wearing my hair in a ponytail if that's what you mean. And I did put on some make up."

Madeleine narrowed her eyes thoughtfully. "No, this is more than just cosmetics or a new hairstyle, though I do like what you've done with your hair. You look so sophisticated with it up like that. It shows off your wonderful bone structure. But it's not the hair. It's like you're . . . glowing from the inside. Oh my God, you're not pregnant, are you?"

"Madeleine!"

"Well, you know what they say about pregnant women glowing," Madeleine said defensively, "and Lord knows, *you* are."

"Let me be the first to assure you that I am *not* pregnant. If I was, I'd be right up there with Mary and Joseph in the miracle department."

Madeleine threw back her head and laughed. "Honey, I just love your sense of humor. It reminds me so much of my own. Well, you look wonderful whatever the reason. If I didn't know better, I'd swear you had a new man in your life, though where you'd meet one around here I have no idea. Now go on in and have a good time. And mingle, honey, *mingle*!"

Kate was almost relieved to move out of the crowded foyer. She was used to Madeleine's effusiveness, but she'd kind of gone off the deep end tonight. All that talk about Kate having a new man in her life and glowing like an expectant mother. The stress of the reception must be getting to her.

Kate handed her cashmere shawl to a waiting maid and then accepted a glass of champagne from a passing waiter. Taking a sip of the ice cold Moet & Chandon—Madeleine's favorite—she strolled through the magnificent, two-story entrance hall and then down three semicircular steps into the living room.

It really was a perfect home for entertaining. It could easily accommodate a hundred people and still look like there was room for more. The rooms on the main floor were all large and airy, the color scheme was muted throughout, and the furnishings and accessories had been professionally chosen to create a peaceful and serene ambience.

And there was glass everywhere. Madeleine often said that she liked to feel that the outdoors was part of the decor—and here in the living room, you certainly could. A long expanse of glass ran the entire length of the west wall and continued on into the custom-designed conservatory, the roof of which was an exquisite glass-topped dome. It had been built that way to allow the maximum amount of sunlight to pour down onto the plants below. Madeleine had never had the slightest interest in horticulture, of course, and had used the conservatory in any number of ways—none of which included plants. Tonight, she was using it as a gallery in which to display the special pieces of art she had commissioned for the show.

Kate spotted her stained-glass window immediately. It was impossible not to, given the prominent location Madeleine had awarded it—and its impressive size. Measuring just over four feet by three and a half, it was one of the largest pieces of stained glass Kate had ever undertaken—and it was certainly the most difficult. She had worked the central pattern in shades of amber, aquamarine, and emerald green glass, while filling in the background with a mixture of plain and frosted crackle. It had been a very long and painstaking project that had tested her mettle as an artist. Kate had loved every minute of it.

"It's a beautiful piece of work," a masculine voice commented from behind her. "The size and combination of colors alone make it memorable, but the skillful way the artist has used beading and touches of metal work in the execution make it truly outstanding. Do you know if—" the man leaned forward to read the name on the brass plaque, "Kate Pedigrew is here tonight?"

The compliment, which was both unexpected and flattering, brought a smile of pleasure to Kate's lips. As an artist, she loved hearing how people felt about her work, especially when the comments were positive. But this man didn't *know* that he was speaking to the artist. He was simply expressing his opinion. And to Kate, that anonymous vote of approval made his endorsement of her work a hundred times more valuable.

She turned around with an expression of thanks already forming on her lips—and never uttered a word. Because the mesmerizing look in his eyes practically made her forget her own *name*, never mind what she'd been about to say.

"Cole? Cole Beresford, is that you?" Madeleine called from across the room.

Her voice was like a dash of cold water, but at least it helped snap Kate out of her daze. Unfortunately it did nothing to restore her equilibrium. She'd never considered herself the type of woman to be easily swept away by a handsome face, but the man standing beside her took the word handsome to a whole new level. Maybe it was his eyes; those rich, dark slumberous eyes that were staring down into hers like he was trying to see into her soul. Or maybe it was the smile; so gentle yet compelling that Kate couldn't help but smile back. Her pulse was racing and she knew the color was high in her cheeks. And she was staring at him like a starstruck teenager. But at least she wasn't alone in that regard. The man was staring back at her in exactly the same way.

"Cole, honey, how in the world did you get by me at the

door?" Madeleine said now, oblivious to the silent communication going on in front of her. "You know I never let a handsome man walk through my front door without saying a proper hello. Especially when he also happens to be an old and very dear friend."

The man addressed as Cole-honey chuckled in a way that had Kate's stomach doing back flips. "It really wasn't difficult, Maddie. You were busy greeting Mr. and Mrs. Lubeck and hearing all about their wonderful trip to Tahiti."

Madeleine grimaced. "As if a trip to Tahiti could be more interesting than you. I swear, you really must come up here more often, Cole. You are surely one of the best-looking men I have ever seen; next to my dear departed Lawrence, of course. Why just looking at those shoulders of yours makes me feel quite breathless. And I see you've met Kate."

"Actually no, I haven't." He turned to smile at Kate again—and sent another series of shock waves rippling up her spine. "I was just asking her if the designer of this stained-glass window was here tonight when you made your appearance."

"You mean . . . she didn't tell you?"

"Tell me what?"

"That *she's* the artist?"

"Really?" He looked at her with new awareness. "No, as a matter of fact, she didn't."

Madeleine sighed. "Kate, honey, how in the world are you *ever* going to make a name for yourself if you don't start blowing your own horn? Cole, allow me to do the introductions. This is Kate Pedigrew, one of our most talented—and certainly most beautiful—artists, and Kate, this is my good friend, Cole Beresford from New York."

Blushing hotly, Kate extended her hand. "Mr. Beresford."

"My pleasure, Miss Pedigrew."

Cole grasped her hand and Kate felt a jolt of electricity shoot up her arm. She was almost relieved when he let it go.

"Kate's the only one who adds a touch of class to these little gatherings of mine," Madeleine confided. "The rest of them are so hopelessly countrified."

"Now, Maddie, you know that's not true."

"Of course it is. I'm not going to have Cole thinking you're as provincial as all the rest, honey. I've always said that your talents were wasted here. You should be working out of a studio in Manhattan, not stuck up here in the boonies."

"My talents aren't wasted here at all," Kate replied good-naturedly. "I have lots of customers in the area, and besides, you know how I feel about New York. I came here to get away from all that."

Cole turned those wonderful chocolate-brown eyes on her again and smiled. "You used to live in the city?"

"Live in it? Honey, her father *owns* half of it!" Madeleine supplied. "He's some kind of a real estate tycoon."

"Madeleine!"

"Well, it's true. Annette Loring told me that, and she knows everything. Besides, what's wrong with telling people what your family does?"

Kate bit back a less than flattering remark about the interfering Annette Loring and struggled to keep the smile on her face. Why did Madeleine insist on bringing up her connections in the city? She spent most of her time trying to forget them.

"I think Miss Pedigrew has an excellent point, Maddie," Cole said unexpectedly. "Most people I know would love to get out of New York if they had some other means of earning a living. Seems to me she's done the smartest thing all round."

The idea of having a handsome man come to her rescue was a new and intriguing one, but it wasn't one Kate intended getting used to. Disappointment inevitably followed on the heels of aspirations like that. "I don't know about it being the smartest thing, but I know I've been happy for the last three years. I like being my own boss."

"I take it you worked for somebody else in the city?" he asked.

"Yes, my father, but it didn't work out. He accused me of being too honest."

"Can you imagine being told you were too honest—by your own father?" Madeleine tutted. "Makes me want to shake my head every time I hear that. But, like I've always said, you can choose your friends but you can't choose your family. Oh and now there's Sophia waving at me again. Must be some kind of problem in the kitchen." Madeleine sighed as she scooped a glass of champagne from the tray of a passing waiter. "You two carry on chatting. I'll catch up with you later."

Cole grinned as their hostess marched away. "Dear Maddie. She never changes."

"No, she doesn't." Intrigued by the note of affection she'd heard in his voice, Kate asked, "Have you known her long?"

"About nine years."

"As an artist or a businessman?"

Cole gave her a keen glance. "What do you think?"

"I'm not sure." Even in three-inch heels, Kate had to look up at him. "You don't strike me as being the artistic type, Mr. Beresford, but if you'll pardon me for saying, you don't look much like one of Madeleine's jet set friends either."

"Actually, you're right on both counts. A business acquaintance turned friend would probably be a better way of describing it. Her late husband, Lawrence, introduced us at a party some years ago."

Cole's voice was deep and sensual, and the more he spoke, the more Kate felt herself being drawn in. He was obviously English, but his accent wasn't in the least arrogant or affected. It didn't grate on her nerves the way some did. In fact, Kate was quite sure she could have listened to him talk for hours . . .

"Would I be out of line if I asked you to show me around, Miss Pedigrew?"

"Hmm?" The unexpected question brought Kate back to earth with a bump. "Oh, no, not at all. I'd be delighted. And it's Kate."

"Good. If you'll call me Cole."

Relieved at how easily they'd moved past that hurdle, Kate smiled and led the way into the conservatory. "So what brings you to a gathering like this, Cole? Does your job include looking at the works of relatively unknown artists in far flung corners of the state?"

The laughter came easily to his lips. "Not as a rule. Truth is, I came to Vermont to do a little antique hunting and to meet an old friend I haven't seen in a while."

"Ah, a rendezvous."

"Nothing so intriguing, I'm afraid. The gentleman is an old university professor of mine," Cole told her. "He keeps a summer place in the area and when I told him about Madeleine's party, he said he might drop by. Although, even if he doesn't come, it will still have been worth the trip." His eyes were warm with approval as they rested on hers. "It's been a long time since I've met an artist who's as beautiful as the work she creates."

Kate felt a rush of warm color flood her cheeks and hastily glanced away. Boy, was she out of practice. She couldn't even flirt with a handsome man without blushing like a schoolgirl. But then, Cole Beresford *wasn't* exactly the kind of guy you bumped into every day of the week either. And he certainly wasn't the type she'd come to expect at Madeleine's upscale gatherings. There was nothing smooth or glib about him, and his interest in the artists and their work was as genuine as her own. As they moved around the room together, Kate instinctively knew which pieces captured his interest and which didn't. And as far as she was concerned, his taste was flawless.

"There are some very talented artisans here," Cole commented when they had gone about halfway around. "I'm impressed."

"Madeleine will be delighted to hear you say so. She may be something of an eccentric, but she's done a marvelous job of promoting the local craftspeople," Kate said generously. "Most of the artists you'll meet here tonight had never done anything more ambitious than display their works on the balcony of the local hotel, or donate things to the Christmas bazaar. Strategic marketing wasn't something these people were into."

"I'd venture to say it's an area in which you excel, though," Cole surmised. "The time you spent working in real estate in Manhattan must have helped."

Kate brushed her hand over a beautifully carved rosewood

egret, her artist's eye appreciating the sculpture's clean, simple lines. "It helped that I knew how to promote myself, but I had no idea what kind of living I could make doing stained glass."

"Why stained glass?"

Kate lifted her shoulders in a graceful shrug. "Probably because I'd been making pieces for my own use for so many years. My brother used to say there was more glass in my apartment than there was at Steuben. Then, some of my friends started asking me to make things for them too. You know, wall hangings, cabinet doors, window inserts. Pretty soon, I was spending as much time working on stained glass as I was selling real estate, and enjoying it a whole lot more." Kate's mouth twisted. "I think I was making more money at it too. So, one day I decided it was time for a career change."

"But how did you end up here? Montpelier's a long way from New York, in more ways than one."

Kate couldn't help but laugh. "Yes, you're right. I was familiar with the area because my family used to vacation here. Mom would bring us up as soon as school let out."

"Us?"

"My brother and me. Dad used to fly in on weekends. He could only take about two days of this place before he started getting antsy. Matt finally moved up here on a football scholarship and I started staying with him during summer vacations. By the time I was finishing college myself, Dad was already laying down plans for me to join the firm. When that didn't work out, Matt told me about an old church that was up for sale, and I jumped at it. The rest, as they say, is history. After that it was just a matter of turning my hobby into a business and seeing whether or not strangers liked my work as much as friends did."

By this time, they had come full circle and were standing under Kate's window again. "And do they?" Cole inquired.

Kate allowed herself a cautious smile. "So far the response has been encouraging."

"Well, if that's a sample of your work, Kate, I don't think you have anything to worry about. In fact, if it's not already spoken for, I'd like to buy it."

*"What?"* Kate swiveled her gaze around to his. "But . . . you don't have to feel obligated to buy it just because you've been talking to me."

"I never feel obligated to do anything," Cole assured her quietly. "In my line of work, I come across a lot of exceptional works of art, but I only buy what I really like. And I hope this won't sound trite but I've been looking for a piece of stained glass in just about that size and those particular colors for some time now."

"Well . . . thank you. And of course, I'm delighted, but—"

"Ah, Cole, there you are," Madeleine said, bearing down on them like a battleship at full throttle. "That gentleman you were hoping to see is here. I've just spent the last five minutes chatting to him. What a fascinating man. Wherever do you meet such interesting people?"

"Connections, Maddie. That's how I met you, remember?"

"As if I'm likely to forget." Madeleine's laughter was a silvery ripple of sound. "You are one of the nicest people Lawrence ever introduced me to. By the by, how are you enjoying my little show? Didn't I tell you I had taken some very talented people under my wing?"

"You have excelled yourself again, Maddie. In fact—" Cole reached into his jacket pocket and drew out his wallet. "I've just told Kate that I want to buy her piece of stained glass. I hope you'll mark it sold before anyone else decides to better my offer."

Madeleine's face flushed with pleasure. "Why, Cole, that's absolutely wonderful! I'm so pleased. But then, I told you Kate's work was exceptional, didn't I."

"The only problem is there doesn't seem to be a price on it." He pulled out a business card and jotted a figure down on the back of it. "Will this cover it?"

Kate took the card and her eyes widened in shock. "About three times over. May I?"

Cole handed her the pen and Kate crossed out the number he had written and wrote in a much lower price over top. "This is more what I had in mind."

Cole took back the card and his eyebrows lifted in amusement. He held out his hand, and the pen exchanged hands one more time. "This is my final offer. Take it or leave it." To Kate's surprise, he handed the card to Madeleine.

"Sold!" she announced with satisfaction. Madeleine winked at Kate and tucked the card into her purse. At the same time, she pulled out a red "Sold" sticker and handed it to Cole. "Be a darling and put that in the corner, will you, Cole. You're so much taller than either of us."

Kate frowned. She wasn't used to being left out of a transaction where her own work was involved. "Maddie, what was the—"

"Well, that was a delightful start to the evening," Madeleine said, clearly pleased with the outcome and seemingly determined to keep Kate in the dark. "But, you mustn't keep your friend waiting any longer, Cole. He said he came here specifically to see you and that he doesn't know how long he'll be able to stay. He mentioned something about having to catch a plane to London first thing in the morning."

Aware that she wasn't going to get anywhere with Madeleine, Kate put her hand on Cole's arm. "Cole, please—"

"The matter's closed, Kate," he said firmly. Then, winking at her, added, "Use the difference between your price and mine to cover the cost of crating and shipping."

"But . . . where do you want me to send it?"

"The address on the front of the card will do," he said, handing her another card. "I'll give you a call tomorrow or Monday to arrange a delivery date."

"Yes, but—"

"Come along, Cole," Madeleine whispered urgently, "Professor Morris is waiting."

"It was a pleasure meeting you, Kate," Cole said as Madeleine drew him away. "I'll be in touch." And then he was gone before Kate even had a chance to say a proper good-bye.

Well, so much for getting to know the charming Mr. Cole Beresford, Kate thought ruefully. She glanced down at the card in her hand, and then at the sold sticker on her window, and wondered what he did for a living. Obviously something that allowed him to drop large sums of money at the drop of a hat.

Unfortunately, the business card told her nothing. The bold black print on the cream, linen-finish card gave her his name, his telephone number, and his addresses in London and New York. But that was it. No company name, no title, no occupation.

Kate tapped the edge of the card against her chin. Funny that a man like that would come all the way to Vermont to do a little antique hunting when he had homes in two of the finest shopping cities in the world. She tucked the card into her purse and moved toward the dining room, curious to see what kind of man he was meeting.

It didn't take her long to spot Cole. Apart from the fact that he stood about a head taller than any other man in the room, he was also the most handsome one there. He had an angular face with a strong jawline and chin, and high, well-sculpted cheekbones. His black, wavy hair was worn stylishly long, and his lips were full and beautifully shaped. His mouth seemed forever poised on the edge of a smile, but it was a natural smile, not like the plastic ones Kate had so often seen at art shows.

He was the type of man who radiated confidence and authority. He stood there talking to the other man, with his legs apart and one hand tucked casually into his pocket. Kate had no doubt that he was completely at home in the elegant and wealthy crowd. His head was tilted slightly forward to hear what his friend was saying, and it was obvious that he was completely immersed in the conversation. It was also obvious that he was a magnet to every female in the room. But if Cole Beresford was aware of the commotion he was causing, there was no indication of it in his manner. He seemed far more interested in the strange little man with the snow-white hair and the bushy black eyebrows, than he did with anyone else in the room.

Kate turned and slowly strolled back toward the conservatory. Funny. She hadn't expected Cole's friend to be the absent-minded professor type. She'd been expecting a polished and erudite intellectual, like himself.

At the entrance to the conservatory, Kate stopped and looked up at her window. To her surprise, other people were looking at it too. Some of them were nodding amongst themselves, and others were stopping to look down at the name on the plaque. She even saw one woman take out a pen and jot the name down on her program.

What an extraordinary weekend this was turning out to be, Kate mused. First she'd found her spinning wheel, and now this. She couldn't help but wonder whether her luck wasn't finally starting to change.

Kate didn't see Cole again that night. She looked for him after giving her brief introductory speech and then again when she was getting ready to leave, but she wasn't able to find him or the professor. It was almost as though they'd disappeared into the warm September night. She had, however, found Madeleine, who was clearly ecstatic over the success of the evening.

"Kate, honey, thank you *so* much for coming. I don't know *what* I would have done without you." Madeleine swept her into another Chanel-laced embrace. "It all went off so splendidly, don't you think? And your speech was absolutely *wonderful*."

Kate had to laugh. She was used to Madeleine talking in superlatives, but tonight, she had it really bad. "Yes, it was definitely one of your more memorable evenings, Maddie."

"But it was for you too, honey. You made quite an impression on Cole Beresford, and let me tell you, he's not a man who's easily impressed. His buying your work was the best thing that could have happened to you."

"It was?"

"Well of course. The man's a connoisseur when it comes to fine art and collectibles. And because of what he does, he has opportunities to see some of the finest pieces in the world. So you can only imagine how impressed he must have been with yours to offer to buy it so quickly."

"Madeleine, what exactly does Cole Beresford do?" Kate asked.

"Didn't he tell you?"

"No. And his business card doesn't say."

"Well, no, it wouldn't. Cole likes to keep a low profile. And his name is well enough known in the antique world that he doesn't have to broadcast it."

Kate tried not to look surprised. "He's an antique dealer?"

"Oh no, he's way more than that. He's an acknowledged authority in the field. He gets calls from historical foundations and archaeological societies all over the world, but he spends most of his time in England and Europe doing research. He's forever going off to this old castle or checking out that old ruin. You'd never know it to look at him though, would you?" Madeleine sighed. "Mercy, what I wouldn't give to wake up and see a face like that on the pillow next to mine. It would almost make mornings worthwhile."

Kate burst out laughing. "Madeleine, you're terrible!"

"I know, but that's one of the nice things about being a rich widow, honey. People *expect* us to say outrageous things. They figure we've got more money than sense, and the richer we are, the more outrageous we're likely to be. I stopped worrying about it years ago."

Kate was surprised to hear Madeleine speak so candidly about herself, but she suspected she was right. She'd been guilty of putting some of Maddie's more . . . capricious tendencies down to her wealth too. And that suddenly brought another thought to mind. "I don't suppose you're going to tell me what Mr. Beresford finally paid for my work, are you?"

Madeleine's lovely blue-green eyes sparkled. "No, I'd rather wait until you get the check in the mail. But I think you can safely say that your days as a struggling artist are over, Kate. Once word gets out that Cole Beresford paid *that* much for one of your pieces, they'll be beating a path to your door!"

• • •

Later that same evening, Cole Beresford sat in his second-floor bedroom at the Maple Tree Inn and thought about Kate Pedigrew. Not just because she was one of the most attractive women he'd had the pleasure of meeting in some time, but because there was something about her he just couldn't forget. He kept remembering the way her deep blue eyes had sparkled when she'd laughed, and the way her lips had curved in that unknowingly sensuous smile. And then there was that maddening little dimple that kept appearing in her left cheek.

Yes, there was definitely something about Kate Pedigrew that would make a man stop and take a second look. He certainly had, and he would have taken a third if Maddie hadn't yanked him away to see Professor Morris.

Cole loosened his tie and poured himself a glass of scotch from the small in-room bar. Interesting family situation too. Her father owned half of New York yet here she was, stuck out in rural Vermont trying to make a living out of designing and building stained-glass windows.

Not that she wasn't good, Cole conceded, because she was. Damn good. He'd seen enough stained glass in his life to know that Kate Pedigrew had an eye for what worked and what didn't, and he was genuinely delighted that he'd been able to buy her work before someone else snapped it up. But it was hard to believe that a lady who had that much going for her would just . . . chuck it all and move to the country. As Madeleine had said, Kate could have easily set herself up in a loft in Manhattan and used her father's social and business contacts to get her business going. Surely she hadn't wanted to get away from him *that* badly.

*Take it easy, Beresford. You didn't come all the way to Vermont to get caught up in the personal problems of an attractive artist,* the niggling voice of his conscience told him.

Cole regretfully lifted the glass to his lips and swallowed a mouthful of the fiery liquid. No, he hadn't. He'd come up here for an entirely different reason altogether, and one which in light of his startling conversation with Professor

Morris tonight, had to take precedence over the beautiful Miss Pedigrew.

Cole fished out the piece of paper the professor had given him and studied the address. He'd already checked out the location of the store with Madeleine and discovered that it was less than an hour's drive from here. He'd head over there first thing in the morning. If what Professor Morris had told him was true, Cole knew he couldn't afford to wait much longer—especially given that his old nemesis Jeremy Davenport was likely following up the same lead.

Cole tossed back the rest of his drink and sighed. It wasn't the first time he and Davenport had crossed paths over a rare piece of art or a priceless collectible, and he knew it wouldn't be the last. Davenport always seemed to know when something was going on in the art world—especially if there were large sums of money to be made from it. And while Cole didn't like or trust the man, he wasn't foolish enough to underestimate his talents.

Jeremy Davenport was one of the best art thieves, the best con men, the best . . . whatever you wanted to call him, in the business. There wasn't a safe he couldn't crack, a lock he couldn't pick, or a security system he couldn't bypass. He had passed himself off as everything from a Swiss count to an American college professor, and his network of suppliers and contacts all over the world made it easy for him to travel around in relative obscurity. He had successfully swindled galleries and collectors from one end of Europe to the other, and had never once been convicted.

One day he'd slip, Cole told himself, deriving a certain amount of satisfaction from the knowledge. After all, even the best grew careless, and all it took was one small mistake to bring an entire operation to a close. But for now Davenport was a free man—and he was looking for the Lockton spinning wheel; a priceless antique which, thanks to some botched paperwork, was out on the market again.

Yes, his contacts in England had really screwed up this time, Cole thought darkly. The antique should never have ended up on the list of general items available for sale after Lady Thelford's death. The spinning wheel was to have been discreetly removed from the house as soon as the owner died. Unfortunately, that hadn't happened, and there was nothing Cole could do about it now. All he could do was try to make sure that nothing else went wrong.

With that in mind, he reached into his briefcase and pulled out a small leather-bound book. It was one he'd had in his collection for over sixteen years and he seldom traveled anywhere without it—which was undoubtedly why the title was all but illegible. He flipped to the chapter dealing with ancient legends centered in the northern part of England and stretched out on the bed. Might as well refresh his memory before he set off in the morning. After all, when it came to something as extraordinary as the Lockton spinning wheel, he couldn't afford not to know exactly what he was talking about!

In spite of the late night, Kate was out of bed before seven o'clock the next morning. She was tired of living in a disaster zone. After nearly six weeks of construction, it was time to start putting her life—and her home—back in order. So saying, she pulled on her faded denim jeans, a loose-fitting white cotton shirt and a pair of old Reeboks. Then rolling up her sleeves, she got out a bucket, grabbed a roll of paper towels, and diligently got down to work.

She tackled the showroom first, which, in the wake of the workmen's departure, was the biggest disaster. The floor of the brand-new sixteen-by-twenty room was littered with empty light fixture boxes, assorted lengths of wire, and broken pieces of wallboard. And everything was covered in a layer of fine, white dust.

In spite of the mess, however, Kate was absolutely thrilled with her new studio. Originally intended as a showroom where she could display and sell her stained-glass art, the newly built studio actually accomplished two things. It provided a bright, sunny room where her pieces of glass could be displayed to their best advantage, but more important, it gave Kate back the privacy of her home. *That* was something she hadn't been able to enjoy in nearly two years. Ever since she'd hung out her sign advertising custom-made stained-glass windows for sale, her home had been public territory.

But now, local people and tourists alike would be able to view the beautiful works of Kate Pedigrew *without* having to tramp through the church's narrow entry hall and walk all through her house. She wouldn't have to keep rolling up the exquisite hand-knotted Persian carpet her mother had given her for her twenty-first birthday, or worry about getting mud stains on the floor or on the buff-colored suede furniture. Instead, her customers would be able to drive around to the back of the church, and walk into the brand new studio from there. Matt had built her a specially carved wooden door, into which Kate had set oval pieces of amber, gold and crimson glass, so that the finished product resembled a tree in brilliant autumn foliage.

Once inside the studio, people would be able to see her works as they were meant to be seen. Rather than have them sitting atop wooden tables, or propped against other pieces of furniture, Kate's stained-glass panels would be suspended from the ceiling against a backdrop of pristine white walls. All in all, it made for a much more professional and artistic presentation.

By noon, Kate had finished clearing away all of the larger pieces of debris and had vacuumed the oatmeal-colored carpet throughout. She had washed the windows, oiled the trim on the display tables and dusted the black, wrought-iron wall supports. So when the phone rang at twelve-thirty, she was more than ready to stop for a break. "Pedigrew Stained Glass?"

"Hey there, sleeping beauty. Found any good spinning wheels lately?"

Kate leaned her back against the wall and grinned. "Matt, don't you have anything better to do than call me up in the middle of the day and hassle me?"

"Come on, sis. How can you yell at me after what you put me through the last few months? Where's your sense of compassion?"

"Floating in a bucket of very dirty water. I've just spent the entire morning cleaning the studio."

"Sounds like fun. How's it going?"

"Great. The studio's beautiful and I'm a wreck."

"Impossible. Mom instilled some kind of neatness thing in you when you were still in the cradle. You never look a mess. Too bad I didn't get any of it."

"No kidding," Kate drawled. "You're just lucky Megan's as patient as she is. I would have told you to clean up your act years ago."

"Yeah, well, I hit the jackpot when I met Meg. But listen, sis, that's what I'm calling about. We're going to have to postpone dinner tonight."

For the first time since she'd started talking to him, Kate heard the note of concern in her brother's bantering tone. "Matt, is everything okay?"

"Well, it's probably nothing to worry about, but Christian's come down with something again and Meg's kind of worried. She just wants to keep an eye on him tonight. Can I give you a rain check on dinner?"

"Of course you can, you know you don't have to ask. But I'm really sorry to hear that Christian's not feeling a hundred percent," Kate said sincerely. "Is it another cold?"

"Who knows?" Matt sighed, and the frustration was evident. "With so many things going around school these days, he's bound to pick up something. But Christian's never been a strong kid and when he gets something, it always seems to settle in his chest. And you know how Meg worries."

"Yeah, I know." Kate could hear the concern her brother was trying to hide and she didn't like it. "Have you taken him to see Dr. Sheffield yet?"

"Not yet, but I will if this doesn't clear up. I'm just sorry we won't get to see you tonight. We were all looking forward to it."

"I was too, but don't worry, there'll be lots of other times," Kate assured him. "You just take care of my nephew and call to let me know how he's doing."

"You bet. Thanks, Katie."

The term of endearment was one Matt only used when he was feeling down, and Kate's heart went out to him. She didn't like hearing that Christian had another cold. That would make four this year, and they all went straight to his chest. Kate knew that kids were prone to picking up viruses, but Matt was right, Christian seemed particularly susceptible. They'd had to put him in the hospital in Montpelier twice, and both times, he'd ended up on a respirator.

Still, her brother and his wife were great parents, and Kate knew they'd do everything they could to make sure Christian got better. Besides, with all the new wonder drugs on the market these days, doctors could cure almost anything.

Feeling somewhat reassured, Kate put down the phone and picked up the box of cleaning materials. The den was her next challenge. Right now it looked like something out of an Addams Family movie. Every stick of furniture, including her desk and her drafting table, was covered with a white sheet. Only the spinning wheel stood unadorned, having arrived after the workmen had left.

Kate looked at it now and sighed in satisfaction. She still couldn't believe her luck at finding it—*and* at only a hundred dollars. She ran her fingers lightly over the wood, amazed at how smooth and unblemished it was. The drive band, a kind of braided cotton cord, looked to be relatively new, and there seemed to be very little wear in the groove where it sat. The distaff was formed of delicate rattan rods, bent and shaped to resemble an open, slightly elongated pear. But it was the intricate carving on the legs and the bench that made it truly unique. Someone had spent hours carving the delicate pattern of flowers and birds into the wood.

Kate had moved the spinning wheel from the living room into the den so that she wouldn't be as likely bump into it. But now, anxious to see how, or if, the mechanism worked, she bent down and pulled out the wooden dowel. Then, dragging over a chair, she sat down in front of the spinning wheel and placed her foot lightly upon the treadle.

"Now, how does this work?" Kate gave the wheel a gentle spin to get it going and watched the footman and the footboard move up and down a few times. When she thought she had the rhythm, she tentatively placed her foot on the treadle and lightly rested her left hand on top of the wheel.

Then, she spun the wheel. Once, twice, three times . . .

At first, the sensation in her fingertips was so slight as to be almost imperceptible. It felt as though she'd dipped them into a can of nearly flat ginger ale. She didn't pay much attention to it however, figuring it was just the friction of her skin against the wood. But as the wheel continued to spin and the feeling suddenly crept up into her hand and wrist, Kate realized that it had to be more than that. The sensation wasn't painful. Nothing like an electric shock or even a burst of static electricity. It was more a kind of . . . tingling. She brought the wheel to an abrupt stop.

The tingling stopped too—but not right away.

Kate's brow furrowed in confusion. If the tingling in her fingers was caused by vibration from the wheel, why hadn't it stopped as soon as the wheel had? Was it possible that the thing was giving off some kind of . . . electrical charge?

Dropping to her knees, Kate examined the spinning wheel from top to bottom. But there was absolutely nothing to indicate that it had ever been fitted out for electricity. There were no wires, no plugs, no switches. Which meant there was absolutely no way it could have been emitting any kind of electrical charge. So where had the tingling come from?

Kate got back on the chair and tried to come up with an answer. Think! She'd just lived through six weeks of construction. Workmen had been everywhere; tearing down walls, putting them up, stapling drywall, installing lighting—

Kate blinked. Lighting? Now *that* was a definite possibility. The electricians had been pulling wires from *everywhere* when they'd been installing the track lighting. Was it possible that they might have forgotten to put a wire back in their haste to get to their next job?

"Oh, that's just great!" Kate muttered. If that was the case, she'd have to call the electrician back and have him lift the carpet to see what he could find. But there was no way she was going to do that today. The last thing she needed was John Burke clumping around her house again.

Besides, it obviously wasn't anything dangerous. She hadn't been electrocuted so far. In fact, the sensation was . . . kind of nice. Kate pushed a few loose strands of brandy-colored hair out of her eyes and tentatively spun the wheel again.

The tingling began on the third revolution. Like before, it started in her fingertips and slowly moved up into her hand and wrist. But this time, it didn't stop. It traveled up her arm toward her shoulder and seemed to radiate out from there. It really was the weirdest sensation.

*So is this funny feeling of disorientation,* Kate thought groggily. It was like she'd had one too many glasses of champagne. When she closed her eyes, she felt like she was . . . floating. She could feel the movement of her chest as it rose and fell in time to the beating of her heart. And she had the strangest urge to smile. She had no idea why. Maybe because she just felt so good. In fact, she couldn't remember ever having felt . . . so good before. So languorous . . . so sleepy . . .

*Yes, come . . . I have waited for you . . .*

Kate nodded, and felt herself falling deeper into the mists. She didn't want to fight it any more. She just wanted to put her head down and turn off her mind. To slip away into the realm of twilight. To close her eyes . . . to dream . . .

*There was a woman in her dream. A woman covered from head to toe in a filmy white gauze that shimmered and sparkled as though it had been woven from the essence of light itself. Her face was veiled too, but through the drape, Kate could see the perfection of her features. She looked to be about twenty years old. And she was smiling. A smile of such beauty, such . . . compassion, that it nearly brought tears to Kate's eyes.*

*"Are you an angel?" she whispered.*

*The vision shook her head. "I am Eleya. I have waited a long time for you to come . . ."*

There was a noise then. An intrusion. Kate felt a shift in the air all around her.

*"What's happening?"*

*"Someone comes. It is time to go back . . ."*

*"No, wait!"*

*Eleya's smile was infinitely gentle. "There will be another time. Now you must return . . ."*

*"Eleya . . . wait!*

*But she was already gone, the brilliant light fading as Kate felt herself pulled back through the mists. The dream was dying . . . she was waking up . . . someone was calling . . .*

Cole.

Kate slowly opened her eyes. She blinked a few times to chase away the remnants of sleep, and then lazily stretched her arms over her head. Funny, she could have sworn she'd just heard Cole Beresford's voice. But that was ridiculous—and it was certainly wishful thinking. He was probably miles away from here by now. He might even be on his way back to New York.

Sighing, Kate blinked again, and then slowly glanced around. Wait a minute—what was she doing sitting on the floor? Surely she hadn't fallen asleep *again*?

"Hello? Anybody home?"

Kate's head jerked toward the front door. She wasn't dreaming now. That *was* Cole Beresford's voice—and it sounded like it was right outside her front door!

"Um—just a minute." She started to get up and then winced in pain as the pins and needles attacked her legs again. Damn it. She really had to stop falling asleep in the middle of the day like this. "I'll . . . um . . . be right there." Kate limped to the front hall, slapping her legs to get some feeling back into them. Why, today of all days, did the most gorgeous man she'd ever met have to just drop by? The house was a disaster, none of her works were on display—

and she hadn't bothered to put any makeup on this morning. She must look a total wreck.

Kate stopped to glance in the mirror. Okay, so she didn't look as bad as she'd thought. In fact, she didn't look bad at all. Her eyelashes must be growing in darker these days. And her skin had a nice, rosy glow. Must be all the water she was drinking. She frantically finger-combed her hair into some kind of order, took a deep breath, and opened the door.

Sure enough, there he was. Cole Beresford. Larger than life and twice as handsome.

"Cole! H-hi! W-what are you doing here?"

He was dressed more casually today in an attractive navy and white sweater over a pair of close-fitting denim jeans. But the look in his eyes and the smile on his lips were every bit as warm and as intimate as they'd been last night.

"I hope you don't mind my stopping by, Kate," Cole said in that wonderfully rich voice, "but I was in the area and thought I'd take the liberty of dropping off your check."

Mind? Did she *mind* having a man who looked like he'd just stepped off a Ralph Lauren ad land on her doorstep?

"Um, no, not at all." Kate hoped he couldn't see how hard her heart was beating. She wondered where he'd gotten the tan. Mexico, maybe, or the French Riviera. She didn't think it would be anywhere as mundane as Florida or the Bahamas.

"You really didn't have to go to all that trouble. You could have just mailed it."

"I know, but then I wouldn't have had an excuse to come over and see this beautiful old church Maddie's been telling me so much about."

Kate's eyes widened in surprise. "Maddie told you . . . where I lived?"

"Don't worry. She didn't divulge any other secrets about you." His grin was as disarming as his words. "But she knows how much I love old buildings, and when we got to talking about some of the stone houses in this part of the state, she told me that I simply had to see yours. She said you were finishing up some pretty amazing renovations."

"Well, I don't know about their being amazing," Kate said

with a grimace. "They've been more of a headache than anything else."

"Renovations usually are. But they're worth it in the long run. Especially on a place like this."

"Thanks." Kate smiled, then paused uncertainly. "Would you . . . like to see inside?"

"I'd love to, if it's not too much trouble. But I won't stay long." Cole took a quick glance at his watch. "I have an appointment at two o'clock and I figure it will take me about forty-five minutes to get there."

"It's no trouble at all." Kate stepped back to let him enter. "Just ignore the ghoulish appearance. The workmen haven't exactly earned the Good Housekeeping Seal of Approval for the neat and tidy way they left the place."

Cole chuckled as he walked into the hall. "Tell me about it. I had some work done on my place in London shortly after I bought it. But I had to go out of town before it was finished and no one thought to put out dust covers."

Kate grinned sympathetically. "Much of a mess?"

"Let's just say, I'm still picking plaster chips out of the furniture." Cole paused on the threshold of the room and glanced at his surroundings with interest. "Wow, this is beautiful, Kate. Early nineteen hundreds and in excellent condition." He glanced up at the exposed beams in the ceiling and then back down at the floor. "Maddie was right. You've done a marvelous job with the decorating. Another one of your talents?"

"Not really. I just kind of follow my hunches—and watch Martha Stewart," Kate admitted sheepishly. "Can I get you a cup of coffee?"

"Only if you're having one." Cole glanced at the bucket of dirty water and the bottles of cleaning fluids and polish. "I get the feeling I've caught you in the middle of things."

"That's okay, I was ready for a break," Kate said as she headed for the compact kitchen. "I've spent the entire morning cleaning my new showroom."

Cole followed her in. "You have a showroom?"

"Yep. Had it built onto the back of the church. I used to display my work in the living room, but when I realized that stained glass was starting to take up more space than furniture, I decided it was time for a change. So I designed a studio."

"That's wonderful. Can I see it?"

"There's nothing to see yet." Kate ground up a special mixture of beans and then poured cold water into the coffee maker. "The official opening's not for another two weeks, so I haven't had a chance to hang anything. But I know where I want everything to go, and it's going to look fabulous. Now if I can just get people to come, I'll be all set."

"Well, judging by what I saw of your work last night, that shouldn't be a problem. Speaking of which," he said, reaching into the pocket of his jeans. "I believe this was the agreed-upon price."

Kate slowly extended her hand. "I don't know what the agreed-upon price was, but—oh my God!" She stared at the check in astonishment. "This is still way too much, Cole."

He shrugged dismissively. "Consider it relief money."

"Relief?"

"Yes. Mine. At finally having found the window I've been looking for. I wasn't kidding when I told you I'd been looking for just the right piece for a long time."

"Yes, but why didn't you commission one? A custom-designed window wouldn't have cost you any more than this."

"Maybe not, but since I really didn't know exactly what I was looking for, it would have been hard to sit down with the artist and tell him what I wanted. When I saw your window, I knew I'd found just what I was looking for."

Kate took another look at the dollar amount on the check, and then sighed. "Well, I can't say that it won't help. Building an addition put a pretty heavy dent in my savings. Thanks, Cole."

He smiled and inclined his head. "You're welcome." His gaze seemed to linger on her face.

Kate put the check in a drawer and then took two stoneware mugs down from the cupboard over the stove. She put out sugar and milk, very aware of Cole leaning against the counter watching her. Funny how much smaller the room suddenly seemed with him in it. But then, at well over six feet, Cole would be a considerable presence in any room. She glanced at him quickly as she poured the coffee. Strange that she hadn't noticed that intriguing cleft in his chin last night . . .

"No sugar?" Cole asked when she only put cream in her coffee.

"Hmm? Oh, not anymore," Kate said, blushing. She *had* to stop staring at him. "I gave it up about the same time I quit smoking."

Cole's mouth twisted. "Me too. After my father's first heart attack, my mother decided to change the family's eating habits. So out went all the comfort foods and in came nutrition with a capital N."

Kate laughed. "How old were you?"

"About fifteen."

"Tough age to be introduced to health food. I think that's about the time I discovered I was a chocoholic."

"You—a chocolate lover? You sure don't look it."

Kate looked up in time to see Cole's eyes resting on her figure—and went hot and cold all over. "Don't let the size fool you. Under this slender exterior beats the heart of a hopeless sweet tooth." She wrapped her hands around her mug so he wouldn't see them shaking. "But you look like you've stuck with the regime."

"For the most part, but it's hard when you travel as much as I do. Restaurant food is guaranteed to put weight on, and though I hate to admit it, there are times when I really love sinking my teeth into a hot roast beef dinner." Cole closed his eyes and sighed. "With mashed potatoes, gravy, and a big slice of apple pie for dessert."

Kate laughed at the longing in his voice. "Your mother would have a fit."

"No doubt."

"What about your father? Has he learned to appreciate your mother's nutritional bent?"

"I think he did, before he died."

Kate could have kicked herself. "I'm so sorry."

"Don't be. You'd think two heart attacks would be enough

to warn anybody to slow down. But not him. He just kept on slogging."

"How old was he?"

"Fifty-three. He died in his sleep."

"Fifty-three." Kate wasn't quite sure what prompted her to add, "Five years younger than my father."

Cole gave her a sideways glance. "Is that a comment on his health too?"

"No, though I'm surprised Dad hasn't had *at least* two heart attacks. He works ridiculous hours. He'd always been a ten-hour-a-day man, but after Mom died, the ten stretched into twelve, then into fourteen, and . . . well, you get the picture."

"That must have been hard on you."

Kate lifted her shoulders in a shrug. "I had my brother. Poor Matt. I don't think he ever planned on taking such an active interest in his sister. We just kind of stuck together after Mom died."

"Do you see much of your brother now?"

"Not as much as I'd like to. Between trying to finish enough pieces for the show, and staying out of the workmen's way, it's been kind of hectic. He and his wife and son live close by though."

Cole's gaze was thoughtful as it rested on her face. "Your father must have been pretty upset when both his son and his daughter moved away."

"I'm not even sure he noticed." Kate smiled sadly. "Dad was spending a lot of time in Europe then, and the comings and goings of his family probably didn't mean all that much. But listen, you didn't come here to listen to me ramble on about my life."

Cole watched her over the rim of his mug. He knew she wasn't playing on his sympathies, but it was pretty hard not to get involved when he heard her talk like that. There was a touching vulnerability about her that made him want to pull her into his arms and hold her tightly against his chest. "No, but now that I have, I'd like to hear more, Kate. Unfortunately, it's not going to be today." He glanced at his watch again and regretfully slid off the stool. "I just stopped by when I realized I'd be going right by your door. I hope you didn't mind me intruding into your day."

"Having someone interrupt me in the middle of cleaning up a work crew's mess is hardly an intrusion."

"Good, then I feel better." He finished his coffee and set the mug on the counter. "Listen, when did you say your show was?"

"Friday, September fourteenth."

Cole thought for a minute, and then nodded. Excellent. He wanted to see Kate again and coming back for her show would give him the perfect opportunity to do that. "That should work out fine. I'll be heading back to New York to-night, and then I'll probably be out of town for a while, but I'll definitely try to make it back for your opening. I'd really like to see more of your work. And I'd love to see how this place looks when it's all back together. Old buildings hold a particular kind of fascination for me."

"Yes. Madeleine told me you were something of an expert in the field of antiquities," Kate said.

His smile was surprisingly humble. "She was exaggerat-ing. Professor Morris, the man I spoke to last night, is the real expert."

"That's not the impression she gave me."

"Well, you know Maddie."

Kate's mouth curved in a smile. "Yes, I certainly do. So, have you had a chance to visit any of the antique stores around here?" she asked as she walked him to the door. "I recall hearing you say that was something you wanted to do."

"Yes, that's right." Cole glanced at her . . . and then away. "I've been trying to track down a particular antique for some time now, and I was told that it ended up in this area."

"That's hardly surprising. People come from all over the States to shop for antiques in Vermont. You're bound to find what you're looking for."

"I hope so. Unfortunately, someone else is looking for it too, so I just have to hope I get there first."

"Well, good luck with your search, Cole. And thanks again." Kate held out her hand, glad that it was steadier than her pulse. "It's been a pleasure doing business with you."

Cole took her hand and held onto it a little longer than was strictly necessary. "I'll be in touch."

Kate stood by the door and watched him pull out of the driveway, then waved as he turned onto the road. *I'll be in touch,* he'd told her.

"Yes, I hope you will, Cole Beresford," Kate breathed quietly. "I most certainly hope you will."

"A spinning wheel, you say?" Mrs. Barrett raised her eyes from the business card in her hand to the face of the tall, good-looking man standing in front of her, and nodded. "Yes, as a matter of fact I did receive one. It came in a few months back with a shipment of antiques from the north of England."

"Would that have been from the estate of Lady Thelford?"

Mrs. Barrett glanced at him suspiciously. "How did you know that? Are you a dealer?"

Cole smiled, recognizing in the woman's voice a true antique dealer's competitiveness. "No, but I happen to be something of an antique buff myself. I notice you have some very good pieces here."

Her wariness eased slightly. "It's good of you to say so, Mr. Beresford. I pride myself on the quality and variety of the antiques I carry. In fact, you may be interested in taking a closer look at some of the pieces I've gathered over the last little while. I have some very fine examples of Regency furniture from the collection of—"

"Mrs. Barrett, I am particularly interested in the spinning wheel you received," Cole broke in gently. "I know that the late Lady Thelford was in possession of two very old ones, and that both of them were sent to America with some of her other belongings. I'm trying to find out which one ended up here."

"Did you know Lady Thelford?" Mrs. Barrett asked.

"Distantly."

"Oh, how marvelous." The lady's lingering reserve dissolved completely. "Do you know, I've never met a member of the aristocracy yet, though I sell their belongings every day!"

Cole was careful to hide his amusement. "I wonder if I might see it."

"What?"

"The spinning wheel?"

"Oh, that." Mrs. Barrett slanted him a curious look. "I've never known a man to spin before."

"I don't intend to use it, Mrs. Barrett. One of the spinning wheels has a rather . . . interesting history and I was hoping to buy it for collecting purposes," Cole explained carefully. "My last source indicated that it might have been shipped here by mistake."

"Well, I did wonder at the time why a spinning wheel would have been included in the shipment," Mrs. Barrett commented. "It wasn't at all in keeping with the rest of the furnishings. I've never seen such a fine collection of Limoges porcelain in my life. Nearly the entire set. And the dining room table and chairs—well, they sold very quickly indeed." She winked at him. "I have an established clientele who are always anxious to know when I receive a shipment from England. I actually had two couples bidding on the—"

"Mrs. Barrett, could I see the spinning wheel please?" Cole interrupted her again.

"I'm so sorry, Mr. Beresford, I do keep getting off topic. But no, I'm afraid you can't see it. I don't have it anymore."

Cole's stomach knotted. "You *sold* it?"

"Yes. A young woman came in one afternoon last week and bought it."

"A young woman?" Cole felt the knot ease slightly. Thank God. At least Davenport hadn't beaten him to the punch. "Can you give me her name?" he asked, reaching into his pocket for a pen and a piece of paper.

"Well, no, I'm afraid I can't."

"You can't?"

"No." Mrs. Barrett looked somewhat embarrassed. "Because I have no idea what it is."

Cole frowned. "Didn't you make out a bill?"

"No. It was all very strange, now that I think about it," Mrs. Barrett said with a self-conscious laugh. "I think I must have been in a bit of a daze. Which is most unlike me because I am usually very levelheaded when it comes to my business. But I can't recall having done anything right that afternoon."

"Mrs. Barrett, did you by any chance spin the wheel?" Cole asked slowly.

"Pardon?"

"The wheel. Did you give it a turn?"

"Well, yes, now that you mention it, I suppose I did. Or rather, the young lady did," Mrs. Barrett amended. "And I must say, it had a beautifully smooth action."

"Mrs. Barrett, can you tell me anything about this woman? Anything at all?"

"Well, I don't know." The elderly woman looked thoughtful for a moment. "What would you like to know?"

"Was she from around here?"

"She might have been, but I'd never seen her before. She wasn't my usual type of client, you understand."

"Do you know if she intended to use the wheel for spinning?"

"As I recall, she just wanted it for decorative purposes. Which I thought rather strange since she seemed very concerned that it have *all* its working parts. Most people who buy a spinning wheel intact do so with an eye to using it."

"What did the woman look like, Mrs. Barrett?" Cole asked. "Can you tell me anything about her?"

Mrs. Barrett paused for a moment to think. "Well, she was very pretty. Fairly petite, slim. And she had lovely hair. Kind of a brandy color, I supposed you'd call it."

Cole marked it all down. Wonderful. That probably described at least a thousand women in the immediate area. There had to be some other way of identifying her.

"How did she pay for the wheel, Mrs. Barrett? Did she give you a check?"

"Oh no. Wimpole-Barrett's doesn't take checks," she told him. "Cash or credit card is our policy. We deal with too many out-of-town travelers, and I hate to say that I've been burned more times than I care to admit. And yet, do you know, I think if she had asked me, I probably would have said yes. I was feeling very queer that day. Very queer indeed."

Cole drew in a deep breath, feeling more and more certain that he'd located the Lockton spinning wheel. "Mrs. Barrett, do you have *any* idea where I could find this woman?"

She regretfully shook her head. "No, Mr. Beresford, I'm afraid I don't."

"Damn," Cole swore softly. Somehow, he had to find out the woman's identity. He was too close to let it slip away now.

He took back the business card he'd given Mrs. Barrett and wrote some numbers on the back. "I'm giving you two telephone numbers, Mrs. Barrett. The first is my cell phone, and the second is my room at the Maple Tree Inn, where I'm staying. If you remember anything at all, I'd very much appreciate your giving me a call. It's extremely important that I find that spinning wheel."

Mrs. Barrett sighed. "I'm sorry I can't be of more help, Mr. Beresford. It's most unlike me not to have prepared the proper paperwork. My accountant will probably take me to task over it." The woman studied the card thoughtfully. "Nice girl, but a bit strange."

"Your accountant?"

"No, no, the young lady who bought the wheel. She thought she was hearing voices."

Cole raised one dark eyebrow in surprise. "I . . . beg your pardon?"

"Voices. She thought I had the radio on, but I don't even own one. Still, as I was saying, I was feeling a little absent-minded myself that afternoon." Mrs. Barrett smiled as she accompanied him to the door. "Maybe it was something in the air."

"Yes, maybe it was." Cole's smile was polite, but distracted. "Well, thank you again, Mrs. Barrett. I appreciate your time."

Cole left the shop and reviewed everything Mrs. Barrett had told him. It *had* to have been the Lockton spinning wheel. The physical description she'd given him had matched, as did the timing of the shipment. Even the absentminded behavior of the people who came into contact with it fit the pattern. Which meant that the *other* spinning wheel in Lady Thelford's possession—the one that had ended up in California—*wasn't* the one he was looking for. He'd managed to get lucky on that score.

What she'd said about the woman hearing voices didn't make any particular sense to him. Maybe she had, but he doubted it had anything to do with the spinning wheel. He'd met some pretty funny people in his life, and hearing voices wasn't the worst of their complaints.

One thing Cole did know, however, was that he sure as hell wasn't going back to New York today. The discovery that the spinning wheel was here and that a woman—possibly a local one—had bought it meant that he had no choice but to stick around. He had to find out who she was and where she lived. Then he had to try to convince her to sell it back to him before the situation got out of control. There was no other choice.

Her very life might well depend on it!

After Cole left, Kate went back to work. She had too much to do to sit around dreaming about cleft chins and amazing brown eyes—even if it was a whole lot more fun than vacuuming up leftover plaster dust. Because once she was done cleaning, she intended to start work on a new piece of stained glass. An idea had been floating around in her head for the past few weeks and while Kate hadn't been able to capture it fully, it was there, a nebulous collection of shapes and colors hovering just beyond reach. She only hoped that when she sat down at the drafting table, the form would finally come to her.

For now, however, art would have to wait. She had promised herself that she was going to get her house in order—and that's exactly what she was going to do. She started by giving all of the furniture—with the exception of the spinning wheel—two coats of polish and buffing them to a glowing shine. She washed the pillow covers and shook out the mats; she even gave the curtains and the vertical blinds a much-needed going over, so that by six o'clock, the inside of the church was sparkling. There wasn't a speck of plaster dust anywhere. Even the slate floor in the kitchen was back to its original shade of green rather than the nondescript gray it had been for so long.

Satisfied that she could live in her surroundings again, Kate put the lid back on the tin of wood polish and picked up her bucket of dirty water. All she had to do now was the windows, and she could tackle those in the morning. That would leave the afternoon free for work. Of course, if she did the kitchen windows now, she would be able to get the rest of them finished that much earlier, and perhaps even get to her new design before nightfall.

It was all the convincing Kate needed. She carried the stepladder into the kitchen and positioned it as close to the window as she could. Then, picking up the bottle of window cleaner and a handful of paper towels, she started climbing.

She was about halfway up when the phone rang.

"For crying out loud!" Kate stopped and glanced at the phone. She was tempted to let the answering machine pick it up. But then, remembering that it might be Matt calling with news about Christian, she quickly scooted back down and answered it herself.

She was glad she did. It wasn't her brother on the other end. It was Cole Beresford.

"Kate, hi. I hope I'm not disturbing you again."

Kate gripped the receiver a little tighter. As if hearing a voice that resembled warm honey could ever be disturbing. "Not at all, I was just finishing up." She heard a sudden crackle on the line, followed by the sound of traffic in the background. "Are you on your way back to New York?"

"As a matter of fact, I'm on my way back to the Maple Tree Inn," Cole told her. "I've decided to spend a few more days in the area. Listen, I know it's terribly short notice but would you . . . like to ha . . . with . . ."

"*Ouch.*" Kate winced at the sudden burst of static in her ear. "Cole, are you there?" She raised her voice to be heard over the noise. "There's a lot of interference on the line."

"Sorry, I'm go . . . wires. I said . . . you like to . . ."

"Cole, you're breaking up. Hello? Cole, are you still there?" Kate glanced at the phone in frustration. "Useless things," she muttered. "Cole? Hello? Cole?" She heard a few more sputters and crackles and then the line went dead.

Great. Just when he'd been trying to ask her something, technology had hit a black hole.

She sighed as she hung up the receiver. That's okay, he'd call back. People always did when they got cut off. She stood by the phone and waited.

Five minutes later, Kate resolutely swallowed her disappointment. He hadn't called back. Whatever he'd wanted to talk to her about hadn't been important enough to warrant fighting with the telephone lines.

She headed back up the ladder and tried to tell herself it didn't matter. It wasn't smart to get hung up on a guy who could have any woman he wanted.

Too bad she didn't believe it.

Kate had just finished spritzing the entire upper portion of the kitchen window with cleaner when she heard a knock on the door. Jeepers, if it wasn't one thing . . .

She resolutely climbed back down the ladder and walked to the front door. Her annoyance vanished completely, however, when she opened it to see Cole standing there, with an apologetic look on his face.

"Sorry I didn't call back," he said, "but I figured there wasn't much point. I've been having a devil of a time with this new phone."

Kate glanced at the palm-sized cell phone in his hand and shook her head. "It's not your phone. It's the area. Lots of people complain about fading in and out around here. It's probably all the trees."

"Well, that's good to know," Cole said as he tucked it into his pocket. "I didn't want you to think I couldn't be bothered to call back."

Kate gave him an overly bright smile and felt the butterflies come back. "Why would I think that?"

He suddenly caught sight of the paper towels in her hand. "I thought you said you were finished for the day?"

"I did. And I am. Well, almost. But I just thought I'd do the kitchen window before I packed it in. It's not a big one so it won't take long."

"Good, because what I was trying to say on the phone was, would you like to have dinner with me tonight?"

Kate's mouth went dry. "Dinner?"

"Yes. I know it's short notice, but I thought you might be ready for a break. If you don't already have plans, that is," he added quickly.

Kate almost told him that she did, when she suddenly remembered that Matt had called earlier to cancel. "As a matter of fact, I don't. And I'd love to have dinner with you, Cole."

His smile practically had her heart rate doubling. "Great. Then why don't I pick you up around seven-thirty. Will that give you enough time to finish what you're doing?"

"It will give me plenty of time to do that," Kate told him ruefully. "I'm not so sure it will give me time to clean *myself* up. I think I've got more dust in my hair than the vacuum cleaner. But . . . are you sure about this? It sounds like you've had a pretty hectic day yourself."

Cole smiled again, exposing a rather devastating dimple in his right cheek. "I think we've both had a hectic time of it. And I can't think of a better way to relax and unwind than with a good meal and an even better bottle of wine. What do you say?"

Without hesitating, Kate turned and threw the paper towels into the bucket. "I'd say, Mr. Beresford, that you've got yourself a date!"

The place Cole took her for dinner was actually an old house which had been turned into a delightful restaurant. The entire first floor had been gutted and then made into three separate dining rooms—each of which held no more than six tables. The Olde House—as it was aptly named—was well known in the area for excellent food, a reasonably priced wine list, and a comfortable, relaxed atmosphere. Kate knew the place by name, of course, but she'd never eaten there. Now, she was glad she hadn't. She liked the idea of coming here for the first time with Cole. It made their date seem more special somehow.

"Is this all right?" Cole asked as he held out a chair for her.

"It's perfect." Kate glanced around the quaintly decorated dining room, noting the touches that made it feel like part of someone's private home, and smiled her approval. "But I'm surprised *you* knew about it. It's a little off the beaten path."

"I happened to drive by it on my way out of town this afternoon," Cole explained as he sat down across from her. "Then when I realized that I was going to be staying in the area for a while, I took the liberty of stopping in on my way back. You haven't been here before, have you?"

Kate shook her head. "I've always wanted to, but going out to dinner hasn't exactly been high on my priority list. The only dinner invitations I get these days are to my brother and sister-in-law's house."

"I can't understand why." Cole picked up the wine list, which was creatively displayed on a large bottle of wine, and cast a discerning eye over the choices. "I know this isn't New York, but I can't believe the young men around here aren't beating a path to your door." His eyes lifted and lingered on her face. "Especially looking as beautiful as you do."

Kate's cheeks colored under the heat of his gaze. She was glad she had decided to dress up a little for the occasion. The long toffee-colored skirt topped with a cream silk blouse was perfect for the casually elegant setting of the restaurant.

"Actually, I have a feeling that my brother may have warned off some of the more eager ones," she admitted. "And the others probably know that I live for my work and hardly ever take time off to play."

A faint glimmer of amusement replaced the heat in Cole's eyes. "What about tonight?"

"You caught me at a weak moment."

He grinned and returned his attention to the wine list. "Remind me to make sure you're always cleaning house when I call to ask you out."

Kate quickly reached for her water glass. Funny, he almost made it sound like there was going to be a next time. And if *that* wasn't wishful thinking, she didn't know what was.

"Hi, there. Can I get you anything from the bar?" the young, fresh-faced waitress asked.

"Yes, I'll have a gin and tonic," Kate told her with a smile.

"And I'll have scotch," Cole said. "No ice, a little water on the side."

The girl wrote it down on her pad. "Would you like to wait a few minutes before you order dinner?"

"I think that might be a good idea." Cole glanced at Kate. "Unless you're starving after all that cleaning?"

She was, but she wasn't about to tell him that. "Thanks, but I'm happy to relax for a few minutes."

Cole winked at the waitress. "Give us about fifteen minutes and we should be ready."

The girl's cheeks went as pink as her sweater. "Yes, sir. I'll be . . . um, right back with your drinks."

Kate quickly turned away to hide her smile. Poor girl. She knew just how she felt. She felt the same way every time Cole smiled at her too. Men like Cole Beresford weren't a common sight around here. Apart from the way he looked, he dressed like somebody who moved in a different league. Tonight he was wearing a pair of beautifully tailored black pants, a light gray silk shirt, and a gray and black tweed jacket that had to have been custom-made for him. Cole wasn't a small man, and there probably weren't many off-the-rack jackets that would fit his broad shoulders and chest as perfectly as this one did. And when you combined all that with ruggedly handsome looks and warm brown eyes you could get lost in, it wasn't surprising that any female would walk away feeling somewhat breathless.

"Do you have the same effect on small children and animals?" Kate couldn't resist asking.

"I beg your pardon?"

"Never mind." She quickly reached for her water glass again.

In a few minutes, another young waitress emerged from the kitchen. This one was carrying a basket of freshly baked rolls, a colorful ceramic pot filled with creamy whipped butter and a tray of assorted pickles. She smiled at Kate as she put each of the items down on the table, but her eyes were on Cole most of the time, leading Kate to believe that some serious chatter was going on in the kitchen.

She wondered how long it would be before the next waitress came out. If nothing else, it was a guarantee of good service.

"So, what precipitated your sudden change in plans?" Kate asked, curious in spite of herself to know more about the man sitting opposite her. "I thought you said you'd done what you came to do and that you were heading back to New York."

"I did. But as a result of something I learned today, I decided to stick around a bit longer."

"Won't your office be looking for you?"

"I've already called them to say I won't be back. This other matter is far more important."

"Oh?" She rested her chin on her hand and smiled at him. "And just what is this other far more important matter that's keeping you here?"

His own smile was enigmatic. "Let's just say it's something which, if proven true, will set contemporary historians on their ears."

Kate blinked. "Now that's an intriguing statement. But it doesn't tell me very much."

"It wasn't meant to."

"So you won't tell me anything?"

The first waitress returned with their drinks and set them on the table. After she moved away, Cole shook his head. "It's not that I *won't* tell you, Kate, it's that I can't. Not right now anyway. But if everything turns out the way I hope, I promise you'll be one of the first to hear." He lifted his glass and held it out to her. "For now, I'd like to propose a toast to the loveliest cleaning lady I've ever seen. And may your opening be a huge success."

"I'll drink to that," Kate said as she raised her glass and touched it to his. "*And* to the handsome gentleman who made me leave my scouring pad behind and gave me such a nice start toward that success. Cheers."

They tipped back their glasses and drank in silence, their eyes meeting briefly over the rims. Kate was the first to look away.

"So, never mind asking me questions, what about you?" Cole said at length. "I don't mind telling you that I find your story a little intriguing."

"My story?"

"Yes. About giving up the glitz of New York to come and live in rural domesticity."

Kate's mouth twisted into a wry smile. "You mean, the poor little rich girl leaves the city to find her own way in life thing?"

"That's not what I said."

"No, but it wouldn't be the first time someone did."

"Is it true?"

"I suppose," Kate admitted. "It's one of the reasons I don't like Madeleine telling people about my background. I prefer to keep a low profile around here."

"In that case, I suggest you lose the Mercedes. It tends to stand out amongst the pick-up trucks and SUVs."

Two spots of color appeared in Kate's cheeks. "Yeah, I guess it does. But it was a birthday present from my father, so I couldn't very well send it back."

"Let me guess. A peace offering?"

"Kind of." Kate sighed. "You were right when you said Dad wasn't too happy about my moving up here."

"I thought you said he didn't notice."

"He had to. After Mom died, I started acting as his social director."

Cole lifted an eyebrow in surprise. "Really? Did he do a lot of entertaining?"

"Not at first. After Mom died, we didn't see much of him at all. He ate out most of the time. He knew how to cook, but I think he just wanted to get out of the condo." Kate took a warm roll from the basket Cole held out to her. "But once he started getting involved in international deals again, the entertaining picked up. He was always bringing clients and business associates home for dinner."

Cole broke his own roll in two and spread a thick dollop of creamy butter on one half. "And that's where you got involved."

"Kind of. My role was to organize everything. I planned the menus and hired the staff. I made sure we had enough glasses and silverware on hand, as well as enough champagne, caviar and cognac to keep an entire football team going for a week."

Cole smiled. "Sounds like your father knew how to throw a good party. Were you required to stay and participate in the evening as well?"

"I was in the beginning. But once Dad realized that I wasn't going to make it as a big-time real estate mogul, he stopped asking. He didn't tell me that I couldn't stay, of course. He just left it up to me to make my own decision."

"And you decided that you had better things to do."

"Pretty much." Kate fiddled with her cutlery. "I've never been good at small talk."

"Does your father still spend a lot of time in Europe?"

"Yes. He is, or at least he was, involved in a huge commercial development in London. My last two birthday presents came from Harrods."

"You miss him."

It wasn't a question, and Kate shrugged. "I miss who he used to be. I'm not sure I even know who he is anymore. Dad doesn't have time for anything other than work. He judges everything and everyone by degrees of success. And as far as daughters go, I guess I was something of a failure."

"As a real estate mogul, maybe, but not as anything else. Look at your life here, Kate. Don't you think you've made a success of that?"

"Cole, I run a small-time craft business out of a converted church in rural Vermont," Kate said bluntly. "That's not exactly big-time success."

"Is that so? Well let's see if I can rephrase your life so that it sounds a little more noteworthy." Cole paused for a moment, thoughtfully tapping his finger against his lips. "Did you have your own place in New York?"

"Yes."

"Was it nice?"

"It suited my purposes."

"Okay. So you left your swanky apartment in New York—"

"I never said it was swanky—"

"To move to Vermont, where you bought a dilapidated stone church and started life over. You carried out an aggressive restoration project, and now that same church could be featured in *Better Homes and Gardens*, or even *Architectural Digest*. There's your first success. Success number two, you taught yourself the art of stained glass and eventually turned your hobby into a business. One that was so successful it necessitated the addition of a studio onto the back of your home. Success number three," he said, counting them off on his fingers, "you earned the respect and support of a woman like Madeleine Carstairs, and success number four, you sold an original piece of art for more money than you've probably made on glass in the entire year. And you're only—how old?"

Kate's lips twitched irrepressibly. "Don't you think that's being a little personal, Mr. Beresford?"

"Of course. Those are the best kind of questions to ask."

Kate laughed at his answer, amused that he was honest enough to admit it—and liking the fact that he could make her laugh. "I'm thirty-two."

"Really. That old?"

"Cole!"

"Just kidding. I like to see you laugh."

A smile tugged reluctantly at her mouth. "Flattery will get you nowhere."

"Pity, I was hoping it might. But I meant what I said, Kate," Cole continued in a matter-of-fact voice. "People judge success by what a person's been able to accomplish. And I'd say you've accomplished a hell of a lot in your thirty-two years."

Kate toyed with her glass. "You don't happen to do a little psychiatry on the side, do you, Dr. Beresford?"

His smile flashed briefly. "No, but some things are easier to see than others, especially given the fact that I'm older than you."

"Oh? And how old are *you*?"

"Sorry. I never divulge that kind of information on a first date."

Kate gasped—and then started to laugh. "Cole Beresford, you are . . . incorrigible!"

"Incorrigible!" This time, it was Cole who threw back his head and laughed. "Good God, I haven't been called that since I was in school. Which I frequently was, I might add. And before you accidentally discover anything *else* about my wayward youth, I think it's time we ordered."

It was undoubtedly the fastest three hours Kate had ever spent with a man. When Cole finally paid the bill and they got up to leave, she was genuinely sorry their date was over. She was amazed at how comfortable she felt with him. It was like they'd known each other for years. He was so easy to talk to, and after a few awkward moments at the beginning, their conversation had flowed like wine.

On the other hand, Kate had never spent an evening with anyone who made her feel more aware of her own femininity either. Every time Cole's gaze fell on her hair, or lingered on her face, she felt a strange pulsing way down deep inside. And all it took was one look from those dark, slumberous eyes to bring the color rushing to her cheeks. It might have been a long time since Kate had had a physical relationship with anyone, but she didn't forget the signs.

Unfortunately, even as she recognized them, Kate warned herself not to get involved. Men like Cole Beresford didn't hang around places like Barre, Vermont for long; they didn't belong here. They belonged in New York City where they lived in trendy brownstones and dated beautiful, successful women who just *flew in* for the weekend. They spent their summers in the Hamptons and their winters in Gstaad, and they did not get involved with stained-glass artists who were trying to scratch out a living.

Kate knew that, because she knew the type. And she knew she couldn't hope to hold Cole's interest beyond a few days. The man was an acknowledged authority in the rarified world of expensive art and elusive treasures. He was used to moving in a different circle. Sure, she came from a reasonably well-to-do family, but she wasn't in his league. She hadn't traveled the world the way he had, or seen the things he'd seen.

In fact, maybe he was already getting bored with her, Kate reflected sadly as they headed back to the church. He'd hardly said a word to her since they'd got in the car. Maybe he was already thinking about getting back to New York, and to the sophisticated lady—or ladies—who were waiting for him there.

Cole *was* quiet on the ride home, but not because of Kate. He'd left his cell phone in the car while they'd been at dinner, and he'd seen the message indicator flashing as soon as he'd got in. Someone had called, but until he dropped Kate off, there was nothing he could do about it. There was no telling who might be on the other end—or what they might be calling about.

He was also finding himself far too aware of Kate as a woman and that was something he wasn't prepared to deal with right now. He didn't like the fact that he wanted to know more about her than just what she did for a living. In the restaurant tonight, he'd hardly been able to take his eyes off her. He'd watched every movement she'd made, from the way her long, slender fingers had caressed the stem of the wineglass in that unknowingly erotic fashion, to the way they had gently tugged at a strand of hair when she was nervous. He'd seen the pulse fluttering at the base of her throat and noticed how her skin seemed to glow like warm cream in the soft light of the candles. He'd even seen the left side of her mouth tremble just a little when he'd complimented her.

And he'd wanted to touch her more than he cared to admit. He'd wanted to reach across the table and run his fingers over the smoothness of her cheek. He'd wanted to press his lips to the tender curve of her neck and then slowly move up to her earlobe. He'd wanted to see those bright, beautiful blue eyes turn dark with yearning. When Kate had brushed by him in the restaurant, Cole had been totally unprepared for the jolt of pure sexual desire he'd experienced. It was so strong he'd wanted to turn around and pull her into his arms and find out just how soft and sweet that beautiful mouth really was.

He hadn't, of course, and he wouldn't. He wasn't the kind of man who got off on casual affairs or one-night stands. He didn't want to get involved with Kate Pedigrew or anybody else because there was just too much at stake. He had to track down the woman who'd bought the Lockton spinning wheel and convince her to sell it back to him. That had to take priority over everything. Which meant that the smartest thing he could do with Kate was to get her home and say good-bye. The problem was, he didn't want to say good-bye. He wanted to say hello, how are you, and a whole lot more. Until he looked at the flashing red light, and remembered what it meant.

That's why, when he walked her to the door, he made no move to follow her inside, as much as he would have liked to. "Thanks, Kate. I had a great time," he said quietly.

Kate fumbled in her bag for her keys, grateful to have something to do with her hands. She always hated these good-bye-at-the-door-after-the-first-date scenes. Things like that were supposed to get easier as you got older, but they never did. She felt as awkward now as she had at seventeen when she'd stood outside her front door and wondered if Philip Alderman was going to kiss her. As it turned out he hadn't, and the rejection had hurt for a very long time.

"Me too," Kate said finally. She'd been planning to ask Cole in for coffee, but changed her mind when she saw the look in his eyes. Mentally, he'd already left. "Well, good night."

"Good night." Cole hesitated for a moment, and then smiled. "I promise I'll give you more warning before I show up on your doorstep next time."

Kate smiled too and watched him walk back to his car. She waved as he drove off and then quietly closed the door. *Next time?* Yeah, right. Who was he trying to kid? He'd find what he was looking for and then head back to New York. She'd probably never see him again.

Which was okay, Kate assured herself as she walked into her bedroom. She didn't need any complications in her life right now—especially in the form of a handsome world traveler like Cole. But she was glad they'd had the chance to have dinner together. They'd shared a few laughs over a delicious meal and Kate had thoroughly enjoyed herself. If nothing else, she would be able to tell Maddie that her friend,

Cole Beresford, certainly knew how to show a lady a good time!

Cole reached for the phone the minute he turned onto the main road. He dialed the four-digit access code, heard the beep, and listened as the first message played back.

*"Hello, Mr. Beresford? This is Mrs. Barrett from Wimpole-Barrett's. The antique shop, remember?"*

Cole's mouth curved in the darkness. As if he was likely to forget.

*"I hope this message is reaching you. I just called to say that I remembered something about the young lady who bought the spinning wheel. It's not very much, but you did say to call if I remembered anything. Well, I recall her saying that she lived about an hour away from the shop. And I think she was married. A nice-looking young man got out of a truck and helped her put the spinning wheel in. I know it's not much, but I suppose it's better than nothing. Well, bye bye."*

That was it? The woman he was looking for lived an hour away and that she might or might not be married? Cole's dark brows knit together in a frown. Mrs. Barrett was right; it sure as hell wasn't much. But it was better than nothing. He now knew that he was looking for an attractive, dark-haired *married or engaged* woman, who lived about an hour from the shop. In which *direction* from the shop, he had no idea—which meant, that he was really no closer to finding his elusive lady now than he was when he'd started out this morning. How the hell was he supposed to track down the owner of a spinning wheel in an area that drew weavers and spinners from all over the—

Wait a minute. Craftspeople. Crafters. Of course! Why hadn't he thought of it before?

Cole abruptly pulled the car over to the side of the road. He reached into his briefcase for his organizer, and flicking on the overhead light, quickly leafed through the pages. When he found what he was looking for, he picked up his phone and punched in the number. Seconds later, he heard her familiar southern drawl. "Hello?"

"Madeleine, it's Cole. Yes, I'm still in the area. Sorry to be calling so late. Listen, I wonder if I could drop by in the morning. I need to talk to you. Is it important?" Cole was glad she couldn't see his face. *Only one of the most important things he'd ever had to do.*

During the tourist season, Kate seldom had time for herself. From the moment she opened her doors at ten until she locked them again at six, a steady trickle of visitors dropped by the church. Some of them were buyers; others just liked to come in for a browse and a chat.

After the first of September, however, Kate adjusted her schedule. She shortened her midweek hours, and was only open on weekends by appointment. And on this particular Monday morning, she had taken no appointments at all. Because it was time to start making her newly built studio *look* like a studio.

She started by moving all of her larger pieces of stained glass out of the living room and into her new room, which on this brisk fall morning was gloriously awash with sunshine. Bright, golden shafts of it poured down through the skylights and passed through a large piece of pink, burgundy and clear glass Kate had already hung, bathing the whole room in a rosy pink glow.

Next to that, she hung a semi circular piece of work in three shades of amber glass set against a dark background, which she called the King's Moon. A larger piece still called The Greenhouse sat on the window ledge until she figured out where to put it. The smaller pieces and the Tiffany-style lamps would come out later.

Kate hummed as she worked, aware of a pleasant feeling of contentment this morning. Whether that was as a result of her house being livable again—or her dinner with Cole last night—she wasn't sure, though she suspected it was the latter. She hadn't enjoyed an evening that much in . . . longer than she cared to remember.

But if it didn't happen again, that was okay. Kate had stayed awake a long time coming to terms with that. She wasn't reading any hidden meanings into the dinner they'd shared. Cole had probably just found himself at loose ends as a result of having decided to stay in town a bit longer, and rather than spend the evening alone or in his room, he'd decided to ask her out.

Simple. She wasn't going to obsess about it. What was the point? Men like Cole didn't just walk into the lives of backwoods crafters and stay there. They passed *through* them like beams of sunlight passing through her windows, making them glow for a few brief shining moments and then moving on again. That's what Cole was going to do. He was going to move on like that elusive beam of sunlight. Sure they'd had a nice evening, and yes he'd told her that he wanted to do it again, but she didn't believe it. He'd probably just said that to be polite.

Besides, her studio opening was in less than two weeks and that's what Kate needed to concentrate on now. She had more than enough to do to get ready for it. And if Cole happened to turn up like he said he might, that was great. If not . . . well, only time would tell. In the meantime, there was no point in daydreaming about what she might like to see take place. Because at times like this, wishing just wasn't going to make it happen.

At about the same time Kate was coming to that conclusion, Cole Beresford was turning into the driveway of Madeleine Carstairs's home. He'd spent the night telling himself not to get his hopes up. In fact, he absolutely refused to indulge himself in the possibility that he might find an answer, because he knew it was a slender chance at best. But that didn't stop him from hoping that Madeleine might be able to give him some of the answers he needed. She was well known in the artistic community, and knew most of the crafters by name. If anyone was in a position to know whose work had suddenly undergone any kind of change for the better, it would be her.

"Cole, honey, this is such a treat," Madeleine said as she warmly kissed his cheek. "I was delighted to hear that you hadn't gone back to New York. And I've been positively dying of curiosity ever since you called."

"There's really nothing much to tell, Maddie," Cole said evasively. "I was just hoping you might be able to shed some light on a problem I'm having. You seem to have your finger on the pulse of what's going on around here."

Madeleine's throaty chuckle echoed around the foyer. "Well, yes, I suppose I do. There isn't much that goes on in this little burg I don't know about. But come on in and sit down. We might as well make ourselves comfortable." She turned and led the way into the sunny living room. "Can I offer you anything to drink? Coffee, tea, bourbon?"

Cole laughed as he shook his head and sat down. "I'm fine, Maddie, thanks, but you go head."

"That's all right. I don't usually start until noon," she said, winking at him. "By the way, before you tell me what this is all about, I want to thank you again for buying Kate's piece of stained glass the other night."

Surprised that she would bring it up, Cole shrugged his shoulders. "You don't have to thank me, Maddie. I bought the piece because I liked it. You know I'm not sentimental about things like that. I can't afford to be in my line of work."

"I know, but it was good of you just the same. Kate's a wonderful girl, isn't she?"

Sensing that Madeleine was more curious about his feelings for the artist than her work, Cole took his time answering. "She's a talented and thoroughly delightful young woman. But I recognize a matchmaking gleam when I see it, Maddie. And I'm telling you straight out, it won't work."

Madeleine pouted. "Oh now, Cole, you can't blame me for trying. Any man as handsome as you is bound to be the object of somebody's matchmaking attempts. And I consider myself to be very good in that particular field."

"I'm sure you are, but if you're so anxious to see someone get married, why don't you start with yourself?" Cole retaliated. "A wonderful woman like you should be married. You need somebody to look after and love, and to love you back."

Madeleine toyed with the heavy gold chain around her throat. "That's easy for you to say, Cole, you've never been married. But I was happy with Lawrence. I loved that man with all my heart and we had some wonderful times together. I don't think I'm ready to roll in his replacement just yet."

"Who said anything about replacing him?" Cole said with a gentle smile. "You'll never *replace* Lawrence, Maddie. He was a fine man, and I miss him too. But that's not to say you can't find happiness with somebody else. There are lots of good men out there."

Madeleine's lovely eyes sparkled. "Yes I know, and I'm trying to get one of them married off right now. Oh, all right, I won't say another word," she said when she saw the warning look in his eyes. "I'll just let nature takes its own sweet course—even if it is slower than molasses in December. Now, what kind of information were you looking for?"

Cole sat forward, resting his elbows on his knees and steepling his fingers in front of his face. "I know this may sound a little strange, Maddie, but do you know of anyone in the area who might recently have bought a spinning wheel?"

"A spinning wheel?" Madeleine stared at him in astonishment. "Good Lord, Cole, that's a strange question. What's this all about?"

"It's a long story and one I can't get into right now, but suffice it to say that I'm trying to track down a lady who bought a spinning wheel from that store I went to the other afternoon. And I couldn't think of a better place to start, than with you."

"Well, I'm flattered, of course," Maddie said, clearly not sure whether she should be or not, "but I don't know if I can help. Lord, Cole, a spinning wheel could have been bought by any one of hundreds of spinners in the area."

"Fortunately, I do have a few small pieces of information," Cole told her. "The owner of the antique shop told me that the lady who bought the wheel didn't know how to spin. She was buying it strictly for decoration."

"Well, I hate to tell you, honey, but that's going to make it even harder to track down. Three quarters of the people around here buy antiques for decoration. Why doesn't the woman who sold it to her simply check her records? She must have made out a bill."

"Apparently, she didn't. The shop was rather . . . busy at the time," Cole said carefully.

"Well, this isn't easy, Cole." Madeleine got up and slowly began to walk around the room. "Ninety-five percent of the population around here own at least one piece of antique furniture, some of which are functional, most of which are not."

"What about the ladies you socialize with? They must be into antiques. Have any of them mentioned buying a spinning wheel?"

"Honey, very few of *my* friends have tastes that run in that direction," Madeleine drawled. "For the most part, *their* type of antiques come from Christie's or Sotheby's."

Cole sat back and raked his fingers through his hair, disheveling the dark waves. "I was afraid of this. It's going to be like looking for a needle in a bloody haystack."

"Cole, if you don't mind my asking, what's so important about this particular spinning wheel? I mean, if you just want a spinning wheel, I'm sure there must be hundreds of them lying around."

"This isn't just *any* spinning wheel, Maddie." Cole rose and shoved his hands into his pockets. "I'm sorry I can't tell you anything more about it right now, but that's the way it is."

He walked toward the window and stood gazing across the expanse of beautifully manicured lawn. There had to be another avenue. Something he hadn't thought of. He needed more than she was giving him. "What about the craftspeople around here?" he asked quietly. "Have any of them displayed any . . . uncharacteristic flashes of brilliance lately?"

"Flashes of brilliance?" Madeleine gave a hoot. "Now that's a good one. Most of them wouldn't recognize a flash of brilliance if it walked up and slapped them in the face. I mean, I love them all dearly, Cole, but the biggest percentage of them are happy just to keep making the things they've been making for the past ten years."

"So you haven't noticed anyone being unusually creative of late."

"Not likely. Kate's the only one whose work has been showing strong signs of improvement, but that's been happening steadily over the past year. I can't say I've noticed any—what did you call it? Flashes of brilliance, in anyone else's work."

It wasn't what he'd been hoping to hear, but then, it had been a slim hope at best. Maddie couldn't be expected to know everything that went on in the area—though Cole knew damn well that she tried. Besides, maybe he was rushing his fences a bit. The woman who'd bought the wheel had only had it a few days. And if she didn't *spin* the wheel, she'd have no way of knowing what it was capable of—or that it wasn't the plain old ordinary spinning wheel it looked to be.

As to Maddie's comments about Kate, Cole had already dismissed her as a possible candidate. For one thing, Mrs. Barrett had suggested that the woman who'd bought it was attached, and to the best of Cole's knowledge, Kate wasn't. Certainly there was no man in her life she was likely to go furniture shopping with. For another thing, he would have seen the spinning wheel in her living room the day he'd stopped by with her check. People usually kept things like that in their main living areas. And while it was true that most of the furniture had been shrouded in dust covers, Cole was sure that he would have recognized the shape of a spinning wheel hidden beneath. Wouldn't he?

"Well, I thought it was worth a try." He turned around and slowly walked back toward Madeleine. "Maybe you can keep an eye and an ear out for me and let me know if you hear anything."

"Of course I will." Madeleine's gaze turned suddenly serious. "You're not kidding about this spinning wheel, are you, Cole? It means a lot to you."

He stared down at the carpet, not wanting her to see the look in his eyes. "More than you could possibly know, Maddie."

"And you can't tell me *anything* about it?"

"I can tell you this much. As hard as I'm trying to find it, so is a man by the name of Jeremy Davenport, whose methods aren't always orthodox when it comes to getting what he wants. That's why I have to find the woman who bought it and convince her to sell it back to me before Davenport gets here. Because if he finds her first, he'll do whatever it takes to get the spinning wheel away from her."

Madeleine stared at him, her expression a mixture of fear and bewilderment. "Cole, are you telling me that this man would use *force* to get it back?"

"The possibility exists, yes."

"But . . . it's only a spinning wheel, for heaven's sake." She laughed uncertainly. "Does this man think there's a fortune to be made selling antique spinning wheels on the black market?"

If it hadn't been such a serious matter, Cole might have laughed too. "I'll keep in touch, Maddie. I'm staying at the Maple Tree Inn. Here's my number. Call me any time you need."

"You're not going back to New York then?"

"Not until I find out where the spinning wheel is. It's best for all concerned that I stay close." *It would certainly be best for the lady who'd bought it,* Cole reflected grimly as he drove back to the inn. Because Madeleine had almost got it right. It wasn't the black market he was worried about when it came to the Lockton spinning wheel.

It was black magic!

By three o'clock, Kate decided she'd done all the cleaning and organizing she was going to. It was time to turn her attention to something she enjoyed for a change. So, after making herself a late lunch and putting her dishes into the sink, she walked into the den and sat down in front of the drafting table.

The blank, white page stared back at her. Kate picked up her pencil, closed her eyes and waited. This was usually how she worked. Rather than use her eyes, Kate *pictured* how the design would look. Then, with pencil poised, she would allow the images to come together, and to blend and take shape. And with her eyes still closed, her fingers would translate the images onto the page.

At least, that's how she'd always done it in the past. But today, nothing came to mind. The tantalizing images that had started taking shape just a few days ago were gone. The blank, white page stayed depressingly white—and depressingly blank.

"Damn," Kate muttered softly. "I was so sure it was starting to come."

She opened her eyes and got up from the table. Why wouldn't the images gel? She was usually so good at coming up with new and interesting designs. She'd close her eyes and the patterns would just *flow* into her head. Why weren't they flowing today?

Kate sighed in frustration as she wandered around the house. She moved from the den into the living room, then to the kitchen, and then back to the den again. She walked around her desk. She sat down in the chair, and got up again. Eventually, she found herself standing beside the spinning wheel, and idly reaching out to touch it. Funny how just looking at it brought her a sense of peace. Maybe because it was a remnant of another time; a time before computers and cell phones and print-on-demand had become the norm.

Kate let her eyes move slowly over the wheel and wondered why nobody else had bought it. It wasn't like any other spinning wheel she had ever seen, and for a lot of people that would have been reason enough. She'd known tons of people in New York who'd always been on the look-out for the new and unusual. And yet, Mrs. Barrett had put it at the back of her shop because she'd believed it wouldn't sell—even at a hundred dollars. Goodness, the intricate carving on the legs alone made it worth more than that.

Her thoughts returning to the problem with her design, Kate absently put her left hand on the wheel and gave it a gentle spin. Maybe if she put on some music. She usually worked in silence, but maybe today some background noise would help.

Kate was so caught up in her dilemma, that it was a few minutes before she noticed that the strange tingling had started again. She glanced down and abruptly brought the wheel to a halt. What *was* it with this thing? Why did it keep doing that? She'd had John Burke in to see about the wiring and he'd assured her that everything was fine. There weren't any loose wires, and there were no open sockets anywhere. So what was making the thing vibrate like a well-tuned pitchfork?

"All right, let's see what this is all about," Kate said briskly. She spun the wheel again, but this time rested the fingers of both hands on top of it. And sure enough, there it was again—the vibration or whatever it was. She felt it move through her fingers into her hands, and then right up into her arms and shoulders. As long as she stayed in contact with the wheel, the sensation continued. And damn it, she was getting sleepy again. Why did this happen every time she came near this thing? Was it giving off some kind of toxic fumes?

Kate closed her eyes, suddenly finding them too heavy to keep open. This was so *bizarre*. It was almost as though something was coming out of the wheel and flowing into her body. She could feel it spreading, making her limbs feel heavy and her mind grow numb.

Finally too weary to resist, Kate just let herself go. She felt the soft caress of a summer breeze lift away her cares. The room and the daylight receded as she was engulfed in a glorious panalopy of shades and ever-changing hues. And the colors . . . dear God, the colors were so beautiful; so rich, and vibrant, swirling around her like a rainbow of precious stones plucked from a king's crown. There were sapphires and emeralds, rich dark rubies, and deeply glowing amber, the colors blending into shapes and the shapes into form.

And in the background, Kate heard the voice. Something

soft, and gentle, reaching out to her, not with words, but with thoughts; filling her mind with pictures and shapes. With colors that intensified and grew bolder. Their edges merged one into another like oils blending on a canvas. A shape was coming into focus. A design . . .

Kate's hands dropped away from the wheel. But this time, she didn't go to sleep. She opened her eyes and walked with slow, measured steps toward the drafting table. Her eyes were fixed in front of her as she picked up her pencil and began to draw, and this time, there was no hesitation. Her hand moved over the paper with quick, decisive movements as she began to sketch out a design. There was no awareness of time; no sounds to disturb her concentration. Only the rasp of her pencil as she sketched out the design in her mind.

Kate reached for her pattern pieces, fitting them into the design, tracing their outline and then moving on to the next. And then came the colors. She selected the pencils she wanted, picking them out with no hesitation at all. She knew exactly what colors she wanted, and exactly where the colors would go.

Two hours later it was finished. Kate put down her pencils and gazed at the design she had drawn. She saw the skillful blending of lines and angles, saw the subtle shading of light and dark, and the texture of the glass where she had sketched it in. But she had no conscious realization of what she had done. She was only aware of an incredible sense of weariness. Her body craved sleep, and it was becoming a physical effort just to breathe.

She turned away from the drafting table, heading for the bedroom. But it was too far away. She staggered into the living room and collapsed on the sofa, falling at once into a deep, almost drugged sleep. And this time, there were no dreams of any kind to disturb her.

The light was flashing on the phone in his room when Cole got back to the inn. He'd been driving around for hours, trying to come up with answers. But now, as he picked up the receiver and dialed the front desk, he had to face the fact that he still didn't have any—and that time was running out.

"Yes, this is Beresford in two-twelve. You have a message for me?"

"Yes, sir." There was a moment's silence before the girl came back on the line. "A Mrs. Barrett called for you earlier. She said you could give her a call anytime up to ten o'clock tonight, and that you had the number."

"Yes, I do. Thank you."

Cole hung up the phone. Mrs. Barrett had called again? He glanced at his watch. Five to ten. He still had time.

He fished the business card out of his other coat pocket and dialed the number. It rang four times. On the fifth, it connected. "Mrs. Barrett? Good evening, it's Cole Beresford."

"Oh, hello, Mr. Beresford, I was hoping you hadn't gone back to New York."

Cole smiled as he slipped the card back into his pocket. "No, I'm still here."

"Well, I thought you might like to know that I had an interesting call today with regard to that spinning wheel."

Cole stiffened. "A telephone call?"

"Yes. A gentleman called me this afternoon to ask if I had received any spinning wheels recently, and in particular, from the north of England."

A muscle tensed in Cole's jaw. "Did the man have an accent of any kind?"

"Yes, he did. I think it might have been German, but I'm not sure. But he was very pleasant on the phone. We chatted for some time. Do you know him?"

A thin smile spread across Cole's lips. "I believe I may be acquainted with the man. Did he happen to give you his name?"

"No, he didn't. I did ask, but somehow, we moved on to another topic before he had a chance to tell me."

*I'll bet he did*, Cole thought narrowly. "What did you tell him about the spinning wheel, Mrs. Barrett?"

"Much the same as I told you. That I had one, but that I sold it to a young lady only last week. Like you, he was very interested in her name and was most disappointed when I couldn't give it to him."

"Yes, I'm sure he was. Did he happen to say where he was calling from?"

"No, but there was a lot of static on the line. Sounded like another one of those car phones."

Cole dropped his head and took a long, deep breath. "Thank you, Mrs. Barrett, you've been very helpful. By the way, you didn't happen to mention my name to him, did you?" he asked, cursing himself for not having thought to tell her not to.

"Dear me, no, I'm afraid I didn't. Should I have?"

"No. The gentleman and I aren't exactly good friends. If he contacts you again, I'd appreciate you not mentioning it."

"Oh. Well, as you like, Mr. Beresford."

"Thank you. Good night, Mrs. Barrett."

Cole hung up the phone and swore eloquently. It had to be Davenport! It was too much of a coincidence to be anyone else. How many other people would call an antique store in Springfield, Vermont to ask if they'd received a spinning wheel from the north of England?

Cole walked toward the latticed window and rested his palms on the ledge. Davenport had probably been calling from his car, which meant that he was in the area and heading this way. That also meant that Cole had no choice but to step up his search. He had to find the owner of the wheel. He'd go door to door if he had to. He couldn't let Davenport get to her first. The consequences could be fatal!

When Kate awoke, it was with no recollection of what she had done. She absently glanced at her watch—and then gasped. *Eleven o'clock!* But that was impossible! The last time she'd looked, it had been three-thirty. She couldn't have slept for seven and a half hours. Could she?

Swinging her feet over the edge of the sofa, Kate stood up—and then abruptly sat back down as a wave of dizziness overwhelmed her. She must have gotten up too fast. She sat still for a minute, waiting for the feeling to pass. Her head felt like it was wrapped in cotton, and there were stars dancing in front of her eyes. If this kept up, she was going to have to see the doctor. The last thing she remembered was sitting at the drafting table, trying to come up with some new ideas for a design. She remembered feeling frustrated that she hadn't been able to get the images right, and that she'd got up and started walking around the house. She vaguely remembered walking back into the den and looking at the spinning wheel. After that, everything went blank.

Kate pushed her hair back and groggily shook her head. There had to be something wrong with her. It wasn't healthy to keep falling asleep like this. Maybe she was missing something in her diet, or she was iron deficient. She wished she'd paid more attention to that article about supplements in *Reader's Digest* last month.

Tea. She wanted a cup of tea.

Carefully, Kate got to her feet. She stood still for a minute to see how she felt. Okay, so far, so good. She didn't think she was going to keel over. She took a tentative step forward. Good, things were starting to settle down. The cotton-head feeling was easing. She shuffled out to the kitchen and leaned against the wall for balance. She wasn't hungry, but she was terribly thirsty. She plugged in the kettle and drank a glass of water while she waited for it to boil.

When the tea was made, she took it and an oatmeal cookie into the living room. She walked by the entrance to the den, and briefly glanced at the drafting table. She stopped and did a double-take. Then she walked into the room and stared down at the table in disbelief.

The drawing was finished. The design she had been laboring over for the past two weeks was done. Complete to the last detail. Every shape, every color, every specification, all there, neatly set out in her own hand. And it was, without question, the most fantastic thing she had ever created!

Kate's hands were shaking so badly she had to put the cup down. This was impossible. When had she done this? Where on earth had such an incredible idea come from? The design was exquisite. She traced the outline of it with her fingertips, marveling at its simplicity, yet astounded by the complex beauty of what she had drawn. It was the idea she'd been tossing around for weeks, but it was more. So much more.

And now, it was finished. But how? She'd been asleep for the last seven hours. When had she had time to create something like this? Her last memory before falling asleep was of sitting at the table with a blank piece of paper in front of her.

How could she have created the most spectacular design of her life—and not even remember how?

Kate spent the rest of that night and most of the next morning staring at the design, trying to make sense of what had happened. But the only conclusion she could come up with was that it didn't make sense. There was no possible way she could have done what she'd done. She had lost nearly half a day of her life—and this was what she had to show for it. But how? And why couldn't she remember? Was her mind suddenly turning to mush? Maybe she'd developed some kind of personality disorder. A Jekyll and Hyde thing. It was a scary thought, but Kate knew she had to consider all the possibilities. Because how could she have created what was on the drafting table when she didn't even remember picking up a pencil?

Kate went out to the kitchen and made herself some fresh tea. What about sleepwalking? Was it possible she'd suddenly started doing that? She knew about people who did, of course, and about all the weird and wonderful things they did while they were asleep. Was that what was happening to her?

Her thoughts far removed from what she was doing, Kate took a mouthful of tea, then winced as the hot liquid burned her tongue. She jerked her hand back, spilling some on her sweatshirt. Then somebody knocked on the door and she upset the rest of it all over the counter.

This really wasn't her day! She hastily grabbed a towel to mop up the worst, then ran toward the front door.

"Hi, sleeping beauty, how are—" The joking tone vanished. As did her brother's smile when he saw the color of her face. "Jesus, Kate, what's wrong? You look like you've seen a ghost."

Kate tried, but she couldn't even coax a smile to her lips. "Sorry, Matt, I just woke up. Guess I'm still a bit dopey."

"You look a hell of a lot more than dopey, kiddo." He glanced at her in concern. "You sure you're okay?"

"Yes, I'm fine. Really. Do you have time for a cup of coffee? I just boiled the kettle."

Matt shook his head. "Thanks, but I don't. I just stopped by to let you know that we took Christian to the hospital last night."

Kate felt a cold, hard knot form in the pit of her stomach. "What's wrong?"

"He had an attack. He's okay at the moment." Matt's

mouth pulled into a grim line. "The doctors had to put him on a respirator again."

"Oh, Matt," Kate groaned. "Did they say how long he'll have to be in?"

"No. They want to bring his temperature down first, and then they'll see. Right now, they're going to keep an eye on him."

"Matt, I'm so sorry. How's Megan doing?"

"Tired. Scared." Matt clamped his hand on the back of his neck and leaned his head back. "Last time this happened, Christian's temperature shot up to a hundred and five. Last night it hit a hundred and six. You know I like to stay positive, Kate, but it's got me worried too."

"Of course it would. There has to be a reason why Christian keeps getting sick like this, Matt. It's not natural."

"I know, and the poor kid just lays there, staring at me with those big blue eyes and I can't do a damn thing for him. It makes me feel so helpless."

"Now stop that. There's no point getting upset with yourself. You've done everything you can."

"Yeah, I know. And the good thing is, Dr. Sheffield isn't panicking. He's started Christian on another new line of medication, so hopefully that will help. I just came over to let you know what was happening." He smiled, trying to mask his concern. "And to apologize for the short cancellation notice on dinner the other night. Hope you were able to make other plans."

"As a matter of fact, I was."

"Oh yeah? Like what?"

"I went out on a date."

"On a date? With a *man*?"

"No, with Cynthia Horton's cat," Kate drawled. "Of course with a man. Is that so hard to believe?"

"Well, yeah, kind of. I didn't know you were seeing anybody right now."

"I'm not. I just went out for dinner with somebody I met."

"Ah ha! A mystery man. So who is he?"

"You don't know him."

"Local?"

Kate shook her head. "I met him at Madeleine's party."

"Oh God, one of her artsy fartsy friends from New York? Or is he more the yuppie stockbroker type? You know, Italian suit, Gucci loafers, and a cell phone surgically attached to his hip?" Matt said, posturing expressively.

Kate laughed, aware that her brother couldn't have been more wrong. "As a matter of fact, he's a good friend of Madeleine's. Her late husband introduced them several years ago. As to what he does, he's something of an expert in the field of art and antiquities."

"Really? Then he should have a field day in this place," Matt replied, glancing around at Kate's eclectic mix of furniture.

"He's also one of *my* new customers," Kate told him proudly. "He bought my big window for *way* more than I was asking."

"Did he? Well, I'm real happy for you, Katie. I know how hard you worked on that. And no doubt he could afford it. None of Madeleine Carstairs's friends seem to be lacking in that department." He paused and glanced around the room. "By the way, what have you been doing in here? It smells great."

Kate shrugged. "Probably all the pine cleaner I used."

"Well, whatever, the place looks and smells great," Matt complimented her. "Nice to see you've done away with the Munster look. Speaking of which, where's the old spinning wheel? I thought you said you were going to put it in your little *nook* beside the fireplace."

Kate rolled her eyes. "Funny, Matt. It's in the den. I haven't got around to finding a suitable home for it in here yet." Then, suddenly reminded of the den—and of what was in it—Kate said slowly, "Matt, would you mind taking a look at something I've been working on? I'd really like your opinion."

"Are you serious? You want *me* to give you an opinion on something *you're* doing?"

"Strange as that sounds, yeah."

"Strange is definitely the word," Matt warned her. "You know Megan says that I'm artistically challenged."

"That's okay, I'll take my chances." Kate turned and led the way into the den. She walked toward the drafting board and turned on the overhead light. "Well, what do you think?"

Matt stood for a moment gazing down at the paper, and then softly sucked in his breath. "Jeez, Kate, I knew you were good, but I didn't know you were *this* good."

Kate felt her pulse begin to race. "You like it?"

"Like it. It's fantastic, even to a philistine like me. You must have been working on this for weeks."

Kate glanced down at the paper again and worried her bottom lip with her teeth. "Yeah, something like that."

"Well, like I said, I always knew my little sister had all the talent in the family. I just got the muscle. But even I can't wait to see this one made up." Matt's eyes went back to the design again. "Looks really complicated though. Are you going to be able to finish it in time for the opening?"

"I'm going to try. You and Megan are coming, aren't you? As long as Christian's okay, that is."

"As long as Christian's okay, we wouldn't miss it. You know that," Matt told her. "And on that note, I'd better get back to the house. Meg was looking pretty worn out when I left. I told her to grab some sleep. She didn't get too much last night."

"Neither did you, judging by the bags under your eyes," Kate said as she walked him to the front door. "But give her my love and tell her I'll drop by soon."

"I'll tell her. And thanks, Katie." Matthew pulled her into his arms and gave her a brotherly hug. "I meant what I said about taking a rain check on the dinner too. We really missed seeing you. We'll have you over to dinner just as soon as Christian's home again. Okay?"

Kate gave his hand an encouraging squeeze. "Okay. But there's no big rush. I'm not going anywhere."

No, until she figured out what was going on here, she certainly wasn't going anywhere.

Cole wasn't sure what made him pick up the phone and dial Kate's number. Maybe it was because he was tired of hanging around his hotel room, waiting for something to happen.

Or maybe it was because he hadn't seen her in three days and he missed her like hell.

Cole hadn't been able to figure out exactly what it was about Kate Pedigrew that made him feel like this. He'd come into contact with lots of women before, but there was something about Kate Pedigrew that set her apart from all the rest. Something that put her in a class all her own.

At least that's the way he saw her, Cole admitted ruefully. The night he'd met her at Madeleine's, she had been the elegant artist. The other day at her house, she'd been the girl next door, complete with bucket and paper towels. Then at dinner at The Olde House, he'd been delighted to find her a witty and intelligent conversationalist with an independent streak as wide as the Mississippi.

Yes, Kate Pedigrew definitely intrigued him. And each time he saw her, she only intrigued him more. She was a fascinating mixture of sexuality and innocence. He thought about the elegant black cocktail dress she'd had on at Maddie's and the way it had clung to every beautiful curve of her body—and then about the flirty little shoes she'd worn with it. He'd always been a sucker for a beautiful woman in high heels, and Kate had the right kind of feet to wear strappy sandals like that. They were small and dainty and the toenails had been painted a dark, almost burgundy red. Then his mind skipped ahead to the next day when he'd dropped in on her unexpectedly to deliver the check. She hadn't been wearing a stitch of makeup, yet she'd looked fabulous. Her clear blue eyes had sparkled like sapphires and the copper highlights in her hair had shimmered every time she'd turned her head. And she'd been wearing those snug-fitting jeans and that oversized white shirt. God, he loved women in tight-fitting jeans. He'd been itching to cup that perfect little bottom in his hands and—

*Hold on, Beresford, you're starting to sound like a teenager, for Chrissake.*

Yes, he sure was, Cole thought darkly. He hadn't thought about a woman in *that* way since he'd been twenty years old. That's when he'd met Ingrid and had ended up following her to the States. They'd had some pretty wild times back then, but hell, he'd only been twenty. At that age your hormones were *supposed* to be raging. Somehow at forty-one, he didn't expect to be thinking about taking cold showers again!

Cole was just about to hang up the phone when Kate finally answered. Her voice sounded slightly breathless—and incredibly sexy. "Hi, Kate. Did I get you from something again?"

He heard the momentary pause. "Cole?"

Was he imagining it, or did she sound pleased to hear from him? "Yes. Look, I'm sorry I haven't had a chance to call you before now, but . . . I was wondering if I could . . . pop in and see you this afternoon?"

Again, a pause. "Sure, that would be great."

Cole heard the hesitation in her voice—and hoped it didn't have anything to do with him. "I can always make it another time if you're busy."

"No, no, I'd love to see you. Really," Kate assured him. "It's just that I have to run some errands this afternoon. I've started working on some new pieces for the show and I need some supplies. Would you mind coming into town with me?"

"Not a bit." More relieved than he cared to admit, Cole glanced briefly at his watch. "I can be there in half an hour. Too soon or too late?"

He finally heard a note of amusement creep back into her voice. "Neither. That should just about give me time to shower and change. I've been living in jeans for the past few days."

Jeans. Cole groaned under his breath. Just what he needed to hear. "I'll see you at two." Then he hung up the phone and foolishly started to grin. She hadn't forgotten him.

Kate hung up the phone and almost felt giddy. Cole Beresford hadn't forgotten her! He was coming by to pick her up in half an hour.

*Half an hour?*

"Ohmigod!" Kate's smile disappeared. She dashed into the bedroom and started rummaging through the closet. Cole couldn't see her looking like this. Not only had she been working for the past three days straight; she'd been wearing the same clothes too.

God, had it really been three days? She'd hardly noticed the passage of time. She'd been so immersed in her work. She had finally finished the painstaking work of preparing the pattern for the new window, carefully tracing the outline of each piece on brown paper and then numbering them all. Then, she'd cut them out and sorted them into piles. Now she could start working with the glass—and that's why she had to go into town.

Kate stepped into the shower and sighed as hot water poured down over her aching body. Her shoulders and neck were one big pile of knots from having spent so many hours bent over the worktable. Even her legs were sore from standing in one place for so long. But she didn't begrudge a minute of it, because she was in the midst of creating a masterpiece.

Kate still couldn't believe that she had actually come up with the drawing herself. Even now, the intricacy of the work astonished her. She'd never thought to use those particular shapes in that kind of pattern before. But now that she had, it all seemed so simple. She wondered why she hadn't thought of it before. And the colors she'd mapped out were perfect! If she could find the right shades of glass, in just the right textures, the finished work would be stunning.

Kate smiled in satisfaction as she rubbed shampoo into her hair and worked up a rich lather. If Cole thought what he'd seen of her work was good so far, wait until he got a load of this!

Cole arrived right on time. Kate heard his car pull into the driveway, and quickly applied her lipstick. Then, grabbing her shoulder bag, she went out to meet him. "Hi, Cole. I'm ready."

Cole was watching a horse and rider trot along the road, and turned at the sound of her voice. "Hi, Kate. How are—" That was as far as he got. The rest of his words died on his lips. He just stood there and stared at her.

Kate smiled up at him uncertainly. "What's wrong?"

"Wrong?" Cole gruffly cleared his throat. "Nothing's wrong. I just . . . haven't seen you for a while. And I don't think I've ever seen you wearing that particular shade of . . . what do you call it?"

Kate glanced down at the sweater she'd thrown on over a pair of off-white jeans and shrugged. "Coral, I guess."

"Right, coral. Is it new?"

"As a matter of fact, it is. First time on. Do you like it?"

Cole swallowed hard. Like it? He loved everything about it, especially the way the silky fabric draped over her breasts. "Yes, it's wonderful. I love what it does for your . . . complexion."

Had it really been that long since he'd seen her? Or was she just having this incredible effect on his senses? Because she really did look fabulous. Her blue eyes were bright and sparkling, her skin was glowing with health, and there was just . . . something about her that made his mouth water.

"It's great. The color is . . . great." Cole cleared his throat again and tried to get rid of the huskiness. "The sweater looks . . . wonderful on you."

"Funny, I thought the same thing when I put it on. I didn't even have to bother with blush today." Kate's laugh was a bit self-conscious. "Maybe I should stock up on clothes in this color. Some days a girl needs all the help she can get. Ready to go?"

Cole nodded, hardly able to take his eyes from her. "So what exactly do you have to pick up in town?"

"Glass and leading," Kate said as she got into his car. "I've started working on a few new pieces."

"That's right, you mentioned that on the phone," Cole said, glad to have something mundane to talk about. "But you're starting them kind of late, aren't you? Will they be ready in time for the opening?"

"I hope so. The designs are considerably more intricate than anything I've done before so I'm hoping I haven't bitten off more than I can chew."

Cole smiled easily. "I doubt it. Every artist needs to push to see exactly what they're capable of doing. They need to grow, and the only way they can do that is by tackling ambitious projects. I've yet to meet a successful artist who was completely satisfied with everything he'd done. Though, I'll grant you, artists are usually their own worst enemies."

"You sound like you've spent a lot of time with creative people," Kate observed.

"I have. A large part of my job centers around artifacts from the past, but I like to keep up-to-date on what's current too."

Kate turned her head to look at him. She had no idea why Cole had called her this afternoon, but she didn't care. She was just going to enjoy whatever time they had together. And she wasn't going to get her hopes up. It was safer that way.

"You've really never told me much about what you do, Cole," Kate said. "How does one go about becoming an expert on antiquities? Where do you pick up your information?"

"From anywhere and everywhere," Cole told her with a smile. "I read everything I can about the past. It's vital to have a thorough knowledge of the various time periods in history so that you know who and what came out of each. From there, you concentrate on the more detailed accounts of furniture, fashion, art, and literature. You come to learn and to appreciate what was valuable and what wasn't."

As he was talking, Kate watched his hands. She noticed how long and slender his fingers were as they rested on the leather steering wheel. She could easily imagine them holding a priceless vase, or rippling along a piano keyboard.

Or caressing the softness of a woman's skin.

Kate's pulse skittered alarmingly. *Get that thought out of your head, lady!* "What about actually seeing the works for yourself? Is that important?"

"Tremendously. And to me, that's the best part," Cole said, his mouth curving upwards in a smile. "I spend a lot of time traveling around the world, validating the authenticity of pieces that are brought into museums and art shops. I'm away about seven months of the year doing that."

"Seven months!" Kate said in astonishment. "That kind of schedule must be hell on a personal relationship."

"It is. That's why I've never had one that's lasted more

than a few months. Now, I don't even bother. I would never expect, or even ask a woman to put up with the kind of schedule I keep. People need time to get to know one another, and you can't do that when you're living at opposite ends of the world."

Kate glanced down at her nails. "No, I suppose not. Still, it must make for a lonely existence at times."

"You get used to it," he said briefly. "And the work is its own reward. I wouldn't do it otherwise."

*So there, Kathryn Pedigrew. You have been warned!*

"But isn't it the same for you, Kate?" Cole asked suddenly. "When you're working on a project, don't you shut out everything else?"

"Yes, I suppose I do," she admitted. "When I'm really into something, Matt doesn't see me for days. I spend hours in the workroom, cutting out glass and grinding it down. He says an explosion could go off in the next field and I wouldn't hear it."

"There, you see. Try explaining that to a boyfriend who wants to see you on a regular basis." Cole slanted her a sardonic look. "Men have outrageous egos, you know."

"So I've heard. Though like I told you at the restaurant, they're not exactly beating a path to my door these days."

Cole didn't want to admit that he was relieved at that. Because it wasn't fair. Why should he want other men to stay away from Kate, just because he had a life that forced *him* to? "What about the time you spent living in New York?" he asked idly. "You must have run into the usual crowd of up-and-coming young executives and ambitious real estate types. Surely there was someone who made you think twice about coming here?"

"I'm here, aren't I?"

Cole turned his head to meet her gaze, and felt something twist in his gut. She was getting under his skin. He couldn't ever remember wanting to be with a woman as much as he wanted to be with Kate. And he sure as hell couldn't remember wanting to kiss a woman as much.

"We're here," she said quietly.

"We are?"

"Uh-huh."

Cole swallowed hard. "That was . . . quick," he said, hoping she hadn't noticed his intense study. He tore his eyes from her face and studied the small plaza they were approaching. "Which one is it?"

"The store right at the end. The Glass Unicorn."

"Whimsical name."

"Would you like to come inside? I think you might find it interesting."

Cole did, and the moment he stepped through the door, he realized that whimsical was hardly the word to describe the nature of the business going on inside. The Glass Unicorn was jumping. All five clerks were kept on their toes looking after a steady stream of customers, most of whom, like Kate, were knowledgeable in their field. He saw her smile at one of the young clerks and then head in the direction of the warehouse. Once inside, she knew exactly where she wanted to go. She led Cole along corridors lined with shelves that were stocked with large sheets of glass in every color, every shade, and every texture imaginable.

"Good Lord, I had no idea there was such a selection to choose from," Cole said in a voice of genuine astonishment. "I'm used to seeing stained glass in its finished stage, not in the raw material one. How do you ever choose your colors?"

"Most of the time, I don't," Kate admitted as they moved out of the range of cool purple and blues into the warmer red and pinks. "I picture the pattern in my mind and try to imagine which colors will work."

"Do you ever make the same pattern up in different colors?"

"Nope. Everything that comes out of Pedigrew Stained Glass is an original. Strictly one of a kind."

"So what colors are you looking for this time?"

"Jewel shades. Like that," Kate said, spotting the exact shade of amber crackled glass she was looking for. "And this one," she pulled out a sheet of fiery red glass with a slightly marbleized finish. "Then I'll have a bit of this, and this . . ."

The process continued until Kate had located all ten colors, mainly in shades of red, gold, and amber. The colors of passion, Cole mused. She'd drift along the row and suddenly stop to pull out a fragment of glass, and then hold it up to the window to see how the light traveled through it. If she was satisfied, she'd put what looked like a small piece of putty in the corner and then carry on down the aisle.

Cole watched her with a growing sense of admiration. He was seeing another side of the artist at work. She moved around the warehouse with a clear sense of purpose; stopping when she found something she liked, moving on when she didn't. They finally returned to the main part of the store where Kate picked up grout, finishing nails and leading, and in less than half an hour, they were back in the car with her purchases. The sheets of glass were individually wrapped in brown paper and marked by color, the large roll of lead piping was in a separate bag, and the other assorted bits and pieces were in a cardboard box. Cole helped arrange the pieces of glass in the back seat and the trunk and then came round to open the passenger door. "Are you always so efficient when it comes to shopping for your supplies?"

"Heavens, no. I usually dither for hours over colors. Today, I just knew what I wanted."

Cole gazed down into her face. She was so beautiful. Her eyes were the most incredible shade of blue he'd ever seen. They reminded him of one of the pieces of glass he'd seen in the shop, a fragment of which he'd picked up and slipped into his pocket. "Are customers allowed to specify colors when they order a piece of work?"

"Yes, of course."

"Good." He pulled out the piece of glass and handed it to her. "Then I'd like you to make something for me using this."

Kate glanced down at the fragment with interest. "Nice shade."

"I'm partial to it."

"Any particular reason?"

"Not that I intend to go into right now."

Kate smiled, but she didn't push. "All right. Did you have anything in mind for a design?"

"Surprise me."

She saw the sudden intensity in his eyes and felt her heart

begin to hammer against her ribs. "All right. I just hope you won't be disappointed."

"I haven't been yet." Cole smiled down into her face and then nodded in the direction of a quaint looking café across the road. "Can I interest you in a cappuccino before we head back?"

Kate hesitated, suddenly afraid to meet his eyes. She would have loved a cappuccino, and she knew that the café across the road made the best one in town. But she wasn't sure she was up to spending any more time in Cole's company today. She still didn't know why he'd phoned her, but one thing she did know was that every minute she spent with him was going to make it harder to say good-bye. She liked everything about him. The little things he said to make her feel special, the genuine interest he showed in her work, and the way he listened to her when she talked. All those things were working against her. The carefully erected barriers she'd built to shut him out were starting to crumble. She was longing for things she couldn't have. Things he'd already told her he couldn't give.

Fortunately, Cole seemed to sense her hesitation. "Perhaps another time," he said quietly. "I guess you're anxious to get back to work."

Kate grasped at the excuse. "Yes, the show will be here before I know it. But thanks for the offer, Cole," she added quickly. "I mean that."

"Sure."

His expression was remote, and Kate knew that she'd offended him, but she was only doing what she thought was best. She was trying not to get involved, and the only way she could do that was by keeping her distance. That's what the man wanted, wasn't it?

Then why did she feel so guilty when she got back into the car?

They didn't say much in the car on the way home.

Cole *was* disappointed that Kate had turned him down. He wanted to believe that the distraction he sensed in her was due to her concern over getting the studio ready for the opening. He knew what it was to work to deadlines, and he knew there was a lot riding on hers. Success demanded sacrifice, everybody knew that. But that didn't stop him from resenting the fact that one of those sacrifices included giving up the chance to enjoy a cappuccino with him on a beautiful autumn afternoon.

At the church, Cole drove the car around to the showroom door and helped Kate unload the glass. "Where do you want these?" he asked.

"On the floor will be fine," Kate threw back over her shoulder. "I'll sort everything out later."

It didn't take the two of them long to unload the car, but it was already getting dark. Feeling that she owed him at least a cup of coffee, Kate went through to the kitchen and put the kettle on. While she did, Cole returned to the car to get his jacket and noticed that the light on his phone was blinking. He checked to see that Kate was safely inside, then slipped into the driver's seat and dialed his access code.

*"Cole, honey, it's Madeleine. Your friend Professor Mor-*

*ris called from England looking for you. Lord only knows why he thought you'd be here. Anyway, he said it's extremely important that you get in touch with him. Something to do with a Lady Thelford, whoever she is. He left a number. He also sent a package for you. It arrived just now by courier. Give me a call when you get in from wherever you are. Here's his number."*

Cole quickly wrote down the telephone number and then hung up. What could Morris have been calling about? Had he learned something new about the spinning wheel? And what was in the package he'd sent to Madeleine?

The clock on the dashboard read six. That made it eleven o'clock in England. He glanced toward the church, and then quickly dialed the number.

"Good evening, Crosshands Hotel," a woman answered in a broad Yorkshire accent.

"Yes, hello, may I speak to Professor Morris please."

"Oh, sorry, luv, the professor's not in at the moment. Can I take a message?"

"Yes, would you tell him that Beresford called from America. He can reach me at the following numbers." Cole gave her both his number at the inn and his cell number, then asked her to repeat them. "Good. Do you know when he might be returning?"

"I'm sorry, Mr. Beresford, I don't. He went out early this afternoon. Said he might not be back until late."

Cole frowned. It was late now. Where the hell was he? "Well, if you'd give him my message as soon as he does come in, I would be most grateful." He hung up the phone and thought for a minute. Morris was in Yorkshire, and he'd couriered a package back to the States. A package he'd obviously felt was worth following up with a phone call. The second number Cole dialed was Madeleine's. "Maddie, it's Cole."

"Cole, honey, how are you? More importantly, *where* are you?"

"I was on my way back when I got your message," he said evasively. "What kind of package is it?"

"Flat and light. And he's scrawled 'Do Not Bend' all over it."

Cole smiled at the interest in her voice. She was as curious as a cat. "Photos, no doubt."

"Cole, this wouldn't have anything to do with that spinning wheel you're looking for, would it?"

"It might. Morris is in the area the spinning wheel came from."

"Oh my, I do love an intrigue. When are you coming over to get this?"

Cole sighed. Kate was making coffee. He hated having to miss it, but . . .

"Right now, if it's not inconvenient."

"Not at all, but only if you promise to tell me what this is all about."

Cole shook his head. "I can't. The fewer people who know about this, the better."

Kate came out to the car just as he hung up the phone. She smiled at him uncertainly. "I've put the kettle on. Do you have time for a cup of coffee?"

He shook his head. "Sorry, Kate, I don't. Something's come up."

Kate hoped her disappointment didn't show. She'd wanted to make up for her behavior in town earlier by offering to fix him something here, but obviously that wasn't the way it worked. "I understand." She couldn't tell him that she wanted him to stay and drink coffee, and talk to her until the early hours of the morning. So she just smiled and nodded. "Well, thanks for taking me into town. And for putting up with the chaos of the Glass Unicorn."

Cole laughed easily. "That was a pleasure. As was being with you." Slowly, the easy-going smile vanished. He glanced down into her face, searching her eyes, looking for . . . he wasn't sure what. Her name escaped his lips as a soft whisper of sound, and then, because he couldn't stop himself, Cole bent his head and brushed his mouth gently across hers.

It was a light, fleeting touch; barely a kiss at all, but it was enough to let him know he wanted more. He took a step closer, wanting to kiss her again. But this time, she stepped away from him, shaking her head. "No . . . Cole, don't."

Immediately, he backed off. He saw that her face was flushed, and he knew he'd upset her. "I'm sorry, Kate," he whispered brusquely. "I suppose I shouldn't have done that. But to be honest, I've been wanting to kiss you all afternoon."

Kate gazed up into his face, confused and shaken by his kiss. What was he doing? She was trying to play by the rules, damn it, why wasn't he? Didn't he understand that the only reason she'd backed away when she had was because she was *afraid* she wouldn't be able to if he'd started kissing her again?

"I'll call you soon," Cole said as he abruptly turned on his heel.

Kate nodded. There was an ache in her throat, as though someone had their fingers around her neck and was slowly squeezing. She wondered if soon would ever be soon enough.

Kate had leftovers for dinner. She didn't feel like cooking. She couldn't even be bothered to order pizza, which was about the only fast food anybody delivered this far out. After that, she poured herself a glass of wine and headed for the living room.

She was restless tonight. It was one of those nights where she couldn't settle to anything. She turned on the TV and flipped through the channels. She got out a deck of cards and played a couple of hands of solitaire. Finally, she slipped a classical CD into the player and stretched out on the sofa, hoping to get lost in the pages of her favorite author's newest book.

But images of Cole Beresford kept jumping in front of the words. The sound of his voice kept blotting out the story. And the memory of his mouth on hers completely destroyed whatever was left of her concentration, until eventually, she just gave up.

What was wrong with her? Why did she suddenly feel like her life was going through an emotional meat grinder? Was this all because of Cole?

Kate angrily threw down the book and got up. Idiot. Of

course it was about Cole. Where did she think these ridiculous mood swings came from? Cole unsettled her more than any man she'd ever met—which didn't make any sense. He certainly wasn't the first handsome, successful man she'd ever gone out with. She'd met lots of them in New York. Roderick Pedigrew was a powerful figure in the real estate business, and as his daughter, Kate had been in demand. The fact that she was bright and beautiful had only added to her cachet. She'd been wined and dined at some of the most expensive restaurants in the city. One enterprising young fellow had even chartered a plane and flown her down to New Orleans for some authentic Cajun food.

So what was there about Cole Beresford that had her longing for a cappuccino in a sleepy Vermont café? What was it about his kiss that reduced her bones to the consistency of jelly?

Kate flopped down into the rocking chair and leaned her head back against the cushion. That was another thing that bothered her. Why couldn't she stop thinking about how good that kiss had felt? It wasn't the first time she'd been kissed. But it sure as hell was the first time the memory of it had lingered longer than the time it took to close the door in her date's face.

Cole excited her. He intrigued her. And she wanted more. But he didn't have any more to give. He'd told her that in just about as many words.

Kate sighed and took a sip of her wine. So what did she do now? Mope around the house? Call up Madeleine and cry on her shoulder? Hardly. What she was going to have to do was just stop thinking about him. Because she had too many other things to worry about. Like the fact that her nephew was sick, and that she had her first professional show to get ready for. She had a whole bunch of new pieces of stained glass to get finished. Thank God she'd at least been able to make some inroads into *that*.

Kate got up and wandered into the den. The spinning wheel was still there by her desk. She'd stared at it so often she knew its graceful lines by heart. But lately, she'd begun to wonder about it too. She'd started thinking about all the strange things that had happened to her since she'd brought it into the house—and she couldn't explain any of them. Like the tingling sensation she got in her fingers every time she touched it. And the bizarre way she kept falling asleep—only to wake up and find herself right beside it. Then, of course, there was the new design she'd apparently created in her sleep.

Kate was beginning to wonder if *sleep* was the right word for what happened to her whenever she went near the wheel.

"You're not just a plain old ordinary spinning wheel, are you?" Kate said quietly, her eyes running over every inch of it. "But if you're not, then what the hell are you?"

The fact that she was talking to the spinning wheel probably should have bothered her, but it didn't. Somehow, it seemed minor compared to some of the other thoughts she'd started having about it lately. She knew it was crazy, or maybe *she* was crazy for thinking about it, but—was it possible that it *wasn't* just a plain old ordinary spinning wheel? Was it possible that it possessed some kind of . . . magical power?

Of course it wasn't, Kate assured herself quickly. It was an inanimate object, for crying out loud. Something that some man had built out of wood and cord. There were no such things as haunted castles or ugly little men who spun straw into gold.

Or enchanted spinning wheels that turned dreams into art.

And yet, wasn't that *exactly* what *this* spinning wheel was doing? Kate thought in frustration. Wasn't it . . . spinning her dreams into reality? It was taking her amorphous shapes and ideas and turning them into tangible art. The proof was right there on her worktable. Or did she truly believe that it was just coincidence that she had just designed the most beautiful piece of stained glass of her entire life?

Kate sighed. No, she didn't believe that. Because she couldn't ignore the fact that her life hadn't started to change until *after* she'd brought the spinning wheel home. But she wanted to know why, and there was only one way she was going to be able to do that.

Kate set her wineglass on her desk and slowly bent down.

She pulled out the dowel that held the wheel stationary, and then she rested her hands on top of the wheel.

*Would it be different this time?* she wondered. She was coming at it from an entirely different direction and with an entirely different mindset this time. She wasn't just casually spinning the wheel because she liked watching it turn. She was looking for answers. She strongly suspected that the spinning wheel did hold secrets of some kind, and she wanted to know what they were. She wanted to know why or if this simple antique was having such a profound effect on her life.

After a moment's hesitation, Kate pulled up a chair and sat down in front of it. Then, holding her breath, she gave it a turn.

As expected, the tingling started straight away. It traveled slowly up her hands, into her wrists, and then up her arms.

Kate spun the wheel again. Harder this time.

Yes, there it was—the smell in the air. A . . . freshness tinged with the delicate sweet scents of rose, jasmine and freesia. Then came the feeling of weightlessness as she began to . . . float and drift away. Her eyes closed of their own volition. And behind her lids, she saw the colors. But this time, they were not the bold vibrant reds and golds she had seen before. They were the cool, clean colors of winter; the deep sapphire blues, and shimmering violets, marbled with slashes of emerald, and the crystal white perfection of diamonds.

And then, as soft as a lover's breath, Kate heard the voice.

It was like nothing she had ever heard before. It was soft and ethereal. Gentle. And it was not in the least frightening.

"Is . . . someone there?" Kate whispered tentatively.

She waited, holding her breath.

A few seconds later, Kate saw her—the hazy outline of a woman appearing through the mists of her mind. She was dressed in a flowing white gown, medieval in style, with long tapering sleeves and a square neck. Her white-blond hair was caught in a jeweled snood at the nape of her neck and what looked like a Juliet cap rested on the crown of her head.

And she was beautiful. So . . . heart-wrenchingly beautiful that Kate felt her breath catch in her throat. The figure drifted toward her and it seemed to Kate that her eyes were filled with light. *"It is I. Eleya."*

"Eleya." Kate whispered in a hushed tone.

*"What is your name?"*

"I am called Kathryn. Kate."

*"Kate."* Eleya nodded, and the air all around her seemed to shimmer. *"It is a good name."*

Her voice was like the soft chiming of distant bells, each note pure and crystal clear. It was surely the voice of an angel. But it seemed to Kate that her face was wreathed in sadness. "Are you . . . unhappy, Eleya?" she asked.

There was silence.

"Eleya, please talk to me. Can you tell me what's wrong?"

*"All in good time, Kate,"* came the otherworldly voice. *"We will speak again."* And abruptly, her image began to dissolve.

"No . . . wait! Eleya, don't go!" Kate cried, as the mists began to fade. "Please don't go . . ."

But she was already gone, and Kate knew the vision was coming to an end. She felt her legs begin to tremble as she fought the inevitable lassitude, desperate to spin the wheel again and call the lady back. There was so much she needed to ask. So much she wanted to know.

But in the end, the effort was too much. She slipped to the floor beside the spinning wheel and, within minutes, was asleep. Again.

Cole studied the picture in his hands and whistled softly. "These are some of the best pictures I've seen. Just look at this detail on the carving."

Madeleine rolled her eyes. "Cole, if you won't tell me anything about this spinning wheel, will you at least let me *look* at it?" She saw him hesitate, and added persuasively, "It might help me to find it if I knew what I was looking for."

Cole sighed. Trust Maddie to come up with a logical argument. "I suppose I can't argue with that." Wordlessly, he handed her the picture.

Madeleine studied the black and white photo in surprise. "*This* is what all the fuss is about?"

"That's it, Maddie. The Lockton spinning wheel. A beautiful piece of workmanship, don't you think?" Cole murmured as he got to his feet.

"Well, yes, I suppose it is." Madeleine glanced at the picture a little more closely. "There's certainly a lot of nice carving on the legs. How old is this thing anyway?"

"Old." *Countless centuries.* "The exact date is a little sketchy."

Madeleine's eyes narrowed suspiciously. "You're not being completely honest with me about this thing, are you, Cole?"

He took the picture from her fingers. "No, but like I said, I will be when I finally track it down."

"Well, now that you've shown me what it looks like, it should be easier to spot. I'll keep an eye out when I start paying my calls."

"Your calls?"

"Yes, I've decided to call up all my old girlfriends and invite myself over," Madeleine told him. "Especially friends whose tastes run to early Americana, and who might be in the habit of collecting things. You know, like old copper kettles or wooden butter churns. Or . . . spinning wheels."

Cole laughed. "You're a sweetheart, Maddie. I'll give you a finder's fee if you track it down."

Madeleine waved his offer aside. "Keep your money, Cole. I've already got more than I know what to do with. I'm far more interested in discovering what's behind all this mystery. So," she said, changing the subject, "what have you been doing with yourself when you're not off chasing after spinning wheels? Aren't you getting a little bored with all this rural tranquility?"

"As a matter of fact, I haven't been in the least bored. I've seen Kate a few times, and—"

"Kate?" Madeleine's eyes lit up. "Why Cole, that's splendid. I knew you liked her."

"You're doing it again."

"What?"

"Matchmaking. I've been to see Kate twice; once to take her shopping for supplies, and—"

"Shopping together! Oh, now that positively smacks of domesticity. And the other? Something more romantic than traipsing around stores, I hope."

"I took her to dinner at The Olde House."

"Now that's more like it. Did you have a good time?"

"We had an excellent time," Cole told her honestly. "She's very easy to be with."

"I've always thought so. So, when are you going to see her again?"

The pointed question took Cole by surprise. "I don't know." He thought about Kate's sudden hesitation outside the café, and the way she'd backed away from him when he'd kissed her, and wondered if he'd *ever* see her again. "I'm not sure that she wants to see me."

"Nonsense, of course she does," Madeleine said briskly. "Kate just hasn't dated for a while, and her signals are probably a little rusty."

"Her signals were just fine." Cole's mouth twisted. "It was the message she was sending I'm not too sure about."

"Well, maybe you went too fast. Kate's not like other girls, Cole, all talk and flash," Madeleine informed him. "She's a serious young woman. For example, I know for a fact that the relationship between her and her father causes her a lot more grief than she lets on."

Cole eyed her speculatively. "Bad blood?"

Madeleine shrugged. "Not bad, per se. She just thinks he's disappointed because she didn't make it big in New York. She figures she let him down."

"Have you met her father?"

"No. He only came up here the one time and I happened to be in Phoenix. It was just after Kate bought the church. He stopped long enough to see where she was living, and to visit Kate's brother and his wife, but he left the same afternoon."

"Very paternal," Cole muttered.

"It happens." Madeleine's tone was philosophical. "From what I've been able to gather, Kate was much closer to her mother than she was to her father in the final years. Clare was the glue that held the family together. When she died, it knocked the wind out of all of them."

Cole thought about that for a moment. "Well, if it makes you feel any better, I don't intend to give up on the daughter just yet."

"I am so glad to hear you say that, Cole. Because I've invited her to dinner here tomorrow night and I want you to come too. And don't you dare try to get out of it by accusing me of matchmaking. All I'm doing is having two of my dearest friends in for a meal. Do you see anything wrong with that?"

Cole was about to, and then abruptly changed his mind. Why should he be a hypocrite? How could he condemn Maddie for arranging something that he wasn't in the least sorry for!

Kate dressed carefully for her dinner at Madeleine's house and tried to ignore the thousand or so butterflies that seemed to have taken up permanent residence in her stomach. Ever since she'd found out that Cole was also going to be there, she'd been on an emotional seesaw. She'd gone through everything from embarrassment and fear, to elation and relief. In the end, she'd just tried to put it out of her mind—which was next to impossible since Cole was rarely out of her mind these days.

Kate took one last look in the mirror, and satisfied with her appearance, sprayed a light touch of perfume to her wrists and the base of her throat. The silk jumpsuit had been an impulse purchase the last time she'd been in New York. It had been outrageously expensive and Kate had a hard time justifying the cost, especially since she'd only just bought the church and she'd known how extensive *and* expensive the renovations were going to be.

But now, as she looked at her reflection in the mirror, she wasn't sorry that she'd broken down and bought it. It was one of those things that made you feel good just by wearing it. The soft, oyster-colored silk did wonders for her skin, and the flowing lines suited her figure to perfection. The narrow-legged style made her long legs seem even longer and the wide black belt drew attention to her slim waist and gently curving hips. The only thing she was a little uncomfortable with was the low neckline which exposed more of her cleavage than she was used to.

Still, it was probably good to wear something daring every now and then, Kate reflected. Madeleine did, and she'd never thought it looked outrageous on her. And if she could get away with it at her age, surely Kate could at hers!

# Nine

Fifteen minutes later, Kate pulled her white Mercedes to a halt in front of Madeleine's house and switched off the engine. She tried to ignore the fact that her heart was thumping like a jackhammer at the sight of Cole's car parked in front of hers—and wasn't happy with herself when she couldn't. She felt like a breathless schoolgirl mooning over the new boy in class.

Grabbing her purse, Kate's eyes suddenly fell on the small brass plate affixed to the dashboard. "To my Katie-bug," she read softly.

Katie-bug. That's what her father had called her when she'd been growing up. She'd always loved the little black and red bugs that had filled their garden. It was the only insect Kate would actually pick up in her hands—and it was the one she made sure Matt never killed. And her father had laughed, every time she'd brought one to him and recited the rhyme. *Ladybug, ladybug, fly away home. Your house is on fire and your children have all flown . . .*

Abruptly, Kate pushed the memories away. Silly. There wasn't any point in thinking about the past anymore. She and her father had been close once, but they weren't any more. He'd wanted his fame and his success, and he'd gotten it.

Whether the price he'd been forced to pay was worth it, only he could say.

The maid opened the door to her knock, and Kate smiled as she handed over her shawl. Then, taking a deep breath to calm her nerves, she walked into the living room with her head held high and a bright, confident smile upon her lips.

"Hi, everyone. Sorry I'm late, Maddie. I was working on a design and completely lost track of—" Kate stopped, glancing first at Madeleine's startled face and then at Cole's. "Is something wrong? You're *both* staring at me like you've never seen me before."

Madeleine was the first to recover. "Kate, I'm so sorry. I really didn't mean to stare." She quickly got up and kissed her warmly on both cheeks. "It's just that you look so . . . lovely tonight. Doesn't she, Cole?"

"Yes, she certainly does," Cole agreed softly, because he couldn't deny that she did. Kate's skin glowed like the finest porcelain, while her eyes, under a fringe of impossibly long, silky lashes shimmered like molten sapphires. Cole had never seen a color like that before. She even moved differently tonight. Her walk wasn't so much a step now, as it was a sensuous, undulating movement across the floor. She was, in every way, the essence of what a woman should be. She was Venus and Aphrodite rolled into one, with a generous helping of Marilyn Monroe sexuality tossed in for good measure.

The interesting part was that Kate seemed completely unaware of it. Her smile was as open and guileless as it had always been. She wasn't consciously trying to act the part of an incredibly beautiful woman. She had simply . . . become one.

"Cole, weren't you going to say something?" Madeleine prompted as the silence lengthened.

"Hmm? Oh, yes, I'm sure I was, but I'm damned if I can remember." Cole laughed softly and shook his head. "Forgive me, Kate, I'm usually better on my feet than this. It's just that I've never seen you looking more beautiful."

Kate flushed. This really was starting to get embarrassing. Every time she set foot out the door these days she was getting complimented on the way she looked. "Thanks. It must be the new outfit."

"Which is absolutely stunning," Madeleine agreed. "Wherever did you get it? Not from around here, I'll bet."

"No, I picked it up in New York the last time I was there. It was in a little store off Fifth Avenue. I really couldn't resist."

"I can see why," Cole murmured.

Kate glanced at him quickly, all too aware of how wonderful *he* looked in his dark sports jacket and open-necked shirt. She saw the strong, tanned column of his neck, and the dark springy curls clustered at the opening of his shirt, and suddenly felt uncommonly warm. The man really was too attractive for anyone's good—and certainly for hers.

"Can I get you something to drink, Kate?" Madeleine offered. "A gin and tonic perhaps?"

"That would be great, Maddie, thanks."

"Cole, how's your drink?"

He held up a half full glass. "I'm fine."

As Madeleine moved off to prepare the drinks, Cole moved closer to Kate. A soft cloud of fragrance seemed to surround her, alluring yet not in the least overpowering. It went to his senses like vintage wine. "So, how's the new piece coming along?" he asked, striving for a conversational tone.

She smiled up into his eyes. "Very well. I've finished the pattern and started cutting out the pieces. I should be able to start putting it together by the end of the week, if I don't start working on the other piece in the meantime."

"The other piece?"

Kate blushed. "You commissioned me to make another piece for you, remember? With that little piece of blue glass. Unless you've changed your mind, of course."

"No, I certainly haven't. I just didn't think you'd have time to work on it before the opening. I know how many other pieces you're trying to get finished. Besides, I didn't give you much to go on."

"You didn't need to," Kate assured him. "It came together in a dream."

Something in the tone of her voice caused Cole to glance at her sharply. "I beg your pardon?"

Kate flushed, and hastily averted her eyes. "I said it came together like a dream."

Madeleine returned with the drinks. "Here you are, Kate. I hope you don't mind, Teresa was all out of lemon so I put a slice of lime in. Personally, I've always thought one worked as well as the other." She caught the tense look on Kate's face, and the watchful one on Cole's. "Did I miss something?"

"Not at all." Cole's voice was smooth. "Kate was just telling me that an idea for a piece of work I asked her to do for me came to her in a dream."

"*Like* a dream," Kate said urgently. "I said it came together *like* a dream."

"Well, I don't know now about you two, but I've always thought that coming up with ideas in your sleep must be a very *nice* way of creating something," Madeleine remarked idly. "And certainly an easy one. My grandmother used to come up with recipes in her sleep all the time."

"Your grandmother dreamed about *recipes*?" Kate asked in amazement.

"Oh yes. She *swore* until the day she died that her prize-winning chocolate cake was a gift from the heavens. And after tasting it, I was inclined to agree."

"Of course, it's not unheard of for creative people to come up with some of their best ideas in their sleep," Cole said casually. "I came up with an idea for a poem once. It wasn't very good. But then, neither was the poetry I created when I was awake."

They all laughed at that, and Kate was thankful that the awkward moment seemed to have passed. "My mother used to have creative dreams all the time," she said.

"Why Kate, I didn't know that your mother was an artist." Madeleine said.

"Not with her hands. She wrote music. She often told me that the songs came to her when she was sleeping. After a while she started keeping a tape recorder by her bed so that she could record them as soon as she woke up."

Cole tapped the edge of his glass with deceptive casualness. "You don't happen to have Celtic blood, do you, Kate?"

"As a matter of fact, I do. On my great-grandmother's side," she said proudly. "Or so my mother told me."

"Dinner is served, Mrs. Carstairs," Teresa announced from the doorway.

"Oh, thank you, Teresa. Shall we go in?"

As Kate expected, the dinner was excellent. She knew that Madeleine loved to entertain, and she did so with style and panache, her skills no doubt learned during her days as a celebrated New York hostess. There were fresh flowers on the table, soft music playing in the background, and the glow of candles everywhere.

It reminded Kate a lot of the dinners her own family had enjoyed when her mother had been alive. And she was surprised to discover that, like her mother, Madeleine had done most of the cooking herself.

"Oh yes, I may not have any particular *artistic* flair," Madeleine admitted, "but I can throw together a decent *poulet à l'orange* when I have to. Actually, I love cooking. It's one of the things I miss about not having anyone to cook for." Her face momentarily lost some of its brightness. "Sometimes it gets to be too much trouble to go to all that bother for one."

"Well, you've certainly excelled yourself this evening, Maddie," Cole complimented her warmly. "That was as fine a meal as any I've eaten."

Madeleine's cheeks flushed with pleasure. "Why, thank you, Cole. Coming from a man who eats in some of the finest restaurants in Europe, I'll definitely take that as a compliment. But if you want a real treat, you should ask Kate to make you some of her special *crêpes suzettes*. They're the best to be had this side of the state line."

Cole raised an eyebrow. "How did you know they were my weakness?"

Kate hardly knew where to look. "Maddie, don't be silly, you've never even *tasted* my crêpes."

"I know that, but I recall your sister-in-law positively singing their praises. By the way, how's your little nephew doing, Kate? I swear he is just the cutest little button of a boy. Cole, you really should see this child, he's absolutely adorable."

"I'm afraid he's not been very well lately," Kate said. "Matt had to take him to the hospital last Monday night. His temperature was a hundred and six."

Madeleine looked stricken. "Mercy, Kate, I had no idea. That's high for a youngster his age. But this isn't the first time it's happened, is it?"

"No, he was bad earlier in the spring too," Kate admitted. "And in the winter. The doctors don't know what's causing it. It comes on very quickly and shoots his temperature way up for a few days. But Matt said it's coming back down so he'll probably be home soon. When he does, I've volunteered to look after Christian so that Matt and Megan can get out for a night together. They really need the break."

"That was nice for you to offer," Cole said softly.

Foolishly pleased by his approval, Kate tried to shrug it off. "It's no trouble. I *am* Christian's godmother, after all."

They touched on a number of other subjects over the course of the next few hours. Kate wasn't surprised to discover that Cole was a lively and entertaining conversationalist. He seemed to know a little about everything and had an endless supply of interesting stories and amusing anecdotes. And she could have listened to him talk about his travels throughout the world all night. Unfortunately, by eleven o'clock, she was having a hard time keeping her eyes open.

"I hate to say this, Maddie, but I think I'm going to have to call it a night," Kate said, reluctantly getting to her feet. "Thanks for a wonderful evening."

"Yes, I suppose I should be heading back too," Cole said. "Dinner was excellent, Maddie, thank you."

"It was my pleasure. I'd forgotten how much I enjoyed cooking for company. I guess I've grown a little lazy of late."

"Well, you can come over to the church and cook for me anytime," Kate told her.

"Thank you, honey, but I think it's Cole you should be inviting over. After all, eating out every night can get pretty monotonous after a while. Can't it, Cole?" Madeleine asked with a wide-eyed look.

Kate transferred her gaze to Cole, and saw amusement flickering in the depths of his eyes. "Oh, well, I—"

"Please don't feel obligated to respond to Maddie's not so subtle hints, Kate," Cole said dryly. "We both know that the woman is a hopeless matchmaker, who just loves to put other people on the spot."

"Cole Beresford, how can you say such a thing!"

"Very easily, my dear, because it's true."

"Well, actually, I did want to thank you for helping me with my shopping the other day," Kate said, hoping she wasn't making a mistake by doing so, "so if you'd like to come over for dinner before you head back to New York, you're more than welcome."

"Will you make crêpes?"

Kate felt her lips twitch. "I think that could probably be arranged."

"In that case, I accept. C'mon, I'll walk you to your car. 'Night, Maddie."

Kate leaned forward and affectionately kissed Madeleine on the cheek. "Goodnight, Maddie. And thanks again, I really had a great time."

"Not nearly as good as I had, honey," Madeleine whispered impishly.

It was a beautiful autumn night. The sky was dotted with thousands of twinkling dots of light, while the brisk night air rustled gently through the leaves. Kate and Cole strolled in companionable silence down the flagstone path, enjoying the lushness of their surroundings, and the peacefulness of the night.

"You know, in spite of Madeleine's unfortunate tendency to meddle," Cole remarked affectionately, "the more time I spend with her, the more I like and admire her." He tipped his head back to study the night sky. "And the more I think it's a terrible waste that she's living all alone."

"I know. I've often felt the same way," Kate agreed. "The image of her being a lightheaded society matron is very much a façade. She's so interesting when you get to know her. And she's got a heart of gold."

"She's also a lot smarter than most people give her credit for," Cole said. "Unfortunately, rich women who don't work are typically labeled as dilettantes, and Lawrence's wealth certainly put Maddie in that bracket. Personally, I think she's gone along with the label because it's easier to laugh at herself than it is to try to make other people see her for who she really is."

"Well, at least *we* know the truth," Kate said with a smile.

Cole watched her for a moment, and his eyes dropped unbidden to her mouth. He wanted to kiss her again, but he figured he'd better not. He didn't want a repeat of what had happened outside her house the other night. But he couldn't deny that the attraction he'd felt for her since their first meeting was growing stronger every day. He was glad Maddie had given him the opportunity to spend time with Kate tonight. He'd send her a very large box of her favorite imported Swiss chocolates as soon as he got back to New York.

As to the remark Kate had made about coming up with the idea for a design in a dream, he'd have to give that one some thought. He still had no reason to suspect that Kate had the spinning wheel, but a few of the things she'd said tonight had started him wondering. "So, you mentioned something about a dinner invitation earlier," he reminded her.

Kate bit her lip, and turned away to hide her smile. "Yes, I guess I did. Would Thursday evening be convenient?"

"Are you serious? The night before your show?"

"Well, I hope by then I'll have everything taken care of. And it might help me to relax a little bit."

For some reason, hearing Kate say that an evening spent in his company would be relaxing made Cole feel pretty special. "In that case, Thursday would be fine. What time?"

"How does six o'clock sound?"

"Perfect. I'll bring the wine." Then, throwing caution to the wind, he bent his head and kissed her quickly on the lips anyway. "See you Thursday, Kate."

Cole worked well into the early hours of the morning. The package Morris had sent him contained far more than just the pictures of the Lockton spinning wheel he had shown Madeleine. It contained a wealth of new information and speculation as to the origin, history and reputed powers of the wheel.

Judging by the information Morris had uncovered, the wheel's last owner, Lady Thelford, had been in possession of the spinning wheel since the late eighteen hundreds. It had been in her mother's family since the end of the seventeen hundreds. Before that, it had had a number of owners, its change of hands usually occurring as a result of death, thievery or some other unknown circumstance.

Cole leaned back in the armchair, and read Morris's letter again.

*. . . effects of the wheel vary greatly from owner to owner. Upon reading accounts of previous owners, which unfortunately, are sketchy at best, I have determined that the wheel accentuates the good qualities in a person, especially with regard to creativity. In each of the cases studied, works developed by the owner suddenly took on a new dimension. Hence, the term, "flashes of brilliance," which you coined so nicely, my friend.*

*Interestingly enough, I have also found out something that you and I had wondered about in the past. Upon tracing the history of one of the owners, the infamous witch hunter, Nathaniel Becker, it appears that there was no marked change, either in his personality or in any aspect of his life. I have my suspicions that it may have had to do with the so-called "blackness" of his soul, however, I am endeavoring to find out more. Regrettably, details about the man's life are almost nonexistent . . .*

Cole put the letter down and reached for another piece of paper that the professor had included. It was a photocopy he had made of a passage he'd found in an old book from a used bookstore in York. The passage made reference to some of the things Cole already knew about the spinning wheel, but it was the last paragraph on the page that really grabbed and held his attention.

> *. . . can reputedly enhance the physical beauty of the owner, especially if she be female, to a noticeable degree to others, yet oftimes, without affecting the person's perception of him or herself . . .*

*Dear God,* Cole thought in astonishment. *That sounded exactly like Kate.* She'd been totally unaware of how beautiful she had looked tonight. When he and Maddie had complimented her on her appearance, she'd just laughed it off, putting it down to the new outfit she was wearing; the same as she'd done with the coral sweater she'd had on the other day. But was it possible that . . . something else was having this effect on her?

The problem was when it came to Kate, Cole couldn't swear that *he* wasn't a big part of the problem too. Because it was getting harder and harder for him to see her objectively. He wasn't sure whether she *was* growing more beautiful by the day, or whether it was his feelings for her that were making her *look* more beautiful. Maybe there was nothing mystical or magical about it.

"For in as much as love grows in you, so beauty grows," Cole quoted softly. "For love is the beauty of the soul."

Unfortunately, he also knew that whatever his personal feelings for Kate, he couldn't ignore the signs. His training was too deeply instilled. The Celtic background, the creative natures of both Kate and her mother, and now the appearance of steadily increasing physical beauty. The signs were all there. All that remained was to see if Kate's newest works demonstrated any flashes of creative brilliance.

And he would get his answers to that soon enough.

Kate tapped on the back kitchen window and peered inside. "Megan? Matt? Anybody home?" When there was no answer, she tried the screen door. Just as she did, her sister-in-law appeared at the top of the stairs, carrying a well-laden laundry basket.

"Kate, I thought I heard your voice." Megan pushed her shoulder-length hair back from her face and sighed. "I hope you haven't been waiting long."

"No, I just got here. I came by to see how Christian was doing. When I didn't see Matt's truck parked outside, I wasn't sure if anyone was home."

"Matt's gone into town to pick up a few things, but he should be back soon." Megan set the basket on the floor and smiled. "Feel like something to drink? I was just about to put the kettle on."

"Sure, that would be great."

Megan filled the kettle with fresh water and set it on the stove. "Matt didn't tell me you'd been away on vacation, Kate."

"I wish. I've forgotten what the word means."

Megan's eyes widened in surprise. "You mean you haven't been away?"

"No, what made you think that I had?"

"Because you look . . . fabulous."

Kate shook her head. Why was she getting so many compliments these days? Had she really looked that bad before? "What's different about me, exactly?"

"In a word? Everything," Megan said enviously. "You look like you've just come back from a month in the Caribbean. Rested, glowing, gorgeous."

Kate frowned. There was that word *glowing* again. "Must be the new cosmetic line I'm using," she muttered. "I've had more compliments in the last week than I've had in the past two years."

"Well, I want the name of it," Megan said as she took two mugs down from the cupboard. "Lord knows, I could use a lift at the moment."

Kate heard the weariness in the woman's voice and wished there were something she could do to help. "How's Christian?"

"He's stable again. Dr. Sheffield called yesterday afternoon and said his temperature had come down enough that he could be released. Matt brought him home last night. Tea or coffee?"

"Hmm? Oh, tea would be great." Kate paused thoughtfully. "Does the doctor have any idea what's been causing these flare-ups?"

"No, but at least he's not calling them colds anymore. He mentioned something about a viral infection, but he doesn't seem to know much about it. I haven't said anything to Matt yet, but I've been wondering whether we shouldn't take Christian to a specialist."

"It might be a good idea, Meg. I know that kids are prone to catching anything and everything that goes around, but Christian is particularly susceptible. And when he gets something, he always gets it worse than anybody else. There has to be an explanation."

Megan breathed a sigh of resignation. "I know. It's just that I hate the thought of him having to stay in some big medical facility with strangers all around him. Goodness knows, he's a brave little soul but even a grown man would quake at the thought of all those tests."

"Still, it's worth it if they can find out what's causing the problems. Because if there is something wrong with Christian—oh, Megan, I'm sorry, I didn't mean to make you cry," Kate said, stricken with guilt.

Megan shook her head as she reached into her apron pocket for a tissue. "That's okay, you didn't. It's just . . . so h-hard for me to face the fact that something might really be wrong with him. He's just a little boy and—" Abruptly, the words broke off again as Megan turned away.

Impulsively, Kate got to her feet. "Everything's going to be all right, Meg. Christian will be fine, you'll see." She drew her sister-in-law into her arms and held her close. "He's just not as strong as most five-year-olds, that's all."

Megan sniffed and dabbed at her eyes again. "I know, and I'm really s-sorry, Kate. I didn't mean to blubber all over you. It's just that sometimes I get so scared."

"And there's nothing wrong with that. You're his mother, you're supposed to worry. But I think you should talk to Dr. Sheffield about sending Christian for those tests."

"I know. Matt tries to tell me it's not serious, but I know he's worried too."

"Sure he is. I saw it on his face when he stopped by the other day. He just tries not to show it."

"He's been so good about everything." Megan managed a wan smile. "I don't know how I would have gotten through this without him."

"Yeah, well, under that burly exterior, my brother's just a big mushball," Kate said, glad to see Meg smiling again. "Now why don't you sit down and I'll make the tea. I stopped at Mrs. Teasdale's on the way here and picked up some of your favorite eclairs. Baked fresh this morning."

"I really shouldn't."

"Yes, you should. And don't even think about the calories." Kate placed the decadent treat on a plate and slipped it in front of her. "This is medicine of a different sort. Grownup medicine."

"Thanks, Kate. I mean it."

"I know, and believe me, Meg, I feel your pain. You and

Matt and Christian are the only family I have. The three of you mean the world to me."

Megan hesitated uncertainly. "Kate, I need your advice about something."

"Shoot."

"You might not like what I'm going to say."

"I'm a big girl. Try me."

"Well, Matt and I were talking last night and, in view of the circumstances, I said that I thought we should . . . tell your father about Christian being sick." She saw Kate stiffen, and added quickly, "He is Christian's grandfather, after all."

"What was Matt's reaction?"

Megan sighed. "The same as yours. He doesn't see any point in bothering Roderick with this either."

"Well, it's not like my father has exactly gone out of his way to bother with us, Meg," Kate said flatly. "I mean, I know he sends us all wonderful presents at Christmas, and he never forgets any of our birthdays. But apart from that, when do we ever hear from him? I don't even know where he's living these days. He might have taken up permanent residence in London for all I know. That's where my last two birthday presents came from. Besides, Matt's right. There's no need to get in touch with him yet. Christian's going to get better and then you'll have worried him for nothing. Right?"

Megan made a valiant attempt at a smile, but her eyes were still troubled. "I suppose."

"Good. And speaking of that, can I see my dear little nephew for a few minutes? I've brought him a new toy to play with."

Megan slid off the stool. "He may be asleep. The medication Dr. Sheffield's given him has been making him pretty dopey, but let's take a look."

Kate followed Megan up to Christian's room and waited while she went in. She didn't want to disturb him if he was asleep. Fortunately he wasn't, but Kate's heart turned over at the sight of him. He was almost as white as the pillow and his tiny, elflike face was pinched and drawn. His big blue eyes seemed to take up most of his face, and Kate didn't need to lift the covers to see that there was precious little of him underneath.

He smiled drowsily at her approach. "Hi, Auntie Kate."

"Hello, sweetheart." Kate bent down beside the bed and took his hand in hers. "How are you feeling today?"

"Okay. Did Mommy tell you I went . . . to the hospital again?"

Kate nodded, biting her lip to keep it from trembling. "Yes, she told me. Were the nurses nice to you?"

He nodded slowly. "They gave me . . . candies. And—and the doctor let me listen to my heart through his ste . . . stefsc . . . the thing that goes in your ears."

Kate chuckled. "His stethoscope."

Megan bent over the other side of his bed. "Christian, Auntie Kate's brought you a pressie. She'll leave it here on your bedside table and you can play with it when you wake up, okay?"

"Okay." Christian yawned, his eyes growing heavy as the drug took effect. "Thanks, Auntie Kate."

Kate kissed him lightly on the forehead. "You're welcome, darling. I'll stop in and see you tomorrow, okay?" She stood up and felt the sting of tears in her eyes. He was so small, she thought sadly. So small and so very helpless.

"I'll be with you in a minute, Kate," Megan said quietly. "Why don't you go and pour us both another cup of tea?"

Kate nodded quickly. "Yes, all right. I'll . . . see you downstairs."

In the kitchen, Kate shed a few tears and then made an effort to pull herself together. Not just for Megan's sake, but for her own. The sight of Christian lying there had shocked her. He hadn't looked nearly as bad the last time she'd seen him. Obviously, the constant illnesses were sapping his strength and his body wasn't getting a chance to recover between bouts. She wished there was something she could do for him, something she could say that would make her sister-in-law feel better.

Kate heard Megan's footsteps on the stairs and hurriedly poured the tea. She wouldn't show her sister-in-law anything but a brave face. But as much as she hated to admit it, she was starting to think that maybe it *was* the time her father was made aware of the situation.

Kate decided not to accept Megan's invitation to lunch. She knew that her sister-in-law needed to rest, and that she wouldn't if she stayed for a meal. She'd bustle around the kitchen making soup and sandwiches and ensuring that everything was perfect. That's just the way Megan was. For that reason, Kate told her that she'd arranged to meet a girlfriend in town, and left as soon as she finished her tea.

On the way back to the church, however, Kate realized that she did need a few groceries and ended up heading into town anyway. Her head was so filled with thoughts of Christian that she didn't realize she'd parked next to a familiar car until she heard an even more familiar voice say, "Kate?"

She turned—and found herself gazing into a pair of concerned brown eyes. "C-Cole." She cleared her throat and tried again. "What are you doing here?"

"Grocery shopping. I thought I'd pick up a few things to keep in my room. Saves running out to the store every time I need a bottle of water or a piece of fruit."

"Right. The healthy eating thing." Kate smiled. "Your mother would be proud."

He grinned. "Yeah, right."

Kate tried to think of something else to say but found herself uncomfortably tongue-tied. Probably because Cole looked so great in a pair of faded jeans and a cream-colored fisherman's knit sweater. The casual attire only accentuated his rugged good looks and healthy build. No dusty antiquities expert had any right to look *that* good, Kate thought.

"Something wrong, Kate?"

"Wrong?"

"Yeah. You looked upset when you got out of your car."

Glad that he hadn't picked up on her reaction to *him*, Kate shook her head. "I just came from my sister-in-law's. My nephew's . . . not doing so great, and I—" She was embarrassed to feel her eyes fill up with fresh tears.

Seeing them, Cole took her arm and ushered her into his car. "Come on."

"W-where are we going?"

"For a cup of coffee. You look like you could use one."

"But the groceries—"

"Can wait until later. Right now, you need somebody to talk to."

With that, Cole drove her down the street to the little cappuccino place they'd been heading for the other day. This time, however, Kate made no demur. She did need somebody to talk to and probably the impartial ear of a third party was best. And the café was the perfect place to do that. It was cozy and quiet and exactly what Kate needed. Gretchen, the jovial owner of the café, quickly appeared to take their order, and it wasn't long before two steaming hot mugs of cappuccino were sitting on the table in front of them.

"You know something, Cole, I don't think I would make a very good parent," Kate said after a long, thoughtful silence. "Christian's only my nephew, but I swear, it tore me apart to see him lying there like that. I can't imagine how Megan and Matt cope."

"When did this all start?" Cole asked, genuinely interested.

Slowly, Kate told him the history of Christian's illness, and how Matt and Megan feared that his condition was getting worse. "But he's so small, Cole. So . . . fragile. He looks up at you with those beautiful blue eyes and believes in his heart that you'll take care of him. But what happens if—"

"Stop right there," Cole interrupted. "The number one rule of being a parent is that you don't stop to worry about the what ifs. You take things one day at a time. You deal with one problem, then you go on to the next. If matters get complicated along the way, you dig in a little harder and draw on resources you never knew you had."

Kate glanced at him in surprise. "You sound like you've been through it."

"I have, and the same way as you," Cole said. "I have an eight-year-old niece who suffers from epilepsy. I don't see her very much because she lives in Scotland, but my sister and brother-in-law have been through some pretty rough times. But they never lose hope. And hope's one of the greatest things we have going for us, Kate. That, and the strength to see things through. That's why your brother and sister-in-law don't give up."

Kate sighed. "They may not give up, but God knows, it must get them down. Megan looked ready to drop today."

"She probably is. But if that little boy were to take a bad turn, she'd be there with the strength of ten."

"I suppose." Kate thoughtfully sipped her coffee. "You weren't a teacher in another life, were you?"

Cole grinned. "I have no idea. Why?"

"Because one of my professors in college had the same gift as you. He always knew the right thing to say at exactly the right time." Kate laughed weakly. "I thought maybe it was a trait teachers shared."

"Well, we're all rumored to have led past lives. Who knows, maybe I was a teacher way back when."

"I wonder what I was?" Kate took a sip of her coffee, and laughed. "A friend of mine did that once. Regression, I think they call it. A psychic took her back into ancient times. Turns out she was a handmaiden to Cleopatra. Must have been a weird experience."

Cole pretended an interest in his coffee mug. "Do you believe in things like that, Kate?"

"What, reincarnation and things that go bump in the night?"

His mouth quirked. "I was thinking more along the line of ancient legends and folklore."

Kate stilled. *Folklore*. Like Rumpelstiltskin and enchanted spinning wheels? She reached for a package of sugar and tipped it into her coffee. "I've never really stopped to give it much thought." *Until recently*. "But yes, I suppose I do believe there are . . . things we can't explain." She looked up to see Cole watching her and forced a smile to her lips. "So, what do you think of this place? Charming, isn't it?"

Cole recognized a ninety-degree turn when he saw it. For the moment, however, he decided to let it go. "Yes, it is. You said the owners were European?"

"Gretchen is German, and her husband, Hans, is Swiss. They emigrated here four years ago and decided to recreate some of their homeland in Vermont. So they opened the

Edelweiss Café. Gretchen whips up dynamite schnitzel and Hans makes the most incredible desserts I've ever tasted. When I'm having a really bad week, I come here for a piece of chocolate hazelnut torte."

"Ah, yes, to sooth the chocoholic cravings."

Kate felt her stomach do a funny little flip. "Don't you ever forget anything?"

"Not the important stuff." Cole let his gaze travel slowly around the room. "Quite an eclectic mixture of furnishings."

"They brought a lot of their belongings with them. Gretchen inherited some beautiful antiques from her great-grandmother."

"Now there's an interesting piece," Cole said, his eyes finally lighting on something across the room. "I didn't realize they had spinning wheels in Germany."

Kate didn't have to turn around to know what he was talking about. She knew the location of every spinning wheel in the region. "Oh yes. In fact, spinning schools were first established in Germany and Holland, but Germanic tribes were already wearing tunics of finely spun linen around 200 BC."

Cole carefully concealed his surprise. "And here I thought you just knew your way around stained glass. Do you spin?"

"No, but a number of my friends do. And when everybody gets together, we talk about the different crafts and the skills required to do them."

"It must be difficult to learn."

"To be honest, I have no idea," Kate told him. "I've watched some of the girls work, but like anyone with a skill, they make it look easy."

"Yes, they do. I remember watching a girl spinning wool in Japan one time." Cole laughed. "I think I was more taken with *her* than I was with anything else. But I still remember the wheel. It was quite large."

"It might have been a hand-turned spindle wheel. I believe they originated in Asia."

Cole's eyes narrowed. "You seem to know a lot about spinning wheels, Kate. Were you thinking of getting one? Or do you already have one?"

The question came at her fast, catching her off guard. "I . . . beg your pardon?"

"A spinning wheel. I asked you if you were thinking about getting one."

Kate laughed, hoping he wouldn't notice the way the edges of her mouth quivered. "I work with stained glass, Cole. What would I want with a spinning wheel?"

He shrugged. "Maybe just as a piece of furniture. I've always liked them myself, and I thought anyone who knew as much about them as you might have wanted to buy one. Especially since they're probably easy to come by around here."

"Yes, they . . . probably are." Kate licked her lips. "Unfortunately, I don't have room for one. You've seen where I live. As Matt says, I've got enough furniture to sink a ship." She finished her coffee and abruptly got to her feet. "Well, I guess I'd better get going. I still have some shopping to do. Thanks for the coffee, Cole."

He gazed up at her for a moment, and then slowly got to his feet. "Right. I have a few errands of my own to run." He dropped some money on the table and escorted Kate outside and into his car.

Back in the café, the bearded, black-haired man sitting in a booth at the opposite end of the room slowly put down his newspaper and carefully pushed aside the lace curtain. He watched Beresford and the young lady leave, paying particular attention to the woman. Then, neatly folding the paper, he signaled to the waitress.

"Yes, sir, will there be anything else?"

"No, thank you, Frau," the man replied, using the polite form of address. "Although, I wonder, the lady and the gentleman who just left, do you know them, by chance? I thought the young lady looked like someone my daughter went to school with in California."

"Miss Pedigrew?" Gretchen shook her head. "I think she went to school in New York."

He smiled. "My mistake. Nice-looking fellow. Her husband?"

"No, I do not know him. I have not seen them together before."

"Interesting. They seem to be quite close. A new boyfriend, perhaps. Now, dear lady, that was an excellent cappuccino," the man said in his most charming fashion. "How much do I owe you?" Then, he added, "Miss Pedigrew, you said? You wouldn't happen to know where I might find her?"

A few minutes later, the man left the restaurant and made his way to the rented black BMW parked around the side. Sliding into the driver's side, he looked at what he had written on the piece of paper. KATE PEDIGREW, 24 ASH GROVE PLACE. He pulled out a copy of the local map he had purchased and quickly located Ash Grove Place. Then, he sat back with a smile.

What an incredible stroke of luck. He'd known that Beresford would be in the area looking for the spinning wheel, but he'd had no idea where. He'd simply been driving through town and stopped at the café to grab a coffee. But when he'd glanced through the front window to see Cole Beresford and a woman getting out of a car and coming in, he'd quickly taken his coffee and a newspaper and headed for a booth at the far end of the room.

And he'd watched them the entire time they'd been there. More to the point, he'd watched *her*, because he was far more interested in her than he was in Beresford. If his gut feeling was right, he'd just located the new owner of the Lockton spinning wheel. And he couldn't have been happier. Given the rather vague description he'd been given by the owner of the antique store, he'd expected to spend days searching for the woman. But now, seeing Beresford with someone who matched the description perfectly, Jeremy Davenport knew he'd struck gold.

"Thank you, Beresford. For once, you have been something other than a royal pain in the ass," he said in a flat, emotionless voice. "All I have to do now is keep my eye on the two of you until I'm ready to make my move. I've waited this long to get my hands on the Lockton Spinning wheel. I can certainly wait a bit longer."

Kate did two things that night, both of which surprised her. The first was to move the spinning wheel into her bedroom. The second was to write a letter to her father, something she'd been thinking about doing ever since she'd left Matt's house that morning.

Kate couldn't remember the last time she'd written to her father. She still sent cards to his office at Christmas and for his birthday, but she didn't get in touch with him otherwise. Despite what Matt thought, Kate knew that her father had a right to know what was happening. Christian wasn't getting better. The sight of him this morning had told her that. There was a lot more to his condition than a simple viral infection. He'd lost an alarming amount of weight, and for a five-year-old who'd never been strong to begin with, the loss of even a few pounds could be dangerous.

With regards to telling her father about the studio show, Kate was of two minds. She hated sounding like a hopeful schoolgirl, asking her father to come to a school play, but on the other hand, she didn't want to sound like a complete stranger either. As a result, the finished product was a blend of sentiment and distance. She briefly advised her father that she'd an addition built onto the house, which she intended to use as a studio for her work, and that the following Friday evening marked the official opening of it. She told him that he was welcome to come.

Kate rewrote the letter three times before she was satisfied with the wording. And even then, she wasn't sure she had it right. She thought about phoning his office on the off chance he might be there, but then quickly discarded it as a bad idea. Rejection in print was bad enough. Hearing it over the phone was even worse.

Kate sealed the letter, stuck a stamp in the corner and put it in her bag. That done, she turned off the living room lights and headed for the den. She worked quickly, gathering up her tape recorder and a blank tape, and carried them into her bedroom. She set the tape recorder on the floor and positioned the microphone on her pillow. Then, she walked back into the den and picked up the spinning wheel.

There was no longer any question in Kate's mind that the spinning wheel was haunted. Okay, maybe *haunted* wasn't the right word, but something paranormal was definitely going on here. It was the only logical explanation she could come up with for the periods of blankness she experienced whenever she touched the wheel—and for the bursts of creativity which followed.

It had happened again last night. She'd sat down at the spinning wheel—and three hours later had woken up to find another completed design on her drafting board; this one in vibrant shades of blue and mauve, the colors of Cole's piece. And while she couldn't remember *everything* that had happened during the encounter, Kate was sure that something or . . . someone had tried to communicate with her.

That's why she wanted to make contact with it again now. She had to find out what was controlling the spinning wheel, and why it was having this startling effect on her life.

Strangely enough, Kate wasn't scared at the thought of what she was about to do. Maybe she should have been. She'd never had any experience with the supernatural before, other than to see the usual collection of box office thrillers, and those usually made her groan rather than long for any type of close encounter with the other side. But for whatever reason, Kate sensed that what she was about to do wasn't dangerous. Whatever the power in the wheel was, she was sure it originated in good.

Kate positioned the spinning wheel close to the wall. The most unfortunate part of her experiences with it thus far was that after only a few minutes she fell asleep. The lethargy that invaded her body invariably kept her from maintaining prolonged contact with it, and the telepathic link—or whatever it was—was broken. Kate hoped that by sitting with her back against the chair and her right side against the wall, she would be less likely to collapse, thereby prolonging the contact once it was established. The tape recorder was there in case she said something during the encounter that would help her to remember it afterwards.

"Okay, here goes," Kate said softly, hitting the record button. "I sure hope I'm doing the right thing." With that, she pulled the dowel from the base of the wheel and set it into motion, watching as it began its slow, silent revolutions.

It happened faster tonight. Kate closed her eyes and almost at once the familiar surroundings of the church began to dissolve. She began to drift through the whirling kaleidoscope of colors until she was there again. In that . . . other place. Perhaps even in another time.

Eventually, she saw the white-garbed figure coming toward her, and knew that this was the person who had tried to contact her. And strangely enough, this time, Kate remembered her name. "You are . . . Eleya," she whispered softly.

*"Yes. I am glad you have come back."*

A tentative smile found its way through Kate's uncertainty. "It seems very . . . strange to be talking to you, like this."

*"It is not the first time."*

"No, but it's the first time that I'm more or less aware of what I'm doing." Kate hesitated, remembering something. "Was it . . . you who spoke to me that day in the antique store?"

*"Yes. It was . . . important that I reach out to you. I had to let you know that . . . you were the Chosen One."*

"I don't know what you mean by that."

*"Your coming was made known to me many years ago,*

*Kate, and I have waited for you. At the time of the summer solstice, I sent a message to you."*

Kate gasped. So that's what had happened. She remembered the inexplicable longing she'd felt at the beginning of the summer to find a spinning wheel. But it hadn't been a whim that had sent her searching. It had been Eleya.

There were so many questions, she hardly knew where to begin. "Why have you waited for me?"

*"I have waited so that I may achieve my Nyada. My spiritual release."*

"Your release from what?

*"From the spinning wheel that binds me to the earth."*

"But . . . how did you come to be here?"

*"My physical body was put to death centuries ago, but my spirit was condemned to live on. I was put here against my will."*

"You mean you're a . . . prisoner?" Kate asked in horror.

*"Yes."*

Suddenly, Kate felt the lassitude returning. The lethargy was pulling her down, and sleep was beckoning. Her head felt like it was too heavy to hold up. She had to fight to keep her hand on the wheel. "I don't want to . . . go," she struggled to say. "There is . . . so much more I need to know."

Eleya smiled with the dignity of a queen. *"And we shall speak again, Kate. But there is one thing I must tell you before you leave. There are those who wish to possess the spinning wheel. Their souls are filled with greed, and they know of the wheel's great powers. They will try to take it from you, but I beg you not to let that happen."*

"But . . . how can I . . . prevent it?" Kate whispered, aware that she was quickly succumbing to the weariness.

*"You must tell no one that you have the wheel. Your life will be in great danger. Because the evil will come in a form that you do not recognize."*

"Then . . . how will I know?"

*"You may not know. Until it is . . . too late."*

When Kate awoke the next morning, it was with total recollection of what had happened the night before. There had been no need for the tape recorder. She could remember every detail of her encounter with Eleya, every word the two of them had exchanged. It was as though a rapport had been established, a telepathic link between this world and the next.

Kate had no explanation for it. How could anyone explain the existence of ghosts or spirits that were trapped in a place that was neither here nor there? All she knew was that Eleya *did* exist—and that the spinning wheel was the means through which they communicated. That meant that under no circumstances was she going to give it up—or let anyone else know that she had it.

Kate didn't know why Eleya kept referring to her as the Chosen One. She didn't know why or how Eleya had come to be trapped inside the spinning wheel. But she knew there was an explanation. It wasn't chance that had sent her searching for a spinning wheel this summer. It had been Eleya calling to her. For whatever reason, their paths had been destined to meet at this time. But why had the spirit warned her to be on her guard?

It was a fascinating and incredible dilemma. Unfortunately, as much as Kate longed to spend every waking hour trying to come up with answers, she knew she also had to attend to the other more immediate concerns in her life. Like making the final preparations for her studio show. It was only a few days away and she had only finished three of the pieces she planned to showcase that night.

There would be five new pieces in all. The largest piece, which she had impulsively named Eleya's Dream, would take pride of place in the studio. It was without question the most magnificent thing she'd ever done, and she was tremendously proud of it. The second new work, which she had entitled Ice Magic, was the piece she was doing for Cole, and she intended to display it close to Eleya's Dream. Kate liked the way the colors contrasted; the rich, passionate reds and golds with the icy blues and greens. The other three pieces would be exhibited in prominent locations around the studio, and she knew that they would all garner praise. All five would be distinguished by the excellence of their design and construction. Because all five had been inspired by the beauty of Eleya.

As a result, Kate spent most of her daylight hours in the workroom, cutting and grinding the fragile pieces of glass, and fitting them onto her work board. She constantly measured and checked to make sure that everything was perfect, and the speed and efficiency with which she worked was astonishing. It was almost as though other hands guided her own. As though she could see her work through another's eyes, and knew what had to be done. She could hardly wait to see what the response would be the night of the show.

Before that, however, she had to get through her dinner with Cole.

Kate had planned the details of the meal earlier in the week and went out Thursday afternoon to shop for it. And if she glanced at her watch once, she glanced at it a hundred times between the hours of one and five-thirty. Finally, at a quarter to six, everything was ready. The roast beef was in the oven, the vegetables were cut up, the rolls were warming, and the big bowl of salad was keeping crisp in the fridge. She'd already set the dining room table with her best crystal and china—after cleaning up a few pieces she hadn't used in years—and had even made an attractive arrangement of colorful fall leaves for the centerpiece.

The very last thing Kate did was move the spinning wheel into her bedroom closet. In spite of her growing feelings for Cole, she couldn't forget what Eleya had told her. She had no doubt that there *would* be others looking for the spinning wheel. She had even begun to suspect that Cole knew of its existence. His subtle questioning of her in the café the other day had certainly left her wondering.

And if that was the case, Cole presented a genuine risk. As an antiquities expert, it was only natural that he would want to see it. He'd want to examine it, and possibly even take it away so that his colleagues could look at it. But now that Kate knew about the secret of the spinning wheel, she couldn't let it fall into *anyone's* hands. Her duty was to Eleya. To find out why she had been imprisoned in the spinning wheel, and to learn how to go about freeing her.

Which was why Kate tucked the wheel into the back of her closet and carefully arranged her summer comforter over it. She had no way of knowing whether or not such precautions were necessary, but she didn't intend to take any chances.

The Lockton spinning wheel wasn't going anywhere.

Cole arrived at a few minutes after six. Kate heard his knock on the front door and nervously glanced into the hall mirror. She hoped he wouldn't say anything about the way she looked. She was starting to get a little sensitive about the whole thing. She thought she'd looked okay before, but suddenly, everybody was telling her how beautiful she looked.

Okay, so maybe her skin *was* looking a little smoother and healthier these days, and yes, her eyelashes did seem to be longer and more luxurious than before. But she was using a different skin care line and she'd started buying that new mascara that made your lashes curl on their own. She was sure that's all it was. Maybe if she just kept the lights turned down low, Cole wouldn't notice anything.

But Cole did notice. As soon as she opened the door, Kate knew. The expression in his eyes said it all. Nevertheless, she gamely put a smile on her face and held the door open wider. "Hi, Cole. Come in."

If Cole's shock at seeing *her* in the elegant cream dress and long tunic was apparent, then Kate's at seeing *him* must have been just as plain. They could have been opposing pieces on a chessboard. Cole's black suede shirt was open at the throat to reveal a dark shadow of curls, while black dress pants molded to his firm thighs and trim waist. His hair was still damp from the shower, and she could smell the clean, fresh scent of his soap. He wore a striking gold and sapphire ring on the third finger of his right hand, and around his neck, a fine gold chain. Kate had never seen him wear jewelry before, but like the stark unadorned black of his clothes, it suited him.

For his own part, Cole moved into the entrance of the

church past Kate, and tried not to stare. He'd warned himself in the car that he'd likely find her looking more beautiful than the last time he'd seen her, and he'd tried to prepare himself for that eventuality. But the carefully rehearsed words of greeting died on his lips the minute she opened the door.

In the flowing cream silk outfit, Kate looked stunning. Cole was reminded of H. Rider Haggard's immortal classic, She, and of the burly Leo's stupefaction at first gazing upon the goddess Asheya, a woman who was said to enslave men's hearts with a single sight of her uncovered face. If ever there was a modern day Asheya, it was Kate.

He suddenly remembered the flowers and the bottle of wine in his hands, and belatedly held them out. "These are for you."

"Oh, Cole, thank you. But you shouldn't have gone to all this trouble." Kate bent her head to the delicate blooms and closed her eyes in pleasure. "Mmm, I love the scent of freesia. And Pouilly Fuisse. How did you know it was my favorite?"

Cole stared at her, unable to look away. This must have been how the sailors felt just before they were lured to their deaths on the rocks by the sirens. They hadn't see it coming either, poor bastards. "I . . . didn't. I—" Cole sighed and shook his head. He was stammering like a schoolboy. "Kate, I'm sorry, really," he said finally. "I didn't mean to stare. It's just that every time I see you, you look even more beautiful than before."

Kate smiled to hide her nervousness, and quickly turned away. Well, at least he hadn't said she *glowed*. "Have a seat in the living room. I'll put these in water."

Cole sensed her withdrawal and cursed his clumsiness. He would have to be careful about what he said to her from now on. If Kate was in possession of the Lockton spinning wheel, it changed everything. "So, how goes the work for the opening tomorrow night?" he asked as he sat down on the soft leather couch.

Kate pulled a glass vase out from under the sink and filled it with water. "Great. I finally finished the last of the new pieces today. Now all I have to do is make up some price tags and I'll be all set."

"Why don't you just hang them without stickers and let people make offers. I guarantee you'll make more money that way."

Kate flashed him a grin. "Maybe, but I don't think I'll run into too many customers like you, Cole. Most people are reluctant to pay the asking price, let alone hundreds of dollars more."

"Ah, but I recognized talent when I saw it. As well as an overly modest artist. You should give some thought to making Madeleine your business manager. She has a definite knack for making money. And unlike you, she puts a realistic value on your talent."

Kate snipped off the ends of the flowers and placed them in the vase. "Sounds great, but I wouldn't be able to pay her very much."

"I think she'd be happy just to have something to do."

"You're probably right." Kate stood back to look at her handiwork and then, satisfied with her efforts, set the vase on the counter. "She's great at taking charge. Now, can I offer you something to drink?"

"What do you have?"

"Well, it's not the Ritz," Kate admitted as she opened the small liquor cabinet, "but I do have rum, rye, vodka, gin, scotch, vermouth, Dubonnet—"

"I thought you said it wasn't the Ritz," Cole broke in.

"It isn't. The list just ran out. The only thing I ever buy is gin. The rest of the stuff I brought with me from New York."

"I'll have scotch."

"No ice, water on the side."

Cole looked at her in surprise. "I'm impressed. I barely remember what people drink, let along how they take it."

"I don't believe a word of it." Kate pulled out the bottle of scotch and a glass. "I have a feeling that you have a very retentive memory, Mr. Beresford, and that you use it to your best advantage."

"You make me sound quite Machiavellian. And I suppose you're going to have a gin and tonic, on the rocks with a twist."

"There, you see?" Kate rounded on him with a smile. "So much for your bad memory." She prepared the two drinks and carried them into the living room. "Somehow I didn't think anybody in your business would suffer from a bad memory."

Cole rose to accept his glass. Kate had beautiful hands. The fingers were long and tapering, the nails neatly rounded and brushed with a soft peachy-pink polish. Piano fingers, his mother would have called them. He also noticed that she wore no rings. Come to think of it, he'd never seen her wearing any jewelry apart from a pair of pearl studs and the heavy gold choker necklace she'd had on the night of Maddie's party. "I take it you're not into jewelry."

"My lifestyle doesn't call for it," Kate said simply. "When I first started doing stained glass, I'd forget that I was wearing a ring until my hands were covered in grout. It used to take me ages to clean up. After that, I just stopped wearing them. Now I tend to forget about them altogether."

"That's a shame." Cole reached out and took one of her hands in his. "Because with hands like these you could be a model for Debeers."

Kate inhaled sharply, unprepared for the touch of his hand. She watched him rub his thumb over her palm, and felt a shiver ripple up her arm.

Cole felt her tremor and reluctantly let her go. "How's your nephew doing?"

"He's . . . holding his own." Kate sat down in the big armchair opposite Cole. A safe distance away. "His condition hasn't worsened since he's come home, but he hasn't improved as much as Matt and Megan were hoping he would either."

"What about the tests?" Cole asked. "Has your sister-in-law decided to have them done?"

"I don't know. Meg still hates the idea of putting him a big city hospital. She thinks he'd be scared to death."

Cole took a sip of his scotch. "More than likely he'll think it's all a big adventure. Kids usually do. Besides, I've always found that medical staff take particular care with children. They usually go out of their way to try to make the experience as nonthreatening as possible."

"I hope so, Cole, because he needs those tests—" Kate broke off and raised the glass to her lips. She wasn't sure that pursuing that topic of conversation was a good idea right now. "So, what do you think of my church now that it's all put back together?"

"I think it's absolutely wonderful. You should be proud of what you've accomplished. I'd love to buy a place like this, and I will if there are any left by the time I get around to it. Old stone buildings like these have become something of a target for young, upwardly mobile executives looking to escape the cities." He looked up at the ceiling with a discerning eye. "What kind of shape was it in when you bought it?"

"Structurally sound, though all of the outside metal work had to be replaced."

"I notice you've put new windows in too. Whoever you hired did a nice job."

"I had one of the young carpenters from the village do it." Kate tipped back her head and smiled. "Which turned out to be something of a coincidence when I discovered that his grandfather was the one who installed the original set of windows."

Cole looked at her in astonishment. "You're kidding."

"Amazing, isn't it? But then, I suppose a lot of the people who were born around here never left. They grew up, got married and had families of their own, and all without ever traveling more than fifty miles away."

"Funny. I don't think I've been *within* fifty miles of the place I was born in years."

There was no particular note of regret in his voice, so Kate felt safe in asking, "And where exactly is that remote and infamous spot?"

Cole chuckled. "You won't have heard of it."

"Try me."

"How well do you know the Lake District?"

"Not very," Kate admitted.

"Then I guarantee the name of the town won't mean anything to you."

"You don't have much of an accent for somebody who was born in England."

"Only because I choose not to." Cole suddenly slipped into an accent that would have gained him admittance to Buckingham Palace. "Sometimes I find it better not to be too easily identifiable."

Kate started to laugh. "Now *that's* an English accent. You sound just like Mrs. Bar—like a lady I met at a craft show one day." She quickly gulped her drink, looking everywhere but at Cole. Had he noticed her unintentional slip? If he had, he wasn't letting on.

"I also do German, French and a credible Italian when called upon to do so," he was saying now.

"I'm impressed."

"Don't be. It's a necessary part of the job. Now, as to your earlier question, I was born in Broughton in Furness."

"Where?"

"I told you so. It's a small village up in the mountains."

"Good heavens, however did a boy from the English mountains end up becoming an authority on antiquities and living in New York?"

"It's a long story on both counts, but in a nutshell, my father started me on my career, and a lady I met in university started me thinking about coming to America."

"Moved by love, no doubt."

"Well, I don't know that I'd call it love," Cole drawled, "but it was certainly enough to get me out of England. Funny though, I've spent more time back there than I ever thought I would when I left."

Kate gazed at him thoughtfully. "I suppose that's not surprising when you consider the age and the history of the country. There are so many antiquities that come out of the British Isles."

"Yes, and the biggest percentage of them end up here."

While he had been talking, Cole had been doing a careful and thorough examination of the room. He'd expected that if Kate had the spinning wheel, she would have displayed it in here, though he could see what she'd meant about not having enough room to bring anything in. The addition of a spinning wheel would certainly have cramped things. Which only left the bedroom and the studio, because after her inadvertent slip about Mrs. Barrett just now, Cole's suspicions that she had the wheel were growing steadily.

"You have some fine antiques yourself, Kate," he complimented her. "You're obviously a knowledgeable shopper."

Kate fingered the gold tassel on her belt. "I think calling me knowledgeable is probably being kind. I buy what I like, and since I don't buy for investment, I can afford to give up age to get a nicer finish or a more complete piece."

"I know what you mean. I'd been looking for a particular type of dining room table, and finally came across one a few months ago. It was in beautiful condition, but when I asked the owner how much he wanted for it, he tried to sell me another piece that was far more valuable, simply because it was older. Unfortunately, some dimwit had painted it yellow to go with his decor. From an investment point of view, it was a much better buy, but since I wasn't partial to yellow and didn't feel like stripping it, I passed it up." He grinned. "The owner thought I was crazy."

"Well, I don't imagine you'll find too much of value in here. Like you, I buy what I like, not always what's the most valuable."

Cole rose, and wandered around the room. His eyes suddenly lit upon a framed photograph sitting on one of the end tables. "Is that your father?"

Kate swiveled around in her chair. "Yes. We were at the Black and White Ball in New York. That was . . . just before I handed in my notice."

"Good-looking man," Cole commented. "But I don't see a strong resemblance between you."

Kate rose and crossed to the mantle. She took down a picture Cole hadn't noticed and handed it to him. "I've been told I look more like my mother."

Cole looked at the photo. It could be Kate in thirty years' time. "Your mother was a beautiful woman," he said softly.

"And you're right, the resemblance between the two of you is very strong."

"I followed my mother in looks, Matt took after my father. That's why Christian was named for him." Seeing Cole's blank look, she said, "Roderick Christian Pedigrew."

"Ah. Are Matt and your father close?"

"No. They have nothing in common. Matt was always into sports, and Dad was into business. When Matt had the car accident and lost his chance at any kind of a career playing professional ball, Dad thought he'd come back to New York and join the firm. Matt didn't and things just kept going downhill from there. That's why Matt doesn't talk about him much now." Kate paused, a pensive shimmer in her eyes. "I've . . . written him a letter, asking him to come."

Cole glanced at her in surprise. "To your show?"

Kate's mouth twisted ruefully. "I hardly think my studio opening would be motivation enough for Dad to come here from wherever he is. But Christian is. Dad loves that little boy. Always has. And he has a right to know what's going on. If anything were to happen to him—" Kate put the photo of her mother back on the mantle. "But rule number one of being a pseudo parent is that we don't talk about the what ifs, right? In which case, I think I'll just go and check on dinner."

Once again, Cole knew that Kate had successfully diverted the conversation away from a subject she didn't want to talk about. But in this case, he couldn't blame her. His own family life hadn't been so memorable that he recalled it with any particular fondness.

In a few minutes, dinner was ready. Cole opened the bottle of wine while Kate mashed the potatoes and put the other vegetables in serving tureens. She tossed the salad with her own homemade dressing and took the bread rolls out of the oven. The last thing she did was bring out the succulent roast beef and set it on the table.

"Roast beef and mashed potatoes!" Cole grinned at her. "You remembered."

"Well, I remembered the way your eyes lit up the day you talked about all the comfort foods you missed so much. So

I couldn't bring myself to serve you linguine with a light marinara sauce."

"I'm almost afraid to ask what's for dessert," Cole groaned. "I've mentioned at least three things I'm crazy about—all of them terribly fattening."

"What makes you think we're not having fruit salad? After eating all this, you should be feeling like something light."

"I should be, but I figure if I'm going to be bad, I may as well be really bad." He rubbed his hands together with glee. "Shall I carve?"

By the time Cole had finished slicing the roast, Kate had lit the candles and put a couple of classical CDs on the stereo. Cole held out her chair, and as she sat down, she detected the delicious smell of his aftershave again. "Th-thank you."

"My pleasure." His hands touched her briefly, lingering no more than a moment as he pushed in her chair. But Kate felt them intensely; their heat burning through the thin silk of her blouse and into her skin. When he reached across the table to pour her wine, her eyes were drawn to the sight of his fingers curled around the bottle. She had a sudden image of those fingers on her body, slipping off her clothes and caressing her skin. She shuddered as she thought of him touching her in the way and in the places she wanted to be touched.

As the hot color rose in her cheeks, Kate wasn't sorry that she had turned the lights way down low.

Kate wasn't sure how she got through the meal. The atmosphere was definitely charged. She could all but hear the crackle in the air every time they looked at each other. She was aware of Cole making light, unthreatening conversation, and of the number of times she laughed. But it was always there. That . . . undercurrent of sensuality.

"Kate, if you ever decide to give up stained glass, I suggest you open a restaurant," Cole said when they finally took their wine back into the living room. "Maddie was right. Your *crêpes suzettes* are about as close to heaven as it gets." He raised his glass to her in a toast. "My compliments to the hostess."

"Thank you, Mr. Beresford. But I think I should raise my glass to you, since you're the one responsible for this celebration."

"I am?"

"Yes, don't you remember?" She sank down onto the couch and tucked one leg under her. "This is my thanks for helping me with my shopping the other day."

"Ah, but I only did that knowing you would feel obligated to feed me," he retorted, sitting down beside her. "And I think I have been adequately repaid." His eyes dropped to the tempting curve of her lips. "So tell me, Miss Pedigrew, what do you do when you're not creating masterpieces in glass. Ski down mountains? Jump out of planes? Ride around town on the back of wild elephants?"

Kate threw back her head and laughed. "I have to admit, it's been a while since I've seen an elephant lumbering along the main street of Barre. And I go green just *thinking* about jumping out of a plane with nothing but a flimsy white chute on my back. But I used to be a skier."

"Ah ha! I knew there was some daredevil blood in you somewhere."

Kate let out a snort. "Daredevil, my foot! The one time I ended up in the moguls, I damaged both knees and put my shoulder out of joint."

"Ouch!"

"That's a polite way of putting it," Kate said ruefully. "So now, I look at the snow from the comfort of my living room, preferably while I'm sitting in front of a blazing fire, with a glass of wine and a good book."

"Sounds like a pleasant alternative to me," Cole murmured. He ran his finger around the rim of his glass, and glanced at her speculatively. "So what about boyfriends? We touched on the subject briefly, but you never told me if there's been anyone special in your life."

Kate shifted a little on the couch. He was moving into the personal stuff, and she wasn't sure she was ready for that. "How far back do you want to go?"

"How far back do you need to?"

"That depends on what you mean by special. Sheldon Carter was very special to me in the eighth grade. That boy could wing a baseball faster than—"

"I was thinking in more recent terms," Cole said, trying to keep a straight face.

"Ah. Well, in college, there was this senior who was majoring in architecture—"

"*After* college."

"After college?"

"Yes. Like in the last five or six years."

"Oh. Well in that case, just one."

"Serious?"

Kate shrugged. "We were engaged."

"That's serious. What happened?"

Kate wrinkled her nose. "It didn't work out. I think my mother liked him more than I did. And I know my father did. He liked the thought of having a doctor in the family."

"Always handy for house calls. So why didn't it work out?" Cole persisted gently. "Lack of compatibility? Interfering mother-in-law? Sexual hang-ups?"

"Mine or his?"

"I don't know." The look in Cole's eyes turned disturbingly sensual. "Are you referring to the hang-ups or the mother-in-law?"

"I think I'm better off avoiding both," Kate said. "But getting back to your first question, I think one of my biggest problems with the relationship was that we never laughed. Everything was always so terribly serious. And appearances were everything. We always had to go to the right parties, and move with the right crowd. It got . . . tiresome after a while. But for the most part, we just never sat down and laughed."

"And that's important to you."

"You bet."

"What else?"

"Cole—"

"What else?"

Kate squirmed a little more. "I don't know. I guess I always wanted to experience that . . . funny feeling in my stomach. You know, the one you get every time you step off the really high diving board?"

"I know the one." Cole grinned. "I was champion high-board diver for three years."

"No kidding?"

"Would I lie about that?"

"No, I guess that's pretty serious stuff."

"So apart from the laughter and the flutters, what else was missing?"

Kate's sighed. "I suppose feeling that I was . . . important to him," she said softly. "That I meant something in his life. Richard always seemed to be able to find time for his work, and his hobbies, even his friends. But sometimes—" Kate broke off and glanced down into her lap. "I don't know. Maybe I was just being . . . selfish."

There was a haunted quality to her voice that tore at Cole's heart. "Now why do I get the impression that you're not the selfish type?" He took the wineglass from her hand and set it on the table next to him. "Why do I get the feeling that your fiancé was the selfish one and that letting you walk out of his life was the biggest mistake he ever made?"

Kate stared up at him, aware that she could hear the sound of her heart thumping in her ears. "I . . . don't know why."

"Don't you?" Cole leaned forward and lightly brushed his lips across hers. "You can't give me an answer for any of those questions, Kate Pedigrew?"

"No, I . . . don't think I . . . can," she said breathlessly.

He kissed her again, his lips lingering a little longer this time. "No answers at all?"

Kate closed her eyes. "I'm . . . kind of at a loss for words at the moment."

He sat back and watched her in silence for a moment. "Is that because I'm going too fast?"

Kate opened her eyes—and felt her breath catch. "I think I should probably be. . . . telling you that you are, but . . ."

"But?"

"But you're not." Kate looked into his eyes and wished it was as easy to see into his heart. "Why do you want to know all this about me, Cole? You . . . told me that you didn't have time for a relationship, so why are you . . . hanging around?"

"Maybe I've changed my mind," he said in a voice that was as husky as hers.

Kate's expression turned suddenly wistful. "I'd like to think that was the case, but I don't. A leopard doesn't change his spots and that's what you're asking me to believe you've done. Something's keeping you here, but I know it isn't me. So . . . what is it?"

Cole gazed down at her face, touched by the silent sadness he saw there, and knew he couldn't tell her the truth. Not now. Not like this. How could he tell her that he was hoping to find a spinning wheel—without admitting his suspicions about her? What was he supposed to say? *Hi, Kate, I'm looking for an enchanted spinning wheel. Oh, you just happen to have one? What a coincidence.*

Yeah, right, he wasn't that naïve. Maybe if there hadn't been any kind of. . . . emotional connection between them, he could have gotten away with it. But that wasn't the case any more. He did care for her, and he was sure that Kate cared about him. He could see it in her eyes, and in the way she responded to him. She wasn't in this for the thrill and neither was he.

But how was he supposed to tell her the truth without making it sound like he was? What would that say about him and the way he felt for her? What would that do to their relationship? What would it do to Kate?

No, it was better that he wait, Cole decided grimly. Tomorrow night was the opening. If the spinning wheel was in the showroom, he'd be able to bring up her ownership of it in casual conversation sometime over the weekend. If it wasn't, he'd just have to ask her straight out if she had it. But he wasn't going to tell Kate anything tonight. They'd had a very special evening together and he didn't want to spoil it.

He'd waited this long to find out where the spinning wheel was. Another few days weren't going to hurt.

The call came first thing Friday morning. Kate was in the middle of typing up labels and price stickers when she picked up the phone, so she didn't pay particular attention to the caller's name the first time he said it. But when he mentioned something about being connected with an art gallery in New York, her fingers stopped dead on the keys. "I'm sorry, what did you say?"

She heard a smooth chuckle on the other end of the line. "Yes, I thought that might get your attention, Miss Pedigrew. I said I'm with the Preston Gallery in New York. Perhaps you've heard of it?"

Kate's eyes couldn't have opened any wider. Of course she'd heard of the Preston Gallery. Who in the art world hadn't? "Yes, I have heard of it, Mr.—?"

"Kline. Oliver Kline," the man said in a cultured English accent.

"Yes, Mr. Kline," she repeated, quickly writing it down. "I'm sorry, but what were you saying before that?"

"I said I'd like to talk to you about the possibility of buying one of your pieces, Miss Pedigrew. It's come to our attention that you do exceptionally beautiful stained glass, and given that we are attempting to put together a show featuring the work of selected artists throughout the eastern states, we thought you might be interested. If we generate enough interest in New York, we hope to send the entire collection on to our affiliate gallery in London."

"London!"

"Are you interested, Miss Pedigrew?"

He had to be kidding. Was she *interested* in having her work displayed in one of the most exclusive private galleries in the city, with the chance of seeing it go on to London? It was the opportunity of a lifetime!

"Yes, Mr. Kline, I am most definitely interested."

"Excellent. Then I think we should set up a meeting. I understand you're having a show on Friday night."

"As a matter of fact I am but—" Kate frowned. "—how did you know?"

"Because we make it our business to know as much as we can about the artists we wish to approach," he said in that same smooth voice. "That being the case, would Saturday evening work for you?"

"Yes, Saturday will be fine." Kate scribbled it down on the pad next to the phone. "Would you like to come here?"

"Actually, I won't be coming at all," he told her. "I'm leaving tomorrow for a week's buying trip in Europe, but I'll be sending my personal assistant, a fellow by the name of Peter Charlton, in my place. Actually, Mr. Charlton has far more experience in the area of glass and crystal than I do, and he handles most of the purchases for the gallery in that area. I will, of course, be looking after all of the business arrangements once the final selection is made. Your compensation, for example, as well as all arrangements for getting you to New York and London—"

"*I* would be going to London?" Kate said in astonishment.

"Well, of course. All of the artists will be flown to both cities at the gallery's expense. This will be a very important show, Miss Pedigrew, and naturally, we'll want you to be on hand for interviews and follow-up work." He hesitated briefly. "I hope that won't cause a problem of any kind?"

"No, none at all," Kate replied quickly.

"You may feel free to discuss it with your husband, if you wish."

"That won't be necessary. I'm not married."

"Ah, well, so much the better," he said.

Kate wasn't sure whether she heard a note of relief in his voice or not. Probably not. What did it matter to him whether she was married or single?

"Well, I won't keep you any longer," Mr. Kline said politely. "I look forward to hearing the results of your meeting with Mr. Charlton when I get back. Oh, there is one last thing, Miss Pedigrew. Given that we hope to achieve something of a first with this show, I think you can appreciate our desire for confidentiality. For that reason, I would ask that you keep what we have discussed today strictly private, even from other members of your family."

"Oh. Well, yes, of course, if that's what you'd prefer."

"It is. Now," he continued, "if I might just get directions to your house, I'll make sure Peter has them, and then he'll see you on Saturday evening at say, seven-thirty?"

"Seven-thirty will be fine," Kate replied and then gave him detailed directions to the house. "And thank you so much, Mr. Kline. I can't tell you what an honor this is."

"My pleasure, Miss Pedigrew. Good-bye."

Kate hung up the phone and stared down at her desk. Then she got up and started dancing around the room, all thought of price stickers and labels temporarily forgotten.

By the time Kate's guests started arriving at seven o'clock, everything was ready. The white wine was chilling, the canapés were in the refrigerator and her best glasses and plates were lined up on the kitchen counter ready to be filled. Kate hoped she hadn't forgotten anything. Her head was still in the clouds as a result of her unexpected conversation with Oliver Kline that morning. Imagine, one of her pieces of stained glass hanging in New York's Preston Gallery! With the possibility of a further showing in London. It was enough to make any artist giddy.

As Kate got dressed for her special evening, she thought about everything that had happened to her since she'd stumbled upon the spinning wheel, and she had to admit that it was nothing short of astonishing. She had created some of the most stunning works of her life, her level of confidence had risen tenfold, and Cole Beresford had walked into her life.

Of course, after last night, Kate wasn't sure what to make of that. It had been a wonderful evening right up until the end when she'd asked him why he was still here in Vermont. That's when everything had changed. A shutter had dropped down over his eyes. And then when she'd briefly mentioned the part about their relationship, he'd gone completely silent. He'd almost looked like he'd been in pain.

But why should he be going through any kind of suffering? Kate asked herself again. *She* was the one whose heart was going through the emotional wringer here. Cole wasn't looking to get involved, and as near as she could make out, he wasn't.

Well, there was one thing Kate did know. Right after the opening, she was going to stay as far away from Cole as possible. Whether he stayed in the area or not wasn't going to be a concern of hers. She was going to get on with her life. And she was going to start by digging into the history of the mysterious spinning wheel.

She'd begin with Mrs. Barrett at the antique shop. The woman had said that her agent would be sending documents about it, which would hopefully include a detailed history. Beyond that, there were libraries and bookstores, historical societies, and of course, the Internet. She would even go to New York if she had to. She had to learn as much as she could about the legend concerning the ancient spinning wheel. She had to find out how to free Eleya.

For the opening, Kate chose a simple but elegant high-necked black gown. The floor-length shift skimmed over her body and fastened behind her neck, leaving her arms and shoulders provocatively bare. She pulled her hair back in a soft, flattering style that drew attention to her cheekbones, and then fastened brushed gold disks to her earlobes. After applying a light touch of cologne to her pulse points, Kate felt ready to face her guests. She went to rise, when she suddenly remembered something else.

Turning back to her dresser, Kate opened her jewelry box and took out a small black box. Inside, was her mother's diamond and sapphire ring, the one her father had given her to celebrate their thirty-fifth wedding anniversary. It had been her mother's wish that Kate have the ring, and as she slid it onto her finger now, she thought back to the day her father had given it to her.

It had been about a week after the funeral, just before he'd left for London. He hadn't said much as he'd handed her the box and Kate thought he'd been mad at her for deciding not to get involved in the business. Until she'd seen the tears in his eyes. Then she'd known better. It was the only time she'd ever seen him cry. He'd pressed the box into her hand and quickly turned and walked away. Kate hadn't seen him again for nearly two months.

"Oh, Dad, why did things have to go so wrong between us," Kate murmured softly. "Why couldn't I have stayed your Katie-bug?" She held her hand up to the light, admiring the play of light between the dazzling white diamonds and the magnificent Ceylon sapphire. She'd had it sized to fit her finger, but it was only the second time she had worn it. She wanted to wear it tonight. Somehow, it made her mother feel closer.

"If only you could have been here tonight, Mom," Kate whispered into the shadows. "It would have made everything even more special." Well, she would have to content herself with the hope that somewhere in heaven, her mother was looking down and smiling.

Kate took one last look at the ring and sighed as she turned off the bedroom light.

Cole had told her she had beautiful hands and that she

should wear more jewelry. Well, tonight she was. She wondered how long it would take him to notice.

The studio looked marvelous. The white walls served as a perfect backdrop for the jeweled panels of glass, while the strategically placed spotlights brought out every glorious color and hue. The five new pieces were finished and hung and each one of them had their own name plaque. There was Eleya's Dream and Ice Magic, The Dove's Song and Candlelight, and the smallest of her new works, Interlude. But as always, Kate's eyes swung back to her showpiece—Eleya's Dream, and she felt a tremendous sense of pride and satisfaction.

Words really couldn't describe how she felt about the piece. It moved her as much now as it had when she'd first seen the design for it on paper. She knew it would be the most admired piece of work in her collection, and that had nothing to do with vanity. Because in truth, Kate didn't feel that Eleya's Dream was hers at all. It belonged to Eleya, the beautiful spirit who had inspired it. She was simply the medium through which the idea had been translated into glass. In truth, Kate felt more like she had stolen the idea than anything else.

With a last satisfied nod, she headed back into the church and closed the adjoining door. She had decided to greet her guests in the living room and then, when everyone was assembled, to take them into the studio in a dramatic "here it is" fashion. As she did, however, her eye fell on something white sticking up between the cushions on the loveseat. Pulling it free, Kate groaned.

The letter to her father! It must have fallen out of her bag. Of all the stupid—she'd addressed it, stamped it, and then forgotten to put it in the mail. Which meant that there was absolutely *no* chance of his coming to the opening now. The chances of his showing up *with* an invitation had been slight at best. The likelihood of his coming *without* one was nonexistent.

• • •

The first people to arrive were Madeleine Carstairs and a pretty young woman by the name of Brooke Asher. Madeleine looked radiant in an exquisite emerald-green Yves St. Laurent ensemble. She gave Kate a hug and a kiss and then stood back to look at her.

"Kate, honey, you look ravishing. What *are* you doing to yourself? Is it something you're taking, because if it is, I want to know *what* it is and *where* I can buy it. Either that, or invest heavily in the cosmetic line you're using. And that dress is absolutely *divine*. What I wouldn't give to have a size-six figure again." Madeleine leaned in a little closer. "I hope you haven't invited any men to this little do tonight, honey, because you've wasted your time if you have. No man in his right mind is going to look at art when *you're* in the room!"

Impulsively, Kate leaned over and kissed Madeleine on the cheek. "You flatter me far too much, Maddie. And I'm not taking anything. I'm just . . . happy with the way everything's turned out and it shows."

"Uh huh," Madeleine replied, the skepticism in her voice plain. "And just how much does a handsome English gentleman have to do with the wonderful way everything's turned out, I wonder?"

Tactfully ignoring the question, Kate turned to greet the young girl standing behind Madeleine. "Hi, I'm Kate Pedigrew."

"I'm Brooke Asher," the girl said in a rapt voice. "It's really an honor to meet you, Miss Pedigrew."

Kate glanced at Madeleine and raised an eyebrow in surprise. "It's nice to meet you too, Brooke. And call me Kate."

The girl's cheeks colored with pleasure. "Awesome."

"Brooke is the youngest daughter of a good friend of mine," Madeleine told Kate. "She's been trying to earn money to go to France next year, and she's been helping out at private parties and receptions. I brought her along tonight because I thought you might be able to use the help. I didn't think you'd thought to hire any."

"Help? Oh, but Maddie, I really can't—"

"Are you serving refreshments?"

"Well, yes. There's wine and a fruit punch for people who'd prefer something non-alcoholic. And I've got cheese and crackers, and some hot appetizers for later. I just have to heat them up and—"

"Fine. Brooke can see to all that," Madeleine said briskly. "You can't be in the kitchen seeing to food and drinks *and* be mingling with your guests."

Kate glanced at the girl in bewilderment. "But how much—that is, what do I pay—?"

"Never mind all that," Madeleine said, dismissing the question with a wave of her hand. "Brooke's services tonight are my little gift to you for the opening of your studio. Her mother and I worked all that out ages ago, didn't we, Brooke."

"Yes, Mrs. Carstairs."

"Well, I don't know what to say," Kate said. She looked from one to the other and laughed. "I really didn't expect anything like this."

"I know that, honey, and that's why doing these little things for you is such a pleasure. You are just so terribly unassuming."

"I think Cole was right when he said I should hire you as my business manager."

"What a marvelous idea! I think I still have a few negotiating skills left over from my days in business. Mind you, that *was* a very long time ago. All right, Brooke. Why don't you run along and get familiar with the kitchen. We'll need wine poured and taken around, and the first batch of canapés ready to serve. You haven't hidden anything away, have you, Kate?"

Kate glanced at her quickly. "Pardon?"

"Will Brooke be able to find what she needs without going through every drawer and cupboard in the kitchen?"

"Oh, yes. Everything's in plain sight. I took the serving dishes and china out earlier and put them on the counter. The new wine bottle opener's there too."

"Fine. Off you go, Brooke. Now," Madeleine said, slipping her arm around Kate's shoulders, "I hope the rest of your guests get here soon. I am positively *dying* to see what you've done in the studio!"

Madeleine's wish wasn't long in being granted. The rest of the guests began to trickle in around seven o'clock, and by twenty after, the church was filled to capacity. Everything was going perfectly. The soothing sound of harp and piano provided soft background music and the candles Kate had arranged throughout the room helped create a warm, intimate atmosphere. Everyone seemed eager for the unveiling. Kate's eyes widened in delight when she saw her brother and sister-in-law appear in the doorway a few minutes before seven-thirty.

"Matt! Megan! Oh, I'm so glad you could both come." She rushed over and gave them each a hug. "I was hoping I might see one or the other of you, but I never expected to see you both." She glanced into their faces anxiously. "How's Christian? Is everything all right?"

Megan nodded. Her eyes bore evidence of the strain she'd been under, but she was holding up admirably. "Mrs. Blair is watching him tonight. We can't stay long, Kate, but we wouldn't miss your opening for anything."

Kate's grasped her hand and squeezed it. "I can't tell you how much this means to me."

"Well, Meg figured we had to show some kind of family support," her brother teased. "I wasn't going to come at all, but I thought you'd probably disown me if I didn't at least show my face."

"You got that right, Matthew Pedigrew. Well, come on in. I was just about to open the studio, but I want you to meet a few people first."

Kate drew them toward the center of the room where Madeleine was chatting with the photographer from the local newspaper. "Maddie, you remember my brother, Matt, and his wife, Megan?" she said.

"Yes, of course I do." Madeleine warmly shook hands with them as the photographer moved away. "Though it's been a while since I've seen either of you. And how is that dear little boy of yours doing? Kate tells me he's not been well."

Megan managed a brave smile. "He hasn't, but the doctors are hopeful."

Matthew put an arm around his wife's slender shoulders. "We got a babysitter in to watch him for an hour or so, then we'll have to get back. But we wanted to be here for a little while."

"And I'm sure Kate appreciates it more than you know," Madeleine told them with a smile. "She's worked very hard for this."

"Huh. I don't know about that," Matt said. "I'm beginning to think Megan was right."

Kate looked at him blankly. "About what?"

"About you taking a holiday. Either that, or you hired somebody to work for you while you skipped off to a spa. When I got home the other day, Megan told me she thought you'd been away on holiday, and looking at you tonight, I can see why. You look fabulous, sis."

Kate bit her lip, remembering that Matt hadn't seen her for a few days. She noticed Madeleine's thoughtful regard and shrugged. "Like I told Madeleine, it's just happiness. And the outfit, of course. Clothes can do wonders for a woman."

"So can love," Madeleine said innocently.

*"Love?"* Megan's eyes danced with curiosity. "Kathryn Autumn Pedigrew, have you been keeping something from us?"

"Of course not." Kate blushed furiously. "Don't listen to a word Maddie says, she just loves to meddle in other people's lives. I do *not* have a man in my life. And now before she has a chance to start any other rumors," she said with a fond wink at Madeleine, "I think it's about time I got this show on the road. Ladies, gentlemen, if I might have your attention for a moment, please."

Kate waited for the sounds of conversation to die down as she glanced out over the crowd of friends and family who were gathered in her living room. She tried not to notice that one person wasn't there. "First of all, I'd like to thank all of you for coming. This is . . . a very special night for me, and I'm so glad to be sharing it with all of you." She glanced at Matthew and Megan, then at Madeleine, with an expression of deep affection. "Some of you I've known all my life; others I've only had the pleasure of meeting since I moved to Vermont. But it was important to me that you all be here to share this moment. Now, if you'll follow me into the studio, I think we're ready to begin."

A smattering of enthusiastic applause greeted her words. As Kate led the way into the studio, she tried not to think about Cole and the fact that he wasn't here. She hadn't spoken to him since he'd left last night, but she hoped that everything was all right.

Kate opened the door to the studio and flicked on the lights. Then, as people began to move through the doorway and into the studio behind her, she went to stand beside Eleya's Dream—and waited.

For a moment, there was a stunned silence as every eye in the room turned toward the breathtaking window. Kate saw the looks of surprise, of admiration, and even of wonder on their faces, and knew that Eleya's beauty had touched them all. Then, the flash of the photographer's camera broke the spell, and everyone began talking at once. Kate was surrounded by people, besieged by questions about how long she'd been working on the new piece, and where the inspiration for it had come from.

Cole stood quietly in the doorway, and felt as though somebody had punched him in the stomach. He'd come in too late to hear Kate's welcoming speech, but not too late to witness the startling reaction to her work. She was standing beneath a breathtaking stained-glass window that literally left him speechless. There looked to be hundreds of pieces of glass in the work, each cut and placed with a precision that was mind-boggling. He'd never seen such a subtle blending of colors and textures before; such a vivid use of colors.

He had never seen the work of contemporary genius—until tonight.

And then there was Kate herself; standing next to her work, completely unaware of her own radiant appearance.

Didn't she see the way people were staring at her? Wasn't she aware that she was the most beautiful woman in the room?

It was all the proof Cole needed. The spinning wheel might not be in the room, but it was definitely here somewhere. He'd found his elusive owner.

Turning to answer a question, Kate suddenly caught sight of Cole standing in the doorway, and her face lit to heart shattering beauty. *You came,* she cried silently. *You didn't forget.*

Cole smiled back at her, his eyes brimming with tenderness and pride. *I wouldn't have missed it for the world.*

Across the room, two other people saw that smile as well.

"Well, I think the nonexistent man in Kate's life just walked in," Megan whispered to her husband. "And no *wonder* she's looking so happy. The guy's *gorgeous*. But I don't think he's from around here."

Matt slipped his arm around his wife's waist. "I'll ignore the comment about his being *gorgeous*, Mrs. Pedigrew," he drawled, "but you're right about him being from out of town. He's one of Madeleine Carstairs's friends from New York. But I sure had him pegged wrong. There's nothing slick or yuppie about that guy."

Unaware that he was being watched by most of the people in the room, Cole slowly walked toward Kate. She was still being positioned for publicity shots, so he smiled at her over the photographer's shoulder. "Hi."

"Hi." Kate's smile lit up the room. "I thought you'd forgotten me, Beresford."

"Forget the lady who made me that fantastic roast beef and gravy dinner? Not on your life. You didn't really think I'd miss this, did you?"

"I thought maybe . . . something had come up."

"Nothing that would keep me from being here tonight." Cole's expression stilled and grew serious. "Congratulations, Kate. The studio looks wonderful. And this—" he said, indicating Eleya's Dream, "—is the most incredible piece of work I've ever seen. I don't think I can even find the words to describe it. Except maybe to say that . . . it's a shame you're not going to sell it. Because it would bring you a great deal of money."

Kate stared at Cole in astonishment. How could he possibly have known that she had no intention of selling Eleya's Dream?

"Hey, fella, would you mind moving over a bit?" the photographer interrupted. "I'd like to get a few more shots of Miss Pedigrew."

The glance Cole leveled at him spoke more eloquently than words.

"But I can do it later, if you like," the man said hastily. He started to move away, when Cole abruptly put out his hand. "No, stay and take your pictures." This was Kate's night, after all, and she deserved every moment of the attention she was getting. He looked at her and winked. "I'll catch up with you later."

Kate nodded, wondering if he'd been able to see the beating of her heart under her dress. She thought she'd been happy when she'd opened the door to her studio, but that was nothing compared to the way she felt when she'd looked up to see Cole standing in the doorway.

No wonder she had to ask the photographer to repeat himself three times before she finally heard what he was saying.

Madeleine made her way to Cole's side as soon as she saw him leave Kate's.

"Well, I was wondering where you'd got to," she murmured in his ear. "She only glanced at the door a hundred times before you showed up."

Cole laughed self-consciously. "I hadn't meant to be so late, but I got a call from Professor Morris just as I was leaving."

"Ah, yes, the professor and his mysterious spinning wheel," Madeleine said dryly. "Are you any closer to finding the elusive owner?"

Cole hesitated, and then glanced into Maddie's eyes. "Let's just say you don't have to visit any more of your friends."

"Well thank goodness for that! I'd forgotten how tiresome some of them could be. So, who is it?"

"I'm surprised you haven't figured it out." Cole leaned closer and nodded towards the stained-glass panel above Kate's head. "Remember what I said about flashes of creative brilliance?"

Madeleine paused, and then she gasped. "Kate! Oh, my God! I never thought—but of course. It all makes sense now. Her new works are so beautiful. They're outstanding. They're—"

"The work of a genius," Cole said softly. "As will be everything else she turns out from now on."

"Cole Beresford. Are you trying to tell me that . . . all this is as a result of Kate owning some old spinning wheel?"

"Did I say that?"

Madeleine rolled her eyes. "I swear, you are the most provoking man I have ever met." She reached for a fresh glass of champagne as Brooke ambled by with a tray. "But I intend to hold you to your promise to tell me what all this is about."

"And I will, Maddie. But not until the . . . difficulties are out of the way."

"Well, I hope they're out of the way soon, because I have a feeling dear Kate may not be a member of this community for too much longer."

Cole glanced at her sharply. "What's that supposed to mean?"

She glanced at him in wide-eyed surprise. "Cole, for a smart man you can be terribly naive sometimes. I'm surprised you'd even have to—oh. Oh, now that is one good-looking man!" Madeleine whispered as she glanced in the direction of the living room. "And he surely isn't from around here. I would have noticed him by now if he was."

Cole turned to see whom Madeleine was talking about—and felt shock slam into his gut. He knew all too well who the man was.

He glanced around for Kate, wondering if she'd seen the late arrival too. When he spotted her a few seconds later, he knew that she had. The expression on her face said it all.

"Cole, honey, why are you looking so serious all of a

sudden?" Madeleine said. "Do you know who that good-looking man is?"

"Oh, yes, I know him, Maddie. Not personally, but I've seen his picture."

"You have?" Madeleine frowned. "Where?"

"On the table in Kate's living room. Because that distinguished-looking man, my dear, is none other than her father, Roderick Christian Pedigrew."

# Thirteen

Kate *had* seen her father standing in the doorway, but she couldn't believe that he was really here. Because there was no reason for him to be. He hadn't known that she was having a studio show and there was no way he could have found out, given that the letter she had written was still sitting in the drawer.

But there he was, standing in the doorway and looking decidedly annoyed.

Taking a deep and unsteady breath, Kate slowly started toward him. He hadn't changed much in the past three years. He still had a full head of hair, though the black was more liberally sprinkled with gray than she remembered, and his eyes were still the same piercing shade of blue. Eyes that looked through you, rather than at you. He was in good shape, which meant that he probably still worked out at the gym, and he dressed in a way that made the most of his build. Roderick Pedigrew knew what looked good on him and he had the money to indulge his tastes. The impeccably tailored Italian silk suit, the crisp white shirt, and the elegant silk tie all bespoke a man of culture and wealth.

But that's what her father had become, Kate reminded herself. The mega-successful business man. The entrepreneur who, at fifty-eight, was at the height of his career because he had put work ahead of everything else. He had made the sacrifices necessary to be the best. Sacrifices that had included the love and respect of his family.

Kate kept putting one foot in front of the other, slowly closing the distance between them. It was thirty, maybe forty feet to the front door, but tonight it felt like a hundred. She finally stopped about four feet away and took another deep breath. "Hello, Dad."

That was it. Simple. Brief. Unemotional. She didn't rush up and throw her arms around his neck, because it wouldn't have been appropriate. They had stopped demonstrating any kind of real affection toward one another a long time ago.

Kate felt his steely-eyed gaze on her now and waited for him to smile. He didn't. He just stood there watching her with those cold, hard eyes. It was like looking into the face of a stranger.

"Hello, Kate."

His voice was still the same; the kind that could silence a room with a single word. Kate tried for some kind of smile, but the muscles in her face felt stiff and tight. "I . . . hardly know what to say. I . . . didn't expect to see you here tonight."

"Obviously."

He could have said anything, but the single-word reply told Kate everything she needed to know. Nothing had changed. She was still a failure in his eyes, and he still had the power to make her feel that way.

"Kate, honey, are you going to introduce me to this handsome gentleman? Or are you going to keep him all to yourself all evening?"

The lighthearted sound of Madeleine's voice, combined with a brief, reassuring touch on the shoulder, was like a lifeline tossed to a drowning sailor. Kate grabbed for it and held on, blessing its comforting familiarity. "Yes, of course. Sorry." She turned toward the older woman and was surprised to see compassion shimmering in her eyes. "Maddie, I'd like you to meet . . . my father, Roderick Pedigrew. Dad, this is my good friend, Madeleine Carstairs."

Madeleine gracefully extended her hand. "This is a real pleasure, Mr. Pedigrew. Kate's told me so much about you, but I never thought I'd have the chance to meet you way up here in Barre."

Her voice was like a cool mint julep on a hot summer's day, and whatever his feelings toward his daughter, Roderick Pedigrew was too much a gentleman—and too savvy a businessman—to ignore a warm, southern greeting from a good-looking woman. "My pleasure, Miss . . . Carstairs?"

"It's Mrs. But all my friends call me Maddie."

Roderick took her outstretched hand in his. "Then it's my pleasure . . . Maddie." He looked past her to the man standing on her left and his smile cooled. "And you are?"

"Cole Beresford," Cole said, extending his hand. His tone was noticeably more reserved than Madeleine's had been and Roderick's eyes narrowed as he returned the handshake. "Are you here as a guest, Mr. Beresford, or are you and my daughter involved?"

The blunt question, so typical of her father's "cut to the chase" style, brought the blood rushing to Kate's cheeks. But Cole took it in stride. "Your daughter invited me to come to the opening of her new studio, Mr. Pedigrew. But I like to think that we're friends as well."

"I see. And are you one of her artsy friends, or do you actually work for a living?"

This time, the caustic tone angered Kate rather than embarrassed her. "That wasn't called for, Dad. Mr. Beresford is a world-renowned authority on antiques and fine art. His clients include museums and galleries all over the world, and I am honored that he accepted my invitation to come tonight. I think you owe him an apology."

"He also bought one of your daughter's pieces of stained glass for his private collection," Madeleine put in softly, "so you might say that Cole's a customer as well."

Roderick briefly inclined his head. "Well, it appears you do it all, Mr. Beresford. My compliments. And my apologies. It seems that my daughter is moving in a better crowd than I expected."

"You mean better than the yokels and country bumpkins

you expected to find her hanging out with, Dad?" Matt said in a voice as sarcastic as her father's had been.

Kate tensed—and waited for the explosion. Matt and her father had always had a volatile relationship, especially since their mother had died. They seemed to thrive on confrontation. It had never taken more than a look or a word to get them going, and it seemed that nothing had changed. To her surprise, however, her father let it go. Other than a brief tightening of his lips, there was nothing in his face to indicate that he was upset.

"I see you haven't changed much since you left New York, Matt. But then, I guess it was too much to expect that you would. How's the construction business going?"

"As if you cared," Matt sneered.

"Well, why don't we all move inside and have a glass of wine," Madeleine said in a purposely bright and cheerful voice. "I'm sure you're anxious to see Kate's work, Mr. Pedigrew—"

"What I'm anxious to see, Mrs. Carstairs," Roderick interrupted, "is my grandson. That's why I'm here."

A stunned silence greeted his words.

"You mean . . . you didn't come for the opening of Kate's new studio?" Matt said.

Roderick shrugged. "I didn't even know she was having one. I came because I received a letter telling me that Christian was ill."

Kate started. "But . . . that's impossible. I never sent the letter—"

"*You* wrote a letter to Dad?" Matt said, whirling on her.

"Well, yes, but—"

"Damn it, Kate you knew how I felt about that!"

"I didn't *send* the letter, Matt," Kate said in exasperation. "It's still sitting in my drawer. I forgot to mail it."

"But . . . if you didn't tell Dad about Christian, who did?"

"I did," Megan said, quietly stepping out from behind Cole. "I wrote to your father and told him what was going on."

Matt stared at her in disbelief. "*You* wrote to my father? But . . . why? I thought we agreed it wasn't necessary."

"We agreed that it wasn't necessary the first time we talked about it, Matt, but not after that. Christian isn't getting any better and I thought your father had a right to know. He's the only grandparent our son has left."

Kate glanced at her brother and knew there was going to be trouble. If she didn't do something fast, an all out family brawl was going to erupt right here in her living room. And that was about the last thing she needed tonight. "Look, let's all settle down and take it easy," she suggested in a low, urgent voice. "I'm in the middle of a show. I have a house full of guests, and I don't have time to worry about my family getting into a fight in the middle of it. So why don't we just get together in the morning and talk about this. Maddie, could I impose upon you to show my father around?"

"Of course, honey, I'd be delighted."

"Matt, maybe you and Megan could—"

"Forget it, Kate." Her brother's face was stony. "We're leaving."

"Good," Roderick said bluntly. "I was wondering why you were both here. If my grandson's that sick, you should be home taking care of him, not standing around here drinking wine and looking at pieces of colored glass."

Kate went white. *Pieces of colored glass?*

"I think your daughter's work deserves more respect than that, Mr. Pedigrew," Cole remarked quietly. "She's a gifted artist and you should be proud of what she's accomplished."

"My daughter had the potential to be one of the top real estate agents in New York, Mr. Beresford," Roderick said tersely. "She had a natural gift for selling and a relaxed, easy way with people. Her earning potential in residential real estate alone would have been in the millions. Do you honestly expect me to believe that she'll earn anywhere *near* that kind of money producing stained-glass panels and Tiffany lamps?"

"Maybe not at first," Cole agreed, "but you know what kind of money galleries are willing to pay for art, and Kate's work is getting better all the time. Take a look in her showroom and see for yourself."

Roderick shook his head. "I'm sorry, Mr. Beresford, but

I've never encouraged Kate to take up art as a profession, and I was disappointed when she did. As a hobby, it's fine, but it's not a way to earn a living. At least, not as far as I'm concerned."

"Doesn't it mean anything to you that she's happy with what she's doing?" Cole asked.

Roderick shrugged. "I'm happy with what I do too, Mr. Beresford, and I make a lot of money doing it. That's because I deal in facts and figures, and on things I can see and touch. Art's too nebulous for me. It's subjective. And while I wish Kate well, I'm sorry to say that I don't think she'll ever realize her true potential as long as she stays out here doing this."

Kate thought her father had said everything there was to say to her *before* she'd left New York—but she'd been wrong. With every word he'd just plunged the knife a little deeper. She saw Cole take a step toward her and numbly raised her hand. There was nothing he could do to help. In a matter of minutes, her father had effectively taken away all of the pleasure she'd felt in her achievements and in the evening. He might as well have taken a hammer and smashed every last one of her beautiful pieces of . . . colored glass.

"If you'll excuse me, I have . . . other guests to attend to," Kate said, her voice sounding strained even to her own ears. "Please . . . enjoy the rest of the evening."

In the uncomfortable silence that followed, no one seemed to know what to say. Cole and Madeleine exchanged troubled glances, while poor Megan, obviously feeling the guilt at having been the one to bring Roderick here, didn't know where to look.

In the end, it was Matthew who broke the silence.

"You know, you really are a bastard, Dad," he said quietly. "The least you could have done was to congratulate her. Look around you. Look at everything she's accomplished, and all without any help from you. But you couldn't even do that, could you? Well, it's no wonder she moved away. In fact, the smartest thing *either* of us ever did was get the hell away from you."

Matt turned on his heel and walked out. Megan cast one

last look at her father-in-law's rigid face, and then quietly followed him, leaving only Madeleine and Cole to keep Roderick company.

"Well, you certainly have a way with your family, Mr. Pedigrew," Cole observed dryly. He bent to kiss Madeleine's cheek and smiled an apology. "Sorry to do this to you, Maddie, but you're on your own. I'm going to go check on Kate."

He found her in the kitchen. She was trying to open a bottle of red wine—and not having much success. "Damned useless bottle opener!" Kate muttered, cursing as the catch slipped off for the umpteenth time. "Why don't they make wine bottle openers that work?"

"They do." Cole gently took the bottle and the opener out of her hands. "But they work a lot better when you hold them the right way." He pressed his thumb against the clip and deftly removed the cork. "See?"

He made it look so easy that Kate groaned. "I guess I should have stuck with my old-fashioned opener, rather than buying a fancy new one. Thanks for coming along before I hurled it *and* the bottle against the wall."

A smile ruffled one corner of Cole's mouth. "You're welcome." He absently sniffed the cork and set it on the counter. "So what are you doing in the kitchen opening wine when you're supposed to be out mingling with your guests?"

"I saw Brooke having trouble with the bottle and told her I'd take care of it."

"Is that the only reason you're in here?"

Kate glanced at him sharply, saw the concern there, and sighed. "That and the fact that I needed a few minutes alone to cool off."

The smile Cole gave her told Kate he'd already figured that out.

"You okay now?" he asked gently.

"I will be." She closed her eyes and tried to forget the ugly scene that had just taken place at the door. "I'm so sorry you had to see that."

"Don't worry about it. It's not the first time I've run into an attitude like that. Your father's a businessman and he's used to dealing in facts and figures. That's where his comfort zone is." Cole reached for another bottle of wine and opened it as easily as he had the first. "All the same, I think he could have gone a little easier on you and your brother."

"My father doesn't believe in pussy-footing around when it comes to his family." Kate smiled but there was a hard edge to it. "He calls a spade a bloody shovel and figures we're old enough to take it. You heard how he feels about my work with . . . colored glass."

"Yes, I did. So . . . do you want me to go over there and punch his lights out?"

The question was so unexpected—and the thought of Cole doing it so completely unimaginable, that Kate actually started to laugh. And when she looked up and saw the glint in his eyes, she knew that's exactly what he'd intended. "Well, I don't now if it would do any good but it would probably make me feel better. And I *know* it would make Matt's night."

"Now there's an understatement if I ever heard one," Cole agreed, chuckling. "Unfortunately, I don't think it's just your father Matt's annoyed with right now."

Kate bit her lip. "I know, and I feel so bad about that. God, I could *kick* myself for forgetting to mail that letter. If I had, maybe I could have prevented the quarrel that I guarantee Megan and my brother are having right now."

Cole picked up the wine bottle and began filling glasses. "Did you really forget to mail it or did you just start having second thoughts?"

"Who knows? I honestly don't remember it falling out of my bag. But whatever the excuse, it doesn't alter the fact that Megan got stuck with all the blame." Kate risked a quick glance toward the living room, and sighed. "And I don't feel good about *that* either. Maddie's being such a sweetheart putting up with my father. *I* felt like telling him to jump in the lake!"

"Well, don't think Maddie isn't biting her tongue too," Cole told her. "I've known her long enough to know that what just happened didn't exactly endear your father to her. Maddie doesn't like anybody hurting the people she cares about, and she happens to care a lot about you."

"We need more white wine, Kate," Brooke said, arriving back with an empty tray.

Glad for the interruption, Kate smiled. "Good thing I just happen to have some ready. How are we doing out there?" she asked, handing the teenager a fresh tray.

"Awesome. Everybody's having a great time. But they're asking when you're coming back out."

"Tell them I'll be right in," Kate said. After Brooke left, she added to Cole, "but first I'm going to go and rescue Maddie. She came here tonight to have a good time—*not* to be saddled with my father."

"I've got a better idea," Cole told her. "Why don't *you* go and talk to your guests, and *I'll* go rescue Maddie."

"But—"

"No buts. You've already lost enough time as it is, and I'm sure your father and I will find something to talk about. I have a few real estate investments in the city. I could always ask him his opinion on those."

"Are you sure? It's a lot to ask."

"Not really. Your father's probably feeling a bit like a fish out of water tonight, so I'm willing to give him the benefit of the doubt. I'm sure everything will be fine. But if it makes you *feel* better, you can treat me to a double helping of your wonderful *crêpes suzette* the next time I'm over."

It was impossible not to respond to Cole's light-hearted teasing, and Kate didn't even try. "You drive a hard bargain, Beresford, but I'm prepared to meet your terms."

"In that case—" Cole reached for a tray and set four glasses of wine on it. "I prepare to do battle."

Kate's lips twitched. "With *four* glasses of wine?"

"Yes. One for each of us to drink, and one to throw at your father if he dares refer to your work as colored glass again."

It must have been the emotion of the night catching up with her. Kate suddenly felt the sharp prickle of tears in her eyes. "Thanks, Cole. For being such a good sport about all this."

He quickly bent down and kissed her cheek. "Forget

it. That's what friends are for. Now get out there and schmooze!"

Kate nodded. She didn't trust herself to speak. She just watched him walk away and tried to ignore the fact that in one simple phrase, he'd told her exactly where their relationship stood. He'd said it all in those five simple words.

That's what *friends* were for.

As it turned out, Kate needn't have worried about Cole and her father going at it. The next time she walked into the living room, she saw Cole standing beside Madeleine—and her father was nowhere in sight.

"Okay, what happened?" Kate asked ruefully. "I didn't hear any sounds of a scuffle, but I can't believe my father went quietly."

"As a matter of fact, he did," Madeleine said, laughing gently as she glanced at Cole, "though I'm not sure Cole wasn't tempted to escort him out."

Cole shrugged. "I thought I did an admirable job of restraining myself, under the circumstances."

"Under the circumstances, you did, honey," Madeleine agreed, patting him on the arm. "But Kate, you never told me that your father was such an emotional man."

"Emotional?"

"Yes. Why, he's got so much bottled up inside, he's damn near ready to burst."

Kate stared at her in astonishment. "Maddie, my father's never . . . bottled up anything in his life. You heard him at the door. He's the kind of man who *gives* ulcers, not gets them."

"Oh, honey, you're just too close to your father to see what's really going on. It's like that old expression, you can't see the forest for the trees."

"Cole, do you think my father suffers from bottled-up emotions?" Kate inquired idly.

"Well, he's certainly suffering from something," Cole remarked as he raised the wineglass to his lips, "but I don't know that it has anything to do with bottled-up emotions."

Madeleine sighed expressively. "Never mind. You're obviously *both* too young and inexperienced to know when people are really hurting. But *I* know because I've been there."

"Well, all *I* know, Maddie, is that I'm relieved he's gone," Kate said flatly. "I know that's a terrible thing to say about my own father, but it's true."

"Well, I guess I can understand," Madeleine conceded. "Things did get a little . . . tense when he first arrived."

"That's putting it mildly. I just hope Matt and Megan aren't having a huge fight over this," Kate said unhappily. "If only I'd remembered to mail my letter. At least then I could have taken some of the blame."

"I don't think it would have made any difference," Cole said quietly. "Matt wasn't angry at Megan because she wrote to your father. He was angry because she did it without telling him. That's what really got him going."

"I suppose," Kate acknowledged. "But it still doesn't make me feel any better. But listen, you two did *not* come here to be dragged into my family problems. You came to help me celebrate my new studio opening. And for the rest of the evening, that's exactly what you're going to do!"

Four hours later, it was all over. The guests started leaving at eleven, Madeleine and Brooke stayed until eleven-thirty to help clean up, and by midnight, Cole was the only one left in a room which only a few hours earlier had been filled to overflowing with people.

Kate was more than ready to call it a night. It had been a highly charged and emotional evening. On the one hand, she had finally realized her dream of opening her own studio. She had filled it with original pieces of art and had seen the surprise and admiration on the faces of the people she had invited to come and share in the excitement with her.

On the other hand, she had been faced with her family's dissension right there in the middle of it. She had seen tensions erupt between her brother and his wife. She had watched her friends try to deal politely with her father's particular brand of cynicism. And she had been faced once again with her father's bitter disappointment in her and in her accomplishments.

It would be a long time before Kate was able to remember the good things that had happened tonight—without remembering the bad ones as well.

"Well, I think you can consider your show a huge success," Cole said as he sank down onto the sofa beside her. "I heard nothing but praise, praise and more praise."

Kate closed her eyes and let her head fall back against the cushions. "Mmm. I guess I should be pleased."

"You guess?"

"I would have liked it a lot better if I'd been able to avoid that ugly scene with my father. That left a very bad taste in my mouth."

Cole laced his fingers across his chest. "Do you think he'll be here long?"

"No longer than he absolutely has to." Kate opened her eyes and stared up at the ceiling. "Dad doesn't like being away from the office. It leaves him feeling out of touch with his world. But that's not to say he won't wreak a year's worth of havoc in the short time he is here. It's a gift he's developed over the years."

Cole turned his head to look at her, and wished that things could have turned out differently. He'd wanted so much to talk to Kate tonight. He knew she had the spinning wheel, there was no longer any doubt in his mind about that. What he had to concern himself with now, was her possible reluctance to sell it to him. If Kate had any idea that the spinning wheel was the source of her newfound talent, she might be unwilling to part with it. She might want to hold onto it, and use it to create more brilliant works; works that would cement her reputation as a leader in her field. Because Cole knew that she would just keep getting better. Soon she would be producing stained-glass windows that would have churches and cathedrals all over the world vying for her time. She would be able to pick and choose her commissions, and to name her own price for them.

Quite a heady experience for a stained-glass artist living in Barre, Vermont.

Cole sighed. No, their conversation about the spinning wheel was going to have to wait. Her father's unexpected arrival had knocked the stuffing out of Kate and left her physically and emotionally drained. Matthew was right. She didn't deserve the treatment she'd received from her father tonight. The least Roderick could have done was to congratulate her. After all, this was supposed to have been her special night. Something she would remember for the rest of her life. But what kind of pride in her accomplishments would she be feeling now? Her father hadn't even *asked* to see her studio, or any of her new works. What kind of memories would that create of her first professional show?

Not good ones, Cole was sure of that. The only *good* thing to have come out of the night was the knowledge that Kate *had* the spinning wheel, and that he could now spend his time making sure Davenport didn't get anywhere near her.

"Well, I guess I'd better hit the road too," he said, reluctantly getting to his feet. "It's been a long day and you must be tired."

"Hmm? Oh, yes, I suppose I am." To be honest, Kate wasn't sure how she felt. Her emotions were so mixed up.

She slowly got to her feet and started toward the front door. To her surprise, Cole headed for the studio. "That's the piece you did for me, isn't it, Kate?" he asked, looking at the winter scene.

Kate's smile reappeared, soft and just a touch wistful. "Yes. I was so busy with everything else tonight I didn't have a chance to tell you. Do you like it?"

"Very much. From an artistic point of view, it's head and shoulders better than the one I already have. But the reason it's so very special is *because* you made it for me. Thank you, Kate."

Impulsively, Cole leaned down and kissed her. He hadn't intended it to be a *real* kiss, but as soon as he felt the quivering softness of her mouth under his, he knew it wasn't going to be anything else. He slid his hand behind the curve of her neck and drew her closer, needing to feel the warm softness of her body against him as he recaptured her lips and kissed her with an intensity that caught them both by surprise.

Locked in the circle of his arms, Kate was helpless to resist. His lips moved over hers with an urgency that demanded a response, and mindlessly parting her lips, she gave it to him. She moaned softly in her throat as his tongue traced the outline of her lips and then moved past them to explore the recesses of her mouth. She felt his arms tighten around her back and pull her into more intimate contact with the lean, hard length of his body.

Kate knew that Cole was aroused, but so was she. She wanted this right now. She wanted *him*. And for someone who hadn't experienced those kind of urges for the past five years, the wanting came as something of a shock.

So did the realization a few seconds later, that he was pushing her *away* rather than pulling her closer. "Cole?" she whispered unsteadily.

"I have to go, Kate," he murmured roughly against her lips. His voice was ragged, the sound thrumming with emotion. "Because if I don't, I swear I won't leave at all. And we both know that won't be good . . . for either of us."

Kate knew what he was saying. It was bad enough that they were getting emotionally involved, let alone physically. That would just open up a whole new can of worms. He could be here one day and gone the next. He'd told her that himself and Kate was too smart to pretend an ignorance of the facts. She'd be inviting disaster if she did.

The problem was, she hadn't felt this way about a man in a long time, and the wanting made her vulnerable. But somehow, she found the strength to do what she had to. She slowly dropped her arms and backed away. "Then I guess you'd . . . better go."

"I'll . . . give you a call." Cole's voice was thick, and unsteady. "In the morning."

Kate nodded. "Sure. Don't worry if you . . . don't get an answer. I'll probably be . . . sleeping late." *And trying to not to think about what I* would *have been doing if you hadn't left.*

"I won't call before nine, but it won't be long after that.

By the way, did I tell you how fabulous you look in that dress?"

The look in Cole's eyes made her go weak at the knees. "I think it must have slipped your mind."

"I can't think how. It's the only thing I've been able to think about all night."

The silence between them lengthened. Kate stood gazing up at him, and Cole tried to ignore the tempting picture she made. Her cheeks were flushed and her blue eyes were as dark as midnight sapphires. Her breath was coming quickly, and he could see the rise and fall of her breasts under the black gown. He didn't want to go. In fact, he wanted to pick her up and carry her into the bedroom. He wanted to run his hands over every sensuous inch of her body, and make love to her all night long.

But he couldn't. Because in the long run, it wouldn't do either of them any good. He had no idea when he'd be in Vermont again. And he had no intention of asking Kate to spend seven months of the year waiting for him.

"I have to go," he said quietly, the passion in his voice suddenly giving way to regret.

Kate felt it too, and a hot ache rose in her throat. "I know. Thanks for being here tonight."

Not trusting himself to speak, Cole nodded and turned to go. At the door, he hesitated. "Oh, and in case I didn't say it before, Kate, congratulations. I think you can safely say that you've made it."

# Fourteen

She'd made it. Kate sat in the kitchen a little while later and stared at her reflection in the refrigerator door. Was this what it felt like to make it? Funny, somehow she'd been expecting something more.

Of course, Cole had been referring to making it in her professional life, not in her personal one. And in that regard, maybe she had. Judging from the response she'd had to her work tonight, she was almost willing to believe it. The compliments, the praise, the flattery. One person had even gone so far as to hail her as a contemporary genius.

Kate had drawn the line at that, of course. While she had mastered some of the techniques that had eluded her in the early days, with the results showing in the complexity of her works, it wasn't her skills alone which had put her in the category she was in now. The inspiration for the new pieces had come from Eleya, and she wasn't about to take credit for those.

Finishing the last of her milk, Kate put the glass in the sink and walked around the house turning off lights. In her bedroom, she slipped off the long black dress and impulsively held it up to her nose. Mmm, yes, it was still there. The scent of Cole's aftershave. She closed her eyes and buried her face in the fabric, letting the lingering fragrance surround her. It wasn't as good as having Cole's arms around her, but at least it made her feel like he was close. And she was alarmed at how much that was beginning to mean.

Poor guy didn't deserve to be treated to any more of her family problems though, Kate reflected grimly. And he'd seen it all tonight. Her father, Matt and Megan, Matt and *her*. No wonder he'd been ready to leave.

Kate put the dress on a hanger and hung it back in the closet. As she did, she caught sight of the spinning wheel tucked away in the back, and paused, aware of a sudden, overwhelming urge to talk to Eleya. Maybe after the harsh realities of the evening, she was ready to lose herself in a flight of fantasy.

Whatever the reason, Kate pulled the spinning wheel out of the closet and set it next to the bed. Then, sitting down, she took a deep breath, and slowly began to turn the wheel . . .

*"You are tired," Eleya said softly. "Your eyes are heavy."*

"I've had a very busy day."

*"And you are unhappy."*

Kate sighed. "Yes, I suppose I am." She hesitated for a moment. "Eleya, do you ever get . . . lonely?"

*"Lonely."*

The wistful echo wasn't a question, but a statement of fact, and Kate caught her breath as two silver tears ran down Eleya's cheeks. "Eleya, I'm so sorry. I didn't mean to make you cry."

*"You did not make me cry, Kate. The memory of . . . he who was to have been my husband is what fills my heart with sadness."*

"Your husband?" Kate had no idea why the knowledge that there had once been a love in Eleya's life should have surprised her, but it did. And she was anxious to know more. "Will you tell me about him?"

The mists shifted and shimmered all around her, and Kate held her breath. But thankfully, Eleya did not disappear. *"His name was . . . Gareth."*

"Gareth," Kate repeated. "I like that. Was he handsome?"

*"He was the most handsome man in the kingdom. He was a prince, and we were to have been married."*

"What happened?"

Eleya's beautiful smile faded as her eyes filled with sadness. *"Another wished to marry me. A powerful man named Alizor, who was covetous of all I possessed. For I was of royal birth, the daughter of a great king. Alizor wanted me for himself, but I would not have him. He knew that I loved Gareth. So when my beloved lay peacefully sleeping, Alizor crept into his room and . . . murdered him."*

"No!" Kate felt a horrible emptiness in the pit of her stomach. For a moment, it was almost as though she could feel Eleya's despondency. "Did Alizor try to . . . force you to marry him after that?"

*"He tried, but I would not have him. I told him that nothing he could do would persuade me to marry him. And so, he said that . . . if I would not have him, no other would have me. He kidnapped me from my father's castle and took me to Gareth's room. And there, using the same dagger he had used to murder my beloved, Alizor took . . . my life."*

Kate wanted to weep for all that the girl had suffered, for all that she had been forced to endure. "But . . . if he murdered you, how did your spirit come to be trapped in the spinning wheel?"

*"Before I drew my dying breath, Alizor called upon the dark powers to set a curse upon my soul. He condemned it to eternal life in the spinning wheel that was to have been my true love's wedding gift. He wanted me to live throughout eternity with the knowledge that I alone was responsible for my fate and for his. For had I but agreed to marry Alizor, Gareth would be alive and none of this would have happened."*

Kate felt tears sting her eyes. It was hard to imagine that any man could be so evil as to condemn this poor girl to live forever with the memory of the man she loved.

"Eleya, is there any way of freeing you from the spinning wheel? There must be . . . something I can do. Surely you wouldn't have looked for me if I couldn't be of help in some way."

*"There is a way, Kate, but . . . it is dangerous, and I cannot be the one to tell you what it is. Only you can do what needs to be done."*

"But . . . how can I do it, if I don't know what it is? Or how to go about doing it?"

*"You will. When the time is right, you will know."*

The mists shimmered then and began to close in around her. The image of Eleya began to fade. The vision was coming to an end.

*"Beware the danger, Kate,"* Eleya's voice whispered from the shadows. *"Always be on your guard, for the dark one comes in a form that you will not recognize—until it is too late."*

And then, she was gone, the veils dissolving like mists in the first light of dawn, the white light fading to darkness. Kate was asleep before the wheel completed its final revolution.

She awoke the next morning to the sound of the telephone ringing. She reached out blindly, fumbling for the receiver. "Mmm, hello?"

"Uh oh. Still too early to call?"

The low, sexy voice had her stomach doing somersaults. "Cole?"

"You were expecting someone else at nine-thirty in the morning?"

"Well, I never know which one of my boyfriends is going to call. Is it really nine-thirty?"

"Sure is. Should I call back later?"

His voice was warm and tender and Kate felt it pour all over her like hot fudge over ice cream. "No, that's okay. It's . . . time I got up anyway." She dragged herself into a sitting position and pushed the hair back off her face. "Sorry I'm so dopey this morning. Guess it's all the excitement of the last few weeks catching up with me."

"That and the fact that you probably didn't go to sleep right away after I left last night."

Kate went very still. "Why would you say that?"

"Because *I* sure as hell didn't." There was brief silence on the line, and then she heard him sigh. "Look, I'm really sorry about the way things ended last night, Kate. You didn't need me coming on to you like that. You'd had a rough enough time as it was, what with your father showing up and all the emotion of the night. You didn't need me messing up your head as well."

Kate shut her eyes, wishing she could make this horrible feeling in her stomach go away. "It's okay, Cole, really. We both got a little carried away. You're right, I was reaching out and you were there. But you did the right thing in leaving. We both know that."

"Yeah, well, that doesn't mean it was what I *wanted* to do," Cole grumbled. There was silence again, and then he said. "So what's on the agenda for today? Are you going to take it easy?"

Kate sighed. "I wish I could. But I think I'd better get over to Matt's and see what's going on there. As much as I'd like to ignore the fact that my father's here, I know I can't."

"Don't let Roderick get to you, Kate," Cole advised gently. "You're a big girl and you've made a success of your life. The fact that it's not in the same line as his doesn't make it any less so. Ask the people who were there last night."

Kate fiddled with the telephone cord. If only it was that easy. "Thanks for the vote of confidence, Cole. I'll let you know how it goes."

There was a brief pause before he said, "Any chance of seeing you today?"

How about right now? Kate felt like telling him. But that was silly. And impossible. "Why don't I give you a call. I may not be very good company after I see my father."

"Why don't you let me be the judge of that?"

"Cole, I—"

She heard him sigh again. "That's okay, Kate. I just wanted you to know that . . . I miss you. And that I'm sorry about last night. You can call me any time you want. Okay?"

"Okay. And thanks again, Cole."

Kate hung up the phone and sat staring at it for a minute. That wasn't her imagination. Cole was definitely starting to sound like somebody who was getting emotionally involved. He'd admitted that he hadn't want to leave last night, and this morning, he was telling her how much he missed her and wanted to see her. But the question still kept coming back to why. If he knew the relationship wasn't going anywhere, why bother to spend time with her? Wasn't that a complete waste of time? She hated to think that the attraction between them was purely physical, but what else could it be? How could they have a meaningful relationship when they lived at opposite ends of the world for seven months of the year?

"And those were your words, Mr. Beresford," Kate said ruefully. "Not mine."

By ten-thirty, Kate was on her way to her brother's place—and her stomach was in knots. She hadn't had any dinner last night, and she couldn't eat a thing this morning. She never could when she got uptight—and she was definitely uptight right now. For one thing, she had no idea what she was going to find when she got to Matt's place. If he and Megan had had a fight, it would likely be a cold, uncomfortable silence. That's the way Matt handled dissension. For all his volatility when it came to their father, he seldom blew up at anyone else—and never at Megan. He just turned inwards, which was why his outburst last night had been so unexpected.

Still, when it came right down to it, Kate knew that it really didn't matter anymore. Her father was here. It didn't matter *why* he was, or who had asked him to come. He was here because Christian was sick. They were all just going to have to get over it.

Kate pulled off the highway and turned left onto the rural road where Matt's farm was located. It wasn't really a farm. Matt just liked to call it that because it had a small barn and a big field out back. It gave him a feeling of privacy and space, and that's what he'd been looking for when he'd left New York. It also gave him room to park his tractor and work on the numerous projects associated with his construction business.

The house itself was charming, an old-fashioned white clapboard with green shutters and two gables up top. It had been a bit of a handyman's special when he'd bought it, but Matt hadn't minded. The price had been right, and he'd started fixing it up as soon as he'd moved in. And when Megan had moved in with him after the wedding, the renovations had taken on a more domestic and decorative tone.

Now, there was white picket fencing around the front and back yards, a neat flagstone path leading to the front door, and flower gardens everywhere. When Christian was born, Matt had built a play area at one side. He'd put in a sandbox, a set of swings and a bright red slide for his son to play with. They'd all been too big for Christian at the time, but now that he was bigger, they were just fine. He particularly liked playing in the sandbox, building towering castles, and floating popsicle sticks in the moats. Or at least he had, until he'd started getting sick.

Kate was about two hundred yards from the driveway when she suddenly saw Matt's dark blue Blazer pull away from the house. It came tearing up the lane and turned left at the road, heading in her direction. And judging from the fact that Kate had to flash her lights three times before it even began to slow down, her brother's mind was definitely not on his driving.

"For crying out loud, Matt, didn't you see me?" Kate demanded as she got out of her car.

Matt jumped down from the truck and slammed the door. "Sorry, Kate. My mind was a hundred miles away. He just makes me so mad."

Kate could tell at a glance that her brother hadn't slept. There were dark circles under his eyes and the whites were red and bloodshot. He hadn't shaved either, judging by the dark stubble of beard around his chin. "He?"

"The old man." Matt jerked his head in the direction of the house. "He's up there now. That's why I had to get out."

Kate's eyes went to the little white house, and she sighed. She wasn't surprised that Roderick was already there. He'd always been an early riser, and he'd never been one for putting off the inevitable. "What time did he roll in?"

"Eight-thirty. Thank goodness he had overseas calls to make or he'd have been there by six."

"I take it things aren't any better this morning?"

"That's why I left." Matt dragged his fingers through his hair. "I swear that man riles me faster than any human being on the face of this planet."

Kate smiled, but it was tinged with regret. "He always did. You two have been going at it since you were thirteen years old."

"Yeah, well, not everybody grows up in a Beaver Cleaver household," Matt grumbled. "Listen, Katie, I'm really sorry about last night. You didn't need me getting mad and storming out like that. It was stupid and immature, and I hope I didn't spoil your evening."

Kate put her arms around her brother's waist and gave him a hug. "You big goofus, of course you didn't spoil it. But I was worried about you. Is everything okay between you and Meg?" Kate looked up into her brother's eyes, and her heart sank. "It's not, is it?"

"Well, it isn't like I don't have a reason for being annoyed, Kate," Matt said defensively. "Meg knew how I felt about getting in touch with Dad. We talked about it for hours, and we agreed to leave it alone. Then what does she do? She goes and writes to him anyway. Is it any wonder I'm feeling a little betrayed?"

"Megan did what she did out of concern for you and Christian. You said yourself that he's not getting better, and Megan knows it. She's scared, Matt. And she has every reason to be."

Matt turned to look at her, and Kate could have wept at the helplessness in his eyes. "I don't want to fight with her, Kate. God knows we need each other right now. But I don't need Dad coming up here and trying to take over either."

"Take over?"

"Yeah. He wants to take Christian back to New York with him. He said he'll get the best doctors in the city to check him out."

"Well, is that so bad?"

"Of course it isn't. But we can't afford the best doctors, "

Matt said in exasperation. "And I'll be damned if I'll ask *him* to cover the costs. You know he thinks I'm a failure. He wanted me to stay in the city and go into real estate the same as he did you. He never accepted that I wanted to play professional ball. And he certainly never accepted my wanting to settle here after graduating, and starting up a construction company."

"Neither did you for a long time," Kate reminded him gently.

Something akin to regret flashed in her brother's eyes. "No. But the accident put paid to any chances of my making it in professional sports, so I moved on. And I don't think I've done so badly. I've got a wonderful family, a house I can afford, and a pretty good business. But Dad still looks down his nose at me and my life here and thinks I've failed. And now he's telling me that I can't look after my own son. Well he can go to hell for all I care, Kate, because I'm damned if I'm going to be beholden to him for anything."

Kate drew a pattern on the road with the toe of her shoe. "Matt, if it's money you need, let *me* help. I've still got some savings leftover from what Mom gave me, and I've managed to do pretty well with the stained glass. And you know I wouldn't think twice about giving it to you."

"I know you wouldn't, Katie, and I love you for even making the offer. But to be honest, it's not just the money. Dr. Sheffield said there might not be anything the doctors can do. He also said that in Christian's weakened condition, a trip to the city might not be the best thing for him now."

"Does he know for sure what Christian has?"

"No. And that's another thing that sent Dad up the wall. He referred to Sheffield as a bumbling country quack and then lambasted me for being stupid enough to put Christian under his care. Needless to say, that's when I left."

Kate nodded slowly. She could understand her brother's frustration, but as much as she hated to admit it, she could understand her father's too. "Well, maybe I can say something to him to help smooth things over a bit. It's worth a try."

"Well, I wish you luck, Kate," Matt said as he climbed

back into the truck. "But don't forget who you're dealing with. And don't say I didn't warn you."

Megan was sitting at the kitchen table when Kate got there. She was staring into an empty coffee cup, her fingers tracing an endless pattern around the rim. Yes, things were definitely tense in the Pedigrew household this morning.

"Mind if I come in?" Kate said softly.

Megan looked up. "Kate, of course not." She got to her feet and headed for the stove. "You know you're always welcome here."

"I wasn't so sure about that after last night." Kate set her shoulder bag on the table and walked over to her. "Are you okay?" she asked, putting her arm around Megan's shoulders.

"Yes, of course, I am."

"Megan?"

"No, really, Kate, I'm . . . fine."

"Megan, this is Kate, remember? The one who walked down the aisle with you and warned you that life with my brother wasn't always going to be easy."

Megan's bottom lip began to quiver. "Oh, Kate." She turned into her sister-in-law's arms and burst into tears.

Kate just let her cry for awhile. Knowing Meg, it was likely the first time she had.

"It's okay, Meg. You need to let it out. It doesn't help to keep it all bottled up inside." Now where had she heard *that* before? "There, doesn't that feel better?"

"Yes, I have to admit it does. I've been wanting to do that ever since we left your p-place last night, but I couldn't. I didn't want Matthew to see me c-cry." Megan sniffed and wiped her nose on a tissue. "You . . . just missed Matt."

"No I didn't. I ran into him on the road."

"You did?"

"Yeah. I thought I was going to have to jump out in front of him to make him stop though. He shot out of the driveway like a bat out of hell."

Megan laughed, but the sound came out as a sob. "I'm not surprised. He was pretty heated up when he left. I think he was about ready to take Roderick's head off."

"That bad, eh?" Kate took a mug out of the cupboard. "So where's Dad now?"

"Out for a walk."

"You're kidding? Dad's never been into passive exercise."

"There wasn't anything passive about it." Meg dropped a tea bag into Kate's mug and poured boiling water over it. "He charged out of here like he was going on a route march."

Ah, now that was definitely more her father's style. Kate looked into her sister-in-law's pretty face and sighed. "He'll get over it, Megan. Matt, I mean. He knows in his heart that you did what was right. He just didn't like you doing it without his knowledge."

"I know. But I was afraid that if I told him what I wanted to do, he'd tell me that I couldn't," Megan said as they sat down. "And then not only would I have been doing something he didn't know about, I would have been doing something he'd specifically asked me not to." She glanced at Kate and lifted her shoulders. "I know it's not a huge difference, but it made enough of a difference to me."

Kate reached out and patted her hand. "What you did wasn't wrong, Meg. That's what I was trying to say last night. Dad had a right to know about Christian's condition. That's why I wrote to him too."

"Oh, Kate, I thought that's what you'd said, but afterwards, I wasn't sure. I thought maybe it was just wishful thinking on my part."

"Trust me, it wasn't wishful thinking. I did write a letter. I just forgot to mail it."

"So you don't think I was wrong to tell your father about Christian?"

"Not at all. Unfortunately, that's not going to help Matt. Sometimes I think he and Dad take opposite stands on things just to have something to argue about. But he'll get over it. And the important thing to remember, is that we're talking about doing what's best for Christian."

"That's what I think too. I don't want Matthew and your dad fighting about this, and I sure don't want *us* arguing about it." Megan's eyes filled up with tears again. "The situation's hard enough to deal with as it is."

"That's why I'm going to talk to Dad," Kate told her briskly. "I know he's worried about his grandson, but he's got to realize that Matt's a father now too. He's got to stop treating him like a kid who doesn't know any better."

"I wish he'd stop treating his daughter that way too," Megan said softly.

Kate looked down at the table. "Yeah, well, don't go adding me to your list of people to worry about, Meg. You've got enough on there as it is. Besides, I'm a big girl and I can't keep letting my father's opinion of me get me down."

Funny, wasn't that what Cole had told her an hour ago?

A sound on the baby monitor alerted them to the fact that Christian was awake, and Megan got to her feet. "I'd better go see my little guy. Do you want to come up and say hello?"

Kate shook her head. "Not right now. I need a clear head if I'm going to talk to Dad, and seeing Christian just makes me all mushy inside." She took another quick sip of her tea and resolutely got to her feet. "Wish me luck."

She found him standing by the barn, staring out across the cow pasture. There weren't any cows in it now. Matt hadn't wanted to make the property a working farm. But Kate knew that in the past, cows had wandered around this field, and somehow, the name had stuck.

She stood there for a minute, watching the man who'd once played such a huge part in her life, and wondered what had happened to them. At one time, they'd been as close as a father and daughter could be. They'd ridden their bikes together on Sunday mornings. He'd taken her to the movies and to the park. He'd even bought her a toy cash register and pretended to buy cereal and cookies when she'd thought she'd wanted to work in a store. But somewhere along the way, all of that had changed. He'd stopped being a father and turned into a businessman.

Maybe it was around the time her mother had started getting sick, Kate reflected now. He'd never been around when Clare had been in pain, and they'd had to call the doctor. Of course, their mother had never complained. Roderick's business was growing and he'd had important meetings out of town. He'd be home just as soon as he could, she'd told them, and there was certainly no point in calling him back before the weekend. Because by then, she was going to be just fine anyway.

The problem was, she hadn't been fine.

Kate pressed her lips together in a tight, unforgiving line. Funny how some things stayed with you. She could still see the look in her mother's eyes and hear the catch in her voice when she talked about her husband. She had loved him so much. He had been her life. And yet, when he hadn't been there, she'd never condemned him. She'd just kept on making excuses for him.

Which was more than Kate had been willing to do. Then—or now.

"Are you going to stand there and watch me all morning, Kate, or did you come down here because you had something to say?" her father asked abruptly.

Kate put her hands into her coat pockets. "I didn't think you knew I was here."

"I always know when you're around." He stared out over the fields, his eyes narrowed against the morning sun. "Did your brother tell you to come?"

"No. I came because I thought we needed to talk."

"What's there to talk about?" Roderick pushed himself away from the barn. "My grandson's sick, my son won't do a thing about it, and my own daughter didn't think it was important enough to get in touch with me."

Kate flushed. "That's not fair, Dad. I wrote you a letter. I just . . . forgot to mail it."

"And I suppose you think that makes it all right. Well it doesn't, Kate. What if your sister-in-law had forgotten to mail her letter too? What was I supposed to do? Wait until somebody phoned me to tell me that my grandson was dead?" he said harshly.

Kate's face paled. "Christian is not going to die—"

"Are you so sure? Can you honestly tell me he looks like a healthy little boy? The last time I saw Christian, he was a bouncing two-year-old with baby fat and dimples. Now he's little more than skin and bones." Her father's face darkened ominously. "Your brother should be horsewhipped for letting the situation get this bad."

"It isn't Matthew's fault," Kate said hotly. "This only happened in the last little while. Christian was . . . fine before."

"Funny, that's not what Megan told me. She said that Christian's been getting sick on and off for some time now but that the doctors around here don't seem to know what it is. But you and my son just let him go on seeing these quacks and praying for a miracle. Well miracles don't happen, Kate. If you want something to happen you *make* it happen. That boy needs medical attention and he needs it fast."

"There's nothing wrong with the doctors here," Kate said defensively, "but they told Matt there might not be anything that anybody could do."

"And you *believed* that?"

"Why would they say it if it wasn't true?" she said fervently. "Dr. Sheffield wouldn't want to see anything happen to Christian."

"Maybe not, but Dr. Sheffield's just an old country doctor. He has no idea what's happening out there in the real world. Medicine is advancing in leaps and bounds, Kate," Roderick said passionately. "The kinds of treatments that are available today weren't even dreamt about when Sheffield was in med school."

"That's not fair. You don't know anything about the man."

"Maybe not, but I do know that if Christian were my son, I'd be moving heaven and earth to make sure he got the best care possible. I'd be taking him to the finest hospitals in the country. And I sure as hell wouldn't be accepting the word of one country practitioner telling me that he may or may not be able to cure . . . whatever my grandson has. Sometimes you have to push the walls, Kate. You've got to step out of your comfort zone and make things happen. But I guess we both know I'm talking to the wrong person about that."

Kate glared at her father with angry, reproachful eyes. At that moment, she hated him for making Matt sound like an uncaring and incompetent father. And for making her sound like the failure he so firmly believed she was.

"Don't talk to me about what you would or wouldn't do if Christian was your son, Dad," Kate said in a voice that quivered with emotion. "Because when it was your turn, how good a husband were you? Where were you when Mom started getting sick? Did you cancel your precious business trips and stay home? Were you there at her bedside when she started throwing up blood?"

Kate saw her father go white and knew that her words had hit home. "No, you didn't. Because you were too damn busy attending to your other life. So don't you *dare* accuse Matt of being an incompetent father, because maybe if you'd shown the same kind of concern for your wife as you are for your grandson, Mom wouldn't be dead!"

The words spilled out in a bitter torrent and Kate hoped that every single one of them hurt. Because this was what *she'd* had bottled up inside, ever since her mother had died.

"Don't you *ever* talk to me like that again, Kathryn," her father said in a low, trembling voice. "You know *nothing* about what went on."

"I know, Dad, because I was there!" Kate shouted, suddenly fighting back tears. "I watched my mother die. Can you stand there and tell me that you did?"

For a moment, Kate thought he was going to strike her. He tore up the hill with such fury in his eyes that Kate automatically flinched and turned her face away.

And that's when her father stopped. He looked at her defensive posture, saw her body braced for the strike, and it was as though something inside him died.

"Do you really think I'd hit you, Kate?" he asked quietly. "Is this what it's come to between us?" When she didn't answer, Roderick shook his head, the fire gone. "I know you're going to hold your mother's death against me for the rest of my life. But is throwing it back in my face now really going to help the situation? Is it going to help Christian?"

Without waiting for an answer, Roderick turned and walked back toward the house.

Kate didn't try to stop him. There was nothing else she could say. She'd said it all in that one angry, emotional outburst. And if she'd thought the gulf between herself and her father was wide before, she knew it was unbridgeable now.

By the time Kate left her brother's house, there was no way she was going to call Cole. She wasn't fit company for anybody, let alone for a man she barely knew—and wanted to know better. Her father's words had cut her to the bone, opening wounds she'd thought long-since healed, and from which she was still bleeding.

And to think she'd gone over this morning in the hopes of making things *better*. All she'd succeeded in doing was driving them further apart.

Kate drove around the country roads for hours, trying to collect her thoughts and to lose herself in the splendor of her surroundings. Mid to late September was a wonderful time to be in Vermont. The huge sugar maples, which would be tapped for the sticky sap that would eventually be turned into sweet-tasting maple syrup, now sported their glorious autumn robes. Their branches were richly garbed in vibrant crimsons, mellow golds, and the bright fiery blaze of orange. The pungent smell of wood smoke hung in the air, and a feeling of change was blowing in on the wind.

Too bad Kate wasn't in the mood to appreciate any of it. She turned on the radio and dialed in some middle-of-the-road country station, and just followed the winding road. Driving usually calmed her nerves. She'd done it a lot when she'd first moved to Vermont. Matt said she'd been a powder keg of pent-up up emotion.

Was it any wonder considering that she'd been working with her father?

As the afternoon wore on, however, and her anger finally began to cool, Kate found herself mulling over a few of the things her father had said. And while she hated to admit it, she knew that he was right. *She* didn't like the idea of sending Christian away to a big city hospital either, but maybe it *would* be for the best. Maybe there were some medical marvels that kindly Dr. Sheffield knew nothing about. Nobody was infallible, certainly not doctors.

Kate had learned that the hard way. While the doctor who had been looking after her mother had been treating one part of her body, the cancer that had eventually killed her had been growing unchecked in another. It wasn't until they'd done an exploratory that they'd found it, and by then, it was too late.

And nobody had been more shocked or disillusioned with their findings than Kate. She'd kept going over and over it in her mind, wondering if maybe they'd asked for a second opinion, things would have turned out differently. Maybe if they had, her mother would be alive today.

And wasn't that *exactly* what her father was saying about Christian now?

Kate wasn't sure how she ended up sitting in front of Cole's hotel. She knew she hadn't *consciously* driven in that direction. Until now, she couldn't even have said where the Maple Tree Inn was. But when she suddenly found herself driving by the big white building and spotted the name on the signpost, Kate abruptly put her foot on the brake and pulled over to the side of the road.

This *had* to be Eleya's doing, she decided. It was too much of a coincidence that she should just *happen* to be driving by Cole's hotel—especially when it lay in the opposite direction from the church. But *why* had the spirit sent her here? Why was it so important that Kate see Cole on this particular afternoon?

Figuring it was better not to question fate, she got out of the car and walked inside.

"Can I help you?" the young man behind the reception desk asked.

"Yes, can you tell me what room Mr. Beresford is in?"

"That would be two-twelve. But I don't think he's in right now, Miss. I saw him go out about an hour ago."

Kate bit her lip. That was strange. If Cole wasn't here, why had Eleya wanted her to come?

"Of course, he might have used the back stairs," the young man said helpfully.

"Can I go up and check?"

"Sure can. Two-twelve's right at the end of the hall, next to the fire exit."

Kate smiled her thanks and made her way up the staircase. The Maple Tree Inn was typical of most bed and breakfast accommodations in New England. Once a rambling old mansion, it had been converted to an inn, and modernized only in those areas that visitors and guests would expect and appreciate. Quaint was big down here, and savvy innkeepers delivered it with a capital Q. They decorated their interiors with floral prints and chintz, and fixed up the outsides of their buildings with gingerbread trim, wide porches, and lots of comfortable chairs. And of course there were antiques everywhere. This place alone could have kept Mrs. Barrett in business for a month.

Kate reached the second-story landing and turned right. She saw a maid's trolley parked at the far end of the hall and the doors to the last two rooms standing open. Cole's had to be one of them. She walked down to the end and saw a maid cleaning in two-eleven, then carried on to two-twelve. She poked her head around the doorway, just as the maid switched on the vacuum cleaner. "Cole?"

Great. If he was here, he'd never hear her over the noise. She took a step inside his room and tried again. "Cole?" When there was still no answer, Kate cautiously ventured in. She let her gaze drift slowly around the room, admiring the big four-poster bed and its fluffy white comforter, and tried to picture Cole in here. Somehow, she couldn't. There was too much lace. The furniture was nice, though. The rich, dark mahogany triple dresser and tall chest had been polished to a deep shine and there was a matching small table and chairs over against the window. The bedside tables each held a small lamp, which would make it pleasant for late night reading. There were even a couple of books scattered about.

Wondering what kind of things Cole liked to read, Kate glanced idly at the covers. *"Olde English Legends and Folklore,"* she read aloud. Interesting. The book *looked* as old as its title. And there was a bookmark.

Curious, Kate picked it up. She carefully opened it to the mark—then gasped as the picture all but leaped off the page at her.

*It was the spinning wheel! Her* spinning wheel. It had to be. Everything about it looked the same, right down to the detailed carvings on the legs and body.

Aware of a buzzing in her head, Kate began to read.

> *Of the many legends said to have originated in this part of the country, one of the most intriguing is the story of the Lockton spinning wheel, a very old spinning wheel thought to have been built by a high witch who lived in the tiny hamlet of Lockton. The wheel was reputed to have been bought by Gareth of Tyne, who intended to give it to his young bride, the Princess Eleya of Brynmore. Tragically both Gareth and Eleya were murdered by an unknown assailant . . .*

Kate looked up from the page in astonishment. This was incredible! It was all here, just like Eleya had told her.

She hastily dropped her eyes to the page again.

> *The spinning wheel changed hands many times throughout the centuries, belonging to rich and poor alike. But like the curse of the ancient Pharaohs, it often brought death and despair to those unfortunate enough to possess it. Nevertheless, men still sought it for its reputed powers. There have been documented cases of people suddenly having the ability to do things*

*far beyond their normal range, such as the case of a mediocre singer suddenly being able to sing opera, or of a young musician excelling far beyond the skills of his teacher . . .*

"Or of a stained-glass artist suddenly being able to produce works of incredible depth and beauty," Kate whispered aloud.

And suddenly, it all fell into place. *This* was why Cole Beresford was in Vermont. He'd told her that he'd come looking for an antique and obviously, this is what it was. The legendary Lockton spinning wheel.

The very one that was sitting in her bedroom closet right now.

Too stunned to move, Kate stared down at the battered book in her hands. It was . . . extraordinary. The very thing she had spent her entire summer looking for was the same thing that had brought Cole to Vermont. The only reason he was *still* here was because he hadn't been able to find it.

It was a sobering thought. Especially since Kate had almost let herself believe that *she* was the reason Cole was still here. But evidence to the contrary was right here in her hands. Whatever he might feel for her came second to his desire to finding the Lockton spinning wheel.

The problem was, what did she do now? If Cole found out that she had the spinning wheel, there was no question that he'd try to take it away from her. He would tell her that because of its great antiquity, it should be in a museum where the whole world would be able to see it. Or worse, he might tell her it had to be examined to see if it really did possess the kind of mysterious powers the book talked about.

But what would happen to Eleya then? If Cole took the spinning wheel away, the beautiful spirit would be trapped. She'd be locked up with the wheel in some glass showcase under lights and cameras, and there wouldn't be a hope of getting to her. She would be condemned to spend eternity alone.

Suddenly, Kate realized that she was in the worst possible place. If Cole happened to come back and find her here—

and with the book open in her hand—No, it didn't even bear thinking about. Which was why she quickly closed the book and went to put it back on the table. Unfortunately, her hands were shaking so badly she hit it against the edge of the table and dropped it.

A single piece of paper fell out. It was folded in four, and Kate could see the marks of a yellow highlighter on the other side.

Praying that Cole would forgive her, she picked up the paper and unfolded it. She skimmed quickly over the notes someone had made in the margin, and then dropped down to the last paragraph. The one that Cole had highlighted. And she suddenly felt the walls of her world come crashing in around her.

> *. . . can reputedly enhance the physical beauty of the owner, whether it be male or female, to a noticeable degree to others, yet oftimes, without affecting the person's perception of him or herself . . .*

Kate heard the pounding of her heart in her ears. Oh God. *This* was what everyone was talking about. She wasn't looking better because of the makeup she was using or the new clothes. It was the spinning wheel. It was somehow *changing* her appearance—and obviously for the better. Madeleine had seen it, so had Matt and Megan.

But what bothered Kate was that Cole had seen it too—and that's likely why he'd been so attracted to her in the first place. The magic must have already been working when he'd been introduced to her at Maddie's house. Maybe if he'd come a week earlier, he wouldn't have given her a second look.

Unfortunately, it wasn't just the knowledge that the spinning wheel was making a difference to the way she'd looked. It was the fact that Cole *knew* why it was happening. Which meant, Kate realized grimly, that she didn't have a hope in hell of convincing him that she didn't have the spinning wheel.

In the room next door, Kate suddenly heard the vacuum cleaner go quiet—and knew that her time had run out. If the maid saw her in here, she'd be sure to mention it to Cole, and if he asked for a description, it would be all over. She swore softly under her breath. What lousy timing! She wanted to stay and go through every book Cole had, but she knew she didn't dare. Every minute she lingered now increased the risk of discovery.

Quickly checking the hallway, Kate stepped out of Cole's room. When she was sure the coast was clear, she opened the fire exit door and went quietly down the two flights of stairs. At the bottom, she stopped to look again, and then made a hasty exit through the back door. It wasn't until she was safely in her car and well away from the Maple Tree Inn, however, that Kate began to feel that she was out of danger.

And that's when she really started to shake.

At about the same time, Cole was in Montpelier finalizing arrangements with a connection of his in London for the arrival of a very special shipment. He instructed the man to make sure that high-security storage was available and that no one other than himself or Professor Raymond Morris was to be given access to it. After that, he spent an hour or two driving around the countryside, trying to figure out what he was going to do about Kate.

He had to talk to her about the spinning wheel. It wasn't a question of whether she *had* it anymore. It was a question of what they were going to do now that he *knew* she had it. He'd have to warn her about Jeremy Davenport, that was for sure. The man had to be in the area now. The fact that he hadn't shown his face simply meant that he was biding his time. Waiting for the right moment to strike. And that made Cole nervous, because he alone knew how dangerous Davenport was. Kate could be talking to him in the supermarket and she wouldn't know it.

That's why Cole had to know where she was and what she was doing every minute. Like it or not, his feelings for

Kate were growing stronger by the day, as were his concerns for her safety. He had to make sure he got the spinning wheel away from her before Davenport found out who she was. He couldn't risk an encounter between Kate and the man whom a frustrated detective friend of his had once referred to as a cold-blooded thief who had neither a heart nor a conscience.

Which meant that he didn't have a choice anymore. He'd have to tell Kate why he was really here. He'd have to tell her that he was looking for the Lockton spinning wheel, and then try to convince her to sell it back to him—hopefully without going into too much detail about why. He didn't much relish telling her the truth.

After all, what was she going to think when he told her he was looking for an enchanted spinning wheel?

With everything that had happened that day, Kate almost forgot that she was supposed to meet with a representative from the Preston Gallery that night.

Fortunately, she happened to glance at her calendar when she got back from the Maple Tree Inn, and saw the name Peter Charlton, and the time, seven-thirty, circled beside it. Thank heavens she'd got home in enough time to get herself ready—mentally *and* physically.

She took a quick shower, then glanced through her closet for something to wear. What should she put on for a meeting like this? Nothing flashy, that was for sure. Maybe her calf length, camel-colored skirt with a black turtleneck and a casual jacket thrown over top. That looked professional, but not stuffy. Charlton sounded like a British surname, and given that Oliver Kline was English, Kate had no reason to suspect that his personal assistant wouldn't be too. And if that was the case, he'd likely be a bit on the conservative side. She pictured gray flannel pants, a white shirt, maybe a tweed vest with a navy tie discreetly tucked inside, and a trench coat. Likely a Burberry.

As it turned out, however, Peter Charlton was *nothing* at all like the person Kate had been expecting. When she opened the door at precisely seven-thirty, it was to see a thin, flamboyantly dressed man wearing a black Regency-style jacket over narrow fitting black cords, a brilliant red silk scarf draped artistically around his neck and earrings in both ears. He had spiky blonde hair cut very short, pale green eyes, and black Buddy Holly type glasses.

"Kate Pedigrew?" he inquired, dramatically tossing one end of the scarf back over his shoulder.

Kate stared at him in bewilderment. "Yes, that's right. Mr. . . . *Charlton*?"

The man's hand shot out. "I can't *tell* you how pleased I am to meet you."

Shocked, Kate put her hand in his and felt the softness of the black leather glove close around it. "T-thank you. Won't you . . . come in?"

"Delighted." The man—who had to be at least six feet tall—strode in, and then stopped dead. "Oh, my God, this is *fabulous*! I just *love* these old churches. Was it like this when you bought it or did you do the work yourself?"

"No, I did it myself," Kate told him, trying not to smile. The man's head was bobbing up and down like one of those mechanical dogs that sat in the back windows of cars. "It's been a challenge but I'm pleased with the results." She almost expected to see his eyes blink on and off when he spoke. "Can I offer you something to drink, Mr. Charlton? I've just made fresh coffee."

"Hmm? Oh, thank you, no. I never drink coffee after dinner." He leaned in close and lowered his voice. "Caffeine does the most *dreadful* things to my moods, if you know what I mean."

Kate bit her lip to stifle a smile. "Yes, I think I do."

"Of course, it comes with the territory," he continued blithely. "There is just so much *pressure* in this business. But you're an artist, you know all about *that*. Now, Miss—oh, bother the formality. Can I call you Kate?"

Kate pressed her lips together and nodded.

"Fabulous. I am *dying* to see your work, Kate. Shall we have a look?"

Kate inclined her head and led the way to the studio.

"By the way how *did* everything go last night?" Peter inquired as he walked beside her. "Oliver told me that you were having a show."

"Yes, it went . . . extremely well," Kate said, trying to forget that, apart from her work, the evening itself had been something of a disaster. "The response to my new work was very encouraging. Well, here we are."

"Oh, this is incredible." Peter stood with his hands on his cheeks and gazed around him like a child on Christmas morning. "What a *fabulous* way to showcase your work. I just *love* all this white. And these are your *creations*."

Kate abruptly looked away. "Yes."

"Fabulous. The balance, the texture, the depth." He moved to stand in front of Eleya's Dream and Kate saw the change in his face. "Oh, now *this* is outstanding," he said in hushed tones. "The startling yet subtle blending of colors. The complexity of the design—well, what can I say?" The piece is simply *breathtaking*. I think dear Oliver would be *very* interested in having *this* piece in the collection."

Kate laughed—and quickly turned it into a cough. Somehow, she couldn't imagine the very correct gentleman she'd spoken to on the phone being *dear* Oliver to anyone—and certainly not to this man. "I'm sorry to disappoint you, Mr. Charlton, but Eleya's Dream isn't for sale. It's a personal favorite of mine, and I don't intend to sell or to show it."

He looked at her as though she had suddenly sprouted two heads. "Kate, Kate, what are you *saying*? That you don't *wish* to have your very *best* piece of work displayed in the Preston Gallery? It would do a *great* deal toward establishing your career as an artist in this milieu."

"I'm sure it would, Mr. Charlton—"

"Peter, please."

Kate smiled. "Peter. But I really would prefer that you choose another piece."

She could see that he was disappointed, and perhaps a little annoyed. Was she blowing the deal right here?

"Well, if you insist," he said, with a sigh that would have done Scarlett O'Hara proud. "I'm sure I'll be able to find *something* else."

Kate slowly let out the breath she'd been holding and directed him toward the piece she was hoping he'd select. It was entitled The Dove's Song, and it was an exquisitely delicate design crafted in pieces of crackled, frosted and white swirled glass. She had created it with the image of Eleya herself in mind.

"Oh. Now this is *very* good," Peter said thoughtfully. "A most unusual blending of textures. And the lead work is excellent. Have you been doing stained glass long, Kate?"

"Yes. Years, actually." Kate had decided that it would be better not to make it sound as though she had suddenly "discovered" the knack. For most people, learning how to create really good stained glass was a skill that took years to develop. "But I admit, I have been working with a few new techniques, several of which I used in this piece."

"Well, I must say, it's very good. The balance and the composition are excellent. And I love the *feeling* it conveys. So celestial." He took a step closer to it. "Is this the price you're willing to sell it for?"

"Yes."

"Fabulous. Then we have a deal," Peter said, beaming. "I'll phone Oliver with the details and have him send out a contract straight away." He took a small leather purse from his coat pocket and counted out three one hundred dollar bills. "This can serve as a deposit. The balance will follow when we come to collect the piece."

"You mean you won't be taking it now?"

His pencil-thin eyebrows arched expressively. "My dear Kate. I *select* the artists' works. I do not *schlep* them around. Besides, we won't start gathering the pieces together until everything is finalized. Oliver will call you himself to finalize the arrangements." Peter rolled his eyes. "He *loves* overseeing that type of thing. Personally, I hate paperwork. Too boring. No room for artistic expression. Well, I think that just about concludes the business part of our dealings. But Kate . . . I wonder . . . would you be willing to show me the rest of your delightful home?"

Surprised that he would ask, but flattered by his interest, Kate agreed. "Yes, of course, though there's not much you haven't already seen." They walked back out into the main body of the church. "This is the living room, of course, and the kitchen and dining room are through here."

"Lovely proportions," Peter commented, peering with great fascination into every nook and cranny. "Are you sure you're not an interior designer as well as a gifted artist?"

"Believe me, I'm not. And this is the den."

"Ah," he said, noticing the drafting table. "The place where the artist creates!"

Kate had to laugh. Honestly, the man should be on the stage. "Sometimes. Other times I move it into the living room, depending on where the light is best. And the bedroom is through there."

"Just the one?"

"Yes. I seldom have guests and when I do, I use the pull-out couch in the living room."

"I see. And is that . . . everything? I'd hate to think I'd missed anything."

"Well, there's just the workroom in the basement and a small, unfinished attic upstairs which I use for storage. But there's nothing artistic about either of them."

"No, of course. Well, then, I won't take up any more of your time. It has been *such* a pleasure meeting you, Kate, and I am *so* looking forward to seeing your work in the collection. Here's my card," he said, whipping it out of his pocket. "If you have *any* questions at all, *please* don't hesitate to call. I'm sure Oliver gave you his number as well, but you're far more likely to get me. The dear man is constantly on the go."

"Thank you for taking the time to come out in person, Peter," Kate said. "As I told Mr. Kline, I was thrilled to be invited to participate."

"Yes, we're hoping it's going to be a *fabulous* show. But we're keeping very quiet about it just now. We don't want any news leaking out in advance." He dropped his voice to a whisper. "That's why we're asking our artists to keep this all very hush-hush."

"I understand. And you have my assurance of complete cooperation."

"I knew I could count on you, Kate. Your professionalism

does you credit. And of course, it always goes down well with the gallery owners. Well—" He bowed to her with a dramatic flourish. "—until we meet again!"

Kate only just managed not to burst out laughing. She watched him walk toward the road, wondering why he'd parked his car so far away, and then glanced down at the card in her hand. It seemed a strangely conventional card for such an unconventional man. The name of the gallery was embossed in gold across the top and Peter's name, phone number and email address were printed in small black letters below.

"Peter Reginald *Augustus* Charlton?" Kate read aloud. Good grief, what a remarkable name. But then, she was used to dealing with remarkable types in the art world.

Jeremy Davenport walked toward the BMW he'd left parked on the road and smiled to himself in amusement. Perfect. She'd fallen for it hook, line and sinker. But why wouldn't she? He had played the part brilliantly. And while he was disappointed that the spinning wheel hadn't been visible, he wasn't concerned. It simply meant that when he paid a return visit to her house, the only rooms he'd have to check out were the basement, the attic and the bedroom.

Pity he hadn't thought to play the Latin lover tonight, Davenport mused. He might have been able to sweet-talk his way into Kate's bedroom. She was an extremely beautiful young woman and he wasn't averse to a little sex on the side of a business deal. But trying to force his way into her bedroom in the guise of a flagrantly gay male would have been completely out of character. And if there was one thing Jeremy never did, it was step out of character.

Still, he could always work on that later, because he *was* going to see Kate Pedigrew again. He'd have to deal with her in person if he wanted to get possession of the wheel, and right now that was the only thing that mattered to him. He'd played the con game long enough. He was ready to retire. Of course, he already had a few million tucked away in various banks around the world, but it wasn't enough to allow him to live the way he wanted to for the rest of his life. That kind of lifestyle took huge amounts of money—and that's what the spinning wheel was going to bring him. He didn't know how yet, but he'd figure that out once it was in his possession.

For now, the main thing was to make alternate plans for getting back into Kate Pedigrew's house, and that wasn't a problem either. Because like his deceptions, Jeremy Davenport was very good when it came to thinking up alternate plans.

After Peter Charlton left, Kate made herself a cup of tea and sat down in the living room, needing a few minutes alone to mull over the rather startling events of the day. She knew she should have been more thrilled that the meeting with Peter Charlton had gone so well, and that The Dove's Song was going to be hanging in the prestigious Preston Gallery. But somehow, her pleasure in it all was diminished by what she had discovered about Cole and the spinning wheel this afternoon.

What was she going to do about him now? The fact that he was looking for the spinning wheel changed . . . everything. It meant that she'd have to watch everything she said or did around him. It also meant that she would have to start giving serious consideration to Eleya's prophesy—something she hadn't consciously thought about until now.

Was Cole Beresford the danger the spirit had told her to beware of?

Kate hated to think that he was, but what or who else could it be? She knew he was looking for the spinning wheel. He'd set out on a quest to prove its existence, and if he was successful in doing so, every museum in the world would be clamoring for his services. Anything Cole ever wanted would likely be his for the asking. Wasn't that reason enough for him to try to take the wheel away from her?

Kate got up and restlessly began to pace. Maybe. But if Cole's interest in the spinning wheel was strictly academic, maybe he'd be able to understand her desire to help Eleya too. Maybe if she told him the truth about the spirit, he would be willing to help her find the answers she needed. After all, he had all the books. He knew what he was talking about.

Then why had Eleya kept referring to a danger that would come in a dark form that she wouldn't recognize? Kate had to believe that the spirit had the gift of foresight, but what was she seeing? Was it Cole she was trying to warn her about?

Kate didn't know. She needed more time. If she could put Cole off for a few days, she might be able to find the answers she was looking for. And if she could physically remove the spinning wheel from her house, she wouldn't have to worry about him stumbling upon it if he did happen to come by and start looking.

Kate reached for the phone and punched in Matt's number. All she needed was a little more time. Just a few more days and maybe she'd know—

"Matt, hi, it's me. Listen, I need a really big favor. Can you come over here first thing in the morning? I need you to take something back to your house. No, it's not the table you promised to fix for me. Would you stop asking questions, I'll tell you when you get here. How early?" Kate took a deep breath. How early was early enough to avoid detection by a certain gentleman who might be driving by? "How does five A.M. sound?"

# Sixteen

"Okay, sis, what's this all about?" Matt asked at 5:05 the next morning. "You'd better have a darn good reason for getting me out of bed at four-thirty in the morning."

Kate buttered two pieces of toast and slathered honey on them. "You always get up at four-thirty, Matt."

"Yes, but I don't leave the house until six."

"Forgive me for disturbing your routine, but I needed your help. And it had to be this early so nobody would see us. Here, munch on this while I fill you in. It might help to sweeten your disposition."

Matt frowned, but nevertheless accepted the toast. "What do you mean you don't want anybody to see you. Are you hiding from somebody?"

"Not exactly. I just don't want to attract attention to what we're doing."

"Yeah, well, not much chance of that," Matt grumbled. "Even the squirrels aren't up yet. By the way, what's the old spinning wheel doing out in the middle of the floor? Trying to see if I can trip over it or what?"

"No." Kate took a deep breath. "*That's* what I need you to take over to your place."

"What?"

"I want you to keep the spinning wheel at your house for

a few days. And please don't ask me a whole bunch of questions, Matt, because I won't answer them. I just have to get it out of here for a while."

"Why?"

"Because I don't want anyone to see it."

"Kate, this is probably going to sound like a really stupid question, but isn't that why you bought it in the first place?"

"Yes, but things have . . . changed since I brought it home."

"And that's the part you won't tell me?"

"Right."

"Okay. Then can you tell me *who* don't you want to see it?"

Kate hesitated a fraction of a second. "Cole Beresford."

"Beresford? You mean . . . that guy you went out for dinner with, and who Dad insulted the other night?"

Kate rolled her eyes. "Yeah. Him."

Matt finished the toast and wiped his hands on his jeans. "So what's the scoop? Does he have some kind of secret fetish for spinning wheels or what? Are you afraid he'll steal this one and hide it in his basement, then run around rubbing his hands and cackling."

"Matt, where do you get this stuff?"

"Saturday morning cartoons. Christian and I always watch them together. Seriously, Kate, what's the problem? The guy seemed pretty decent to me. I liked the way he came to your defense when Dad started being his usual jerky self."

Kate shuddered at the memory. "Don't remind me. But yes, Cole is a good guy and—"

"Do you like him?"

"Matt!"

"Well, Megan wanted me to ask. She thought he was pretty dishy."

"Dishy?"

"Her words, not mine."

"Well . . . yes, I suppose he is." *Although gorgeous came to mind before dishy did.* "And yes, I do like him. In a professional way, of course."

"Of course," Matt repeated with a straight face. "So has he tried to put the moves on you?"

*"Matt!"*

"C'mon sis, if a guy's messing around with my sister, I've got a right to know."

"You do not! Being my brother does *not* entitle you to dig into my personal life. I'm a big girl. I can take care of myself."

Matt snorted. "Yeah, right. Like you took care of that jerk from Baltimore a few years ago."

A blush ran over Kate's cheeks. "That was different. He was drunk."

"Yeah, and if I hadn't shown up, he would still have had you down on the floor and all your clothes off."

"Matt, just drive the truck around to the studio door, will you?" Kate said tersely. "I have no intention of standing here at five A.M. talking to you about my sex life."

"Okay, have it your way. Don't tell your big brother what's going on," Matt said, pretending to be hurt. "Just don't come running to me later on when it's too late for me to do anything but say I told you so."

"Matt. Go get the truck."

Thankfully, he did.

"Okay, all kidding aside," Matt said as he helped Kate load the spinning wheel into the back of it, "why don't you want Beresford to know you've got the spinning wheel?"

Kate sighed. Honestly, he was like a dog worrying a bone. "Because you were partially right when you joked about Cole wanting to steal it. The only reason he's in Vermont is to find this spinning wheel."

Matt stared at her in disbelief. "You're kidding!"

"Dead straight."

"But . . . why would a guy want a spinning wheel?"

"Because it's not just a spinning wheel. It's very old and something of a . . . collectible," Kate said carefully. "And I need your word that you won't tell anybody you've got it."

"Hey, no skin off my nose," Matt said. "I'll keep it under wraps until you tell me you want it back. And if anybody asks, I have no idea what a spinning wheel looks like or why anyone would be looking for one."

"Thanks, Matt. For a brother, you're not half bad."

"Ain't it the truth. Hey, listen, does this code of silence thing extend to Meg too?"

Kate bit her lip. "I guess it would be pretty hard to keep something like this from her, wouldn't it?"

"Probably, but if you'd rather she didn't know, I can always put it down in the furnace room. She hardly ever goes in there. Spiders, you know."

Kate grinned, and nodded. "That might be best. Oh and Matt, one more thing. There's a small wooden dowel that stops the wheel from turning. Under *no* circumstances are you to pull it out. Okay?"

Matt shook his head as he walked around to the driver's side. "Kate, I don't mind telling you, this spinning wheel's got me real curious. But I won't ask because I know you won't tell." He jumped into the truck and closed the door. "You always were good at keeping secrets. I'll just try to make sure I keep it under wraps *and* that the little wooden dowel doesn't come out."

Kate put her hand on his arm and smiled. "Thanks, Matt. I really appreciate this."

"I know." Giving her chin an affectionate punch, Matt dropped the truck into gear. "Take it easy, Katie."

Kate sighed as she watched her brother drive off with her precious cargo.

She hoped to God that she was doing the right thing.

Kate was in the kitchen when Cole phoned—which was lucky since only moments before she'd been downstairs working on her grinder. And if she hoped to convince Cole that she wasn't feeling well enough to work—or to have visitors—picking up the extension in the workshop wouldn't have helped. "Um, hi, Cole," she said.

There was a short pause. "Kate, are you okay?"

"Actually, no. I woke up with this terrible migraine and I can hardly see straight. It's been a totally useless morning. I just got up to make myself a hot drink and then I thought I'd go back to bed."

"Oh." There was a slightly longer pause. "So I guess you're not up to having company this morning."

Awkwardly, Kate cleared her throat. "I'm really not. If it was just a regular headache I'd take two aspirin and say see you in an hour. But it doesn't work that way with these things. I have to keep very quiet. Right now even the ticking of the clock is making me wince." She hoped she wasn't laying it on too thick and held her breath as she waited for his answer.

"I understand. I'm just sorry I won't get to see you today."

"Yeah, me too," she said faintly.

"Can I check on you later? I really do have to talk to you about something important."

Kate sighed. So much for hoping that his wanting to see her had anything to do with romance. "Sure, call me tonight. Hopefully I'll be feeling better by then. Bye."

"Kate?"

"Hmm?"

"Keep your doors locked today, okay?"

She blinked in surprise. "You want me to lock my doors?"

"Yeah. You know that thing New Yorkers do in their sleep."

"Cole, there's no need for me to lock my doors around here. This isn't New York, nobody's going to break in."

"Just do it for me, will you, Kate? I'll feel better knowing that you're safely locked in."

It must have had something to do with the fact that he lived in New York, Kate decided. And she could understand that. She'd been a little paranoid when she'd lived there too. "Okay, Cole, I'll make sure they're locked."

"Thanks. I'll call you tonight."

The line went dead, and Kate replaced the receiver. Funny, he'd sounded kind of tense today, which was unusual for him. Cole Beresford was one of the calmest people she'd ever met.

Shrugging, Kate went back downstairs to the workroom and turned on the grinder. She looked at the pieces of glass that were sitting there waiting to be smoothed—and then abruptly turned the grinder off again. She wasn't in the mood to work on glass anymore. Instead, she went back upstairs and sat down at her computer. Seconds later, she was connected to the web.

It was time she started doing some homework.

In his room at the inn, Cole hung up the phone and swore softly under his breath. Damn. What a lousy time for Kate to get a migraine. He needed to talk to her, and he needed to do it now.

He stood up and restlessly began to pace. This enforced idleness was driving him crazy. He should be doing something. If he couldn't get his hands on the spinning wheel, he should be making sure that Davenport couldn't either. Which was another reason Cole didn't like being away from Kate. She was all alone out there. He'd told her to lock her doors, but that wouldn't stop Davenport. The best Cole could hope for was that it might slow him down long enough to give Kate time to call the police if she heard someone trying to get in.

Of course, that wasn't to say that Davenport *knew* Kate had the spinning wheel. And that was the *only* thing that was stopping Cole from mounting a twenty-four-hour guard on her door. Davenport didn't know Kate from Eve—and if he was going by Mrs. Barrett's description, he never would. There were lots of tall attractive women with dark hair in town. Cole knew. He'd checked out every one of them himself!

No, for the time being, they were probably okay. With luck, it would take Davenport a while to find out that Kate had the spinning wheel. And by that time, Cole hoped to have it out of the country. In the meantime, it probably wouldn't hurt to do a little checking himself. Davenport would have to ask questions if he wanted to find Kate, and that meant he'd be out on the streets.

Cole grabbed his jacket and his keys and headed out to his car. Might as well be out there too.

• • •

To Kate's disappointment, the Internet told her nothing. She spent the better part of four hours working through every major search engine, scanning through hundreds of sites, and linking to hundreds of others, but in the end they just kept on giving her the same answer.

No matches found. Whatever information was out there about the Lockton spinning wheel obviously wasn't in the public domain. Which meant, Kate realized, that she was going to have to do it on foot. And that was okay too. She could get up early in the morning and head into Montpelier. Then, after browsing through the city's bookstores, she could take a leisurely drive back home, maybe stop for dinner somewhere along the way—and then roll into the church around ten. Hopefully too late for Cole to come visiting.

When the phone rang, Kate was so caught up in her plans that she forgot to sound like she was suffering. "Pedigrew Stained Glass," she answered crisply.

Fortunately, it was only Madeleine. "Kate, honey, I'm so glad you weren't sleeping."

"Maddie, it's three o'clock in the afternoon. Why would I be sleeping?"

"Because Cole told me you had a dreadful migraine and that you were spending the day in bed."

Kate glanced up from the screen and inhaled sharply. Was Cole at Madeleine's house now? "You spoke to Cole?"

"Uh huh. He called me from his hotel this morning. Said how disappointed he was that he wasn't going to get to see you today, and that he was going out for a few hours."

Kate started to breathe again. "Yes, well, I was feeling pretty rotten when he called, but it's easing now, so I thought I'd get up and start moving around a bit."

"In that case, do you feel like coming over here for dinner? I could use some company."

Kate had to ask. "You don't think Cole might just . . . drop in unannounced?"

"Honey, Cole never drops in unannounced. He's British—he wasn't raised to do things like that."

Nervously, Kate nibbled at her bottom lip. Did she dare? She did feel like getting out, and Maddie had always been able to make her laugh. "Well, if you're sure it's no trouble."

"It's no trouble at all, I'd be delighted to have you. Sometimes a person gets tired of being on their own. You know what I mean, Kate?"

She didn't need to ask twice. "Yes, Maddie." Kate turned off the computer and glanced around her empty house. "I know exactly what you mean."

As always, Madeleine welcomed her with open arms. "Honey, I am so glad you're here. How are you feeling?"

"Better thanks," Kate said as she slipped off her jacket. "I guess a quiet day at home was just what the doctor ordered."

"Mmm, I can't really say I was surprised to hear that you were feeling off color. You've been pushing yourself too hard these past few weeks. And then with your father arriving like that—well, I've been wanting to talk to you about it ever since. But I didn't want to pry."

"You're not prying, Maddie, you were there," Kate said simply. "It's only natural that you'd be curious."

"Well, I like to think it's more concern than curiosity," Madeleine said as they walked into the living room. "How have things been going with your father anyway?"

"Not well." Kate sat down in a dark-green wing chair. "He's practically ordering Matt to let him take Christian to New York."

"And Matt doesn't want him to."

"It's not so much he doesn't want him to. Matt wants what's best for Christian too, but he resents Dad coming up here and ordering him around. He's not a kid anymore."

"No, but sometimes men act like kids when their pride gets in the way." Madeleine sighed. "I know. There were times when Lawrence—God rest his soul—would do the silliest things, and only because his pride was offended. Men's egos are very fragile things, honey. Better you know that going in."

Kate ran her finger along the piping at the edge of the chair. "Maddie, when you first met Lawrence, did you . . . know that he was the one for you?"

"Good Lord, what makes you ask that?"

"Well . . . I know how much you loved your husband, and I wondered if it was something that you knew right from the start. Or do you remember?"

"Oh, I remember to the *day* the first time I saw Lawrence Carstairs III," Madeleine assured her. "I'd gone to New York to spend a weekend with a girlfriend. Jeannie was always telling me that I should get out and see what the rest of the world was doing. So I did. Anyway, she had tickets to a play. I don't remember what the play was, but I sure do remember meeting Lawrence." Madeleine smiled. "It was during intermission. We were standing with our backs to each other, and when he turned around, he knocked my champagne glass clear out of my hand. Well, I turned around to see who this clumsy oaf was and—there he was. And that's when I knew."

Kate stared at her in astonishment. "Just like that?"

"Just like that."

"Did Lawrence know too?"

"Oh yes. On the day we got married, he told me that he'd known that very night that we were going to be together for the rest of our lives." Her smiled faded. "We just didn't know how short that time together was going to be."

"You miss him, don't you?"

"Very much," Madeleine admitted. "But it gets easier as the years go by. But . . . why this sudden interest in how I felt when I met Lawrence, Kate? Is there something going on in *your* life that you want to talk about?"

Kate hadn't intended to tell to Madeleine about her feelings for Cole. All she'd wanted to know was whether it was possible for a person to develop strong feelings for someone else in a relatively short period of time—like two weeks. But somehow, in the peaceful atmosphere of the living room, she found herself confiding in the older woman.

"I don't know if there's anything going on or not," Kate said truthfully. "But I've been having some very mixed up feelings about Cole and to tell you the truth, I have no idea what to do about it."

"Cole!" Madeleine's eyes sparkled. "Well, that's wonderful. I'd be lying if I said I wasn't hoping that something like this would happen between the two of you."

"But that's just it, Maddie. I'm not sure that anything *has*. I mean, I know I like Cole. He's funny, he's charming, he's got a great sense of humor—"

"And he's drop dead gorgeous."

Kate laughed. "Yeah, that too. But it's more than all that. Whenever I'm with him, everything around me seems . . . brighter somehow. I feel so incredibly alive. Even though my stomach is doing somersaults the whole time."

Madeleine smiled in satisfaction. "That's how I used to feel when I was with Lawrence. It was like I couldn't get enough air. Then he'd look at me and I'd go hot and cold all over. Sound familiar?"

"More than I like to admit."

"Welcome to falling in love, Kate. Isn't is wonderful?"

"I don't know about it being wonderful," Kate muttered. "I just wish I knew what was going on in Cole's head."

"Well, tell me what the signs are."

"The signs?"

"Sure, there are always signs, honey. Does he look at you in a very intense way?"

Kate thought about that for a moment. "I suppose he has, a couple of times."

"And does he call you first thing in the morning and last thing at night?"

"He's only called me once in the morning. And that was the day after the show."

"Was it early?"

"Not really. But I'd slept late, so—"

"So he called before you were out of bed."

Kate blushed. "Yes."

"And he's taken you to dinner."

"Did he tell you that?"

"And you went shopping together."

"He told you *that* too?"

"Now don't go getting all embarrassed, Kate," Madeleine said with a laugh. "Cole's a good friend of mine. Of course he'd tell me things like that. Especially when I ask him."

"You *asked* him?" Kate gasped. "Maddie!"

"Well, I couldn't help myself. I love both of you so much and I think you'd be wonderful together. And what you've told me tonight only confirms that."

"But it's not that simple," Kate said in frustration. "Cole told me that he doesn't lead the kind of life that lends itself to relationships. Did you know that he's away seven months of the year?"

"Seven months!" Madeleine's smooth brow furrowed. "Lord, I knew he spent a lot of time in Europe, but I didn't know it was *that* long. Still, Lawrence was traveling a lot when I first met him, and that didn't stop *him* from proposing. But I know you and Cole will find a way around it too, honey. I'm so sure you're meant to be together."

"But what if Cole doesn't feel the same way about me? I think he likes me," Kate admitted, "but it's a long way from liking someone to making a commitment that's going to change the rest of your life."

"You'd be surprised, my dear, at how short a distance it really is. Oh, good, there's the dinner bell. Come on, Kate," Madeleine said, getting to her feet, "the only thing I like better than talking about love, is talking about it with a glass of wine in my hand!"

The discussion continued over a long and leisurely dinner, and Kate was given yet another glimpse into Madeleine's multifaceted personality. The woman turned out to be a marvelous listener with a grasp of human dynamics and an understanding of feelings and emotions that went far beyond anything Kate had expected.

"Maddie, why are you wasting your time playing godmother to a bunch of artists in Vermont?" she asked as they carried their coffees back into the living room a few hours later. "You should be working in New York. Counseling all those lovelorn people out there."

"I'm not sure I'm ready to know *that* much about life," Madeleine said with a grimace. "I only like helping people I really care about. But I think you and Cole have what it takes to make a relationship work, Kate. That's not to say there won't be compromises. You both love what you do and you're both very good at it. And if you decide you want to be together, there will have to be some sacrifices. But believe me, if Cole's the right man, you won't think of them as sacrifices at all."

Kate was pondering that when the doorbell rang.

"Now I wonder who that could be," Madeleine said. "I'm not expecting anyone tonight."

*Please don't let it be Cole,* Kate whispered inwardly. *I really don't want to have to explain why I'm here.*

Fortunately, she needn't have worried. A gentleman had come to call on Madeleine, but it wasn't Cole Beresford. It was Roderick Pedigrew.

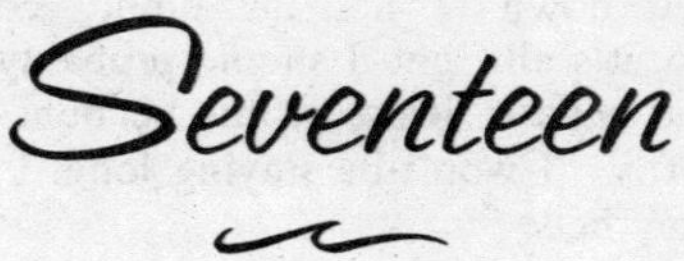

"Dad!" Kate got awkwardly to her feet. It was the first time she'd seen him since their argument in the field, and to be honest, she wasn't sure how to react. The anger she'd felt toward him at the time was gone, but she still felt a little on edge. It was kind of like waiting to hear the bang after the gun was fired. "What are you doing here?"

To her surprise, her father looked a little embarrassed. "Well, I found myself driving around the area and remembered that Mrs. Carstairs said she lived in the neighborhood. So when I saw the house I thought I'd stop in." There was a hesitation in Roderick's voice when he turned to Madeleine and said, "I hope you don't mind."

"I don't mind at all. The only thing I'm going to insist on if you stay is that you call me Madeleine. Kate knows I don't stand on formality, and I'm sure as hell not going to call you Mr. Pedigrew anymore," she said flatly.

Her reply seemed to amuse him. "Thank you, Madeleine, I will."

"Good. Now, can I offer you a cup of coffee?"

"I wouldn't want to impose—"

"It's no imposition. Two things a southern lady always has on hand are bourbon and coffee. I'll just go and ask

Teresa to put on a fresh pot. Kate, honey, can I freshen that up for you?"

Kate stared down at her half-empty coffee cup and frowned. "No, it's all right. I should probably go—"

"There's no need to leave on my account," Roderick interrupted gruffly. "I won't be staying long. I just wanted to stop in and say hello."

"Oh." Kate blinked. "Well, I suppose it wouldn't hurt to have another cup for the road."

Madeleine smiled as she picked up Kate's cup and walked out, leaving father and daughter to face each other in silence.

"I hope I didn't interrupt your dinner," Roderick said abruptly.

"Um, no, you didn't. We were . . . already finished."

"Good. It's just that I was in the area and thought I'd stop by."

Kate nodded. Had he seen her car parked out front? "That was nice of you."

Roderick shoved his hands into his pockets. "Madeleine seems like a nice person."

"Yes, she is."

"Is she from around here?"

"No. She moved here from New York after her husband died."

He looked surprised. "She's a widow?"

"Yes."

"I'm surprised she would have left the city. Seems to me there'd be more for her to do there."

"I suppose, but she keeps herself busy and she's made a lot of new friends."

"I can see why. She's very pleasant company." Roderick pulled his hands out of his pockets and crossed his arms over his chest. "I went into Barre for dinner. There's a good German restaurant on the main street."

"Yes. The Edelweiss Café."

He glanced at her quickly. "You know it?"

"I eat there frequently."

"They do a pretty good Hunter Schnitzel."

High praise from her father indeed. "Yes, Gretchen's an excellent cook."

"The pastries looked good too."

Kate looked at her father in amazement. If she didn't know better, she'd swear he was actually trying to *make* conversation. "Desserts are her husband's specialty. I often stop there for a piece of chocolate hazelnut torte."

"You would. You always did love hazelnuts."

Kate stared at him. Now how in the world had he remembered that? Not that it mattered, of course. "So, where are you staying?"

"The Willow Inn. Nice place. A little too much chintz for my liking, but it's clean and comfortable."

Kate allowed herself a smile. "Chintz is very popular up here."

"I gathered. Anyway, I wasn't ready to go back and immerse myself in all that pink and white so I decided to go for a drive. And when I saw the street name, I thought I'd . . . stop in."

Kate nodded. By the sounds of things, even if he had seen her car, he wasn't going to admit it.

"Well, here we are," Madeleine said, breezing back into the room. She carried a silver tray with three cups of fresh coffee on it, along with a generous slice of pie. "I thought you might like something to go with your coffee, Roderick, so I brought you a piece of Teresa's apple pie. I don't know how she does it, but her apple pies are surely the best I've ever tasted."

"Thank you, Madeleine. Kate knows I never turn down pie."

Madeleine set the tray on the coffee table and then glanced at them. "Is there any reason why the two of you are still standing?"

"No." Kate promptly sat down. "We were just . . . chatting,"

Her father sat too. "Yes. I was telling Kate that I didn't feel like going back to my room after dinner, so I went for a drive. And when I found myself on Cherry Tree Close, I remembered you saying that you lived here."

Madeleine smiled. "Funny, I don't remember telling you the house number, but then, I forget a lot of things these days. Sugar?"

"Just cream."

Madeleine poured a drop into his coffee, then handed it and the pie across. "I hope you enjoy it."

"I'm sure I will." Roderick glanced at his daughter's averted face, and then gruffly cleared his throat. "Actually, I . . . didn't know which house it was. But when I saw Kate's car parked in the driveway, I took a chance. I figured it was unlikely she'd have two friends living on the same street."

Kate took a quick mouthful of coffee. So he *had* recognized her car. Was that why he'd come in?

"Well, I think this is delightful," Madeleine said, seemingly unconcerned with the reasons for his visit. "We didn't get a chance to talk much at Kate's the other night, and I'm pleased to have an opportunity to do that now." She dropped two lumps of brown sugar into her own cup and then sat back against the cushions of the cream and gold brocade sofa. "So, what are your plans while you're here, Roderick?"

"I don't have any fixed plans," he admitted. "Other than to see as much of my grandson as I can. I was supposed to be in London closing a deal on a retail development, but when I got back to my office and found Megan's letter, I postponed the trip and came straight here."

"It was good of you to show such concern," Madeleine said quietly. "I don't imagine you get to see very much of your grandson."

A muscle jumped in Roderick's cheek. "No. It's difficult with Matt living up here. And I haven't been . . . close to the family since Clare died."

Kate felt a lump the size of a golf ball rise in her throat.

"Yes, I know how hard Clare's death was on all of you," Madeleine said in a soft, sympathetic tone. "Kate and I have talked about it many times, haven't we, Kate? It's never easy losing someone you love. I lost my own dear husband a few years back, and I know what it's like."

"Yes, Kate told me. I'm sorry to hear that," Roderick said genuinely. "And you're right, losing a family member is never easy. That's why I'm so angry at Matt for not doing more to help his son."

Kate heard the warning bells go off. "Dad, I really don't think this is the time to bring it up."

"Why not? I'm sure Madeleine knows what's going on. Anyone can see that the boy needs help." Roderick stood up, his eyes suspiciously bright as he clasped the back of his neck with his hand. "He's dying, damn it, and nobody seems to care."

Kate heard the gruff note of anguish in his voice and hastily put down her cup. "Maddie, I'm sorry, but I think it's best I go. Thanks for a lovely dinner, and for listening to me. It meant a lot."

"Oh, honey, you don't have to thank me," Madeleine said warmly. "You know you can come over here any time you like."

"Thanks. No, that's okay, don't get up, I can see myself out." Kate turned to face her father and sighed. There was so much she wanted to say—and she had no idea where to begin. All she knew was that they were both hurting—and that they were both too stubborn to admit it. "I don't know if I'll see you before you head back to New York, Dad, so I'll say good-bye now."

He didn't reach out. He just stood there and looked at her. And when he finally said good-bye in that cool, controlled voice, Kate turned and walked out.

*Damn it,* she didn't want it to be like this. She wanted to believe that she'd seen something in his face just now. A tiny flicker of regret, perhaps. Something to show that he wasn't as indifferent to her as he seemed. She knew she shouldn't have expected anything, of course. She shouldn't even have looked for it. But just once, couldn't he have said something *nice* before she left? Was that so much to ask?

It was raining by the time Kate got to her street. She switched on the wipers and listened to the rhythmic thump of the blade as it swished back and forth across the window. The wet air seemed to suck all the brightness from her headlights—just like being with her father sucked all the happiness out of her.

Kate thumped her hand on the steering wheel in frustration. Why did it always have to be like this? Why couldn't they have just kept on talking the way they had when he'd first arrived? He'd talked about everyday things, like how great Gretchen's cooking tasted, and what a nice person Maddie was. He'd told her about the place where he was staying and about how much she liked hazelnuts, for crying out loud. And then in the space of five seconds flat, whammo! They'd been back at it again. All it had taken was that one careless remark.

The rain started coming down harder. Kate dashed unexpected tears from her eyes and nudged the wiper up a notch. She was glad she was almost home. It was a bad night for driving and her nerves were shot. But when she rounded the last bend and her driveway came into view, she started to frown. Why wasn't the light over her sign on?

As soon as she turned into the driveway, Kate knew something was wrong. The entire place was in darkness. The light on the front porch was out, and so was the one in the kitchen. Had there been some kind of power failure while she'd been away? She pulled into her usual spot at the side of the church—and that's when she saw him. A man, caught for a split second in the dull glow of her headlights. He had stepped away from the back of the house and was bolting toward the trees.

Kate slammed on her brakes and jumped out. "Hey, you! Stop! *Stop!*" She couldn't see much in the darkness, but she knew he just kept on running. Minutes later, she heard the sound of a car starting up in the road.

Oblivious to the rain, Kate turned and made a mad dash for the road. If she could just catch a glimpse of the car, something to identify it by—but again she was too late. She reached the end of the driveway just in time to see red taillights disappear into the murky night. She didn't even have a chance to see what kind of car it was.

For a minute, Kate was too darn angry to be scared. How dare some . . . hooligan kid try to break into her house!

Didn't they have anything better to do with their time?

Then, she blanched. Her glass. Eleya's Dream!

"Oh my God!" Kate tore back down the driveway. *Please don't let him have broken my beautiful glass.* She dug her keys out of her purse and headed for the studio door.

It was already open.

Heart pounding, Kate stepped over the threshold. She slid her hand along the wall, feeling for the light switch and turned it on.

Nothing.

She flipped it up and down a couple more times. Dead.

Knowing that she had to, Kate stepped into the studio, then closed and locked the door behind her. She stood still for a minute, letting her eyes adjust to the darkness. Then, she started forward, waiting with every step for the crunch of broken glass beneath her feet. Thankfully, it never came. She reached the door into the living room and holding her breath, pushed it open.

At first glance, everything looked to be fine. She could make out the familiar shapes of her furniture, and nothing seemed to be out of place. She continued on to the kitchen, and taking a flashlight from under the sink, she flicked it on, steeling herself for what she might see.

But she saw . . . nothing. The couch hadn't been shredded, the table and chairs hadn't been overturned, and all of her paintings and ornaments were still hanging on the wall. Everything was exactly the way she'd left it.

Kate turned and headed for the fuse box. Had she been lucky enough to stumble upon the intruder *before* he'd had a chance to do any damage? She shone the light into the hall closet—and gasped. The cover was open—and every circuit had been thrown.

Kate stared at the box grimly. So it hadn't been a quick in and out. Whoever had been here had taken the time to find the fuse box. He'd wanted the place in darkness. She flipped the switches back to the "on" position.

Immediately, the light in the kitchen came on. From the den, she heard the sound of her computer re-booting, and out on the road, she saw the light over her sign flash on.

After that, Kate methodically went through every room in the house. She turned on every lamp and every fixture, she examined every closet and every drawer. But the results were the same throughout. Nothing. No damage of any kind. Nothing had been broken, nothing had been moved. There was nothing to indicate that anyone had even *been* in the house.

Then what had the intruder wanted?

Kate picked up the phone and started to dial the sheriff's office. Thank heavens her father *had* turned up at Madeleine's house tonight. If he hadn't she might have stayed longer, and God only knew what kind of damage she would have found when she finally did come home.

If she'd found any damage at all.

Kate stopped with the receiver halfway to her ear. Wait a minute. What was she saying? That whoever had been in her house tonight *hadn't* been looking for money or valuables. Then what—

"Oh, *no*!" Kate whispered aloud. "Oh, God no, please not that!"

The shudder started deep down and spread until her whole body was shaking. *No, it wasn't possible.* Surely . . . *Cole* couldn't have broken into her house looking for the spinning wheel!

No, there had to be some other explanation. He wouldn't treat her like this. It was true he'd come to Vermont looking for the spinning wheel, but she couldn't believe that he would resort to something underhanded like this. She couldn't have been *that* wrong about him.

Unfortunately, Kate couldn't ignore the facts. Someone had been in her house, and not a single thing had been stolen. Which either meant that the intruder hadn't had time to do what he'd wanted—or that he'd never intended to *take* anything in the first place.

It didn't take long for Cole to figure out that Kate was avoiding him. She wasn't answering her phone—and when she did, her voice went from warm honey to pure ice in two seconds flat. And he didn't like it one little bit.

"What are you doing here?" Kate asked when she opened

the door to find him on her doorstep two days later.

Cole had been expecting surprise. He hadn't been expecting blazing hostility. "I want to talk to you."

"Well that's too bad, because I don't want to talk to you."

"Tough." He was inside before she had a chance to slam the door in his face.

"Cole!"

"You've been avoiding me for the past two days, Kate, and I want to know why."

She lifted her chin in defiance. "I don't know what you're talking about."

"Yes, you do. You won't return my calls and when I do manage to speak to you, I have to thaw my ear out for an hour afterwards. Why are you avoiding me?"

"I'm not avoiding you. I've just been . . . busy."

"Bullshit! You found time to go out with me when you were really busy. Now you won't even talk to me on the phone?"

"Cole, why are you here?"

"I told you. I want to find out what the hell's the matter with you."

"I didn't mean why are you *here*," Kate said in exasperation. "I meant why are you in Vermont? What did you come here looking for?"

Cole wasn't worried that she'd see his surprise. He'd spent too many years learning how to hide it. "I told you that too. I'm looking for an antique."

"And have you found it?"

Cole looked into her eyes and was astonished at the pain and disillusionment he saw there. "I think you already know the answer to that," he said quietly.

"Maybe, but I'd still like to hear it from you." She could see that the anger had gone from his eyes, but she wasn't willing to part with hers just yet. She'd need it to get through this. She wanted him to admit that he was looking for the spinning wheel. And she wasn't going to let him off the hook until he'd told her everything.

"I think it's time you told me *exactly* what you're looking for."

Cole was silent for a long time. Finally, he nodded. "All right. I came to Vermont to find a spinning wheel. One that I've been searching for for a very long time."

"Why? What's so special about it?"

"It's very old. And it has some unique carving on it which makes it a valuable collector's piece."

"There must be more to it than that, Cole," Kate said in a low voice. "I hardly think an old spinning wheel with a bit of carving on it would set contemporary historians on their ears. And that, as I recall, was how you phrased it."

Cole glanced at her sharply. What kind of game was she playing here? She wasn't willing to tell him that she *had* the spinning wheel, but she wanted to know why he was looking for it. Which meant that she obviously hadn't made the connection between what was happening to her and the spinning wheel.

"All right, I'll tell you." He paused for a moment, and then took a deep breath. "The Lockton spinning wheel *isn't* just an ordinary spinning wheel. It's over five hundred years old, and there have been . . . rumors about it for just about as many." He waited for a moment. "Aren't you going to ask me what the rumors are?"

"It's your story."

"The spinning wheel has special . . . powers," Cole continued after a moment. "It has the ability to accentuate certain abilities of the person who owns it. It makes them better at what they do. Or more attractive than they were before."

A pulse began to beat at the base of Kate's throat. "Why didn't you tell me this before?"

"Because I had no reason to. Until I knew where the spinning wheel was, there wasn't any point. I don't make a habit of going around telling people about enchanted spinning wheels, Kate. But now that I *know* where it is, there's no reason not to tell you."

Kate swallowed tightly. "What do you mean?"

"I know you have the Lockton spinning wheel. It's obvious, in the way your work has changed, and in the way you have. Plus you let a few things slip. Like the fact that an idea for a piece of work came to you in a dream, and that you had Celtic blood. Then there was that hastily retracted comment about Mrs. Barrett."

Kate floundered under the intensity of his gaze. She couldn't tell him, not yet. Not until she knew it all. "That's a pretty incredible story, Cole. If I . . . had a spinning wheel like that—and I'm not saying that I do—what would you try to do?"

"I'd try to convince you to sell it to me," Cole said without hesitation. "Because every day it remains in your possession, the danger to you increases."

There it was again. The mention of danger.

Kate turned so that her back was toward him. "Are you trying to tell me that the owner of this spinning wheel is at some kind of risk?"

"Yes. Because I'm not the only one who's looking for it."

Kate whirled around. "You're not?"

"No. And the man who is won't hesitate to do whatever's necessary to get it."

Her bravado crumbled. Dear God, somebody *else* was looking for the wheel too? "I don't understand. Who—"

"His name is Jeremy Davenport," Cole said quietly. "He's an American, and something of an authority in the art world. But Davenport's a criminal. He has absolutely no scruples when it comes to getting the things that he wants. And he wants the Lockton spinning wheel."

"What does this Jeremy Davenport look like?"

"You might as well ask me what a shadow looks like," Cole said in a harsh voice. "The first time I saw him, he had short red hair, blue eyes and a light, freckled complexion. He spoke with an Irish accent and walked with a limp. The next time I saw him, he had long black hair, brown eyes, and a swarthy, olive skin. He spoke French like a native and moved with the agility of an athlete. The man can change appearance and accents as easily as you or I change shoes. And he has an underground network of suppliers that provide him with passports, visas, arms—"

"Arms!"

"Anything he needs to do his work."

"And you're saying that he . . . knows the spinning wheel is here?"

"He knows it's in the area. He traced it to Wimpole-Barrett's the same as I did. I just got there a few days earlier. But by the time I did, the owner of the store had already sold it to a young woman. Fortunately, she couldn't give me her name."

Kate gulped. "Fortunately?"

"Yes. Because she couldn't give it to Davenport either."

"So this man likely doesn't know where the spinning wheel is?"

Cole's look implied the negative. "The only reason *I* know you have it, is because I've seen the changes. Davenport hasn't. All he knows is that he's looking for an attractive young woman with dark hair who lives about an hour from Mrs. Barrett's shop."

Kate thought hard for a minute. "Cole, if I asked you a question, would you give me an honest answer?"

"Yes."

"How do I know that?"

"Because you have my word."

That was good enough for her. "Two nights ago, did you try to break in here?"

Cole went deathly still. "Somebody broke in?"

"Yes. I'd been away at Madeleine's. It wasn't late when I got home, but when I turned into the driveway, I saw someone running away from the studio door."

"Did you recognize him?"

Kate shook her head. "It was too dark. But he had a car waiting on the road."

Cole steeled himself to say the words. "Was anything taken?"

"No. I'd left some money in the studio, but it was still there when I checked."

Cole nodded tersely. He didn't care if she saw his relief, because the game had suddenly changed. It wasn't him against Kate anymore. It was the two of them against Davenport.

"To answer your question, Kate, no, it wasn't me. I was

in my hotel room making some calls. I can have the manager verify the times and the numbers if you'd like."

"No. You gave me your word, and that's good enough for me," Kate told him, relief evident in her voice. "But I had to ask. Because I thought—"

He turned to look at her. "You thought what?"

Kate felt the heat rising in her cheeks. "I . . . thought it might have been you, and I wanted to know for sure."

"You thought I'd break into your house?" he asked in disbelief.

"I didn't want to," Kate told him desperately, "but think about it, Cole. I knew you were looking for the spinning wheel, so it only made sense that—"

"How did you know that?"

"P-pardon?"

"How did you know I was looking for the spinning wheel?" Cole's voice was deathly quiet. "You knew that I was looking for some kind of antique, Kate, but even a wild guess wouldn't have put it at a spinning wheel."

Too late, Kate realized what she had said. "I . . . I—"

"The truth, Kate. It's too late for lies."

Cole was right. It *was* time for the truth—all of it. "I . . . saw the book on the bedside table in your hotel room," Kate whispered. "And I . . . read it."

There was an ominous silence. "You were *spying* on me?"

*"No!"*

"Then what the hell were you doing in my room?"

"It's not what you think!" Kate cried. "I'd had an argument with my father. I went out for a drive and ended up outside your hotel. I don't know how or why. But once I was there, I realized I wanted to see you, so I went in. The maid was vacuuming in the room next to yours, but your door was open too. I called but when you didn't answer, I went inside. I thought maybe you couldn't hear me. That's when I saw the book laying on your bedside table."

"And you read it."

"Sections of it, yes."

"Which *sections*?"

"The ones you'd bookmarked."

Something dark and dangerous flashed in Cole's eyes. "So you *knew* all along why I was here and you didn't let on."

"I . . . needed time to think," she said awkwardly.

"About what?"

Kate could feel her heart thundering in her breast. She desperately waited for a sign—*any* kind of sign that would tell her that she was about to make the biggest mistake of her life. But the universe was silent. There were no gentle voices whispering in her head, telling her not to say anything. The decision was hers to make. And for better or worse, she made it.

"About whether or not to tell you that . . . I *was* the woman who bought the spinning wheel from Mrs. Barrett."

# Eighteen

"I can't believe it." Cole walked over to the couch and sat down. "After all this time. I've spent so many years looking for this thing that—" He gazed up at her in wonder. "I can't believe the search is finally over."

Kate didn't move. She just stood there and watched him. "Why didn't you tell me about the spinning wheel before, Cole?"

"Because I didn't want you to think I was crazy."

"You—crazy? You're one of the sanest people I know."

"Oh yeah? How many grown men have come up to you and asked you to believe in a fairy tale?" he said ruefully.

She smiled. "Okay, you've got me there. But seriously, why didn't you want to tell me?"

"I told you. Until Friday night, I had no way of knowing whether you knew what the wheel was capable of. And if you didn't, and I'd told you, what were you likely to think?"

"That you had a very vivid imagination?"

A faint light twinkled in the depths of his eyes. "Something like that. I also didn't want to alarm you if I didn't have to. Because I meant what I said about the risks, Kate. Davenport's looking for the spinning wheel and you're not safe as long as you have it."

"All right. I understand that there's a risk involved," she

said slowly. "But you still haven't answered my question. What do you intend to do with the wheel once you have it?"

"I'd like to take it to London. There are people there who'll want to examine it, date it, that sort of thing. Then, depending on the results of their findings, it might end up in a museum."

"Or?"

He glanced at her sharply. "What makes you think there's an *or*?"

"There always is when people have a choice."

"I'm not really sure you want to know."

Kate walked over to the couch and sat down beside him. "Cole, you kept a secret from me, now I'm keeping one from you. I *need* to know what the *or* is. If you won't tell me, I'll do everything I can to stop you from getting the wheel."

He was startled by the look of grim determination on her face. "You're not kidding about this, are you?"

"No, I'm not."

Cole got up and slowly walked across to the fireplace. Resting one foot on the hearth, he put both hands on the stone mantle and stood with his back to her. "Depending on what my associates find, the Lockton spinning wheel may end up in a museum."

"Or?"

"Or it may very well be destroyed."

Kate stared at him in open-mouthed disbelief. "Destroyed! Are you serious? This is . . . a piece of history, and an incredible piece at that. You've spent years searching for this. And now you're just going to let somebody else destroy it?"

"It doesn't always matter what *I* want, Kate. But it's possible that the spinning wheel is dangerous. And sometimes, when something's too powerful, it has to be neutralized."

"Oh great. Now you sound like you're talking about a monster out of a B-grade sci-fi movie."

He turned around to face her. "All right then. How about defused? Deactivated. Made safe for human consumption."

Kate sprang to her feet. "Cole, you said yourself that historians know very little about the spinning wheel. So who's to say that it's evil?"

"And who's to say it's not? Kate, this thing has . . . unnatural powers. It can physically *alter* a person's appearance and abilities. I don't know about you, but I find that a rather intimidating concept."

"But from what I understand, the changes are always for the good."

"So far, but who's to say that the power doesn't have a dark side too?" Cole asked. "Do you think a man like Jeremy Davenport would bother with it if it could only be used for the good of mankind?"

"How do you know what his plans for it are?"

"I can guess." Cole's voice was harsh. "I know the nature of the beast."

"Yes, but *I* know something about the spinning wheel that no one else does!" Kate said passionately.

"Then tell me!"

"I can't!"

"Why not?"

"Because . . . I made a promise to someone that I wouldn't."

She saw the surprise—and the alarm—in his eyes. "You *told* someone else about this? Do you have any idea what kind of risk you took?"

"It's not like that—"

"The more people who know about this, the greater the chances of something leaking out to the wrong people."

"Cole, I said it's not like that. I can't explain it any better right now. You'll just have to trust me."

Kate saw the tensing of his jaw and knew that he was frustrated. There were a hundred questions he wanted to ask—and none that he'd get an answer for. "Can I at least see the spinning wheel?" he asked finally.

"Yes. But I'll have to take you to it."

"It's not here?" he asked, shocked.

"No. I didn't feel it was safe."

"Kate, I don't understand. If you didn't know about Davenport, what were you afraid of?"

"I told you." Kate slowly lifted her eyes to his. "You."

• • •

As it turned out, neither her brother nor her sister-in-law was at home, a fact for which Kate could only be thankful. She was nervous enough about what she had to do. She didn't need an audience looking on. She opened her wallet and took out Matt's house key.

"Does your brother have a key to your place as well?" Cole asked.

"Yes. We thought it was a good idea that we be able to get into each other's houses. You never know when it might come in handy."

"Like now."

"Yeah." Kate opened the door and walked in. "Like now."

Cole followed her into the kitchen and glanced around. "Nice."

"Meg's doing," Kate told him briefly as she locked the door behind them. "If it was up to my brother, you wouldn't be able to move for dirty dishes. Come on, the spinning wheel's downstairs."

Breathless with anticipation, Cole followed Kate down to the basement. It was hard to believe that in a few minutes, he would actually come face-to-face with something he'd spent the last nine years of his life looking for. It was like the culmination of a dream.

"Matt told me he put it in the cupboard behind the furnace," Kate said as they moved past shelves stocked with Megan's homemade preserves. "He figured it would be out of everybody's way there."

Cole didn't say anything. The sense of expectation was too great. He watched Kate open the cupboard door and carefully extract the spinning wheel from its hiding place. Then, as she flicked on the overhead light and stepped back, he finally found himself looking at the legendary Lockton spinning wheel.

For a moment, Cole was too overcome with emotion to say anything. He felt an incredible sense of awe at being this close to something that had fascinated him for years. His heart began to pound as he reached out his hand and ran his fingers lightly over the wheel. He touched the spindle assembly and the distaff, his eyes absorbing every line, every minute detail of the spinning wheel's construction.

"I've touched history before," he said reverently, "but never anything like this. To quote a phrase, this is the stuff of which dreams are made."

He bent down to examine the spinning wheel more closely. It looked for all the world like any other spinning wheel he'd ever seen. The construction was the same; the three legs, the cross bar, the treadle assembly. But he noticed that the wood felt unusually smooth and warm to the touch. "What happens when *you* touch it?" he asked.

"Nothing. It has to be in motion before the show starts," Kate said, forcing a smile. "I pull out the dowel there, and give it a spin."

"And?"

"And I start to . . . feel things. I get a kind of . . . tingling sensation in my fingertips and arms. It's almost as though something's flowing out of the wheel into me. It's hard to describe, especially since that's generally when I lose consciousness. Oh, and there's a smell—"

"A smell?"

"Mmm. Like I'm standing in the middle of a mountain forest, breathing pure, clean air. Other times, it's more like perfume. Something sweet and exotic."

Cole gazed at her in fascination. "What happens next?"

"It varies," Kate said carefully. "But that's when I usually start seeing colors and shapes."

"Shapes?"

"Yes. The images that make their way into my designs." Kate stroked her fingers lightly over the wheel. "That's how I created Eleya's Dream. I saw the images and the colors in my mind, and then I just . . . drew it."

"You drew a complicated design like that in your *sleep*?"

Kate laughed softly. "I know it sounds strange. And I normally draw my designs with my eyes closed, but I've never done it in my sleep before. And being asleep, or in some kind of trance, was the only explanation I could come up with. I remembered walking toward the spinning wheel—and then seven hours later when I woke up, the design was finished. It was sitting on my drafting table complete to the last detail. And I had absolutely no recollection of having drawn it. That's happened to me three times now."

"So that part of the legend is true," Cole said more to himself than to her. "It takes the existing talents of the owner and enhances them. But *how* does it do that? What kind of . . . power allows it to get inside a person's mind? I've never heard of a telepathic link between a person and an inanimate object before—at least not one that originates with the inanimate object."

Biting her lip, Kate turned away. She wasn't about to tell him that the telepathic link wasn't with the spinning wheel, but with Eleya. Until she knew what Cole's plans for the wheel were, she wasn't breathing a word. "Do you think it might have anything to do with the fact that it once belonged to a witch?" she asked instead.

Cole considered it. "It's possible. That would certainly account for its magical powers."

"So you believe in witchcraft?"

A glint of amusement appeared in his eyes. "I don't *disbelieve* it. I've seen too many things in my life to dismiss anything out of hand. And there *were* documented accounts of an old woman who lived in a town called Lockton and who professed to be a witch. Of course, most English villages had their resident witch, who in the majority of cases turned out to be an eccentric old woman with knowledge of plants and herbs. It's a billion-dollar industry today, but back then it wasn't the prescribed way of doing things."

"So you think it's possible that the Lockton witch really *was* a witch."

Cole lifted his broad shoulders in a shrug. "It's possible. Legend has it that the yarn she spun was finer than any to be had in the land. But I guess we'll never know." He moved in closer to examine the intricate carvings on the legs. There were flowers and animals, birds and insects, even signs depicting the various constellations. They had all been carved by hand, and no two patterns were the same. "Kate, have you ever experienced any feelings of . . . danger when you're in one of your . . . trances? Have you ever felt threatened in any way?"

"Never," Kate said emphatically. "The feelings I have are ones of peace and harmony. Of happiness."

Cole sat back on his heels and rested his forearms on his knees. "This is so unbelievable. I wish I could make you understand what this means to me." He touched the wheel again, and it was almost as though he were touching a lover. "The sense of wonder that surrounds it. The mystery and the magic. This spinning wheel has survived for five, maybe six hundred years. It's seen wars and battles, probably been moved a thousand times. And yet, in all that time, it's hardly suffered any damage. Look at it. It's almost as though something's been watching over it. Protecting it." Cole slowly got to his feet. "I hope you don't mind, but I'd like to call Professor Morris. An even bigger part of his life has gone into the search for this and I know he'll be anxious to hear that I've found it. Without some of his research, I doubt we'd be looking at it now."

"I don't mind at all. But Cole," Kate put her hand on his arm, "please, I hate to sound like a broken record, but you still haven't told me where we go from here. What are you going to do?"

"To be perfectly honest, I don't know," Cole admitted. "I do know that you and I need to talk about it some more. I'm not going to pretend this isn't one of the biggest finds of the century, but you have a personal stake in it too. So I promise I won't do anything until I've discussed it with you." He held out his hand. "Deal?"

Kate slid her hand into his. "Deal."

It wasn't exactly what she'd wanted to hear, but it was good enough for now.

Cole placed the call to Professor Morris from his hotel room that very afternoon.

"But that's splendid, my friend, splendid!" the professor's voice rang out. "When can we expect to receive it in London?"

"I'm not sure. Kate isn't willing to let it go anywhere at the moment."

"Kate?" Cole could hear the surprise in the professor's

voice. "You mean the young woman who bought it?"

"Yes. She was willing to show it to me, but not to let me take it away."

"Is she aware of the wheel's special powers?"

"Yes, but I don't think that's the problem. I get the feeling there's something she's not telling me. Something very important."

"Cole, dear boy, what could be more important than bringing a discovery like this to the attention of the world?"

"That's what I have to find out, Professor, and it's part of the reason for my call. Is it possible that we might have missed something?" Cole asked slowly. "Some small piece of research that might refer to some other capability the spinning wheel has?"

"Well, I can double check a few of my sources, of course," Professor Morris said slowly. "But I don't know that I'm likely to turn up anything new. We've already gone through everything with a fine tooth comb."

"I know, but it's worth a try. I gave Kate my word that I wouldn't do anything without talking to her first."

There was a long silence at the other end of the phone. "I hope you're not making a mistake here, Cole. You know that Davenport will be close."

*Too close,* judging by what Kate had told him. "That's why I'm going to do everything I can to keep her safe," Cole assured him. "I've told her to be on the lookout for *any* kind of suspicious characters."

"That's all well and good, but being on the lookout didn't help Davenport's victims in the past."

Cole didn't need reminding of that either. "Trust me, Professor, I don't intend to let Davenport get anywhere near her."

"Good. Because you know that he can only take the wheel from her in one of two ways. The first is by crossing her palm with silver in a fair and equitable sale. The second—"

"Yes, I know what the second is," Cole interrupted, his face darkening. The second didn't even bear thinking about.

• • •

Megan gently picked Christian up out of his bed and held him close. Dear Lord, he was so small. He seemed to be eating well, but it obviously wasn't enough to keep the meat on his bones.

"I'm tired, Mommy."

"I know, sweetheart." Megan kissed his forehead and brushed the hair back from his face. He smelled like baby oil and lollipops. "Do you feel like chicken for dinner?"

Christian shook his head. "Spisgetti."

Megan smiled. Christian loved his spaghetti. Probably because he had more fun playing with it than he did eating it. "All right, spisgetti it is. Let's go downstairs and get a bottle of sauce."

Megan kept all her preserves in the basement. She would have preferred to have them upstairs but there simply wasn't room, so Matt had built her shelves in the room next to the furnace. The problem was, Megan had already filled every one of them with canned fruits and vegetables, and as a result had been forced to store her last batch of tomato sauce in the furnace room—a room she usually avoided at all costs. That's where the biggest spiders always seemed to be, and she hated spiders with a passion. The day Matt had moved her washer and dryer upstairs had been a banner day in her life. Unfortunately, Matt wasn't home right now, and she needed a jar of tomato sauce.

It was as she was carefully reaching for one of the bottles close to the cupboard behind the furnace, that she noticed the door to the cupboard was open. Funny. She was sure it had been closed the last time she'd been down here, although that had been a while ago. She set Christian down and went to close the door, and was surprised when she couldn't. "Matthew Pedigrew, what have you stashed away in here now?" she murmured. Glancing around for any marauding six-legged creatures, Megan gingerly opened the door. She was astonished to see not a bulky power tool tucked away inside, but a lovely little spinning wheel. "Well, for heavens sake, what's that doing here?"

"What's that, Mommy?"

"Hmm? Oh, it's a spinning wheel, Christian. It's what

women used to use to spin wool into yarn to make their clothes."

"It's nice." Christian toddled over to it and put his hand on the wheel. "Pretty."

"Yes, it is," Megan said, admiring the delicate carving on the legs. She'd never seen anything like that before. "My great grandmother used to have one of these. And when I was a little girl, I'd sit for hours and watch her spin the soft fluffy wool into yarn."

Suddenly, Meg wondered if she had stumbled upon a secret. She'd once told Matt that she'd wanted a spinning wheel. Was it possible that he'd picked one up at one of the local auctions and hid it here, intending it as a surprise for her? After all, their wedding anniversary was coming up soon.

"Mommy, can I have the . . . spinging wheel in my room?" Christian asked.

"No, sweetheart. I think Daddy bought this as a surprise for Mommy so we mustn't tell him we know it's here. It will be our little secret." Megan carefully pushed the spinning wheel back into the cupboard. "But if you're a good boy, I'll bring it up to your room during the day so that you can play with it. Okay?"

Christian's pale little face lit up. " 'Kay."

"That's my boy." Megan closed the cupboard door and quickly took a bottle of sauce from the floor, her eyes peeled for spiders. Then, breathing a sigh of relief that she hadn't seen any, she took Christian's hand in hers and slowly walked back upstairs, thinking what a very lucky young woman she was.

Not surprisingly, Kate felt much better for having told Cole about the spinning wheel. It was almost as though a weight had been lifted from her shoulders. She only hoped she hadn't made a terrible mistake. She trusted Cole, and she believed him when he said that he wouldn't do anything without talking to her first. But she also knew that he was concerned about her safety. She had a feeling that if push came to shove, he would do what was best for her, rather than for the spinning wheel.

And that's what she had to be careful of. She couldn't afford to let Cole make arbitrary decisions regarding the wheel. She'd just have to hope that this Jeremy Davenport kept his distance until she'd figured out what to do.

When the phone rang, Kate answered it in a bright and cheerful manner. All that changed, however, when she heard the voice on the other end. She listened in silence for a few minutes, her spirits sinking with every word.

In the end, she just nodded. "Okay, Matt, I'll be right over."

The argument was well under way by the time Kate got there. Her father was standing rigidly beside the sink, her brother was leaning against the fridge with his arms folded across his chest, and her sister-in-law was sitting quietly at the table. Megan's eyes were dry but judging by the red, swollen lids, they hadn't been that way long.

"Oh, wonderful," Roderick snapped when Kate walked in. "Don't tell me you had to call in reinforcements, Matt?"

"I won't let you take Christian away, Dad," Matt said stubbornly. "You don't have the right."

"And if you had any sense, you'd realize that it's the smartest thing you could do. The boy needs help and he's not getting it here."

Feeling it was time to step into the role of peacemaker, Kate said, "I understand what you're saying, Dad, but Matt and Megan have a right to make their own decisions about Christian—"

"Not when it affects the boy's life!" her father interrupted. "Damn it, why can't any of you see that? Have you all become desensitized living out here in the sticks?"

"Dad, it's really not—"

"Kate, it's okay," Matt cut in abruptly. "Look, Dad, I took you to see Dr. Sheffield like you asked. And you heard what the results of Christian's tests were. They tested his blood, his urine and anything else that could be tested, and nothing showed up. The fact is, they don't know what they're fighting!"

"Then take him to somebody who does!" Roderick cried. "Damn it, Matt, how many times do I have to tell you?"

"And how many times do I have to tell you that I don't need you interfering in our lives! I'm sick of it, Dad. Dr. Sheffield's doing everything he can for Christian and until *he* tells me to, I'm not sending our son anywhere. I won't have that poor kid scared out of his mind. Because I know what they do, Dad," Matt said angrily. "They'll hook him up to machines, and then poke and prod at him. They'll take blood from him six times a day and put him to sleep with pills. Then they'll wake him up and give him more pills. Well, I'm not going to let that happen. Until I hear that it's *necessary* to send Christian to see a specialist in New York, he's staying here. I have complete faith in Dr. Sheffield's ability."

"Yes, just like I had complete faith in the doctor that was looking after your mother—and I wish to God I'd asked for a second opinion before it was too late for her!"

Kate heard her brother's sharp intake of breath, followed by a startled gasp from Megan. It was the first time they'd heard Roderick talk about the doctor who'd looked after Clare. And it was the first time they'd heard him admit that something went wrong.

A tense silence enveloped the room. Kate tried to think of something to say, but it was Megan who stepped into the breach. "Matt, maybe we . . . should let your father take Christian to New York. It can't hurt to have another doctor look at him."

Matt turned anguished eyes toward Kate, and she could see the pain in their depths. "What do you think, Kate?"

"I think it's a good idea," Kate said as gently as she could. "After all, we owe it to Christian to do everything we can for him. Maybe the doctors in the city will be able to turn up something new. And if Dad's willing to cover the costs—"

"Damn it, money's not the issue here," her father said angrily.

"If Dad's willing to cover the costs," Kate repeated, "let him. We can work on paying him back later. Right now, we have to get Christian better."

Kate watched Matt sink down into a chair and drop his head into his hands. It was like watching somebody let the air out of a big, happy-face balloon. It was all she could do not to run and put her arms around him the way she'd done when they were kids.

"Make the arrangements," Matt said finally. "Christian can go to New York with you, Dad." He looked up at his father and there were tears in his eyes. "I won't have anybody say that I didn't do everything I could for my boy."

By the time Kate got home, she was utterly exhausted. The battle that had raged between Matt and her father, and the bitterness that had followed, had left her emotionally spent and physically drained. She didn't like scenes at the best of times, and she hated scenes that involved her own family.

It was too early for dinner, but Kate wasn't hungry. She stripped off her clothes, ran a brush over her teeth and fell into bed. She needed sleep. She needed to escape for a while. She needed to dream . . .

*She was standing in a large room. There were windows all around her and she was surrounded by glass. The room seemed familiar, yet she couldn't place it. She just kept looking around, trying to figure out where she was.*

*The spinning wheel was there at the other side of the room. A man was standing beside it. Faceless in black, he stood between Kate and the spinning wheel.*

*There was something familiar about the man, but Kate couldn't say what it was. It was almost as though she knew him, but not why he was here. Then she glanced down and saw the gun in his hand. A gun that was pointed at her.*

*The man reached his other hand toward the spinning wheel. He wrapped his fingers around the slender rods of the distaff and slowly began to squeeze. Then, he began to laugh.*

Don't let him break the spindle, Kate, *a silvery voice cried out to her.* He mustn't be the one to break the spindle . . .

*Kate started toward him. She tried to run—but it was like dragging herself through waist-deep water. Her legs felt like lead and every step was an effort. She could barely lift her feet off the ground. And the man just kept on laughing. His fingers were closing, squeezing. She could hear wood splintering.*

*Suddenly, Kate heard an explosion. She felt something slam into her body, knocking her backwards. Her chest was on fire. She looked down and saw blood. Blood . . . on her hands . . . on her clothes . . . on the floor.*

*She heard a man shout. A woman screamed, but it meant nothing because she was falling, sinking down into the murky darkness.*

*But the man with the gun wasn't finished with her yet. He was coming closer. Kate's eyes were closed but she could feel his presence. She could sense the evil.*

*The danger was here. Just like Eleya said. It had come in a familiar form and she had not recognized it. She slowly opened her eyes and looked up.*

Just as something came down hard on her temple and sent her plummeting back to unconsciousness.

# Nineteen

Someone was banging on the door.

Kate went to sit up, and then groaned in pain. Oh, God, her head hurt. No, it didn't just hurt, it throbbed. She slowly reached a hand to her temple and gingerly touched the spot where the pain was centered. She felt a hard lump, and something . . . sticky. She brought her hand back down—and saw blood.

Kate blanched. *The dream.* The one in which she'd been shot. The dream where she'd been bleeding.

But this wasn't a dream. She wasn't imagining the blood on her fingers. This was real.

Someone banged on the door again.

Kate came fully awake as fear obliterated the last vestiges of sleep. She glanced toward her bedroom door and shuddered. Someone had been here last night. Someone had broken in and knocked her unconscious.

*You have to get to the front door. You have to get help.*

Pushing back the covers, Kate swung her feet over the side of the bed. She slowly got to her feet—and almost collapsed as a wave of dizziness broke inside her head. She tasted the bitterness of bile in her throat and thought she was going to be sick. Thankfully, the moment passed and when she felt strong enough to take a step, she started toward the door.

She got as far as the kitchen. The room was spinning so badly she had to stop and lean against the wall. She was having trouble breathing. The lightheaded feeling was coming back. If she didn't get help fast, she was going to pass out.

"Who is—" Her voice cracked. "Who is it?"

"It's me, Kate. Cole."

Cole. Oh, thank God! Kate staggered to the door and opened it with hands that trembled. "Cole . . ."

He took one look at her and his face went white. "*Jesus*, Kate. What happened?" He caught her as she fell forward into his arms. "Kate!"

Megan sat at the side of her little boy's bed and hastily brushed away her tears. He'd had another bad night. One of the worst so far. He'd started crying around three o'clock, and hadn't gone back to sleep until dawn. But he'd woken up again at seven, then at eight, until finally, about an hour ago, he'd gone back down. His face was flushed and Megan didn't like the way he was breathing. It was probably just as well that he was going to New York with Matt's father tomorrow.

Matt had gotten up in the night too, of course. He'd taken turns carrying Christian around the bedroom until Megan had convinced him to go back to bed. Matthew needed his sleep. His company had just been given the contract for the new library extension and while they'd both been delighted, they'd known what it would mean. Matt would have to be on site to supervise every stage of the construction.

The long hours left him bone tired, but he never complained. He came home and had dinner, helped Megan with the dishes, and then went upstairs and played with Christian. But she knew it was taking its toll.

That's why last night when he'd volunteered to stay up with Christian, Megan had said no. She didn't need two sick men on her hands. Besides, looking after Christian wasn't a chore. This bright, beautiful boy meant everything to her. He and Matt were her life, and there was nothing she wouldn't do for them.

Now as she watched, Christian's eyes, big and blue like his daddy's, and fringed with the longest, silkiest lashes Megan had ever seen, slowly drifted open.

"Hi there, sweetheart," she whispered. "How's my little man feeling?"

The big eyes looked up at her and the mouth trembled. "My head hurts, Mommy," he whispered.

Megan sighed. It wasn't the first time Christian had complained about pains in his head. She touched her slender fingers to his cheek. His skin felt warm, but not feverish. The same as always. "Do you want Mommy to read you a story?"

At his weary nod, Megan got up and went to the bookcase. "What would you like to hear?"

"Something from . . . the red book," he told her in a quiet voice.

The red book contained most of Christian's favorite fairy tales. He'd heard all of them a hundred times but never seemed to tire of hearing them again. And Megan never got tired of reading them. "How about Peter and the Wolf?" she asked, flipping through the pages.

Christian glanced down at the book, and suddenly pointed. "Look. Spinging wheel."

Megan stopped. Sure enough, there was a spinning wheel. The story was "Rumpelstiltskin" and the page Christian was pointing to showed the ugly little man standing beside the queen's spinning wheel, with a pile of straw on one side of him, and a sparkling mound of gold on the other.

"Spinging wheel," Christian repeated.

"Yes, just like the one downstairs. You like the spinning wheel, don't you, sweetheart?"

Christian nodded, but his eyes never left the page.

"Well, if you're a good boy, I'll bring it up after Daddy goes to work and you can play with it, okay?"

Christian nodded again, then snuggled back down under the covers. Megan kissed him on the forehead and picked up the book. "Once upon a time, there was a miller who was poor, but who had a beautiful daughter. Now it happened that he got into a conversation with the king and said to him,

"I have a daughter who knows the art of turning straw into gold . . ."

Sometime later, Kate woke up. She felt something cool and soft against her temple and looked up to see Cole watching her, his eyes dark with concern. She managed a weak smile. "Will I live, Doctor?"

"Looks that way." One corner of his mouth lifted. "But you might like to change your hairstyle for the next week or so. That bump's the size of a goose egg already." His smile faded as his voice grew serious. "Can you tell me what happened, sweetheart?"

Sweetheart. Had he really called her sweetheart?

"Someone was . . . in my room last night." Kate hardly recognized the husky voice as her own. "I don't know what time it was. I was having this . . . terrible dream. And when I opened my eyes, I saw something coming at me. That's all I remember."

Cole kept a gentle pressure on the cloth, but Kate saw the muscles tense in his neck. "It had to be Davenport. He's obviously discovered our secret."

Kate closed her eyes and wished that the room would stop spinning. "How?"

"I wish I knew. But the hows don't matter anymore, Kate. I have to get the spinning wheel out of here as soon as possible."

Kate shook her head. "I can't let it go, Cole. Not yet."

"It's not up for discussion. I'm not going to risk your life over a spinning wheel."

"But it's not just any spinning wheel."

"I don't give a damn. Once Davenport knows you don't have it, he'll leave you alone."

"But you don't understand." Kate ran her tongue over lips that felt dry and cracked. "I can't let you take it away until I've done . . . what needs to be done."

"You're talking in riddles, sweetheart. Nothing needs to be done."

"Yes, it does. You don't know about . . . her."

"Her?"

To her dismay, Kate felt tears spring to her eyes. "If you take the spinning wheel away, she'll be trapped forever."

Cole glanced at her in bewilderment. "Who'll be trapped? What are you talking about, Kate?"

"Eleya! The source of power behind the wheel. It's always been Eleya."

Cole's hand froze above her temple. "You're not referring to Princess Eleya from the legend, are you?"

"Yes. She was supposed to marry Prince Gareth but the evil one, Alizor, murdered him in his sleep. And when Eleya wouldn't agree to marry him, Alizor murdered her too. But he condemned her spirit to live in the wheel. She's been there for centuries. And I have to find a way to set her free."

Cole pressed the cloth to her forehead again. It was the wildest story he'd ever heard—and he'd heard a few. "Kate, you don't know what you're saying. The person you're talking about—if she ever existed at all—died over five hundred years ago."

"I know, but you have to believe me, Cole," Kate said desperately. "This is what I didn't tell you before. This is the secret I was keeping. The reason I can't let you have the spinning wheel is because I have to save Eleya. I'm the only one who can do it."

"Kate, this is crazy. There isn't any spirit living in the wheel. You've taken a hard knock to the head. Your mind's playing tricks on you. Either that, or you've been dreaming."

"Cole, please! I'm not dreaming and I'm not making this up." Kate fixed her eyes on his face and begged him to understand. "There *is* a soul trapped within that spinning wheel. She's there. I've seen her. She speaks to me during the trances. She reached out to me that very first day in Mrs. Barrett's store. She told me that . . . *I'm* the one she's been waiting for." Kate reached for his hand and held it onto it tightly. "You have to believe me, Cole, I'm not making this up. I'm the only one who can set Eleya free. I am . . . the Chosen One!"

It was a long time before Cole was fully able to grasp what Kate was telling him—and even longer before he could bring himself to believe it. An entity trapped within the wooden framework of the spinning wheel?

It was almost too incredible to be believed. Cole had heard of houses or buildings being haunted by the spirit of someone who had died there, but he'd never heard of a soul *attaching* itself to a piece of furniture. Or of someone *putting* it there.

The problem was, as bizarre as it sounded, it did make a certain amount of sense. It explained why the spinning wheel had survived through the centuries. If what Kate had told him was true, a spirit had protected it. The spirit of Eleya: the ethereal creature for whom Kate had named her first new work. A woman of indescribable loveliness and indomitable spirit, but one whose life had been tragically cut short by an evil man whose desire for her had destroyed everything she'd held dear.

And now, this same spirit had somehow reached out to Kate and told her that their lives were woven together in a way that even Kate didn't fully understand.

It was extraordinary. Inconceivable. Unimaginable. And if Cole had been anybody else, he wouldn't have believed a word of it. But because of who he was and what he had seen, he opened his mind to embrace the concept. After all, if he couldn't deny the powers of the wheel, how could he deny the source behind them?

Cole leaned against the window in Kate's bedroom and stared out at the field. So where did he go from here? Kate certainly hadn't solved his problems by telling him about Eleya. He understood her reasons for not wanting to let the spinning wheel go, but that didn't lessen the danger to her life. Because somehow or other, Davenport had found out that Kate had the spinning wheel. Cole had no idea how, but it was the only logical explanation for the two break-ins.

Unfortunately, as a result of last night's night attack, Davenport now knew that the spinning wheel wasn't in Kate's house. Which meant that he was going to have to step up his efforts to find it and then to get her *and* the wheel together. And Cole didn't like that one little bit. Davenport was like a snake. He moved in the darkness and struck when you least expected.

Restless now, Cole pushed himself away from the window. He walked back toward the bed and stared down at Kate's sleeping form, and felt a rush of tenderness so strong that it all but turned his insides out. She was so beautiful. Even without the benefit of the spinning wheel, Kate Pedigrew was a beautiful woman, because hers was a beauty that came from within. It went far beyond the superficiality of physical appearance. She was a sweet and compassionate woman who cared about her friends, and about the people who touched her life. She was a loving sister and a devoted aunt. And she was a daughter who grieved for the loss of affection between herself and her father.

Cole knew it was true whether Kate wanted to admit it or not. She ached to reach out to him. She needed that connection. She needed what she'd lost when her mother had died.

He gently sat down on the edge of the bed and watched her sleep. Her hair fell loose upon pillow, reminding him of rich maple syrup poured over crisp white snow. His gaze touched briefly on the softness of her mouth, on the lush sweep of lashes across her cheeks—and he knew that he was in love with her. He'd seen it coming for a long time. This wasn't some passing fancy. It had awakened a part of him he hadn't even known existed. He wanted to sweep Kate up in his arms and to keep her safe. He wanted to see the light dancing in those sapphire eyes and to watch her laugh, and make her happy.

And he wanted to shake Roderick Pedigrew until his teeth rattled. Why couldn't he see what a treasure his daughter was? Didn't he realize how much he was hurting her? All she wanted was to hear him say that he loved her and that he was proud of what she had accomplished in her life. Surely that was little enough to ask?

"Cole?"

Kate's voice was a sleepy whisper—and a maddeningly sexy one at that. Cole smiled as he watched the slow rise of dark, silken lashes, and then caught his breath at the soft, unguarded look in her eyes. It was there for a heartbeat and then gone; replaced by an awareness of where they were, and who they were supposed to be. But just for a moment, Cole had seen something in her eyes. Something that made him hope.

"Hello, sleeping beauty," he said gently. "Feeling better?"

Kate moved her legs under the blankets. "I think so. My head still hurts but not as much as it did." She glanced at the clock and then back at him. "You didn't have to stay."

"I know." Cole tenderly brushed a stray piece of hair back from her forehead. "But I wanted to. I had a lot of thinking to do."

Kate met his eyes, and misunderstanding, nodded. "What are we going to do about the spinning wheel?"

Cole smiled again, but let it go. "Well, one of the first things I'm going to do is get in touch with Professor Morris. He knows more about the wheel than I do and it's possible he may know something about the . . . spiritual force. He's never mentioned it before but that doesn't mean he doesn't know about it."

Kate bit her lip. "What about Davenport?"

"All I can do is alert the police and tell them you've had two break-ins and one with aggravated assault. They'll have to take it from there. I can't tell them what Davenport looks like and I'm sure as hell not about to tell them what he's looking for."

In spite of her injury, Kate grinned. "No. You might be an expert in your field, Beresford, but I think the moment the words 'enchanted spinning wheel' left your mouth, your credibility would be shot for good."

"Which is why we have to keep this to ourselves. And why I'm not letting you out of my sight."

"Me or the spinning wheel?"

He took her hand and turning it over, pressed a tender kiss into her palm. "The spinning wheel's a legend, sweetheart. You're the real thing. And losing you would be a thousand times worse than losing it."

He leaned forward and kissed her on the lips then, and it wasn't tentative or gentle. It was a kiss of fierce possession that left Kate as dizzy as the knock on her head—only much more pleasurably so.

"I . . . have to get the spinning wheel out of Matt's house,

Cole," she said when she was finally able to catch her breath. "Davenport knows that it isn't here, and if he's as desperate as you say, he'll start looking around. And I won't put the safety of my family at risk."

Cole was inclined to agree. "It's also better that we have it somewhere we can both keep an eye on it. In the meantime, I'm going back to the inn and pack up a few things. I'm going to move in here until this is all over."

She couldn't have heard that right. "Did you say . . . move in?"

"Yes. I can sleep on the couch in the living room. But I'll feel better knowing that you're not alone. Right now I have to get in touch with Professor Morris," he said, getting to his feet. "We have to do what has to be done as quickly as possible."

He'd said it in a brisk, almost businesslike manner, but that didn't stop Kate's heart from leaping clear into her mouth. Cole was going to be staying with her? Day *and* night?

She wondered what Madeleine would have to say about that!

Luckily, Professor Morris was in his room.

"Are you sitting down, Professor?" Cole asked.

There was a short silence before Morris said, "Is the news that startling?"

"You tell me." In a nutshell, Cole relayed the details of what Kate had told him about Eleya—and not surprisingly, his story was greeted by an even longer silence.

"So, at long last, we find out what's really at the heart of the legend," Professor Morris said, seeming to find it easier to accept than Cole had. "Do you know what this means, Cole?"

"It means a lot of things, not the least of which is that Kate's life is more at risk than ever," Cole said bluntly. "She won't part with the spinning wheel until she finds out how to free Eleya. Do you know *anything* about that part of the legend, Professor?"

"I wish I did, but I haven't a clue. This is totally out of

my area of expertise. But I know of someone who might be able to help."

"We have to be extremely careful," Cole said urgently. "If word of this got out—"

"You needn't have any concerns about the person I want to contact talking to anyone. She's as anxious to avoid publicity as you are. But what we're dealing with here goes far beyond the realm of the normal, which means we have to go beyond it too."

Cole frowned. "I'm not sure I follow."

"You will. Where can I get in touch with you?"

"On my cell phone. I'm going to be on the move over the next little while."

"Fine. Tell Miss Pedigrew to be on her guard at all times, Cole. Under no circumstances must Davenport be allowed to get his hands on her and the spinning wheel together."

Cole's brow darkened and his voice was harsh. "You don't have to tell me twice."

Megan opened the cupboard door and carefully took out the spinning wheel. She could hardly wait to see the look on Christian's face when she took it into his room. She'd had to wait for Matt to go to work, but now that he'd left, she felt comfortable about taking it upstairs. She didn't want to spoil her husband's surprise, but putting the spinning wheel in Christian's room was like taking something out of his favorite story book and putting it right there beside him. She just hoped she'd be able to get it upstairs all right.

Fortunately, the spinning wheel was lighter than she'd expected and she had no trouble carrying it up the basement stairs. She bumped it once against the edge of the kitchen door, but not very hard. Certainly not enough to do any damage. She carried it up the second flight of stairs to Christian's bedroom, and didn't even notice the small piece of wood that dropped off and rolled under the refrigerator. . . .

Cole was in his car on his way back to Kate's when Morris called. Unfortunately, what the professor had to say wasn't exactly what Cole had been hoping to hear.

"I have to take Kate to *New York*?" he echoed in dismay. "Why? What's in New York?"

"Sadina."

"Who the hell is Sadina?"

"She's a psychic I've been in touch with about the spinning wheel."

"A psychic?" Cole put his foot on the brake and quickly pulled over to the side of the road. "You want me to go to New York to see a *psychic*?"

"Sadina's not just any psychic, Cole. She's as well traveled as you or I and she's made a study of old legends and folk tales. But her psychic powers have enabled her to find answers that no one else can."

"Professor, you know I have a pretty open mind when it comes to these things, but do you really believe that a psychic can help?"

"Yes, I do. Because when I called Sadina and told her about the Lockton spinning wheel, she didn't voice any kind of surprise. She told me that she could help but she flatly refused to speak to anyone about it over the phone."

"Why can't she come here?"

"Because she's close to eighty and hardly ever goes out of her apartment. I offered to cover all of her costs for getting to Montpelier but she said she's not up to the trip."

"So if I want answers, I'm going to have to go to New York."

"I'm afraid so. But I urge you to go, Cole. Sadina is no ordinary psychic. You have my word on that."

Cole thought about it, and then nodded. "All right. If that's the only way, I'll talk to Kate. I'm on my way there now."

"Good. Sadina's waiting for your call. Here's the number."

Cole pulled out his pen and wrote it down. "I don't know how Kate's going to take this," he said, tucking the piece of paper into his breast pocket.

"She really doesn't have a choice. She's the one who's looking for answers, Cole," came the professor's answer. "And I firmly believe that Sadina has them."

• • •

"A *psychic*?" Kate stared at Cole in bewilderment. "*That's* what Professor Morris came up with?"

Cole held up his hands. "I know it sounds weird, Kate, but he told me that this Sadina wasn't an ordinary psychic and that she . . . knew things. And he believes she has the answers we need."

"A psychic." Kate shook her head. "I never thought it would come to this. But then, given everything that's happened over the last few weeks, I suppose I shouldn't be surprised. Going to a psychic's far more routine than finding old spinning wheels that are inhabited by the spirits of long dead princesses."

"I thought you'd see it that way," Cole said dryly. "Besides, it will get us away from here for a couple of days. And we can take the spinning wheel with us. That way we don't have to worry about Davenport getting up to any mischief while we're gone."

"But what if he gets wind of what we're doing and follows us to New York? He may try to ambush us on the way. There are plenty of stretches of deserted highway between here and New York," Kate pointed out.

"I know. That's why a friend of mine is going to be following us in his own car."

"A friend?"

"Yes. The same one who's been parked outside your house for the last day and a half."

Kate gasped. "You've had somebody watching my house?"

"I wasn't taking any chances."

"But who—?"

"A friend of mine who happens to be an undercover cop. He owed me a favor, and I called it in."

Kate was stunned. "You were that worried about me?"

"I told you I wasn't taking any chances. Now, are you coming to New York with me or not?"

There was a certain gruffness to Cole's voice but Kate was learning how to read beyond it. She looked into his eyes—and at the heartrending tenderness of his gaze—and got the answer she needed. "When you put it like that," she said softly, "how can I refuse?"

Megan washed up the dinner dishes and put them in the cupboard. There weren't many to do. Matt had phoned a little while ago to say that he'd be late and to eat supper without him. Megan had, but she'd put his dinner on a plate in the oven anyway. She wanted it to be nice and hot when he got home. She glanced at the clock over the stove and sighed. Nearly nine. It was a long time since Matt had worked this late. Not since before Christian had started getting sick in fact.

She turned her head and smiled as she heard the whirring sound coming from the baby monitor—then she gasped. She'd forgotten to take the spinning wheel back downstairs! If Matt came home and found it in Christian's room, his wonderful surprise would be ruined.

Flinging the towel onto the counter, Megan raced up the stairs. Christian had been sleeping peacefully the last time she'd checked on him. She'd read him a story and once he'd gone to sleep, she had tiptoed out of the room. She was hoping he might have slept through the night, but if he was playing with the spinning wheel again, he was obviously awake and likely to stay that way.

Megan carefully opened the door. To her surprise, Christian wasn't awake. He lay quiet in the bed, his face turned away from her and his right arm stretched out so that his fingers were touching the spinning wheel. He couldn't have been asleep long. The wheel was still moving. Megan smiled and quietly walked in.

It took all of three seconds to see that something was wrong.

"Christian?" Megan flicked on the overhead light, and quickly rolled him onto his back. "Oh my God! *Christian*!"

The little boy's face was blue—and he wasn't breathing.

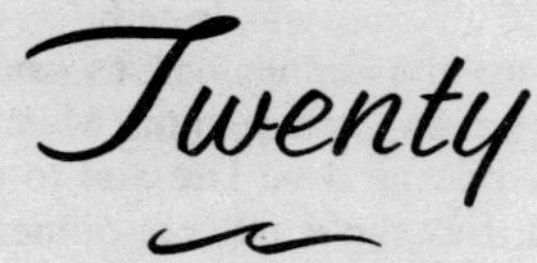

Cole pulled up beside the red van parked in Matt's driveway. "Do you want me to come inside?" he asked.

Kate shook her head. "Matt's truck isn't here, so I won't be long. I'll just pick up the spinning wheel and tell Megan we'll be gone for a couple of days. Funny. I wonder who owns the red—" She broke off as her sister-in-law came flying out the kitchen door, but it was the panicked look on her face that had Kate jumping out of the car. "Megan, what's wrong?"

"Oh, Kate, I'm sorry. I didn't mean to startle you, but when I saw a car coming up the driveway I thought it might be Matt."

"Why, what's happened? Whose car is this?"

"Dr. Sheffield's."

Icy fear twisted around Kate's heart. *Christian!*

Cole quickly got out of the car. "Kate, what's the matter?"

"It's Christian." Kate reached for her sister-in-law's arm. "Let's get inside. Megan, tell us what's happened."

As it turned out, there wasn't a lot to tell. "I went into Christian's room to see how he was," she began unsteadily, "and I thought he was sleeping. But when I got closer, I realized . . . he wasn't breathing. That's when I called Dr. Sheffield."

Kate felt her heart turn over in her breast. "What did he say?"

"He said that Christian was breathing, but in such a shallow way that it was barely visible. I guess I was so terrified when I thought he wasn't breathing at all that I didn't stop to check."

"Have you called Matt?"

Megan sank into the chair. "I couldn't. Of all the days for him to leave his pager home, it had to be today. But he called around eight-thirty, so he should be here any time. Oh, Kate, I was so scared. I didn't know what to do."

"You did the right thing." Kate took off her coat and set it over the back of the chair. "Can we go up and see Christian?"

"Yes, of course. The doctor's still with him."

Kate and Cole anxiously made their way upstairs. They could hear someone moving around in Christian's room but they didn't hear any voices. "Dr. Sheffield?" Kate said.

"Hmm? Oh, hello, Kate." The doctor took the stethoscope from his ears and put it back into his bag. "Come in, dear, it's all right."

Kate stepped into the room—and nearly fainted.

The spinning wheel was standing right beside Christian's bed.

"Dr. Sheffield, what's wrong with my nephew?" Kate asked when she was finally able to tear her eyes away from it. "Is it serious?"

"To be quite honest, I don't know what's wrong with him." The elderly man looked and sounded tired. "I've never seen anything like this in my life. I've called for an ambulance because I want Christian in the hospital for observation. He's sleeping peacefully right now. Too peacefully, I'm afraid."

Cole frowned. "Too peacefully?"

"Are you saying he's in a coma?" Kate whispered.

The doctor shook his head. "It's like a coma but the boy's eyelids keep flickering. And every now and then, his lips move, so it's obvious that he's dreaming and that his mind is still alert. I just can't wake him up."

Kate stared at the spinning wheel. She took a step closer to the bed and gasped.

The wooden dowel was gone.

Meanwhile, from the kitchen, they heard the sound of the side door opening, followed by muffled conversation and then anxious footsteps on the stairs. Seconds later, Matt burst into the room. "What's happened? How's my son?"

"It's all right, Matt," Dr. Sheffield assured him. "Christian's sleeping at the moment. I've called for an ambulance."

"But . . . what's wrong with him?"

"Why don't we all go back downstairs. Megan needs to hear this as well."

"You two go ahead," Kate said quickly. "Cole and I will be along shortly."

She waited until the two other men had disappeared and then turned to look at Cole. "The dowel's gone," she whispered.

Cole glanced down at the wheel. "Did you know the spinning wheel was up here?"

"I had no idea. I thought it was still in the basement. Megan must have found it and brought it up for Christian to play with."

"Do you think it has anything to do with what's happened to him?"

Kate glanced at her nephew's still form. "I have absolutely no idea."

"But if he spun the wheel, would it harm him in any way?"

"Eleya wouldn't intentionally harm him, I'm sure of that," Kate said softly. "But the fact that he's sleeping so deeply just may be a reaction to . . . whatever happened. I know what an encounter with Eleya does to me, and I'm a lot older than Christian."

"So you think it's possible that she may have communicated with him in some way?"

Kate bit her lip. "I wish I knew, Cole. I truly wish I knew."

"Well, there's nothing more we can do here," Cole said gently. "Come on, I think we'd better get back downstairs and hear what the doctor has to say."

Unfortunately, what the doctor had to say didn't help anyone.

"I wish I could tell you more," Dr. Sheffield said to the anxious group gathered around the kitchen table. "But the truth is, I can't. Christian's sleeping peacefully. He's breathing normally, his color is good, and his heartbeat is steady—"

"But you can't wake him up," Matt said helplessly.

"That's right. And to be honest, I'm afraid to try too hard in case I harm him. That's why I want him in the hospital. They can monitor his vital signs there and if anything changes, they have the staff and the equipment necessary to deal with it."

"Dr. Sheffield, have you ever seen anything like this before?" Cole asked.

"No, son, I haven't," the doctor admitted. "I've seen people in comas and drug-induced states, and I've seen patients in shock or paralyzed by stroke. But I have never, in all my years of practice, seen anything like this. And I'm sorry to say that I don't know what to do for the boy. Ah, good, there's the ambulance. Matt, Megan, I think you should go along." Dr. Sheffield picked up his medical bag. "I wish I could give you better news, but I think we're just going to have to wait and see what happens."

The next ten minutes were hard on everyone. Kate watched in silence as the ambulance workers brought Christian's sleeping form down on a stretcher and wheeled him out to the ambulance. Once he was safely tucked inside, Megan climbed in after him. Matt headed for his truck. His face was set in grim, anxious lines.

"Will you call Dad for me, Kate" he asked as he started it up. "The number's on the fridge door. I'm not in the mood to deal with him or his recriminations right now."

"No problem, I'll take care of it, Matt. And I'll be along myself soon."

Kate watched as the three vehicles headed down the driveway, and then turned back to face Cole. "I can't go to New York with you, Cole. Not now. If anything were to happen to Christian after I left—"

"I know," Cole interrupted gently. "And under the circumstances, I wouldn't even ask you to. But I'm not leaving you here alone either." He pulled her into his arms and held her close. "We'll wait until the morning. See how things are then."

Kate shook her head. "We don't have time to wait. We have to know what the psychic has to say. Sadina can tell you what we need to know and you can phone me. I just know I can't leave here right now. I love that little boy and if anything were to happen to him—"

"Do you really believe anything will?"

The underlying question was there and Kate didn't know how to answer it.

"Anyway, you need to be here with your family," Cole continued. "I'll make sure my buddy stays close."

"Your buddy?"

"The cop. No point in his driving to New York with me. I'd rather know he's here keeping an eye on you. Just be careful, will you?"

He drew her into the solid protection of his arms and Kate buried her face in his shoulder, wishing she could stay there forever. She felt so damned helpless. There was so much going on and she couldn't control any of it. Christian was in the hospital, Davenport was closing in and Cole was leaving her to go to New York. And always there, hovering in the background, was the fear that in the end, she wouldn't be able to find the way to help Eleya.

She tightened her arms around Cole and felt tears of frustration slip down her cheeks. "I'll be f-fine," she whispered, not wanting him to see them. "I'll take . . . extra care and I promise I won't do anything foolish."

"That's what I wanted to hear. But where will you be tonight? I don't think you should stay at the church alone, even with a car parked outside."

"Maybe I can stay at the hospital," Kate said after thinking about it for a moment. "I'll drive over in Meg's car and I can put the spinning wheel in the trunk. I doubt anyone would attempt to break into a car in the middle of the hospital parking lot with the sheriff's office two doors down. Besides, if what you tell me is true, Davenport needs me as much as he needs the wheel."

Cole put his hand under her chin and gently titled her face up to his. That's when he saw the tears—and knew it was all an act. Kate was trying to show him a brave face, but the emotional anguish of the past few weeks was catching up with her and the cracks were starting to show. Now with Christian's sudden and inexplicable illness, she was losing the battle to pretend that she was taking it all in her stride. And that's when everything became clear to Cole. He felt the last of his doubts disappear, and while he knew it was a hell of a time to tell her, he needed her to know how he felt. He wanted her to know.

"I love you, Kate Pedigrew," he said simply, and with complete honesty.

Kate stared at him in disbelief. "You . . . *love* me?"

"Yes. I know my timing's lousy, but—"

"You *love* me? I didn't know . . . I mean, I never thought . . . you *love* me?"

Cole's laughter was a throaty rumble of sound. "Yes, I love you. So don't go doing anything stupid before I get back." He kissed her hard then, as though branding her lips with his. "We have a lot to talk about. Now, let's get the spinning wheel and put it in the car."

Somehow, Kate managed to climb out of her euphoria long enough to remember what was going on—and more importantly, what she had to do. "No, it's all right, Cole, I'll do that. You just get on your way."

"I don't like the idea of you being here alone."

"I'm not going to be, I promise. I'm going to call Dad and then I'll put the spinning wheel in Meg's car and get straight over to the hospital."

"All right. I'll call my friend and tell him to get over here—and not to let you out of his sight until I get back. And keep your cell phone on at all times."

"I will. And Cole?"

"Yes?"

"In case you didn't know—" her mouth curved in a beautiful smile, "I love you too."

• • •

As soon as she saw Cole's headlights disappear down the road, Kate went back into her brother's house. She locked all of the doors and turned on all the lights. If Davenport was in the area, he sure as hell wasn't going to get in unnoticed. Then, she walked into the kitchen and after glancing at the telephone number Meg had taped to the side of the fridge, picked up the phone and dialed.

"Yes, room three fourteen please." She waited for a minute, then took a deep breath when she heard her father's voice on the other end. "Dad, it's Kate. No, I'm fine, but I'm calling to tell you to get over to the hospital. Christian had some kind of attack tonight and Matt and Megan are on their way there with him now. Yes, Dr. Sheffield was here and called the ambulance himself." Kate tried to keep her voice as emotionless as possible. "I don't know what's wrong, Dad. Matt will fill you in when you get there. Just . . . go easy on him, will you? He's about as strung out as I've ever seen him. Yeah, I'll be heading over in a few minutes myself. Okay, see you there."

Kate hung up the phone and anxiously bit her lip. Her father had taken the news better than she'd expected, but that didn't mean there wouldn't be trouble. Roderick had been predicting all along that something like this would happen—and now it had. She just hoped he wouldn't rub Matt's nose in it when he got to the hospital. Her brother *was* strung out and the last thing he needed was his father taking a run at him. They hadn't come to blows yet, but she wasn't sure it wouldn't happen tonight if Roderick pushed too hard.

Still, she'd done what her brother had asked her to. Now she had something of her own to take care of. She climbed the stairs to Christian's room, and once there, pulled down the shade in front of his window and drew the pretty blue and white curtains across. Then, kneeling down in front of the spinning wheel, Kate put her hand on the top of it and whispered a desperate plea as she closed her eyes and started it spinning.

"Please tell me what I need to know, Eleya. Please tell me that he's not going to die!"

• • •

In a hospital six miles away, a little boy tossed restlessly in his bed. His eyes were closed, but behind the lids, the eyeballs moved rapidly back and forth. His mouth formed words as though he was speaking to someone, but no sounds came out.

Suddenly, he reached up his arm and stretched his fingers toward the ceiling as though trying to grasp the hand of an angel. His cheeks grew flushed and his heart beat escalated. He remained that way a few minutes longer. Then, his arm slowly dropped back down to his side. The rapid movement of his eyes stilled and his mouth stopped working.

And through it all, not one of the monitors on the wall had registered any change at all.

It was nearly forty-five minutes before Kate finally got to the hospital, but she didn't regret a moment of the delay. She had been able to contact Eleya, and during her brief telepathic link, she had learned everything she needed to know. Christian *had* reached out to the wheel, and Eleya, sensing the spirit of a child, had gone to meet him. And through her wondrous magic, she had healed him.

Kate suddenly knew what it felt like to be Santa Claus.

She rushed through the front lobby of the building and made her way to Pediatrics, where she found her brother sitting alone in the hallway outside Christian's room. "Matt?"

"Hey, kiddo, I was just starting to worry about you." His relief was obvious as he got to his feet and enveloped her in a bear hug. "I thought maybe you'd had trouble with Megan's car and was wondering whether I should go back to the house and get you."

She smiled as she hugged him back. "Everything's fine. I just had a few things to do before I left the house. How's Christian?"

Matt sighed. "No change. The hospital's top pediatrician examined him about half an hour ago, but he seems to be as puzzled as Dr. Sheffield was. He has absolutely no explanation for Christian's condition."

Knowing that he wouldn't, Kate just nodded. "Where's Megan?"

"She went downstairs to get some coffee. And Dad's around here somewhere."

"Dad?" The casual mention had Kate's stomach muscles clenching. "I'm almost afraid to ask but . . . how's he taking it?"

"About a hundred times better than I thought," Matt admitted with a reluctant smile. "I don't mind telling you, Kate, I was ready for a fight when he got here. I expected the old man to start yelling the minute he walked through the door. But he didn't say a word. He just asked me how Christian was, confirmed it with the doctor, and I've hardly heard a peep out of him since. To tell you the truth, it's like he's a whole different person."

Kate frowned. It sounded too good to be true but she wasn't about to look a gift horse in the mouth. Maybe Eleya had worked more magic than she'd thought.

"Maybe Dad realized that yelling at you wasn't going to make this any better and that it was time to start pulling together as a family," she said instead.

Matt lifted his muscular shoulders in a shrug. "I'd like to think that was the case. All I know is that he surprised the hell out of both of us. Megan was even wondering whether *he* shouldn't see a doctor while he was here. But listen, Katie, you may as well go home and get some sleep. There's no need for all of us to be here. Meg and I will stay with Christian tonight, and then tomorrow if you like, you can come back and spell her."

"You need your rest too, Matt."

"Yeah, but I'm not going anywhere until I hear something. I want to be here when my son wakes up."

Kate didn't miss the slight quiver in Matt's voice, and knew that she had to tell him. Whether he believed her or not wasn't important. The least she could do was try to reassure him. "I love you with all my heart, Matt, and you know that I've never lied to you. So please don't ask me how I know this, but . . . Christian's going to be all right."

Matt sighed. "I wish I could believe that, Katie. But the doctors won't say—"

"Matt, trust me. I wouldn't tell you this if I didn't know because I wouldn't dream of getting your hopes up. But I *know* he's going to be all right. You have to believe me when I say that."

Matt gazed down into her eyes. "Kate, all these . . . changes that have been happening to you in the last few weeks. The way you look, the incredible stuff you're doing, and now this sudden burst of . . . intuitiveness. It wouldn't have anything to do with that—"

Kate held her breath. *Please don't ask me, Matt. Please don't ask me what I can't tell you . . .*

But she needn't have worried. Matt only laughed and shook his head. "Nah. Guess I'm just being silly. But they say the power of positive thinking helps, so I'll try to take your word for it. Are you going back home now?"

Relieved that she'd gotten off so lightly, Kate shook her head. "No, you can reach me at Madeleine Carstairs's. I don't feel like staying alone at the church tonight, so I phoned her and asked if I could stay there." She stood on her tiptoes and gave him a kiss on the cheek. "Say good-bye to Megan for me and tell her I'll be back in the morning. I'm going to look for Dad."

It was some time before Kate was able to find her father, but when she did, it was in the *last* place she had expected to. "Dad?"

Roderick didn't turn around. He just kept staring through the window at the three rows of cots lined up in front of him, each of them containing a tiny bundle of life wrapped in a cozy pink or blue blanket.

"You know, I'll never forget the first time I saw you lying in one of these, Kate," he said, more to himself than to her. "It was around three-thirty in the morning. Your mother had just gone through twelve hours of labor and I'd gone through three packs of cigarettes. And there you were, lying in your cot looking completely unfazed by the whole ordeal. You stared up at me with those incredible blue eyes and I thought I was the luckiest guy in the world."

Roderick sighed and shoved his hands into his pockets in the gesture Kate knew so well. "You know, Kate, having children can sometimes be a mixed blessing. The first time you see them, they're just like this: helpless bits of humanity completely dependent on you for everything. Then, you watch them start to grow up. You try to teach them all the things they'll need to know, and you watch them take their first stumbling steps. And your heart breaks every time they stumble and fall. But you pick them up and start them off again, knowing they'll have to find their own way in the world eventually. And when they do, you pray that what you've taught them will stand them in good stead all the years of their life. But sometimes, just sometimes, the urge to interfere in their lives becomes too strong to resist. You find yourself telling them what they *should* be doing rather than letting them find out for themselves. You justify it by saying that you want to spare them the mistakes you made—and maybe still are making—in your own life. And that's wrong. Because everybody has to find their own way." He finally turned to face her, and Kate could have wept at the look of despair in his eyes. "That's what I've been doing to your brother, Kate. And it was wrong. I had no business telling him how to look after his own son."

"I don't think you were wrong to *try* to tell him, Dad," Kate said softly. "I think it's more the *way* you tried to tell him that caused the problems. We know you're worried about Christian, but telling Matt he was a bad father because he didn't do things the way you thought he should was wrong, and it was hurtful."

Her father nodded. "Yes. Especially given that I didn't do any better when it came to looking after your mother, as you so bluntly pointed out."

Kate felt her cheeks burn. "I never meant to hurt you."

"I know that. But you said what was on your mind and that was good. Because you were right."

She stared at him. "I was?"

"Of course. What's more, I knew it all along. But sometimes it's easier to bury the truth than it is to face it." Roderick closed his eyes and ran a hand over his face. "I loved your mother, Kate. More than I can ever tell you. When we were first married, every hour I spent with Clare was precious. In fact, I used to complain that I couldn't spend enough time with her. But as the years went by, I started to forget that she was the most important thing in my life, and I let myself get caught up in the busy-ness, as I call it, of making a living. I spent more and more time away, and Clare, bless her heart, never condemned me for it. She stayed at home and did a wonderful job of raising you and your brother, and she never complained. And I grew complacent," Roderick admitted heavily. "I threw myself into the work more and more because I wanted so much for my family. But at the same time, I was losing the person who had been my reason for doing it all in the first place."

Roderick walked across the hall and sat down in one of the green vinyl chairs against the wall. Almost afraid to say anything, Kate followed and quietly sat down beside him. She sensed that her father wanted to talk, and that as hard as it was for him to say some of the things he was saying, he needed to get them out into the open.

"I never thought your mother was a strong woman, Kate. She was like a beautiful flower that needed to be cared for and loved. And like a beautiful flower, she gave back so much. But I found out later that for all her softness, she had a will of iron. And she was brave. She never told me about her illness. At least, not in the early days," Roderick admitted now. "I knew she wasn't feeling a hundred percent, but I also knew that she was raising two children on her own and I figured she was just tired. By the time I discovered what was really happening, it was too late. And then, because I didn't know how to deal with it, I avoided it." He looked at Kate with a haunted expression. "That's a terrible thing to say about the person you love, isn't it, Kate?"

"Everybody has a reason for doing what they do, Dad," she said, trying to find the right words. "And at the time, we like to believe that what we're doing is right."

Roderick's smile held more than a trace of sadness. "You have wisdom beyond your years, my dear. Yes, at the time, I believed I *could* justify what I was doing. When I knew that Clare was ill, I convinced myself that she was better off without me hanging around, so I put her under the care of the best doctor I could find. I comforted myself with the knowledge that she didn't have to worry about me, and that she was well looked after. But I was wrong, Kate. I was so damned wrong!" he said in a tortured voice. "I should *never* have left her alone so much. I should have been there with her. Maybe if I had I would have seen that whatever the doctor was doing for her wasn't enough. But I didn't. And we lost your mother because of it."

The heart-wrenching confession had tears shimmering in Kate's eyes. "You can't blame yourself for Mom's dying, Dad," she said huskily. "Dr. Constantine was one of the best in his field. You had no reason to doubt his reputation, or his expertise."

"No, but I've always prided myself on my ability to stay on top of things, and that's what I should have done. I should have kept on asking Clare how she was feeling, and how she was responding to whatever treatment the doctor was giving her. And if she *wasn't* responding, I should have gone back to *him* and demanded to know why. That was where I failed your mother, Kate." Roderick got to his feet, but not before Kate saw the wetness of tears in his eyes. "I hated myself for a very long time after your mother died. But I hated myself even more every time I saw the recrimination in your eyes."

"Oh Dad, I never meant—"

"I know," her father said gently. "You may never have meant for me to see it, but I did nevertheless. Don't forget, you were my beautiful baby girl. The apple of my eye. And when I suddenly saw you looking at me in a way that . . . wasn't so special anymore, I didn't know how to deal with it. So I avoided it. I threw myself into the business and told myself that you and Matt were capable of looking after yourselves. I told myself that I had no place in either of your lives, which was easy to believe since neither of you wanted any part of the firm."

Feeling guiltier with every word, Kate got to her feet. "I never meant to make you feel that way, Dad. But emotionally, I didn't know how to reach you either. You'd become so . . . distant. We never knew where you were or when you were coming home. Sometimes we wondered if you ever *were* coming home again."

"I know. And yet, when I received the letter from Megan telling me that Christian was sick, my first reaction was anger," Roderick said quietly. "I was *angry* that neither you nor Matt had bothered to contact me. But as usual, I buried it. I told myself it wasn't important, and that as long as I knew about Christian's illness, it didn't matter *how* I knew. But it did. Because the only explanation I could come up with as to why you hadn't written, was that neither of you *wanted* to see me. And that was a . . . pretty hard blow for a father to take."

When her father's voice broke, Kate didn't stop to consider the consequences. She just took two steps forward and wrapped her arms around him. She wasn't sure whether she was doing it for him or for her. All she knew was that it felt right and that it was long overdue. It was time to close the wounds. And when his arms came up and held her close, Kate knew they'd taken their first steps in that direction.

It was some time before either of them could say anything. Finally, Kate gently stepped back and smiled up into her father's face. "I have to go, Dad, but before I do, I want you to know that everything's going to be all right."

"I'd like to think so, Kate," he said gruffly. "I really would."

"Count on it, Dad. And . . . Christian's going to be all right too," she added hesitantly.

A tiny flicker of hope brightened her father's eyes. "Has there been a change? Has the doctor found something?"

"No. But I have a gut instinct about this, and you know what you always used to say about gut instinct being the best measure of a situation next to a Geiger counter."

Roderick chuckled. "I remember that, but I'm surprised *you* would."

"You'd be surprised at the things I remember. I also think you should get back upstairs and talk to Matt the way you just talked to me. I know how much he'd like that."

Roderick slowly began to smile. "You know, Kate, when you were little, you always used to come to me with your broken toys, and I always seemed to be able to fix them. Sounds to me like you've taken on the role of the fixer now."

"I think we *both* fixed this one, Dad." Kate leaned over and kissed his cheek. "Because I sure couldn't have done it if you hadn't wanted to put the pieces back together again too."

# Twenty-one

"Kate, honey, I'm so glad you're here," Madeleine said as she opened the front door. "I was beginning to wonder where you—oh my Lord!" She broke off at the sight of the spinning wheel in Kate's arms. "What in the *world* is that?"

"It's called a spinning wheel, Maddie," Kate said with a grin. "Okay if I put it down in the living room?"

"Well, yes, of course but—are you going to tell me what this is all about?"

"I think I'll have to before the night's out. And I'm sorry I'm late getting here but I've been at the hospital."

"The hospital! Oh my, what's happened?"

"Megan went up and found Christian unconscious. She called Dr. Sheffield, and when he couldn't bring Christian around, he called for an ambulance and took him in straight away."

"Oh, honey, I am so sorry to hear that. But if that's the case, shouldn't you still be there?"

"There's no need," Kate assured her. "He's going to be fine."

"Oh, well thank God for that. Did the doctors tell you what he had?"

"No, because they still don't know."

Madeleine frowned. "Then . . . how can you be sure that he's going to be all right?"

"Because I just know." Kate hesitated for a moment. "Is Teresa here tonight, Maddie?"

"No, it's her night off. That's why I put the security system back on after you came in. I don't like leaving it off when she's not around."

Kate silently let out her breath. Good. At least if anything unusual happened tonight, she wasn't going to have to try to explain it to the maid as well.

Madeleine suddenly glanced at the spinning wheel and frowned. "Kate, where's Cole?"

"He's on his way to New York to see a psychic."

*"What?"*

Kate sighed. "Sit down, Maddie. I think it's time I told you *exactly* what's been going on."

It was probably the most amazing story Madeleine had ever heard. It was certainly the most unbelievable one. But Kate had to give her credit. She listened to the story from beginning to end, in complete silence and without making a single interruption. Only the expression on her face gave any indication of the shock, disbelief and fascination she must have been feeling.

"And that's why I'm here," Kate told her in conclusion. "The church isn't safe for me and neither is my brother's place. But with your state-of-the-art security system, I figured I could keep Davenport at bay until Cole gets back with the information we need."

Madeleine got up and crossed to the liquor cabinet. Taking out two glasses, she poured a generous shot of bourbon into each and handed one to Kate. "Here, honey, drink this. It'll help calm the nerves."

"My nerves are fine."

"It's not your nerves I'm talking about." Madeleine tossed back the bourbon and went back for a refill.

Kate took a few cautious sips. She wasn't usually fond of strong spirits, but she had to admit that it helped take the edge off. Within minutes, she could actually feel some of the tension seeping out of her bones. "Thanks, Maddie, I think that was a good idea."

"I've always thought so," Madeleine said, resuming her chair. "Well, Kate, that's . . . quite a story. I knew that something was going on, of course, when Cole told me that he was looking for this funny old spinning wheel. But I had no idea it was *anything* like this. I have so many questions I don't even know where to begin. And frankly, I am flabbergasted at how calm you're being about everything."

"Believe me, Maddie, calm is the last word I'd use to describe how I've been feeling. I've seen and heard and . . . experienced things I never even dreamed were possible. And then with the break-ins, and suspecting Cole—well, I don't mind telling you, it's been rough. I've felt a lot better since I told Cole the truth."

"And now he's off to New York to talk to a psychic."

"Yes. According to Professor Morris, this woman may have some of the answers we need. And that in turn will get rid of the danger. Once I've set Eleya free, the spinning wheel becomes worthless and Jeremy Davenport will go merrily—or not so merrily—on his way."

"When do you expect Cole back from New York?"

"Tomorrow. But I should give him a call right now," Kate said abruptly as she got up and headed for the phone. "Now that I know Christian's safe, maybe he can come back and I can go to New York with him. I'll just call him on his cell and—"

"Put the phone down, Miss Pedigrew," said a familiar voice from the hall. "You're not calling anyone tonight."

Kate's hand froze on the receiver. Behind her, Madeleine uttered a startled cry and jumped to her feet. "Who the hell are you!"

"Why don't you ask Miss Pedigrew?" the intruder said quietly. "I think she knows my real name . . . now."

Kate closed her eyes, her stomach churning with fear and disbelief. *No, it wasn't possible.* She couldn't *possibly* have made such a horrible mistake. She wasn't stupid. She'd called the telephone number on the business card, she'd checked his references. Surely she hadn't let herself be taken in by an imposter?

But the moment Kate turned around and saw the man's unsmiling face, she knew that she had. There was nothing in the least effeminate about the black-garbed figure standing in front of them now, or about the gun in his hand. Cole was right. The man was a master—and she'd been completely deceived. "Jeremy Davenport!" she whispered.

"Yes, I've surprised you, haven't I, Kate?" he said, smiling at her coldly. "You never suspected that the flamboyant Peter Charlton was actually the man your friend Beresford had warned you to be on the lookout for, did you? But that's why I had to do something to throw you off track. I certainly couldn't have approached you looking the way I did the last time Beresford saw me."

Kate swallowed with difficulty, but eventually found her voice. "So Oliver Kline was a fake as well."

"Ah yes, the debonair gallery director. I enjoyed playing the part," he admitted. "Although I have to admit, the role of Peter Charlton gave me much more room for artistic expression."

"Well, I don't care who or *what* you are," Madeleine broke in angrily. "I'll thank you to get the hell out of my house! How *dare* you burst in here pointing a gun! How did you get past the security system anyway?"

Davenport shrugged negligently. "Another one of my many skills, Mrs. Carstairs. But rest assured, your system would foil most would-be burglars."

The fact that he knew Madeleine's name surprised them both, but she admirably stood her ground. "Well, if it's money you're after, take what you want and get out."

But Davenport only laughed and took another step into the room. "On the contrary, Mrs. Carstairs, this isn't about money, as your good friend Miss Pedigrew knows. You've led me a merry chase, my dear, but I will have what I want in the end."

Kate raised her chin in defiance. "I won't give you the spinning wheel."

"Of course you will. One way or another." He reached

into his pocket and withdrew two gleaming silver coins. "We can either do it the easy way, or the hard."

"What's the easy way?" Madeleine asked with a frown.

"Miss Pedigrew accepts my offer of silver in fair exchange for the spinning wheel."

"And the hard?" Kate asked warily.

"I shoot you through the heart and take the spinning wheel without your consent."

Madeleine blanched. "Dear God, what kind of a monster are you?"

"Hardly a monster, Mrs. Carstairs. But what you don't understand, is that the innocuous-looking spinning wheel over there has the power to make me a very wealthy and powerful man. No one will be able to touch me once I have it in my possession."

"You can't make the wheel do evil," Kate said, taking a casual step closer to it.

"Ah, but I can. And I will. Stay away from the wheel, Miss Pedigrew," Davenport warned. "I'm won't have you doing anything to jeopardize my chances now."

Kate did stop, but only because she heard the sound of a car screeching to a halt on the road outside the house. Seconds later, she heard a door slam and then footsteps running up the walk.

"It seems you have company, Mrs. Carstairs," Davenport said quietly. "If you don't want anything to happen to your friend here, I suggest you get rid of them as quickly as possible."

He kept the gun trained on Kate as he and Madeleine moved toward the door. Then, he positioned himself behind the door with his back to the wall. When the chimes rang, he signaled Madeleine with his head. "Remember," he whispered as she put her hand on the doorknob, "say the wrong thing and your friend Kate dies."

Madeleine went white, but somehow, she managed to compose her face and open the door. Kate nearly fainted when she saw Cole standing in the doorway.

"Cole!" Madeleine gasped, surprise catching her off guard

too. "What are you doing here? I . . . thought you were on your way to . . . New York."

"I was." Cole strode forward, his eyes on Kate as Madeleine closed the door behind him. "I got near the outskirts of town and something told me to turn around. I have no idea what. I just knew I had to come back. And that I had to come . . . here." He glanced at Kate's white, silent face, and frowned. "Kate, what's wrong? Maddie—" he turned around, and saw Davenport standing in the lobby.

"Nothing's wrong, Beresford." Davenport said, casually locking the front door again. "Just keep your hands up and walk quietly into the living room. You too, Mrs. Carstairs. Nobody goes near the spinning wheel. Stand over there beside Beresford."

Cole's eyes were hard in an expression that was like granite. "How the hell did you get in? Where's Banks?"

"If you're referring to your friend in the car down the road, I took the liberty of disabling him."

"You son of a bitch!"

"Relax, Beresford, he's not dead. I just put him to sleep for a few hours. Now, Miss Pedigrew," Davenport said, turning back to Kate, "you have your choices. And I advise you to think very carefully, because I will pull the trigger if you force me to."

"Davenport, I swear, if you so much as touch a hair on her head, I'll—"

"Shut up, Beresford! And don't move! I'm holding the gun this time, and I told you I'd have the spinning wheel."

"But how do you know that it will do you any good?" Cole challenged. "Kate said that the power in it is good. It won't work for somebody like you!"

"Even good can be turned to evil if the owner so desires." Davenport's mouth twisted. "You've read the history books, Beresford. You know the legend as well as I do."

"What about Nathaniel Becker? The wheel did nothing for him."

An unbecoming flush suffused Davenport's face. "Nathaniel Becker was weak."

"Nathaniel Becker was a murderer!" Cole taunted. "He

was responsible for the deaths of twenty-four innocent women, every one of them burned at the stake after being convicted of witchcraft. But in the end he was beaten to death by one of the dead girls' brothers. Your precious spinning wheel didn't help him, did it?"

"If you're looking for similarities, you're wasting your time." Davenport's lips pulled into an evil smile. "I haven't murdered anyone yet."

"But your soul's as black as his was," Cole said quietly. "That's why the wheel won't do *you* any good either."

For the first time, Kate saw a flicker of doubt in Davenport's eyes. She didn't know whether Cole was trying to discourage him or if he was just keeping him distracted. She did know that Cole had seen her inching toward the wheel. Now she was barely six feet away from it. A few more steps and she'd be able to touch it. But what good would that do her? She still didn't know what she had to do—and time was running out.

*Help me, Eleya,* Kate pleaded silently. *Tell me what I have to do. You must know what I have to do—*

Suddenly, Davenport whirled. "Stop right there, Miss Pedigrew!" he snapped. "One more step and I'll fire—"

Kate halted in her tracks. She glanced at Madeleine, then at Cole, and knew that she'd run out of time. Davenport was waiting for her answer. If she didn't accept his terms, he'd pull the trigger. Which meant that if she was going to do something to save Eleya, she'd have to do it now. But . . . what, damn it! What?

*Break the spindle, Kate,* came the softly spoken answer in her mind. You *must be the one to break the spindle . . .*

Kate almost felt like crying. At last! Eleya had finally told her what she had to do. She had to get to the spinning wheel and break the spindle.

But . . . how could she? Davenport had the gun trained on her. Even now his finger was poised on the trigger. If she took so much as a step toward the wheel, he'd shoot.

Something wasn't making sense, Kate thought desperately. She wasn't supposed to die. She couldn't be dead *and* break the spindle. Besides, she didn't *want* to die; she wanted to live. She had so much to live *for.* Cole loved her, and after this was all over, they were going to talk about getting married and having a family. But Eleya had told her that she *had* to break the spindle. And if she did, Davenport was going to shoot.

"I don't have all night, Miss Pedigrew," Davenport snapped. "You have until the count of three to make up your mind."

"Give it up, Davenport!" Cole shouted. "You can't get away with this—"

"One . . ."

Kate glanced at Cole in desperation. Why was this happening? Surely it wasn't supposed to end like this?

"Two . . ."

"Kate, for God's sake, tell him you'll take the money!" Madeleine cried.

Kate glanced over at the spinning wheel. She knew that Jeremy Davenport was the danger Eleya had referred to, just as he had been the black-garbed figure in her nightmare. If she let him take the spinning wheel now, Eleya would be trapped inside it forever, condemned to spend all eternity in a nightmarish existence where love was nothing more than a memory. And Kate knew she couldn't let that happen. Not now when she knew what it was like to love someone with all her heart and soul.

In the time it took Davenport to say three, Kate reached the spinning wheel.

"Kate, *no*!" Cole cried desperately. "Don't!"

Ignoring his pleas, she reached for the spindle and jerked her hand down hard—snapping the fragile piece of wood in two.

And at exactly the same moment, Davenport screamed in rage—and fired.

Kate felt the thud of the bullet in her chest. The impact knocked her backwards, sending her crashing down on top of the wheel. She heard the sound of wood splintering beneath her and felt a fiery burning in her chest. Blood seeped from the hole where the bullet had entered. She could see it running down the front of her clothes, spilling onto the carpet.

And she heard Cole's scream, a sound that seemed to be torn from the very depths of his soul.

*Eleya,* Kate called into the gathering darkness. *Eleya, can you hear me?*

There was no answer. Kate prayed that it was because the spirit had already found her freedom. Eleya had saved Christian's life, and now, in a curious twist of fate, Kate had ended up giving her life in exchange for Eleya's. She couldn't bear to think that her sacrifice had been in vain.

She was dimly aware of Madeleine rushing toward her . . . of her crying out her name, but it was becoming . . . increasingly difficult to see. The darkness was descending in waves, and the light was growing dim. Kate felt Maddie's soft arms close around her and knew that she was dying. She couldn't feel any pain. The spinning wheel lay broken beneath her. She still clutched one part of the spindle in her hand. She closed her eyes and let it fall to the floor.

*I love you, Cole,* she whispered silently. *I'm so sorry it had to . . . end like this. Remember me . . .*

And then there was nothing.

Across the room Cole watched in stunned disbelief as Madeleine cradled Kate's lifeless body in her arms. He watched the blood pour from a bullet hole in her chest and heard Madeleine's sobs fall unheard against the girl's hair. It was over.

The spinning wheel was worthless. And his beloved Kate was dead.

Shock yielded to fury as Cole felt hatred burn a hole in his heart. The need for revenge, primal and deep, rose in his breast as he turned to face her murderer. Nothing mattered now but that he kill the man who had done this to Kate.

But Davenport was gone. The front door was open. The man had bolted.

"You son of a—" Cole made a dash for the door. If it took him forever, he'd find Davenport. He'd hunt the bastard down and make him pay for what he'd done to Kate. For what he'd done to him.

*No . . . there is no need.*

Cole stopped dead in his tracks. What was that? What had he just heard? A . . . voice? It had seemed to come from the air all around him, the sound soft, and infinitely gentle. He turned back towards the living room—and saw something that couldn't possibly be.

The figure of a woman was hovering over Kate's body. A woman so . . . radiant, so incredibly beautiful, that Cole knew he had to be looking at an angel. He slowly dropped to his knees, and stared at her in wonder.

She was dressed all in white, her long, flowing robe shimmering as though woven from beams of sunlight. Her long blond hair drifted around her face and her glorious eyes were filled with the wisdom of the ages. He had never seen such beauty, such radiance before. And in that split second, he knew. "*Eleya!*" he whispered reverently.

The spirit did not speak. She only smiled as she slowly reached her hand toward Kate and touched her head. And for the first time in his life, Cole witnessed a miracle.

He saw a dazzling white light flow from Eleya's hand and watched it encompass Kate's entire body. It surrounded her, flowing into every part of her body until she was shimmering like Eleya's robes.

It was like nothing Cole had ever seen before.

And then, in a body he'd feared stilled forever, he saw . . . movement. He saw a sudden rise and fall as empty lungs filled with air and drew breath again. Into cheeks which had been as pale as death, he saw the softest blush of pink return as the lifeblood began to flow.

Kate did not open her eyes, but Cole heard the softness of her sigh. And suddenly, the light began to increase in intensity. It centered on Eleya and radiated outwards, filling the room with a blinding white light. It was like standing in front of a row of spotlights with all of their beams aimed at one point. Cole had to close his eyes, to cover them with his hands, and eventually to turn away from it altogether. There was no heat with it. Just dazzling white light. And the air was filled with the most incredible perfume. Sweet and exotic, just as Kate had said.

And then, as abruptly as it had begun, it ended. The blinding light vanished, as though a switch had been thrown, plunging the room back into darkness.

It was a few minutes before Cole could open his eyes. And a few minutes more before he could see past the stars that were dancing in front of them. He shut them again tight, and then blinked a few times. When he opened them again, Eleya was gone.

Cole slowly got to his feet. He still wasn't sure what he'd just seen. Had he been dreaming? Whatever it was, it had been an incredible experience—even for a man who thought he'd seen everything.

His legs were unsteady as he walked across the room. Madeleine was out cold. She was lying on her back, close to Kate. Cole dropped to his knees and touched her cheek, relieved to find it warm and healthy. Then he turned to Kate.

For a moment, he just stared at her. He watched the rhythmic rise and fall of her chest, and listened to the gentle sound of her breathing. She should be dead, but she wasn't. He saw the hole where the bullet had pierced her blouse, but underneath the skin was soft and unblemished. And the blood was gone. There were no signs of it anywhere.

Cole slid his hands under Kate's arms and gently pulled her into his arms. He ran his fingers over the softness of her lips, traced the outline of her eyes, her nose, her cheeks. He felt the reassuring warmth of her body against his, warm and alive and fully well.

And with none but the shadows to see him, he dropped his head and let the tears begin to fall as he thanked God for the miracle that had brought her back to him.

# Twenty-two

Snow started falling early on the morning of December 21st. It drifted down in huge white flakes, covering the mat of gold and crimson leaves. It continued to fall throughout the day, until by four o'clock, the countryside lay hidden under a thick mantle of white. There was a hush across the land, and in the air, the promise of Christmas.

Kate stood at her bedroom window and gazed out at the beauty all around her. The golden hues of autumn had finally given way to the crisp, white shades of winter, and on this bright snowy day, only four away from Christmas, she was filled with a sense of deep and abiding peace. Because today, she was to marry the man she loved.

It was hard to believe that nearly two months had passed since the night of the fateful shooting; a night which had changed all of their lives forever. Kate knew that she would never be able to fully understand what had happened in Madeleine's living room that night. Cole had told her as much as he could the next morning, but that hadn't made the actual experience any less mystifying. And poor Madeleine hadn't known *what* to think. She still didn't.

But there was one simple fact that none of them could deny. They had all been part of a miracle. And ever since that day, Kate thanked God for the gift of her life.

Jeremy Davenport had met with his own particular fate. On the news the day after the shooting, Kate had learned that the police had been called to the site of a fatal car accident which had taken place at approximately one o'clock that morning. The driver of the car, a tall, blond-haired man in his late forties, had been killed instantly when his car had veered off the road and crashed headlong into a tree. No explanation had been given for the accident. The man hadn't been drinking, and the weather conditions had been fine. There were no skid marks on the road to indicate that he might have braked hard or swerved to avoid anything in the road.

It was likely the lack of evidence had led the sheriff's office to conclude that the accident had been a suicide. And the fact that the man was carrying no identification of any kind had prompted the sheriff's office to ask for assistance from anyone who might have been familiar with the man.

Cole had said little about the accident. None of them had. They had known that it was Davenport who had died that night, and Cole alone had gone to identify the body. He'd told the police that he had known the man by reputation, but not as a friend, and had filled in the necessary paperwork and signed the appropriate papers. Then, he had returned to Madeleine's house where Kate was still resting, and had never mentioned Jeremy Davenport's name again.

Nor had they gone to New York to meet with Sadina. There was nothing the psychic could tell them now. It was enough that a painful chapter in their lives had come to an end. One that neither Kate nor Cole was willing to look at again.

But today, another much happier chapter was about to begin.

"Thank you, Eleya," Kate whispered.

She hoped that Eleya heard her, because were it not for that gentle spirit, Kate knew that she wouldn't be getting married today. It was Eleya who had brought her and Cole together, she was sure of that now. Though some might call their meeting a coincidence, Kate knew it had been fated to happen. The only regret she had was that she'd never had a chance to thank Eleya for what she had done, and to say good-bye.

"Are you ready, honey? They're all out there waiting for you."

Kate turned away from the window and smiled at the woman who had become such an important part of her life. Madeleine looked wonderful today. The elegant black and gold jacket over a long black velvet skirt was perfect for the small, intimate ceremony. It set off her ash blond hair and lovely blue-green eyes perfectly.

"I guess it wouldn't do to be late for my own wedding, would it?" Kate said.

"Well, it's tradition for the bride to be a few minutes late, but I don't think poor Cole will be able to wait much longer than that," Madeleine told her. "He's been counting the hours since the day you agreed to marry him. And he sure is going to be proud when he sees you walking toward him. I vow, child, you have never looked more beautiful."

Kate glanced in the full-length mirror beside the bed and wondered if this was really happening. She and Cole were getting married today. They were to be joined as man and wife right here in the church, with only a few of their closest family and friends to witness the occasion.

She gazed at the beautiful wedding gown that she had had made and knew that it was perfect. The style was simple and elegant; the design reminiscent of the medieval gown Eleya had worn. The luxurious white velvet dress fit close through the body and waist, and fell in soft folds to the floor. Its long, tapered sleeves and square neckline provided a perfect frame for the stunning diamond and pearl necklace Cole had given her, and she wore a coronet of white roses in her hair. Her bouquet was simple, a fragrant arrangement of white lilies, freesia, and delicate white baby's breath.

The last thing Kate had done was to slip her mother's engagement ring onto the ring finger of her right hand. That was the only thing that was missing today, she thought sadly. Her mother should have been standing out there with the rest of her family, taking part in this wonderful day in that special way that only a mother could.

"She's up there watching you, Kate," Madeleine said softly as she came forward to arrange the folds of Kate's veil. "Somewhere in heaven, Clare is watching her beautiful daughter get married. And I know how proud of you she is."

Kate felt the moistness of tears in her eyes and nodded quickly. "If I had one wish, it would be that she could be here, Maddie. We always used to talk about . . . my wedding day and how beautiful it would be. But you're right, I do believe she's up there somewhere. If nothing else, my experience with Eleya has assured me that. But if Mom can't be here today, I'm glad that you are."

"I'm glad too, honey. And for what it's worth, I couldn't be more proud if you *were* my own flesh and blood."

"Maybe one day soon you will be," Kate said with a mischievous smile. "Given the amount of time you and Dad have been spending together lately."

"Now hush, child!" Madeleine scolded, though a charming blush appeared in her cheeks. "Don't you go getting any ideas like that. Your father and I have only been out to dinner a few times—"

"Six."

"You've been keeping track?" Madeleine gasped.

"You bet. *And* you've been to movies and to the opera, which tells me that this is far more serious than you're letting on. My father doesn't go to the opera with just *anyone*, you know."

There was a discreet knock on the door, followed by a call of "Are you decent?" in a deep masculine voice.

"Speak of the devil—" Kate put her arms around Madeleine and hugged her tight, "I think it's time to go."

"Yes, I guess it is. Oh, honey, I'm so very happy for you," Madeleine said as she hugged Kate back. "I'll see you after the ceremony. Come in, Rod."

The bedroom door opened and Kate saw her father standing in the entrance. He looked handsome and just a little nervous—and Kate couldn't have been more proud. "I'm ready, Dad."

"That's my girl," Roderick said as he walked in. "I was afraid I was going to have to wave smelling salts under

Cole's nose if you were much longer. Maddie, you look absolutely stunning."

"Why, thank you, Roderick. I do enjoy getting compliments from handsome gentlemen." Madeleine picked up her jeweled evening bag and headed for the door. "And I am on my way. I just had to tell Kate one more time how beautiful she looked."

Roderick glanced at his daughter and there was no mistaking the pride in his eyes. "Of course she's beautiful. She's a Pedigrew." Then, to Kate's delight, he leaned forward and kissed Madeleine on the cheek. "Now off you go. I want to have a few words with my daughter before I give her away to another man."

Kate felt a warm rush of love for the man standing in front of her and marveled that so much could have changed in such a short time. The bitterness and distance had all been forgotten in the wake of Christian's recovery and the family had grown close again. Roderick made a point of coming up to Vermont every second weekend, and while he usually stayed with Matt and Megan—who were only too happy to have him—every now and then he checked into a bed and breakfast in Montpelier. Kate figured that's when he slipped away to visit Madeleine, and that was okay with her. She'd never seen Maddie look better. The woman seemed to be blossoming under the care and attention her father was only too willing to lavish upon her, and Kate couldn't have been happier.

Even Cole had no more reservations about her father. The two men had spent an afternoon together at a sports bar in Montpelier, and although Kate had never been able to get either of them to talk about it, they'd come out the best of friends, albeit looking a little worse for wear.

As for Christian, the little boy had made a full recovery, as Kate had known he would. The doctors had no explanation for the startling turnaround, and in the end, they'd simply put it down to one of those inexplicable freaks of nature that happened every now and then. Matt hadn't said anything to her about it, but Kate knew that he wondered. Sometimes she'd catch him watching her with a pensive, thoughtful expression in his eyes.

But the most wonderful part of her life now, was Cole. The bond they shared was almost mystical. Likely because it stemmed from what had happened on the night of the shooting. What they had suffered in those few agonizing moments, when they had been separated from each other by the thin curtain of death, was something neither of them would ever forget.

"So, Katie-bug, any last minute fears?" her father asked as he turned to face her. "Because if there are, now's the time to tell me."

"I'm the happiest girl in the world, Dad." Kate leaned forward and pressed her lips to his cheek. "No regrets at all. Only my most sincere thanks to you for being here to walk me down the aisle."

Roderick swallowed hard as he reached for her hand and held it between his own. "The thanks go to you, Kate, for asking me to come, and for giving me a second chance to be a father. You'll never know how proud I am of you, sweetheart."

"Oh, Dad—"

"No, let me say it, Kate. I should have told you this a long time ago, but my own foolish pride kept getting in the way. I'm glad you had the courage to walk away and make a new life for yourself. And I'm proud of what you've accomplished. You're a gifted artist with a beautiful home and your very own studio, and you have friends and family who love and respect you. I can't tell you how happy and how proud that's made me. And now that we've got that clear," Roderick said brusquely as he took Kate's other hand and tucked it into the crook of his arm, "I think we'd better get this show on the road. There's a handsome young gentleman out there who wants to tell you how much *he* loves you too."

The ceremony was perfect. Kate walked out on her father's arm, and smiled at the few special friends and family who had gathered in her living room, which had been beautifully decorated with clusters of white roses, red poinsettias, and fragrant pine bows.

There was Madeleine, radiant in gold and black, and Matthew, looking very handsome in a new suit and a smart white shirt. Beside him, Megan looked as pretty as a picture in a stylish cream satin suit, and next to her, Professor Morris, looking extremely dapper in his tweeds, and with his bushy black eyebrows trimmed for the occasion. And dear little Christian stood by the minister, looking as proud as a peacock in his very first suit, and even prouder that he got to carry the white satin pillow upon which sat two very special rings.

And there, standing at the front of the room and smiling at her as though there was no one else in the room, was Cole. The man she loved with all her heart, and whose wife she was about to become.

The minister began to speak and a hush fell over the room. Cole and Kate had written their own vows, and when the time came to say them, they did so with quiet grace and deep sincerity. They pledged their lives to one another in reverent words of love that touched the heart of every person present. And as they shared their first married kiss, Kate knew that the joy she felt could have filled the room a hundred times over. She was starting out on the most exciting journey of her life, with the man she had waited her entire life for.

That night, when they made love, Kate knew that it went far beyond the simple joining of two bodies. It was as though their souls were united as well.

In the flickering glow of the candles, Cole caressed her with his eyes, and then with his hands. His movements were slow and deliberate. He ran his fingers over the smoothness of her belly and then up over her rib cage. His hand brushed the underside of her breast, and then closed over it.

Kate gasped with pleasure. Her body began to hum as Cole's thumb lazily circled her nipple, coaxing it into a hard bud. He smiled and lowered his mouth to taste her, and Kate moaned softly in her throat, aware of the heat beginning to pool in her abdomen. She reached out her hands to caress him, loving the feel of his skin. It was so warm and smooth beneath her fingers. She felt the muscles in his shoulders and his arms, and buried her fingers in the dark, silken curls on his chest. She touched him everywhere, her fingers lightly stroking, gently teasing, always arousing.

And Cole touched her back. His hands burned a trail wherever they touched, scorching the silken white skin of her inner thighs, and lingering there to explore. Kate groaned when she felt his fingers touch her, and unable to resist, she began to move softly against him.

"Ah, Kate," he whispered against her ear. "My beautiful, Kate."

Then, ever so slowly, Cole changed their positions so that Kate was lying fully beneath him. She smiled up into the dark, smoldering eyes above her and tilted her mouth up for his kiss. She felt the heat and the hardness of his body against her, and slowly opened herself to take him. Her groan of pleasure was swallowed by his mouth as he submerged himself in her softness. And together, they began to move, their fingers entwined, their hearts beating as they expressed their love for each other in the most simple and timeless of ways.

This was how it was supposed to be, Kate thought silently. The passion and love that flowed between them was like a precious gift to be given, and to be received. She would never be lonely as long as Cole was near. And even when they were apart, the special connection they felt would close the distance between them, and keep them in each other's hearts.

And later, much later, when she fell asleep in his arms, Kate knew that nearly everything she had wished for had come true. Cole's love had filled her with a sense of complete and abiding peace. Only one other thing would have made her life and her happiness complete.

If only she'd had the chance to say good-bye.

Sometime in the night, Kate drifted up out of sleep. She slowly opened her eyes, not sure what had woken her. And then she saw the soft glow emanating from the living room. "Eleya," she whispered breathlessly.

She glanced down at Cole, relieved to see that he was still sleeping peacefully beside her, and quietly slipped out of bed. Wrapping the flowing silk robe around her, Kate padded out to the living room—and felt a tremendous rush of joy at the sight which met her eyes.

*Eleya!* Ethereal and radiant, her beautiful face shining with a joy that came from within; her entire being was surrounded by a glistening white aura.

"You came back," Kate whispered happily. "I was so hoping you would."

*"I came back to wish you joy,"* Eleya said, her smile, if possible, even more beautiful than Kate had ever seen it. *"And I waited until this day, knowing that it would be special for both of us."*

"I never got to thank you for saving my life," Kate said, her voice hushed.

To her surprise, Eleya shook her head. *"It was my life that was saved, Kate, by the sacrifice of your own. Alizor's hatred could not exist in the face of such selfless devotion. Your ultimate sacrifice broke the bonds that held me, and it was my gift to you, that you be made whole again. Now I am together with my beloved Gareth, and beyond the reach of Alizor, and for that I am eternally grateful to you."*

Kate wished that she could have expressed all of the feelings and emotions that were in her heart, but the sentiments went too deep. "This is the most wonderful wedding present you could have given me, Eleya," she whispered unsteadily. "Thank you, for coming back."

*"We have both received a wonderful gift, Kate. And on this your wedding day, I bless you with two more. The serenity of peace, and the knowledge of eternal joy."*

The vision was coming to an end. Kate saw the shimmering curtain of light begin to fade, and knew it would be the last time she ever saw the beautiful spirit. "Farewell, Eleya." Her voice was barely above a whisper. "I will miss you."

*"And I will miss you, Kate. But we will always have our memories. And you will always be here . . . in my heart."*

Kate stood in the center of the room and watched until all that remained of the light was a faint glow. When that too disappeared, she closed her eyes and let the tears run down her face, not sure whether they were tears of joy or tears of sadness.

"You got to say good-bye after all," Cole said softly. He came up behind her and slipped his arms around her waist. "I know that's what you wanted."

Kate leaned back against her husband's chest and knew that now, finally, the circle was closed. "Did you see her?"

"No. But I saw the glow from the bedroom, and knew that she was here."

"Ever since that night, I've wanted to thank her for saving my life," Kate told him quietly. "And yet tonight, when she came back, it was to thank me for saving hers. She even knew that this was our wedding day."

Cole smiled and nestled his face into the soft curve of her neck. "Which is likely why she chose to come today. Eleya's happiness and yours have been closely intertwined, Kate. You share a spiritual bond. I think that wherever Eleya is, she will always be able to feel your joy."

Kate turned around in his arms and studied his handsome face in the moonlight. "Do you ever regret losing the spinning wheel, Cole? Are you sorry you didn't get to be the man who went down in history as the one who proved the legend of the Lockton spinning wheel true?"

"No." Cole pressed his lips against the smoothness of her brow, loving the smell of hair and the taste of her skin. "I've never wished for notoriety, Kate. It's enough that I found out that it *was* true, and that through you, I discovered the amazing source of its power. But in all honesty, I can't say I'm sorry that it was destroyed."

"I've always wondered how you felt when you saw the spinning wheel that night," Kate admitted. "To have survived all those years, only to shatter like a piece of glass when I fell on it."

Cole shuddered and drew her closer. "Don't remind me. Even if the wheel hadn't ended up broken, I wouldn't have kept it. The wonder and the fascination I'd felt for it all those years died when I saw you lying next to it. After that, it would only have served as a reminder of what happened."

"There's one thing I'll always be grateful to it for, though."

"What's that?"

"That it brought me to you." Kate raised her hand to lovingly stroke his cheek. "If you hadn't come looking for the spinning wheel, our paths would never have crossed. You would have gone on authenticating antiques in London and New York, and I would have gone on making stained glass in Barre, Vermont."

"Do you really believe that, Mrs. Beresford?"

Kate smiled, and the happiness shimmered in her eyes. "I like the sound of that, Mr. Beresford. But to answer your question *with* a question, don't you?"

Cole rested his chin on the top of her head and gazed out at the stars. "I like to think that, like Gareth and Eleya, you and I were destined to be together. If we hadn't met here, we would have met at some other place at some other time."

Kate's smile held a touch of whimsy. "Maybe I would have seen you in my dreams."

Cole laughed, and the deep, sensual sound of it sent shivers up Kate's spine. "Mmm, I'd rather have you here in my arms than in my dreams, sweetheart. Because as far as I'm concerned," he said as he tilted her mouth up to his, "the dream doesn't even come close to the real thing."